EV 2.00

W9-CPB-452

"[Black] excels . . . in creating engaging main characters and unleashing them in the middle of a killer's nightmare. The unexpected ending leaves the reader with a thirst for more."
—*Library Journal*

Devastatingly sexy and deceptively lethal, Nora Clay moves undetected through New York City, shadowing her unsuspecting prey. Once she has seduced her victim, she will leave him sweating, hungry for more. Until she stabs out his life in a flash of fury and steel. That is how TV producer Paul Anderson meets his grisly end.

In the middle of Manhattan's worst heat wave in twelve years, sex crimes detective Conrad Voort is assigned the disturbing case. At the murder scene he finds a taunting message scrawled on the wall: *I know you.* And the killing is far from over. For Nora Clay "knows" other men. Including Conrad Voort. Now, as he pursues one of the most elusive and brilliant killers he has ever confronted, the hunter becomes the hunted.

Other Ballantine Books by Ethan Black

THE BROKEN HEARTS CLUB

IRRESISTIBLE

Ethan Black

BALLANTINE BOOKS • NEW YORK

A Ballantine Book
Published by The Ballantine Publishing Group
Copyright © 2000 by Ethan Black

www.ballantinebooks.com

ISBN 0-345-43348-3

Manufactured in the United States of America

First Hard Cover Edition: April 2000
First Mass Market Edition: August 2001

10   9   8   7   6   5   4   3   2   1

A very special thanks to Ted Conover, Phil Gerard, Peter Gethers, and Esther Newberg.

For Wendy, with love

ONE

"**I** know everything about you, but you don't even know I exist. I know what terrifies you, what makes you stay up nights, craving. I know when you break laws, or hurt people, to get what you want. Your nightmares are my reading fare. Your secrets my lunchtime companions."

The woman, naked, paces in her apartment.

"You think I'm making this up? I know about the three million dollars you've hidden from your wife, in your Chilean bank account. I know the secret deal you've concluded with the Japanese, to sell your optics company, and fire your employees. I know all of you, the liars, phonies, the tricksters, the fools."

The woman grows more agitated.

"If you're a scientist, I've learned each detail of the drug you just invented, against baldness, which is not even on the market yet. If you're sick, and trying to hide it, I know which disease infects you; and whether your surgeon thinks you will live or die, screaming, in pain, as tubes carry fresh blood into your body and poison out."

The woman towels herself off, wet from the shower. She is alone.

"And after all that, we've never met."

She addresses a voice-activated tape recorder, on a maple table under a window shielded by iron bars.

"My knowledge comes from science, not magic." She reaches for a glass filled with gin and ice. "The system that delivers you into my hands begins every weekday at nine A.M., outside my apartment, on 108th Street and Riverside Drive, where I am right now. A brown van double-parks on the far curb. A man in a uniform gets out, holding an eight-by-eleven cardboard envelope. My palms start sweating when I see it. I am an addict waiting for my drug, information about you."

She glances at a loud, wind-up clock on the second-hand dresser. She is in a rush this evening. She must hurry to get downtown.

"The man's name is Louis Vale. After ten years of deliveries, we've never really conversed. But I know him anyway. He lives in Queens, at 1297 Kennedy Turnpike, with an angry wife and two children. He loses half his pay on horses at Aqueduct, which is why his wife filed for divorce, why he started taking cocaine, why a labor dispute erupted at work. Louis is about to be fired.

"Well, fuck you, Louis. You brought it on yourself, like all men."

The room is small, but lovingly put together; with a single bed, oddly childlike for an adult of thirty years, and cheap but polished maple dresser, mirror, rocking chair. There are ferns everywhere, on the cracked sill, by the roach traps, half obscuring a sticker on the refrigerator that says ONE DAY AT A TIME. There's a light-colored remnant carpet, and floor-to-ceiling bookshelves along two walls, packed with hard-back novels, non-fiction books, and manila folders, so many files that they, not the woman, seem to be the primary occupant of this studio apartment.

The only decorations on the walls are magazine photos—a baby in a carriage, a different baby on a swing, a third baby in a field of grass and daisies—and there is a black laptop computer on the maple dining table, against a far wall.

The woman eyes a handwritten list—four names and addresses—beside the laptop. The first name is AN-DERSON, PAUL; the last, CONRAD VOORT.

"I know you all."

She upturns the last of the bottle and sucks the remains of the gin from the plastic glass.

Nora Clay begins to dress.

First comes the garter belt and real stockings, not panty hose. Then the tight, black, short skirt of fine cotton that molds itself to her petite hips. A pullover sleeveless blouse in white defines her flat belly. Black high heels lift her ass, jut her breasts. Bracelets, silver hoops, dangle from her wrist, bright as fishing lures.

"Dr. Neiman said to keep this diary."

The provocative clothes are unlike the rest of the wardrobe hanging in the half-open closet. The dresses on hangers, older, less recently purchased, are long and de-mure . . . calf length, with floral prints. Big orchids or roses, the kind an old woman might wear. There are button-up sweaters and silk scarves to hide her neck. The outerwear is old, long coats in gray or blue, bulky, to conceal the shape of the body. The shoes are flat-heeled. The hats are plain stocking caps.

"Dr. Neiman told me not to drink. Well, fuck you too, Doctor. I happen to know you failed your medical board certification the first two times. And you're about to de-fault on your mortgage. But back to my envelope, and to the horrible thing that happened when Louis Vale came this morning, the thing he said.

"He said, 'Looks like something "personal" for you today too. Not just the usual.' And he handed me *two* envelopes, one with a return address on it that I never wanted to see again. With a lawyer's note inside, a bracelet and earrings. And a note that said, 'Darling, you were right.'

"I slammed the door on Louis. I ripped open the other envelope, the daily one, but today, even the information inside didn't improve my mood. I couldn't stop weeping.

"You were right?"

Nora Clay is small and gorgeous. She is a petite package of sexual power. Her lean, shapely legs, her walk, her huge brown eyes, her black silky hair cut short above the ears, her Cupid-shaped mouth, which looks mashed, kissed, draws men's glances. She exudes ripeness. She has always made men—if she was not careful, if she wore even a little makeup, dressed even a little attractively, gave them the slightest, most minuscule, most ridiculous excuse to think she might be interested in them—grow so intoxicated they would call out to her in the street, follow her home like dogs, push through crowds in subways to chat with her, beg telephone operators to provide her unlisted number.

"Maybe you do something to encourage this behavior," Dr. Neiman had said two months ago, at their final meeting.

"I don't anymore."

"Considering your past, don't you think it's a little possible you might be using this attraction as power?"

"No."

"Nora, even your walk. The way you move is—"

"Excuse me?"

"I've never seen a walk like that. It's like a dance."

"Are you coming on to me?"

A pause. "To tell you the truth, I don't know."

Now Nora Clay does what she does every night, when she finishes her journal entry.

She pulls the tape from the recorder and violently unravels it, yanking the brown ribbon out in whorls. She drops it in the day's trash, and the trash goes into the can outside when she steps into the street.

"That's the beauty of keeping a diary," Dr. Neiman had said. "You can say anything you want. Tell people you hate them. That you think about killing them. It's just between you and the tape. You're not actually *doing* anything, just letting off steam."

"I'm leaving you, Doctor."

"What I said before . . . I didn't mean—"

"Good-bye, Doctor."

"Nora, at least promise me you won't drink. You do bad things when that happens."

Now Nora Clay walks east on 108th, on the kind of mission she reserves for the worst nights, when she is really upset.

She catches the number 1 train at 110th and rides it south, under the groaning city, through dark tunnels, beneath the yuppie Upper West Side, beneath the gigantic towers of Midtown pressing down on the subway. She gets off in Chelsea, in southern Manhattan, a trendy neighborhood filled with art galleries, boutiques, new restaurants.

She tells herself, *I'm just going to watch him, that's all.*

When she climbs to the surface on Eighteenth Street, the air is fetid, the night hot with a cloying grittiness that only a metropolis or factory town can produce. "It's the worst heat wave in the last twelve years," a radio announcer says from the open window of a Saab going by. The temperature is over one hundred degrees. Cars glide through a sooty, choking air so dense that when she looks up or down Seventh Avenue, it obscures buildings a mile away, even on a "clear" night. There are no clouds, yet the stars are invisible. She's sweating, walking past renovated buildings that were tenements ten years ago. Then the gays moved in. Then the professionals. Now sushi can be delivered by bicycle to your apartment here.

A man calls to her, from a car, "Want a ride, beautiful?"

She keeps walking.

Another man, in an expensive suit, stops in front of her, on the sidewalk outside a Korean grocery. He's got a bouquet of tulips in his hand, for, obviously, his wife or girlfriend. But he holds them out to Nora and says, grinning, "Be still my beating heart."

Nora ignores him, refuses to return his friendly smile or even to look at him. She just strides past and enters a bar. WANDA'S, the purple neon overhead announces, after the supermodel who allegedly, according to news reports, owns it. Wanda is the hottest new fashion phenomenon in New York. Blond discovery Wanda, a skinny sixteen-year-old in a Czech mining town three years ago, is a multimillionaire today gracing the cover of *Sports Illustrated*.

More photos of Wanda cover the west wall of the packed room, like idols for about two hundred nouveau riche lawyers, doctors, real estate investors, Wall Street brokers, successful art dealers, business executives, and German or Scandinavian tourists whose money goes twice as far in the United States as it does at home.

The stock market is booming at the moment. Wanda's is pulsating with frantic energy. People have to shout over the currently hot single, "Burn Me," blaring from quadraphonic speakers overhead.

"Buy you a drink?"

"No thanks," Nora tells an older, nervous man in a gray summer suit. Divorcé probably, making the pathetic discovery that he's aged since he was single last time around.

Her eyes search the crowd.

Where is he?

Someone taps her on the shoulder. She turns to see a model-handsome, dark-haired man in a beige light-weight summer jacket and open-neck blue shirt. A killer brunette with hair parted in the middle, like a 1930s Nazi, and two drinks in his hands. An amber liquid, scotch probably, and a clear drink with a wedge of lime smearing the glass. He offers her the clear drink, his smile charming enough to sell forged oil leases to a Rockefeller. His tanned hand, holding the drink, has a Rolex on it. Woman at the bar, young and perfumed, dressed in clothing costly enough to feed a family of five for months, glance enviously between Nora and the man.

"I thought you might like something cold," he says, in a radio host quality voice and an accent; German, she thinks, or Swiss.

"Sorry. I'm meeting someone."

"A girlfriend?" he asks hopefully.

A seat has miraculously opened at the bar, and she takes it. Watching the boisterous crowd, she thinks, I know you people, and you are nowhere near as happy as you seem. You are afraid you will miss an opportunity; to find love, or make money, or make a business contact.

The unforgiving city, rushing past, gives its people, at most, five minutes to take advantage of opportunities. New York runs in five minute increments, she knows. Love and fortune collapse between ticks of a clock. Deals slide by, unnoticed. Young singles are unattached only a few short moments between love affairs. Everyone in this bar feels the unforgiving urgency, and beneath their casual gaiety it makes them scared.

She tells herself, Now I will look left, in the mirror, and he will be in the third seat from the end. There will be a pint of Guinness in front of him. He will be trying to keep from looking obvious, scanning the bar.

Bingo!

Her heart beats faster. She loves being right about things.

Nora, why do you follow these people around?

It's Dr. Neiman, in her head. She sees him in his big brown chair, too young to be so bald, blinking at her through his thick wire-rimmed glasses.

She tells him, in her head, to go away. She says to him, "They're in my files. When I see them it makes reading about them more real, that's all."

But in her head, he won't stop bothering her. "Nora, what about the people on your 'list'? Your 'special people'? Is that the only reason you want to see *them* up close too?"

No answer.

"You told me you think about harming the people on the list."

No answer.

"It bothers me that you won't tell me their names. What are the names of the people on the list?"

"What difference does it make?"

"Well, it makes me wonder if you're more serious about hurting them than you realize. Otherwise, why not share their names? Are you afraid, if you harm one of them, I'll read about it in the paper?"

"Time's up," she'd said to him that day.

The memory is so powerful, so rattling, that she almost leaves. But at that moment the bartender appears, a big, red-haired, red-faced drinker at an early age, a heart attack waiting to happen, a twenty-five-year-old with his nose ballooning. A future member, if he's going to have any chance in life, of AA.

"Gin and tonic!" she has to shout.

The bartender gets it for her and is already turning away, too busy to notice anything except his orders.

The gin calms her. The man at the end of the bar, "Paul Anderson" on her list back home, is eyeing her in the mirror now. She glances away. Her heart beats faster. She crosses her legs. She never wears provocative clothes when she follows someone, and she realizes she only did it tonight so he would notice her.

The bartender puts another gin and tonic on the bar.

"From the gentleman on the other end."

And now the script that she knows, that she's memorized, begins.

She thinks, I'll accept the drink, and he'll get up, and when he comes over he'll say, "I've never seen you here before."

A voice behind her says, "I've never seen you before."

She swivels slightly, with her head, not her body. Close up he's more imposing than from down the bar. He's thirty to thirty-five years old, powerful-looking, slightly shorter than average, but he makes up for it with wide shoulders and long dirty blond hair in a ponytail, ending six inches below the collar of his black Italian jacket. His white Donna Karan cotton shirt, with its stylish wrap-around collar, sets off his deep tan, which she knows he picked up on the beach, in Long Island, by his fully owned two-story shingle summer home in Sag Harbor. The white jeans come from Bergdorf, like the Loafers.

She tells him, "Oh, I come here now and then."

She has never spoken to someone on the list before, and it is exciting in a dangerous way. Paul Anderson wedges himself in beside her, on a bar stool. He pushes back the irritated woman behind him. He gives off a whiff of Calvin Klein cologne.

"I'm Paul."

She lies. "Emily."

He'll bullshit me awhile, talk about weather, and shift the topic to the network where he works.

He starts chatting. The heat is awful, he says. Wanda's, so trendy at the moment, will be empty, passed on by the hordes, in six months, when some other equally fatuous watering hole seizes their limited attention. Paul Anderson is a man, she already knows, who applies his high intelligence to trends, not substance.

"We did a story on these flash-in-the-pan places at the network," he says.

"Oh, you work for TV?" she says, letting her eyes shine with interest, leaning forward, watching her fingers come to a stop half an inch from his hand, on the bar.

"I produce *New York Nights* at NBC," he says, shrugging. "The hottest places. We tell ya first."

"I love that show!" She's never seen it. "And I never met anyone who works in TV."

Now he'll tell me the story about his time as a producer in Bosnia. How his best friend was killed by a mine, and how it ripped him up.

"My buddy, the guy who got me into the business," Paul Anderson says a half hour later, "got killed by that mine."

"That must have been awful," she says.

It was the worst moment of my life.

"It was the worst moment of my life."

She is so proud and happy in her knowledge. Her files back home are perfect. Being with this man is like singing an old familiar song.

Now he'll look sensitive and say, "I'm having a little trouble here, in this kind of place, talking about my dead friend."

"This is the wrong place to talk about him," Paul says. "I don't suppose you feel like getting out."

Dr. Neiman's voice says, in her head, *Leave. Now. Alone.*

But she tells Paul, "Yes, let's go."

The drink is working on her. The recklessness is rising. She puts her hand on his wrist. She knows how this will raise the heat in him, and she is right. She has not touched a man in five years, and it takes all her self-control not to pull her hand back from the wiry hairs, the coarse skin.

He says, "I know a coffeehouse near here, and usually it's pretty packed about now, but maybe there will be a table."

I don't suppose you'd want to go back to my apartment. The terrace overlooks Gramercy Park.

"Or you wouldn't want to go back to my place," he says. "I know we just met, but it has a huge terrace. It's quite beautiful, the way you can see Gramercy Park."

Dr. Neiman urges her, in her head, to stop. Dr. Neiman repeats that sometimes he worries she might actually hurt someone.

But she says, "That would be lovely."

And now she is actually walking out of the bar with Paul Anderson. A taxi drifts from the seedy mist and she slides in first, knowing the movement hikes her skirt up, feeling his eyes on her legs without having to look, demurely pushing the fabric down when she reaches the far side of the taxi. She's uncomfortable with the fact that she has no inkling of whether he will try to kiss her in the cab. Her files are blank on that point, but it turns out he's a gentleman, at least at the moment. He doesn't try to touch her. His pink sausagy fingers lie on the seat cover inches from her skirt, and stay there until the cab pulls up before a beautiful pre–World War II, Tudor-style high-rise apartment building across from the city's most beautiful private park.

"Our doormen are on strike," he says, using his key.

In the elevator she feels slightly nauseous, fights off the urge to leave again. The sound of the pulley system is like fingernails dragging across slate. But when the doors open directly into his apartment, even though she knew what she would see, she gasps at the view, the wall of picture windows, floor-to-ceiling, across the ornate living room. The smeared, fogged-in lights of the city out there. As bright as they are blind.

You should never drink, the doctor's voice in her head says.

"I want a drink," she tells Paul Anderson.

"You betcha," he says, happily, mixing another tall gin and tonic at the sideboard, showing her around the apartment as she knew he would, starting in the living room, like his file said he would, wooing her with his money, terrace outside, baby grand piano, Katz paintings, black leather furniture and glass coffee table and built-in entertainment center and not a single book. The kitchen, remodeled in a country style, has a butcher block table and an array of knives attached magnetically to a wall.

Knives.

He shows her, quicker now, eager to get to things, the den, guest bedroom, office, with his three Emmy awards, his Dupont awards, his photos of himself with two Presidents, a Cy Young–award-winning baseball pitcher, the singer Michael Jackson, the famous criminal Charles Manson, in prison.

He'll say, Manson scared the shit out of me.

"Manson scared me to death. Let's go out on the terrace."

She likes knives.

And it is on the terrace that he makes his move, like his file said he would. She hears the light shuffle of his leather soles as he slips up behind her. She is at the railing, bending over, outlining her ass to him as she looks down at the dark two-block-long park below, with its spiked iron fence. Suddenly she feels rough hands on her hips, and soft lips on the nape of her neck.

"You are beautiful," he says.

Dr. Neiman's voice, fading now, a last piece of advice, says, do not sleep with this man.

Fuck the doctor, fuck everything.

The two of them go at it like animals, ripping at each other's clothes, on the terrace. The dirty city air is like liquid, smearing them. Paul Anderson pushes her back against the terrace wall. Her legs wrap around him. His tongue, tasting of alcohol and dissipation, is in her mouth. She bites his lip.

"Ouch!"

She bites harder.

"What are you doing?"

They go back to kissing. His jacket comes off, sleeves inside out, a tumble of discarded fashion, tailor-made sex appeal crumpled on the tile floor. The buttons rip on his cotton shirt. Her blouse is half over her head, and his hands squeeze her breasts. She feels hot all over. She thinks, I love this. She opens his zipper and grasps his penis, and pulls him inside her.

"Now. Harder," she says.

They are beasts joined above the power of the city. It is as if all the life below them, and fury, has entered them and driven them to new heights. Energy seeking outlet. Passion seeking the object. Species seeking continuation. Desire seeking ruin.

They fuck against the wall and on the floor and he carries her, bodily, into the bedroom. It is a huge, gigantic bedroom, a pillow for sex, and he falls, with her, onto the king-sized bed. She wants to come. She wants it to go on forever. She feels the polluted joy of his penis, ramming her.

"Come with me!" she cries.

And he does.

They lie there, breathing heavily. The sounds of the city come back to her. There is a horn honking down there, and the drone of an airplane. Over the hum of central air-conditioning comes the jagged sound of male breathing, and she detects the sour odor of alcohol, and the rank odor of sex, over the aroma of linens and furniture polish in the room.

Now he'll start talking about commitment.

"That was great," he says. "You hungry?"

She thinks, rattled, You're supposed to talk about commitment!

But he starts in about the network again, the way it's being sued by some Pennsylvania supermarket chain. The way there's a big legal battle in the courts. The way, if the network loses, it could change the nature of investigative reporting.

She can't stand it, that he's departed from the script. Could the file be wrong?

It scares her, but then she hears him say, "You know what I think about sometimes. It sounds silly to say it. A whole world in one word. Commitment."

She relaxes.

"Commitment?" he continues, rising, putting on a black silk bathrobe. "I'll tell you about commitment. I'm with you now and that makes me happy. I feel like I've always been with you, even when I didn't know you yet."

And she says the line she's been rehearsing. "It's early to fall in love."

And he answers in the general way she'd been warned about. "Commitment is better than love. Love is just a four-letter word these days. I'm talking about knowing, in here," he says, touching his chest, "at the beginning of a relationship, that it's going to mean a lot."

"Excuse me," she says. "Gotta pee."

She stands and gazes down at him, considers his face, the stubble of blond hair she now notices starting to bulge from the cheeks, the band of slight fat beginning to form at the waist, not a tire yet, just a fatty, spongy presence. An unattractive bit of saliva, froth, a residue of excitement, dotting the right corner of Paul Anderson's mouth.

It makes her feel filthy inside.

Her reckless feeling has turned to shame.

In the bathroom she runs the hot water and burns herself washing. She looks at the red, ruined color down there. She thinks, disgusted, What if Paul Anderson, since I started his file, started researching him, collecting news clips on him, "running into" his old girlfriends and chatting with them about "old boyfriends," contracted AIDS?

On the way back to the bedroom, she detours through the kitchen, stops before the shiny knives, stares at them, runs her finger over one. She selects a paring knife, the smallest, from the rack, and keeps it hidden at her side as she pads back into the bedroom.

Paul Anderson is propped up on a pillow, eyeing her breasts as she closes the distance to the bed.

"Feel better now?" he says.

Sitting on the bed, she slides the knife below the covers. She can feel the extra-fine cotton sheet, still damp with human fluids, against the bottom rim of her fist.

"Tell me more about commitment," she says.

"It's . . . uh . . . caring and sharing," he says.

"Did you just make that up?"

"The words came into my mouth," Paul Anderson says.

Her hand, beneath the covers, glides back and forth, a small movement like the waving fin of a fish in water. She persists, "But you meet someone and three hours later you say those words."

"I know it sounds nuts, but people always told me, when you know something, you know. I didn't believe it before."

"And now," slightly more harshly, "you do."

Her tone alerts him that something has changed. His forehead shows the tiniest frown. "What are you, upset?" he says. "And what are you sitting all the way over there for?"

"Because we're talking," she says. "About commitment. If you're so committed, tell me a secret."

"A what?"

"A confession," she says.

"Confession," he repeats, his puzzlement a little funny, actually. He'd planned on working the conversation around to condoms, she knew. To birth control, to protecting himself next time around.

She kisses him on the forehead, feels the bones beneath the white, damp skin. "Pick something to confess. It's a game. It's the hard part of commitment. It's sharing bad things, not just good. Tell me what you might need to confess. Something you need forgiveness for."

"What are you, a religious nut?"

She laughs. "It's a game."

"Well, I don't want to play."

She leans forward, close, so he can see her perfect breasts, small and firm, distracting him just beneath the line of his vision. They excite him, and there is a fresh smell, a woman smell from her, and she sees that Paul Anderson feels himself, despite his irritation, getting hard again.

She kisses him, on the mouth. She thrusts her tongue in his. His mouth tastes of liquor.

She says, "Nothing to say, not even one little thing?"

"Look, I have to go to work early. We're doing a show on drugs in nightclubs. It'll be a great piece."

"That's nice."

"Why not come to the studio sometime, and see us put the thing together."

"When?" she asks.

"Uh, soon," he says. "I'll take your phone number."

She reaches and squeezes his right nipple with the tips of her thumb and index finger. The edge of her nail slides around the nipple and then left, over the bicep, to the boney clavicle over Paul Anderson's pounding heart.

His eyes grow hazy, his pupils larger.

"Is confession over?" he says, aroused, reaching for her.

"Yes," she says. "And you don't know anything about commitment."

He has not seen the knife, since her hand is hidden, and with one swift, powerful, and accurate motion, she brings the razor-sharp instrument out and plunges it into the thick artery pulsating along the left side of Paul Anderson's neck.

He gags, too shocked, even in the face of bald evidence, to believe what is happening to him.

By the time he gets his hand up, she has drawn the honed blade halfway across his throat. He thinks, This isn't happening. He thinks, This happens to other people. He thinks, I have to make that one o'clock meeting. He thinks one word, and the word is *Why?*

Her expression, which has been honeyed, fascinated, adoring throughout the evening, is, he sees through his diminishing senses, twisted and hating now.

The blade rises, falls, steady, rises. The man tries to fight, but shock, surprise, and pain have overcome him already.

He falls sideways, still in bed, still weakly trying to fight, or cry out, to hold his throat, to save himself through the fine red spray in the room, a mist obscuring his vision, coating the linens and walls and the creature in front of him, the female smeared with running rivulets of blood.

Normally he would be the stronger person here, but he has never used his power for real combat. At work, at the network, he's fond of phrases like "rip the throat out of the opposition." "Tear their guts out." But like the white-collar men he works with, brags with, drinks with, he has no idea how to defend himself against an actual, knowledgeable physical attack.

He wants to say, Why are you doing this?

He cannot speak.

She is everywhere, in a fury. She has ten hands, ten knives, and they are all hitting him, tearing at him. He has to get up, he tells himself, to get away, to reach the door, or at least the telephone.

The life is running out of him.

He trips, trying to struggle out of the bedcovers.

The rug lies against his downturned face.

And now Nora Clay stands over the inert body, straddles it, standing, watches it, and at length kneels and turns it over and performs the next act of surgery that, she decides, this particular purification requires.

She is breathing hard. She is bathed in sweat. The man's blood is everywhere, in her hair, on her hands, on her skin, in the cracks beneath her toes.

She goes into the bathroom. She stares at herself in the mirror, studies, as if she is another person, her face, the round cheekbones and small nose, the pretty brown eyes. The way her skin glistens in the light. The way the knife glitters.

My God, I really did it.

The CD on the stereo keeps playing. A merry Mozart waltz throbs in the apartment.

Paul Anderson had told her, tonight, as he put on music, that you could play the piano in the apartment at two A.M., scream, even fight, and the neighbors would not hear it because of the thick, soundproofed floor.

So she starts to clean.

She takes her time. There is no rush.

There is a terrible odor in the apartment, blood and viscera, but she has smelled much worse, and she finds gloves and cleaning fluid in the sink, Mr. Clean, the big, happy sanitizing giant. She finds a rag and she carefully goes over the bathroom, backing away from each section as she works.

Bathtub, curtains, toilet, floor.

In the bedroom closet she finds a vacuum cleaner, eyes the floor and calculates if the apartment is really as soundproof as Paul Anderson said it was.

She vacuums the place up, unclips the barely filled dust bag and folds it into her purse.

Meticulous, she wipes the phone, puts highball glasses in the dishwasher, pours in soap and starts it running. Like she's the maid and Paul Anderson will return from a trip soon and desire a spotless apartment. She takes the bloody sheets off the bed, concerned not with the stains, which have soaked into the mattress anyway, but with any hairs she may have left. She folds the blanket, sheets, and pillow cases neatly into a shopping bag. She will take the bag when she leaves.

As an afterthought, she locates Anderson's wallet and takes money from it, eight hundred dollars in cash. Maybe that way the police will think it was a robbery.

She showers, a really hot steamy shower, scrubs every touch of him away.

One last thing to do.

She finds her purse, and extracts, from its meticulously neat recesses, a black Magic Marker.

Going to Paul Anderson's bedroom wall, the un-bloodied part of it, in long looping letters, she begins to write.

TWO

Voort opens his eyes, looks left, in his big hundred-year-old Dutch feather bed, and sees the white, round shoulder of Camilla. He is filled with joy. After a seven-month separation, they're back together again.

He relishes the way her long, white-blond hair spreads over her pillows, adores the lean runner and kayaker's shape of her body beneath the Hudson Valley handmade antique quilt. He fills in, in his mind, the slope of her torso, the bump of her ribs, the way her breasts jut, aureoles swelling, in sleep, when she dreams. Her long legs taper to thin ankles. Her slender hands are adorned with jewelry even in bed, and she crosses her wrists in front of her chest, as if protecting herself.

I am so lucky.

In his thirty years he's never loved anyone the way he loves Camilla. Never been with someone who made him so alive. At St. Patrick's today, he will pray, *God, let me make her as happy as she makes me.*

After she left him, he'd done his best to forget her. But then last night they'd run into each other at a Hudson River environmental fund-raiser, in SoHo. They'd taken a stroll after the rock music/modeling show.

"I never stopped thinking of you," she'd said, over iced cappuccino and a blueberry bagel.

"I went to the fund-raiser because I thought you'd be there," he'd replied.

They'd only come back to Voort's town house to talk, not sleep. But they'd never been able to keep their hands off each other. The instant he'd locked the front door, the combustion had exploded, as if no time had passed.

Now he has a vision of her on top of him, head back, hands behind her ass, massaging his penis. He lifts her with each thrust, and they buck and plunge on the bed. He reaches for her bouncing breasts.

"I can commit now, Voort," she'd said.

Commitment, he thinks, wryly, can mean love or incarceration. The whole city seems to be running from commitment. Lawyers break contracts. Husbands leave wives. Lovers write kiss-and-tell books. Even advertising people pitch slogans like, "Afraid of commitment? Try our product for only one week!"

Manhattan is so pressurized not because so many people live there, but because they are trying to run away from each other at the same time.

And now, Voort the cop knows, linked to his city even in its unconscious rhythms, Manhattan is waking. Lights go on in locked apartments. Radios blare the weather to men and women who do not even glance outside. They'd rather relish a last instant of privacy before acknowledging the existence of millions of strangers out there.

Voort kisses Camilla's shoulder, bringing her slowly awake. She groans happily and her hand seeks his belly, glides lower and . . .

. . . the touch of flesh wakes him up for real this time.

He is not in bed beside Camilla, but Shari, the woman he has been seeing, on and off, since Camilla left his life.

Voort feels sick. It is a brutally clear moment. His dream was so vivid that the loss feels as wrenching as it did on the day Camilla told him, "I need time, Voort."

Take all you need.

"I need space."

Space means nothingness.

And Shari's up now too, drowsy, loving. He can see himself reflected in her black pupils. He is a blond man with lean hips, good shoulders, and taut muscles from workouts. His round Dutch features are topped by hair falling over his wide forehead. His eyes are as blue as the porcelain basin that sits on the antique night table, beside the marble cherub, booty plundered from a British frigate during the Revolutionary War by Voort's ancestor, Admiral Voort of the Continental Navy of the brand-new United States.

Shari says, "Zia has the girls for the whole week. I can come back tonight."

Voort knows he must hide the sick feeling coursing through him. He must make this woman, who loves him, happy to be here.

She is gorgeous; small, nut-brown, firm, enthusiastic. And last night's date was a good indicator of the rhythms of their uncommitted relationship. They'd met downtown, in Battery Park, after she left work at Apple Bank in Sheraton Square. Their first date in two weeks. They'd strolled by the river, hand in hand, catching up, past the dock where Voort's cabin boy ancestor had come ashore with sea captain Henry Hudson in 1609, where Voort's police commissioner ancestor had set up security for the Statue of Liberty opening celebration, where Voorts, for almost three hundred years, first as night watchmen and later as official police, had caught criminals and made the city safer for the people of New York.

An August night, smoggy from the Greenhouse Effect, so the lights across the river in Hoboken were dulled, like the barges on the Hudson. They'd had dinner in Tribeca and caught the Marsalis jazz show at the Vanguard.

They'd had a nightcap by the piano bar at Wilmer's, strolled back to Voort's town house, along the same streets he'd just dreamed about. They'd made love twice, and fallen asleep in each other's arms.

Now Shari smiles and her small, slender hand reaches for him, but Voort intercepts it, kisses it, knowing his feigned happiness is not fooling her. He says, "Breakfast in bed for you."

He wraps his big, fluffy terry-cloth robe, a gift from Shari, around him, and the richest cop in New York makes his way to his huge Dutch kitchen, down two flights of stairs.

I can't keep seeing her.

Voort the sex-crimes detective. Voort who stalks the stalkers, who spends his shifts tracking people whose hearts blew from passion, or loss, or inability to express themselves. Whose envy drives them to violence. Who walk the streets at three A.M., making phone calls and hanging up, climbing fire escapes, trying locked windows.

I'll leave her today.

Make a list, Voort thinks ruefully, and Shari, the banker, is perfect for me. She's smart and slender and happy and curious. She's good to travel with. She adores her kids, as do I. She's caring. She loves sex. She's a good pal. She's loyal in an emergency.

What good is a list on paper, beside a broken heart?

Voort turns on the converted gas lamps in his giant kitchen, puts on the morning news, Channel 4, Camilla's station, and hears the announcer talking about a murder in Gramercy Park.

A producer from this network was found knifed in his apartment, the announcer says, as a head shot of the dead man fills the screen, thirtyish, alive.

Voort opens the industrial-size refrigerator and pulls

out ingredients: shiny red peppers from Balducci's, fresh Italian mushrooms, shallots, Vermont cheddar cheese, basil, sourdough rolls they bought, hot and fresh, as they strolled home last night.

"Police have no leads," the announcer says.

Voort puts on Jamaican Mountain coffee, Shari's favorite. He heats croissants and gets orange marmalade from the refrigerator. He pulls copper pans from their pegs, spreads sunflower seed oil, lets it simmer till it bubbles, and drops in the other ingredients before the eggs.

"Paul Anderson was single and had no children," the announcer says.

He gets out the fresh sourdough rolls, butters them and puts them in the oven.

"Anderson's stories put many people in jail."

Voort's wealth comes from inheritance. He lives, day to day, on his detective's salary and his excellent investments, but the house and land it was built on were bequeathed by the Continental Congress to Admiral Conrad Voort, who blocked a British landing off Cape May in the Revolutionary War. The original land grant hangs, framed in the living room, on the brick wall near a fireplace designed to warm the whole massive downstairs.

Voort had memorized the words by the time he was ten.

"For actions beyond the call of duty, and in lieu of payment, Admiral Voort and his ancestors are hereby awarded, in perpetuity, lot 28 on the island of Manhattan, in the City of New York. The land or any structure on it will never be taxed, by federal, state, or city authorities. Home and land may be handed from generation to generation. This edict will remain in effect until the last Voort dies, or sells the property, at which time all monies from such transaction will remain in family hands, not to be subject to any tax levied by any U.S. government authority, federal, state, or local. Thank you, Admiral Voort. Signed and witnessed."

The announcer on TV says, "Anderson was being sued, with the network, over an investigative piece he produced attacking Allan Foods."

George Washington's signature is included on the land grant to the Voort family, along with that of Thomas Jefferson, Alexander Hamilton, John Adams.

According to an auctioneer from Christie's who was here a year ago, just the piece of paper is worth a couple of hundred thousand dollars. And the furniture—the original Dutch oak tables and bedroom set—the Federalist living and dining room, the oils in the bedroom, the man said, salivating, would go for six times that.

"I have no reason to sell," Voort had told him. "I grew up in this house."

"You live here all alone?"

"There are two hundred Voorts in the New York area, and any of them stay here when they're in town."

Voort had shown the man the portraits lining the stairways. "They're Voort policemen. They were commissioners, captains, sergeants, beat cops. The man with the muttonchops, Bartholomew Voort, arrested the O'Brien Hudson River pirates in 1801. The man on horseback was a sergeant who worked with Teddy Roosevelt and later became commissioner. The twins helped break up the conscription riots during the Civil War."

"And the paintings in the other rooms?" the auctioneer had asked. "The winter scenes in old Brooklyn? The skating scene in Central Park is over 140 years old. They're priceless! How'd your family get them?"

Voort had steered the man back downstairs, toward the Hudson River Project fund-raiser, and Camilla, his girlfriend at the time; Camilla who, when he saw her, made his heart jump in a way that no physical possession could.

"We bought them. The painters were street artists then."

Now Voort slides the finished omelettes onto Dutch china plates, the coffee goes into a hundred-year-old ceramic pot. The orange juice, fresh-squeezed, fills the Chippendale crystal pitcher with matching long-stemmed juice goblets. The well-done slices of juicy ham come from a Voort farm in the Hudson Valley, in Columbia County, near Albany and the Massachusetts line.

"A hot day to be alive," the announcer is saying. "A killer heat wave is causing heart attacks and aggravating tempers. Police sirens kept me up all night."

When Voort reaches the master bedroom, Shari is up, bare-breasted, dressed in a beige pants suit from the waist down, sitting at his mother's old makeup mirror, bulbs glowing. She's applying lipstick. Her crisply ironed slacks outline the excellent curve of her rump.

The phone starts ringing.

"You talked in your sleep," she says.

Voort puts the tray on the bedside table.

The ringing does not stop.

Shari says, brushing her short blue-black hair, "You were pretty racy, actually. I thought you were talking about me, but then you clarified things. You looked a bit disappointed when you woke up."

"I can't control a dream," Voort says.

"Nice-looking breakfast," Shari says in a dead voice.

Voort resists saying, It's not you, it's me.

"Excuse me," he says, picking up the phone.

"Con Man," says the man on the other end, a middle-aged voice with the last remaining trace of a Brooklyn accent, softened by voice lessons, but never gone.

Shari nibbles at a ham slice and closes her eyes, in pleasure or pain. Or both.

Mickie's voice says, "We got a big one. You see the news this morning?"

"Gramercy Park?"

"The two-one has detectives there already. I'm at the Williamsburg Bridge, on my way in. I'll swing by in ten minutes."

Voort detects the slightest hesitation in Mickie's voice.

"What aren't you saying?" he asks.

"Nada, Con Man."

"Mickie!"

"What is it with you? I say two words and you're all over me. Who are you, Claudio the mind reader? Let's get you on stage if you are."

Shari is wiping her right eye with an index finger.

"All right, goddamnit," Mickie says. "We were asked to be there. Actually, *you* were requested, specifically."

"By whom?"

"Camilla." And Voort's heart speeds up.

Mickie continues, "The victim worked at her network. So she-who-must-be-obeyed calls NBC's president and *he* calls the commissioner, saying they want the best guy possible, the guy who saved their beloved Valkyrie last year and broke the Bainbridge case, blah blah blah. And the commissioner calls the chief of detectives. *Jawohl*, news network! We can't have the NYPD fail to kiss NBC's ass when the commissioner wants to run for mayor."

Voort's sick feeling is back, but there is something else there too now. Excitement.

I'll have to interview her.

"She knew Anderson?" Voort asks, remembering the victim's name from television.

"It's bad up there, Con Man. He was sliced up."

Mickie, never at a loss for words, hesitates this time. "Like John Wayne Bobbitt, if you know what I mean."

Voort feels a sudden slicing pain, in his groin area.

"Shit."

"Ouch."

They are silent. They are horrified over the mutilation more than the death. It is as if the murderer has attacked both of them, men everywhere, the very nature of what it is to be male.

When they hang up, Shari is brushing her short hair with quick, feminine flips of the brush.

She says, in a quiet voice, "I know. You have to go."

"Are you free for dinner? How about that Spanish place you love? The Sevillâ."

"Who got killed?"

"A producer at NBC."

"Someone you knew?" Which means, Voort knows, Did you meet this person when you went out with Camilla?

"No."

"Was he gay?" Meaning, Was he Camilla's lover? Is Camilla involved in this?

"I don't know if he was gay."

"You said usually, in sex crimes, a man does it."

"That's right."

Shari's blinking again. "Voort, you never pretended to feel anything you didn't. And the ham's pretty good."

"It's from cousin Matt's farm, up the Hudson."

Stupid, ridiculous small talk to anesthetize pain.

Shari looks smaller now, and the fitful way she breathes when she's holding in tears gives the room an ugly feel. The tumbled contents of her overnight bag, strewn on the bed, add to the notion that her presence here is only temporary. There's her compact and lipstick and hair dryer and clothing, the Metro card, the gold-colored, tear-shaped bottle of perfume she upsides to dab on.

He doesn't want to leave her now. He wants to make her feel better, but it is impossible to do that without telling a lie. And how can he stay when he has to go?

She repeats, dully, "You want to have dinner. My favorite breakfast and my favorite dinner. The condemned person always gets dinner in the movies. A steak, then they pull the switch."

"Oh, Shari," Voort says, "you're not a condemned person. We'll just eat. We need to talk about things, you know, clarify them."

But they both know that he is about to do to her what Camilla did to him. The whole city feels like it is fracturing into pieces that smash into each other—people, jobs, relationships, all splintering and colliding over and over again.

"Okay, we'll talk about things," she says. "Like that I'm pregnant."

Voort feels a ballooning in his chest. Panic, fear, and beneath that, far beneath that, almost not there at all, a stirring of pride and happiness.

Mickie should be here any minute.

Pregnant, Voort thinks. I'm going to have a child.

THREE

The city grows steamier. The sun, even at nine A.M., torments anything living. Pigeons gasp for air on ledges overlooking asphalt canyons. Leaves droop from dying maples in Central Park. Drivers roll up windows on the West Side Highway, beseeching the god of air-conditioning for relief. It is the worst August in Voort's memory. All the pent-up indoor smells of New York blow from cooling units, open windows, sewers, steel pipes, and off five million humans hurrying toward their offices, rushing to escape the sickly yellow rays of the sun.

Mickie parks the black Chevy beside a hydrant across from the dead man's apartment and puts the police ID on the visor. It's an exquisite block, one of the loveliest in New York. Sealed from nonmembers by a spiked iron fence, Gramercy Park is a privatized oasis of grass, oak, and white-pebble-covered walkway. Nurses wheel elderly patients in wheelchairs, or infants in carriages, periodically leaning in toward their wards, wiping sweat off their brows.

"What are you staring at that baby for?" Mickie says.

"No reason."

"You never saw a baby?"

"Yeah," Voort says. "A big one. You."

Mickie tells him, as they get out of the car, "I sold

31

the Chile fund, and I'm into collectibles. Doubloons from 1500. They're gorgeous, and Con Man, they're going up."

Mickie's been Voort's best friend during the six years they've been partners. And between Mickie's genius investments and millionaire-surgeon wife, he's wealthy too. They're the two richest cops in New York.

"Anyway," Mickie says, "there's a Christie's auction Saturday. They're selling one of the first medical sketches, a Dondis. You gotta see the way doctors carved patients up back in 1475! Two hundred spectators crowded around the operation. No masks. No anesthesia. They just slice the guy up."

Mickie's shorter than Voort, but more broad-shouldered. He exudes power in the way he strides rather than walks, and in the conservative, expensive way he dresses. His suit of light gray summer wool is British, Savile Row and double-breasted. His shirt is matching lightweight pearl-gray, from Armani, and his tie, a deep Prussian blue silk, sets off his tan. He spends weekends in the Hamptons, in a three-bedroom "cottage" that once belonged to the chairman of Merrill Lynch—now another one of Mickie's investments.

Voort's in a lightweight jacket of Pima cotton, an open-necked sport shirt and khaki trousers. When the mercury hits ninety, Voort loses the tie.

"I'll take the right side," he says as they approach the building.

Moving, looking right, Voort scans onlookers behind the yellow tape, any one of whom could turn out to be important in the investigation. Sex killers often hang around the scene, or return to it, because, Voort knows, it gives them a thrill to relive the emotion of a murder.

He notes the bare-chested white man with a boom box, a gigantic Panasonic, balanced and blessedly silent, on his shoulder. The trio of teenage girls in shorts and halter tops, at this hour, should be in school. His gaze passes over the Chinese delivery kid straddling a bicycle, the lady dog walker, the dark-haired woman in sunglasses. The black man in a beige suit, with an attaché case, and the man snapping photos, not a reporter, because he's in raggy shorts.

Wait a minute, Voort thinks. A Chinese restaurant delivering at nine in the morning?

Voort talks to the kid. It turns out he's delivering cough medicine to another building, and he shows the prescription and bottle to Voort. He works for a drugstore.

Reporters in the crowd bull up to Voort.

"Hey, Voort! It's Charlie Hodge! From Channel Seven! Any leads?"

"Charlie, you know it's too soon to talk to you."

As soon as they're inside the double glass door, soothing air-conditioning washes over them. They flash their shields at the out-of-place-looking "doorperson," an elderly white-haired woman in an oversized uniform, who's manning the door during the strike.

"I killed him," she confesses, stricken.

She's a foot shorter than Mickie, frail as a paper origami sculpture, with waxy skin and a trembling hand. She's wearing heavy makeup and her watery blue eyes must be at least seventy-five years old. She speaks so softly Voort has to strain to hear her educated accent. European or retired actress, he thinks. Maybe she hangs out at the Player's Club, the actors' club, across the park.

"I'm responsible," she insists.

Voort can see Mickie believes her no more than he does. Seventy-five-year-old women with Parkinson's disease don't usually kill healthy middle-aged men with knives, not to mention cutting off their dicks. And they especially don't, after the carving, do volunteer work in their building. Voort guesses this woman has already "confessed" to other police, who left her here anyway. Which means she had nothing to do with whatever happened last night.

But you check every lead, so Voort says, "Why do you say that?"

"Oh God," she says, and Voort recognizes self-blame in the tone, which he hears from innocent people— stricken parents or friends—too often after killings, as they tell him things like, "I shouldn't have let my daughter take the car. I shouldn't have let her stay out late. I shouldn't have locked my son out when he didn't come home last night. I should have spent more time with him when he was a boy."

Mickie, the ex-Marine, is exquisitely polite to old ladies. "Ma'am," he says, taking the woman's arm, steering her to the doorman's stool, which is several inches too high for her. He helps her up, gentle as a puppy.

"Just talk to us," Mickie says.

"I told the other policemen. I should have known better. The doormen are on strike, and I'm head of the condo association."

"Go on," Voort says, nodding, attentive, pouring water for her from a crystal pitcher on the doorman's stand. Ice floats, clinks against glass.

She says, "The condo association voted to take turns at the door, to substitute for the doormen instead of hiring scabs, until the strike is over."

"What's wrong with scabs?" Mickie the gut Republican asks, meaning it, but also trying to distract the woman from her grief.

Surprised, she says, "We didn't want to offend the doormen."

"If they're striking, who cares if you offend them?" Mickie says. "Some people don't appreciate a good job. No one likes to commit to work anymore."

"Oh, we couldn't do that! It's just some silly argument over benefits. And Mr. Cervantes, the head doorman, is so nice to everyone."

Mickie snorts, and Voort says, "So you took their shifts."

"And I okayed each one, because I'm the head of the association." Voort notes the flowery, theatrical arm movements. "Last night Mr. Jerard, 2B, was supposed to be on duty. He's a retired lawyer, but since his divorce he drinks a little. He was supposed to come on at eleven, but he drank some beers and fell asleep."

"You're saying no one was at the door."

"No one saw Mr. Anderson go in or out. Or who visited him. If someone had, we might be able to help you."

Voort says, gently, "It's not your fault if someone drinks."

But she shakes her head. "It is! The board argued about Mr. Jerard's suitability for the door. People said he's not reliable. But I didn't want to hurt his feelings. So we let him have the late shift. No one wanted it anyway."

Beyond the woman's shoulder, Voort spots a bank of tiny Sony TV screens behind the doorman's stand, and his spirits lift. Cameras are mounted, permanently, he realizes, in this building's elevators, laundry room, and over the rear exit door.

"Does your closed circuit system make tapes of people coming in and out?" he wants to know.

"It only shows what's going on at that second. I tried to talk the board into spending the extra money but we had the new roof to finance. I guess we'll buy a new system now. Too late for Mr. Anderson."

She starts to cry.

Voort puts his arm around her, feels the shift of a featherweight elderly body against his. Her grief is not acting. He soothes the woman. "Ma'am, it's possible someone else in the building saw something last night. We'll canvass the apartments, shops, restaurants. And you're a good neighbor. The way you're working the door. A lot of people wouldn't bother. I'm sure you do plenty for people here, and they appreciate it."

She sniffles. "Take the left-hand elevator to reach the penthouse. Mr. Cobb's operating it during the strike. He has a little trouble stopping it at exactly the right spot."

"Thank you. By any chance, do I recognize you? Are you an actress?"

She brightens. "You remember me?"

"Of course," Voort lies. "You were terrific."

Voort and Mickie proceed into the building. The lobby is marble, paneled in oak, filled with Persian rugs and potted palms. Oak pews stand against the walls, looking churchlike and uncomfortable, decorative rather than functional. This building has money, all right. The owners were just too cheap to buy a videotape system.

The elderly elevator operator stops the elevator perfectly, and needs a key to open the elevator door at the penthouse stop, which means, probably, that the victim let his assailant into his home. Voort and Mickie step out, into a foyer, past yellow tape, past a blue guy, a uniformed patrolman guarding the scene, and into the penthouse where Paul Anderson has been killed. Voort smells the corpse from this far away.

He hears someone throwing up, in the rear of the apartment.

Detectives, medical examiners, and crime scene specialists comb the place, making sketches, taking photos.

Anyone touching things wears plastic gloves. Voort and Mickie pause in the front hallway, an immense, rectangular area done in clay-colored tile, southwestern style. Living room and picture windows straight ahead. Dining room to the left. Library or sitting room to the right, and bedrooms down a long hall, in the rear of the apartment.

Fighting off the dread that never goes away when he enters a murder scene, Voort heads for the bedroom, ground zero. The body lies beneath a tarp, in front of the kingsize bed, feet trailing out of the blue plastic, arms out, as if clawing ahead, Voort sees when he lifts the plastic. Paul Anderson, in agony, had been trying to pull himself away from his attacker. His back is riddled with knife wounds: slashes and punctures. Blood streaks the carpet, crusting against the straw basket and parquet floor, seeping into the thick Bokhara rug, collecting in dulled pools on either side of the body. More droplets fleck the wall, their dried, rust-colored tails confirming the direction the man was crawling from.

The killer went crazy, stabbing this man in a frenzy, probably even after he was dead.

Voort checks the fingernails, the dead hands, already stiffening, marblelike and tobacco-stained. But there's no smell of smoke in the apartment, and he's seen no ashtrays, so he guesses Anderson did not smoke at home, or recently quit. Otherwise there would have been time for the tobacco-stained skin to be shed.

"Who found him?" he asks the precinct detective who had the case before he was ordered to hand it off; a competent man, whom Voort knows, named John Luo, and who looks slightly resentful.

"Your girlfriend got you assigned to this?" Luo says. "Can she get me a raise?"

Voort just repeats, "Who found him?"

Luo's a compact man, bowlegged, with thick black hair, and he wears a powder-blue summer off-the-rack suit. He chews gum constantly. "Anderson was supposed to meet a network limo and be driven to the studio at Rockefeller Center at four A.M. When he doesn't answer the buzzer, the studio phones him. He still doesn't answer. They contact another producer, Lois Shaw, who lives in apartment 5B and has a key."

"In this building?"

"They both own apartments here. She waters his plants when he travels, she says. She says she knocked. No answer. She entered. As a favor, NBC's holding off on the mutilation details, but they'll probably leak. Journalists can't keep their mouths shut."

"And what was Lois Shaw doing last night?"

"She has a cousin visiting. They both slept in the same bed, they say."

"Was she Anderson's girlfriend?"

"She says no, but we'll check. Or I guess *you'll* check, since I'm out of it, huh, Voort? Or maybe you'll hire servants to do it for you."

Voort slides the tarp higher on the body and turns it, slightly, to get a glimpse of the wound on Anderson's front side.

"Christ."

He makes it to the bathroom, where he throws up, where he knows he will never get that bloody gash out of his mind. And where, when he straightens, he sees three words written on the wall, in black Magic Marker, beside the mirror.

I KNOW YOU.

He stares. The words seem a promise. A taunt. They are scrawled with angry stems and slashes. But what do they mean?

Voort keeps back from the sink. He's angry at himself for touching the toilet. He has to rely on mint spray to make his mouth feel livable for the moment, but a foul aftertaste lingers.

He goes back to studying the writing. There is no way of knowing, from the handwriting, if the author was a woman or a man.

Mickie says, coming up behind him, "Whaddaya think?"

Sex crimes are about power, domination, humiliation.

"Someone found out something about him, a secret," Voort says. But they both know there are a thousand maybes. It's just a way to talk, to get a conversation started.

"I just hope," Mickie says, "he was dead when the surgery started."

A pause. "Where's the missing part?"

"Nobody knows."

"Trash chute?"

"They're looking."

Voort remembers the discolored area around the knife wounds. He has learned, over the years, that the size and shade of a bruise helps indicate the strength of the blow.

"A weak guy did it," Mickie guesses, in sync with Voort's line of inquiry. Odds are, they both know, that in this kind of knife killing, this crazy sex violence against a man, the murderer is gay.

"Or a strong woman," Voort says.

"Right-handed either way. And the apartment was vacuumed and wiped. Half the room had *no* prints, not even Anderson's." Mickie muses, "Maybe Colombians might do a little surgery if they're pissed off."

Voort shakes his head, remembering a case last year in Queens, home of the Colombian drug gangs. "If they do something like this, they don't clean the scene. Prints?

They don't give a damn. Whoever did it already flew home."

Mickie nods. "And those guys come in for a reason, so they don't mess up a whole place, don't have to clean it afterward. Colombians find the guy, do the guy, walk away, one, two, three. They don't write on the wall. Forget I brought it up."

Tough talk, but they're rattled. Usually, when detectives get personally involved in a case, the victims are women or children. Kids are helpless, and seeing their little bodies, limp, ravaged, can send a detective into a rage. Women are more vulnerable. The city might dress them in power clothes, might build their muscles in gyms and exercise classes, might teach them, in management classes, the proper legal threats to make against a man at an office, or a courtroom, or board meeting. But put a woman on a dark street, in stiletto heels, against a two-hundred-pound Iraq War veteran—and the armor of civilization falls away.

Voort sees the corpses regularly, the stylish women who thought they were protected, who the city eats up and throws away.

He looks down at Paul Anderson, at the way the head tilts wide, off the neck.

"Maybe Mr. Clean has his trophy in a glass of fruit juice," Mickie says.

"You can use an attitude adjustment, Mickie. And I'm not sure the killer was gay."

When his partner looks dubious, Voort explains. "It's the combination of the fury of the attack and the way the cleaning went on afterward. Cool. A guy who gets crazy, who loses it, doesn't get methodical so fast. He stays nuts."

"You mean, a normal guy."

"What century do you live in?"

"Let's see if the apartment confirms it," Mickie says, meaning, Let's see if we find gay letters, gay art.

Voort keeps his hands in his pockets as he moves around the apartment. He notes potential criminal entry points, double-checking what the precinct detectives probably already looked at. Windows locked. Sliding doors locked.

The living room abandons the southwestern motif. He is struck, looking over the modern glass tables, the mahogany entertainment center and black leather furniture, by a trio of large, original Katz paintings, highlighted by track lights, depicting good-looking men and women lounging on beaches, gazing disinterestedly into the distance, as if something better lies elsewhere.

The work holds the viewer away, impresses with youth but pushes off emotion. One canvas shows a pair of gorgeous women in designer evening gowns, staring in opposite directions, clearly knowing each other but not acknowledging it. Without the frame around them, they might float off, getting tiny.

Modern. Stylish. Alone.

The apartment strives for emotional coolness, yet its owner died in the opposite way.

Dining room untouched. Pantry neat and clean.

Voort notes, in the kitchen, that nothing was left cooking on the stove. There's no smell of food, no glasses out, or plates. The dishwasher is filled, its cycle over. It's not warm, so Voort has no idea what time Anderson, or the killer, cleaning up, turned it on. He finds two highball glasses inside. Did Anderson invite someone he knew here last night, pour drinks, chat awhile, even clean up before the violence began?

Or Paul, did you bring home someone you just met? Did the evening start out pleasurably? What made it turn bad?

What does "I know you" mean?

In the den, Voort finds a veritable gallery of photos of Paul Anderson: on shelves, on the coffee table, by the stove-size television. Paul at the wedding of a rock star, Paul with his arm around a famous talk show host. Paul, on location in South America, in a jungle, in fatigues, with expressionless Indians, who perhaps suspect they are Paul's trophy. And Paul, fishing for blues, grinning into the camera, on a twelve-foot Boston Whaler on Long Island Sound.

There are no photos of family, girlfriends, children, animals.

Paul liked himself quite a bit, Voort decides.

But he wills himself not to jump to conclusions. The apartment is like the man who owned it, part illusion, part fact, revealing only what Paul Anderson wanted you to see.

Back in the bathroom, he sees only one toothbrush in the holder.

He remembers that the toilet seat was up before, not down, so the last person to use it, unless it was cleaned, was male.

Afterward, the detectives compare notes about Anderson's letters, found in the den, and private phone book, found in the desk. They will canvass the names inside, evenly divided between men and women, as well as relatives, friends, bartenders in the neighborhood, shopkeepers. And, of course, coworkers at NBC.

Mickie says, "Who handles Camilla, you or me?"

"Me."

"Con Man." Mickie's tone conveys the warning. She's bad for you. She screwed you up. Stay away from her. Shari's in love with you.

They take a last look at the body, and it is impossible

not to imagine what a blade would feel like, sawing at them, cutting them.

Mickie stands over the lumped-up police tarp.

"I don't care what he did," he says. "Only a rapist deserves this."

FOUR

By four o'clock the temperature is still rising. Mercury climbs toward numbers it has never reached before in New York. At La Guardia Airport heavy air causes airplanes to have trouble lifting off runways. At Shea Stadium, outfielders pull hamstrings from dehydration, racing for balls. Hospital emergency rooms fill with old people suffering respiratory ailments. And at Rockefeller Center, where Voort parks the Chevy, even the statue of Atlas, holding up the world, seems to have trouble with the weight of it, seems drained by the late summer sun.

Time to see Camilla.

Voort's heart beats faster. He tells himself it is from the heat.

He strides past the Banana Republic store at street level, around the ice-skating rink—an outdoor café in summertime—and through the double bronze portals of Rockefeller Center. He used to meet Camilla here, after work, and now every sight, no matter how unremarkable, reminds him of her—from the Depression-era murals dominating the marble lobby, powerful-looking farmers and factory workers—John D. Rockefeller's vision of desirable employees—to the private NBC guards at the network's elevators, who wave Voort past when they see his badge.

At night, when Camilla was working late, he'd bring her roses. She'd lock her office and they'd make love, on her desk, couch, leather chair, bathed in moonlight, in the anonymous glow of the city.

Voort, you feel so good.

Now the receptionist at *Target!*, Camilla's weekly magazine show, brightens when he appears, even though he has not met her. "You're that rich cop. I read about you in the *Daily News*." She sits beneath the show's logo, a bull's-eye with a face on it, flanked by life-size photos of the show's male and female hosts.

"Two assholes," Camilla used to say.

The receptionist says, "You sued the city for trying to take your town house away, trying to break your tax-free status. You won millions and donated money to unseat the mayor. Are you a guest here this week?"

"I'm here to see Camilla Ryan," Voort says. "Not as a guest."

He knows the way to her office; past the receptionist and through a warren of cubicles and semicircular desks lined with computer terminals, where junior staff members, associate producers, writers, and bookers sit.

The scene is surprisingly mundane compared to the glamorous finished product. Voort's struck as always by the fact that news television, dedicated to stripping away illusion, is, in fact, built on it.

Now his blood races faster as he approaches her corner office. She's at her window, looking out, talking into a cell phone. She's lovely even from behind: white-blond hair down to her waist, over her black, silk Armani jacket. Matching silk pants, sharply creased, suggest long legs beneath.

She barks into the receiver. "We have the fucking First Lady on tomorrow and you won't even do a promo on the *Today* show? How about coordinating something right for once?"

"Still the gentle voice of reason," Voort says as she clicks off.

She whirls. She's wearing a white cotton blouse and a single strand of pearls, which Voort gave her. Seeing her tan, he feels a stab of jealousy, because when she goes to the beach she doesn't go alone. He can't read her expression. But she says, "Voort. It's good to see you. But not like this." She puts her arms around him. He smells her perfume, as he has, right here, many times before.

But this time there's no sex in it. Her touch is an act of comfort, simple human connection. When she pulls away, her blue eyes, at a six-inch distance, are red with grief.

"I can't believe he's dead," she says. "Find the bitch who did this."

"A woman, eh?" Voort says. Mickie had been sure it was a man.

"Who else but a woman," she says, "would do such a horrible thing?" She knows about the mutilation, since a network producer found the body. By tonight, Voort guesses, the news will leak to the rest of the press.

Voort tells himself he must ignore his emotions and treat Camilla like any source.

We'll do our best, he tells her, giving the answer he's used hundreds of times before, not adding that he has, at most, four to six days to solve this killing before the sheer volume of new crimes in the city drives Paul Anderson from his active basket and into his files. Also after a few days, statistically, the chances of catching a killer begin going down.

Voort leans back against the lip of her desk, like he did when she used to unzip his fly here, reach into his underwear, pull out his penis and get down on her knees and take him in her mouth.

She seats herself on the Haitian cotton couch on which he used to straddle her, and pull up her skirt.

Her knees are pressed together. Her hands lie demurely on her thighs. Her posture is always perfect, her makeup always in place.

Of all the questions he wanted to ask her during their separation, one he never considered was: "Tell me about Paul Anderson."

"He was a great friend," she says, yet it occurs to Voort that during their months together, she never mentioned this "great friend."

"He helped me when I was in trouble."

"What kind of trouble?"

Camilla's eyes flicker down, away from Voort. Her formidable social skills do not include deception in personal matters.

"Nothing that has to do with this."

Voort must conquer the strong emotions buffeting him. It's hard to think with her near. This special "friendship" with a man he's never heard of before makes him suspicious. Or is it jealous? He's unsure if he's interested in a professional or personal way. He leans back, wills himself to concentrate.

"Tell me about him. Everything is helpful," Voort says. "If I have specific questions, I'll ask them as we go along."

"I used to wonder how you interviewed people, and now you're interviewing me. It's strange how things work out," she says.

She launches into her description, the public relations part, as homicide detectives call it. The litany of praise that generally pours from the deceased's family and friends, at least at first. Paul was kind. He was gentle. He was a genius investigator who worked long hours, days in a row sometimes, and never gave up on an investigation until it produced results.

"He sent mob and union leaders to prison, and broke the story of that Hong Kong heroin ring last year, in Midtown. He risked his life during the war in Iraq, crossed into the fighting zone with his cameraman, against orders."

Voort jots notes as she speaks. "I'd like to see the investigative pieces. And any original notes, phone lists, interviews."

"You think someone he investigated did it?"

Voort shrugs. "Was he working on an investigation now?"

"His new show is entertainment. But you'll have to talk to his staffers to be sure. Paul could have been doing an investigation on the side. He was capable of it."

"The TV this morning said something about him being involved in a lawsuit."

Camilla nods. "Last year he had two of his reporters get jobs at Allan Foods, in Pennsylvania. You know, hidden cameras in the warehouses." She frowns. "It was disgusting. They didn't clean the meat. When the piece aired, Allan Foods sued the network. He had 'em dead on the facts, so they skipped a libel action and claimed the reporters used fraud to get hired. We won, but upstairs," Camilla says with typical producer disdain for network lawyers, "they wanted him transferred out of investigations."

"And Paul didn't like it."

"He was furious. Who wouldn't be? He argued."

"Who was responsible for transferring him?"

Camilla names a network vice president, Roger Martin. "But if you're thinking the death had anything to do with the suit—"

"Camilla, how do you *know* he argued with Roger Martin?"

She meets his eyes, with new understanding. "When Paul was mad, everybody knew."

Voort switches subjects. "Tell me about his personal life."

The question makes her uncomfortable. She crosses her legs, and arms. "He was generous with his private time. He volunteered to work with injured kids at NYU Hospital."

"Good. But I meant, girlfriends."

"I didn't sleep with him, if that's what you mean."

"I asked you who his girlfriends were, not who they weren't," Voort says, feeling the pull between them, the tension, that is always there when they are together in a room.

She blushes, and Voort follows her gaze as it flickers to a color photo on her desk, in a silver frame.

It's new. It shows Camilla and a man; she in an evening gown, he in a tuxedo. A barb moves into Voort's belly. The couple is leaning against each other, shoulder-to-shoulder. Their arms encircle each other's waists.

"That's Paul," Camilla says, realizing where Voort's looking. "It was taken at the Emmys. The network bought a table and we sat together."

"Were you his date?"

"I *said* I didn't sleep with him."

Voort keeps his tone level. "The question is, did you date him?"

"That's hardly relevant," she says, guarding her private affairs with an iron face.

But the truth, he knows, is that it is extremely relevant. She has just become more of a suspect. And at the very least she must be cultivated as a source. He says, with more reasonableness than he feels, "Camilla, I'm sorry he died. But you asked for me to be assigned here, and I have to ask these questions. You're his friend. Your insights can help. I know it's hard for you, but I have to ask about your relationship to the deceased."

"He's not the 'deceased,' " she snaps. "He's Paul!"

Camilla burst out crying, something he's only seen before on the day she left him.

Then she says, "I'm sorry. You're right. I just can't believe what happened!"

She's really crying now, folded over, hugging herself. She needs physical comfort. An arm around her shoulder. A warm body against hers. Voort has performed the service a hundred times, with grieving parents, friends, lovers, children. You get more information from a friend than a stranger. Touch her, he tells himself. Soothe her.

He does not move.

At length she dries her eyes, dabs them with a tissue. "I never dated him. I had no romantic interest in him. You want to know why I put the picture there? It's going to sound stupid."

Voort waits.

"I look good in it, that's why."

Despite himself, Voort bursts out laughing. It's vintage Camilla, exactly the reason she'd put a photo on her desk, whether the person beside her had leprosy or two heads or was Charles Manson the murderer.

It makes me look good.

Voort thinks, You are so beautiful.

He says, "Tell me about his private life."

Camilla's eyes come up, more cooperative now. She moves into the part of her description that Mickie calls the "reality check," the part where the dead person's reputation gets tarnished and the human frailties come out.

"He could never commit to a relationship," she says.

"He was working on it, but at bottom, he had trouble with commitment."

She reddens, because her words on the day she left Voort seem to hang between them.

I can't commit just now.

She says, "He was thirty-five but acted ten years younger. He dated a lot of different women. He met them at parties. He went to singles bars. He picked women up on the road. It was easy for him. He'd complain that there was nobody good out there, but he was like a lot of grown-up babies in TV. Brilliant professionally. Retarded personally. He treated women great at first, but as soon as they responded, he'd start thinking they were too fat, or clingy. *Something.*"

"Every week, another love. Every *other* week, he couldn't wait to escape."

"Did he ever mention any of these women getting angry?"

"He didn't stick around long enough to hurt anyone that much." She sighs. "But I guess time doesn't have much to do with it, if you love someone," she says. "If a woman believed his bullshit, it would have been pretty bad."

"Do you know the names?"

She frowns. Camilla, a TV journalist, spends her days ordering reporters to ask exactly this type of personal question. She sends them after politicians, errant husbands, corporate presidents, famous actors. But now that an inquiry touches her personally, a friend of hers, she seems to disapprove of it.

"I'm sure no one here hurt him," she says.

But she writes names down anyway, and hands him a piece of paper.

And Voort pops the question he was saving. "Was he gay?"

"*Paul?* Are you kidding? What did you find out about him?"

"I'm just asking."

"Believe me, Voort, that man was not gay." Which is the answer Voort's been getting all day.

But he keeps pushing. "And you," he says delicately. "Do you mind telling me where you were last night?"

All the blood drains from her face, and she says in a flat voice, "Asleep. Alone."

As they wrap up, he sees her office is basically unchanged. The couch is half covered with shooting scripts and stuffed moose. The bookshelf contains videos and publishers' freebies, promo books on sex problems, relationships, self-help, which Simon & Schuster or Random House are trying to get publicized on TV. There's a basket of candy samples, more freebies from gum and bakery companies. Camilla, who never eats sweets, leaves them for other staffers to nibble on during the day.

There's a joke calendar on a corkboard, a Stephen Phillips cartoon called "Modern Math Problems." In it, a teacher stands at a blackboard, where she has drawn two huge groups of men and women, just standing around.

"If Dick sleeps with Jane," the teacher is saying, "and Jane slept with three other men, and *they* each slept with three other women, and *they* slept with three other men, how many chances does Dick have of catching VD?"

Ha ha ha.

Call Shari.

Voort excuses himself, finds a phone in an empty office and punches in her work number. He's been trying to reach her since this morning, every time he had a break. First she was in a "meeting," her prissy-sounding assistant informed him. Then she was "out." Then she was "at lunch," the assistant said haughtily, as if Shari confided in her, as if the two of them were punishing him.

This time the phone just rings. He imagines her on the number 2 train, on her way home to Brooklyn.

She never called back, all day, even on Sky Page.

"Voort?"

Camilla's standing in the doorway, just outside the office, as if she's been listening.

"Need anything else?" she wants to know, her eyes moving from the phone to his face. "Want me to help you find those women he dated?"

She's recovered, he sees. Her posture is sure again, her makeup back in place, the only tension remaining is in the corner of her beautiful mouth, where he sees the barest curve of the smallest muscles.

"Thanks, but I'd rather do it alone."

"Sure thing. And Voort?"

His damn heart starts up again. The crazy hope blooms in him.

She says, "I know you had to ask that question before. That favor he did for me?"

"Yes?"

"It had to do with a story we worked on, together, a long time ago. That's all."

Voort pats her shoulder, like a parent, or an old buddy, and he turns away, stomach churning, from love, and lust, from the certainty that she's just lied.

Hours later Voort's on the 2 train, heading to Brooklyn. He's still not reached Shari, and he's decided to show up at her house. He won't use the Jaguar, not tonight, because there are no pay lots near her house, and it is inadvisable in New York to leave a seventy-thousand-dollar vehicle on the street, even in a good neighborhood.

As the train rocks he knows that back at One Police

Plaza the night shift's been handed the information he and Mickie gathered about Paul Anderson, hundreds of facts, a dozen directions, nothing concrete, but enough ex-girlfriends, pissed-off network executives, resentful convicts in prison, all of whom trace their misfortune to Paul Anderson—to fill a small auditorium.

The subway is packed with people who are sweaty and sullen after a day at work. It drops Voort at Grand Army Plaza, in central Brooklyn. He climbs the steps to the surface and, emerging, even in the heat, feels part of the dreadful sense of Manhattan's compression fall away. This part of Brooklyn is tree-lined, off Prospect Park, and filled with brownstones. Writers, brokers, and lawyers with families live here.

The pace is slow, or at least slower by the standards of Manhattan.

But the heat hasn't abated. It wilts leaves on the oaks and boils the pollution, laying a sick yellow film over parked cars, stop signs, and the marble arch commemorating the Union soldiers who fought in the Civil War.

Voort walks through the residential section, to the gray stone cathedral on Sixth Avenue. Mass is over but he slides into the second pew, folds his hands, bows his head.

God, I want to do the right thing, he prays.

Voort hears footsteps coming down the aisle, toward him.

She loves me. She's a good person. I don't want to hurt her. And I sure don't want to hurt a baby, and that's what the life is inside her is, whether or not it's only the size of two cells, hers and mine.

He feels someone sit down beside him.

Thank you for my life, my big family, and my friends, and for Shari. Help me remember all the good things I have, and share them. Help me to not require perfection. Help me to remember that it takes effort to be good. Also, if you don't mind, God, if you can give me a hand tonight, that would be great.

"Hello, Voort," the priest beside him says.

"Hi, Freddy."

"Got a problem?"

"I'll work it out."

"I was heading to the confession booth. Maybe you want to join me. I'd know your voice anyway, you know. Coupla Hail Marys does wonders for the ill at ease. Best deal in town."

"I never say confession, Freddy."

The priest rises. "See you at teen basketball on Wednesday then," he says. "Otherwise, you know where to find me. Man in a box."

Voort watches the fifty-year-old priest disappear into the booth, and a woman in shorts and a halter top rush into the one beside him. Voort puts two hundred-dollar bills in the poor box, and lights two candles beneath the new statue of St. Augustine, who seems to be looking back.

"I have a kid," he says, addressing, in his mind, his parents, who died when he was nine. Voort prefers to believe they hear him. As a cop he requires evidence. In church, desire will suffice.

He tells his parents, "You have a grandchild."

Voort leaves the church, passes strolling couples on Seventh Avenue, who are avoiding the outdoor cafés tonight, in favor of any place that offers air-conditioning. He walks up President to Eighth, and then to Montgomery, and rings the top floor buzzer on a spankingly well-kept ninety-year-old brownstone, diagonally across from Prospect Park.

"Who is it?" says the voice of a young girl, not yet a teenager.

"Open up, criminals! It's the police!"

The girl squeals in delight and the buzzer rings. Voort pushes inside, through the inner foyer door, and up three flights to where Shari's six-year-old daughter Aya waits in the open doorway of their three-bedroom apartment. The pigtailed girl has Shari's small features, same blue-black hair, same lean look that will elongate into a beautiful woman. Now she's wearing an apron that drops to her ankles.

"You missed dinner. We had hot dogs."

If the kids are here, instead of at their father's, if Shari went and picked them up, if she is too upset to be alone, things are bad.

Aya steps aside to let him in. "When can we go to a Mets game again?"

"Saturday, if your mom says it's okay."

In the dysfunctional city Voort sees all the time, kids lack parents. Love lacks object. The city fractures into individual components. Husbands and wives claim separate time with their offspring, separate cars, furniture, baseball tickets.

Celebrating isolation, Voort hears Sammy Davis Jr. singing, from the adjacent apartment, "I Gotta Be Me."

Voort finds Shari in the kitchen, wiping dishes. The electric dishwasher has broken, and anyway, Con Edison is asking people to go easy on appliances, fearing a brownout with the need for air-conditioning so high.

Shari's barefoot, back to him, in tight jeans and a flame-colored cotton pullover. He knows she senses him standing there. At length, she looks up. There is no expression on her face, and it breaks his heart.

"I got your messages. But I needed to think," she says.

The TV seems louder from the living room.

"It's not a good idea that you came here tonight," she adds.

"Let's take a walk," Voort says.

"Who'll watch the kids?"

"I'll call the sitter."

"No."

"Okay then, how about we talk here?"

"So talk," Shari says in a dull voice.

Voort moves close, and smells, over the dishwasher odor, and the carbon smell of burnt hot dogs, a fresh nutmeg scent, Shari's.

Her hand, holding a soapy saucer, is trembling.

Voort tells her what he wants to do.

"Are you crazy?" she says.

"It would work," he says.

"You spent last night dreaming about your old girlfriend. You woke up wanting to break up with me. Didn't you?"

"Yes."

"Then don't you think getting married is a little out of line?"

There is an invisible barrier between them that makes her face seem farther away. Voort does not touch her, but he has thought about his decision, and he is quite serious.

"Things changed," he says.

"Now you love me?"

"I didn't say that."

"What exactly *are* you saying? That you feel guilty?"

"Shari, I never lied to you about how I feel. And we're both responsible for the pregnancy. If you have to know if you're in love with someone before you sleep with them, then no one would ever do anything in the world."

"This isn't a debate. It's a decision."

"Look, you're upset that I didn't propose right way, when I found out, in the first second. I understand that."

"I'm upset," she says, with feminine disdain, "about more than you can imagine, mister."

Voort picks up a dish rag and starts wiping dishes. "Fine. But let me ask you a question. When did you learn you were pregnant?"

"Yesterday. I took the home test."

"And why didn't you tell me at that exact second, when you found out, what happened?"

She says, wearily, "Because I needed to absorb it, if you don't mind."

Voort says, finally putting his hands on her shoulders, feeling the flinch, "Then all I'm asking is for you to give me the same privilege. A day absorbing it."

She softens a little. She takes off the apron, leads him into the living room by the hand; her touch, even tentative, an improvement over the mood so far. She shoos the girls out, tells them to watch TV in their room.

She switches the news on, so the sound will mask their conversation. On screen, Voort sees the police commissioner's chief PR flack, Jack Moseley, at a podium, with an insert photo behind him, reading, GRAMERCY PARK MURDER.

"Voort, you're a good person. I'm not blaming you for not being in love. But marriage is a bad idea."

Moseley is saying, "We have no leads."

Voort takes her hands. "Remember our first discussion, in the park, that first evening?"

They both go back to it. He'd met Shari during the Bainbridge investigation, in which he'd saved Camilla's life. At the time, Shari had worked in a bank in Greenwich Village where the murderer had once been employed. She had recently left a bad marriage, and had built up her courage, after he interviewed her, to call and ask him out.

"I'm getting over someone," he'd said.

"Would it be too forward to tell you that I'd like to see you, if you do get over her?"

Voort had told the little banker, "It would be nice."

Later, on their first date, they'd strolled in Central Park. No actual physical contact yet, except for an accidental touch of swaying hips.

He'd been amazed to learn that Shari, educated at Princeton, had entered into an arranged marriage at the age of twenty-two, seven years earlier.

"Who arranged it?"

"We did," she said. "Zia and me. In America people get a feeling, lust or chemistry, and they fool themselves into thinking that is love. Then they assume everything else will follow. In Pakistan our tradition, my parents' at least, was to look at everything *else* first—background, suitability—and if the list was right, they figured *love* would follow. Considering the divorce rate here, who is to say what is right?"

"But how did you meet Zia?" Voort had asked, fascinated. "Did you put an ad in the paper?"

"I was born in America. I dated American men, but nothing happened. So I tried our way. Pakistani friends knew a man in London. He flew here to meet me."

"All the way from London for a blind date?"

She'd burst out laughing. "See? You have no concept. Neither of us said the word marriage, but both of us understood that for me to let him come, and for him to buy this ticket, this was a serious situation. We walked, talked. We had similar interests, and he was very handsome."

"So you just got engaged," Voort said, astounded.

"The whole family got involved at that point. Asians

stay married, as a rule, longer than Americans. But in our case we weren't really Pakistani anymore. We'd grown up in different countries. We didn't really have the same culture, and that was the base on which we were trying to build this particular marriage. He was formal. To me, he was very British. I was looser. Easygoing. In the end, we realized we'd fooled ourselves. We didn't really know each other. Zia was a lovely man, but too hesitant for me, too fearful of life, in the way he wanted to live, to raise the girls, to take vacations, even to take a walk at night. He would have played it safe until he died. I couldn't live like that."

As Voort had digested it, Shari laughed and took his arm. Her hands had felt silky, her touch exciting.

"Don't worry, Detective Voort. I know the difference between taking a walk with a New Yorker and a Pakistani."

Two weeks later they slept together for the first time.

Now Shari's fingers move against Voort's palm, slowly, rubbing. She is touched by his offer. "You want to pretend you are a Pakistani man. But you're an American man. An arranged marriage, between you and me, would make us resent each other from day one."

"Not if we work on it."

"I'm having an abortion," she says, and folds her arms.

On TV the commissioner's PR flack says, "The information you have, that his hands were mutilated, is a rumor."

"But it's a baby," Voort protests. He sees, in his mind, an infant in a blanket. He sees a small blond boy on the floor, in his house, in the second story nursery, playing with a toy truck. He sees a little girl in a dress, carrying a textbook. He had never planned a child, but it is alive to him now.

"Don't you think I know?" she says. "I can't stand

this. I talked with my sister. I simply can't raise three kids. I just can't do it. *I can't!*"

"Then I'll raise him, if you don't want to get married. Or we'll do it together."

"I'm not walking around sick for nine months," Shari says, furious, "to give away a baby."

Voort keeps his voice low, modulated. "I'll hire help, or stay with you myself. You and the girls can move into my house. I'll do this any way you want."

"What I want," she says, "didn't happen. And how would you feel if we did this thing and then you and I broke it off, like Zia and I did. I can just see it. Zia coming to pick up *his* kids on alternate Saturdays. You coming to pick up *your* kid on alternate Sundays."

Voort, watching her fight tears, is encouraged by the words "if we did this thing." She says, "You have no idea what it means to bring up a baby. It's not something you do on a schedule. Not something you hire someone for. Children get sick. They hurt. They break your heart with worry. They change your life."

"It's too late for this to be about convenience. And anyway, it sounds to me like the baby is *already* breaking your heart."

"Detectives working on the case are confident," the PR flack on TV lies, as the phone rings.

"Promise me you'll think about it," Voort says. "For a week. Hold off for that long. Okay?"

The phone sounds shrill, over shouting reporters on television.

"I won't do anything until we talk about it again," she says as the PR man tells reporters, "No more questions."

She adds, "Now maybe you should go." The TV switches to sports news.

He rises, holding back his arguments as Shari answers the phone, and he sees the exhaustion in her eyes harden.

She stares at Voort, and tells whoever is calling, her tone devoid of emotion, "He's here, all right."

She extends the receiver.

"It's Camilla." Shari's look says, I can't believe you gave her my number. "She thought of something important. Or at least that's what she says."

FIVE

Nora Clay, in the grip of a nightmare, twists and sweats on her single bed. She is fully clothed. Her mouth is open, as if she is screaming, but no sound comes out. Her fists clench the white cotton blanket. Her legs are locked, straight ahead, like a five year-old's, trembling.

"Please," she forces out, in a long moan, as the intercom rings.

"Don't hurt me."

The buzzer keeps screaming, yet the high-pitched noise does not rouse her. It is bright in the apartment, gold with morning light. Sunbeams slice through the iron bars outside, bathe the plants and worktable and file-filled bookshelves and form a lattice pattern on the tortured woman, shaking her head in sleep.

"Oh God," she says. "Stop."

And now the relentless electric whine begins to penetrate. Her eyes open, uncomprehending that she has made a transition to consciousness. Her stomach feels sour, her head pounds. Her throat is parched from the dream, and from dehydration; from the gin, which sucked away more useful fluids from her tissues, her blood.

I can't remember what happened last night.

Panic fills her. The apartment is different! The window moved to the wrong side of the room!

But then she sees that she is lying backward on the bed, her stockinged feet on rumpled pillows, her head half off the bottom of the mattress.

Jesus Christ. I'm still dressed.

She also realizes the buzzing in her head is the intercom. She tries to sit up but a wave of nausea pushes her down.

Who the hell could be down there so early?

She presses her palms to her ears, but the noise is a jackhammer, hooked to her synapses.

I can't even remember the dream.

Finally she manages to stand, the movement sloshing the acid in her belly. She lurches toward the intercom, steadies herself against the wall, yet misses the button on the first try.

She cries, into the intercom, "Go away! Whoever you are!"

Nora envisions a street person down in the locked foyer, a homeless person, needing shelter, or a carpet to sleep on, or a victim to rob.

The buzzer rings again and the voice crackling at her through the intercom says, "It's Louis Vale! With your delivery!"

"Louis?" She cannot believe the idiocy of this man, bothering her this early. "You're not supposed to come till nine o'clock!"

"It's ten-thirty! I came back a second time!"

And now the pulse *really* starts up in her belly. Ten-thirty is impossible, she tells herself. It simply cannot be ten-thirty. She *never* wakes up that late. She rises each morning at seven-thirty, almost exactly, to the minute, in an absolutely unbreakable routine. She doesn't even need an alarm clock.

Seven-thirty. Not ten-thirty. The big hand is on the six when she wakes, and the small one on the seven. And each morning, at *seven-thirty*, she puts on her terry-cloth robe to retrieve the day's delivered *Times* from outside her door, from the welcome mat. She brews Danish blend coffee, and puts two teaspoons of white sugar in it. She butters a cinnamon croissant and cuts it in half, lengthwise. She waters the plants and listens to the morning NPR program. All of this an hour and a half before Louis Vale arrives with her envelope.

But now, when she twists her head toward the big wind-up clock on the dresser, blinks through the pounding pain, she sees that Louis is right.

"Oh God."

Time itself has always been one of the walls of her apartment. Now it is like the wall is missing. Like anyone can see inside today.

She buzzes Louis into the building. The ticking clock seems thunderous, each slam like the weight of a sledge-hammer against her eardrums, reverberating into her brain.

"Your package, Ms. Clay. Sign please."

Louis Vale, filling the doorway, is gaping at her disarray, at the apparition of dissolution that has answered his knock. As she scribbles, she sees that there is a bright sheen of masculine interest in Louis's dark gaze, which travels down her crumpled blouse and short skirt, down the long rip in her left stocking.

She shuts the door on him.

Fuck all men.

And with that rage, an image inserts itself into her head. Just a flicker of a picture, of a rack of knives, magnetically fixed to a kitchen wall.

Whose kitchen is that?

But she cannot remember. She wants to remember, but

when she tries, her panic grows worse. She tells herself, in a mantra of attempted self-control, I got drunk. I fell asleep. I had a bad dream.

The knives must have been from that dream.

She insists, fighting the thing in her head trying to get out. I will start my day. I will shower and open the envelope. I will see whose life has been delivered into my hands. I will learn valuable, fascinating secrets, as I do every day.

Go to work.

In the bathroom, she strips off soiled clothing, each movement sending fresh waves of nausea up her throat. She drops the sweaty skirt and blouse in the hamper, the ripped stocking in the trash, the jewelry on the sink. She washes her face, and steps into the scalding shower, soaps up, a really big lather, covers every inch with bubbles. She uses a washcloth on her whole body, scrubbing, especially her genitals, so hard that they hurt.

Under the needle shower, Nora looks down at her skin, which is red from the heat and pressure. A whole body red as a vagina.

Clean.

But as she towels off, another image comes to her, this time a man's face. A blond man who stands on a terrace high above the city.

She sees herself kissing the man, which is disgusting.

She shuts her eyes. *That image must be part of the nightmare I had.*

But trying to push away the growing sense of disaster doesn't make her feel better. Neither does her normal routine: brushing her teeth, which replaces the rancid taste with a minty one, or choosing a bright yellow sundress, crisp and laundered, or making her way to the freezer, finding Danish blend coffee, the way she does every morning, measuring three teaspoons into the filter and waiting while the Braun coffeemaker begins to bubble.

Blessed coffee. The mug is her chalice. Caffeine in hand, at the worktable, and little computer, she upends the day's envelope and watches two plastic cassettes drop on the blotter, beside the list of four names. The first name on the list is ANDERSON, PAUL.

She hears the blond man in her head say, "Now I understand commitment."

He is not a dream. He is memory.

The phone screams.

Nora, reaching for it, suddenly sees a hand, her own white hand, in her mind, take a paring knife off the rack on the blond man's kitchen wall.

"Hello?"

It's Nora's broker, at PaineWebber, ignoring Nora's shaky voice because she's too excited about something. She's babbling about some stock that's soared, an explosion of money Nora's earned. "It's up twenty points!" Ruth Poole says as Nora reaches for that voice as an anchor, a fact and truth to fight panic with, a tool to dispel other thoughts.

Nora has never met Ruth Poole, but she knows the twenty-six-year-old broker has a corner office in Darien, Connecticut, with a window that looks out on a meadow, and the meadow is spotted with oaks. She knows Ruth is married, and that her husband, Kenneth, commutes to his commodities broker job in Manhattan on the 5:45 train every morning. She knows that Ruth hates sushi, and loves Indonesian knickknack art—wooden angels with movable arms, antique tea chests from Java, of mahogany.

The broker tells her, "Your tip was gold! Jackson Electric went up fourteen points. Let's sell it now."

"Not yet. It's going to split," Nora Clay says.

She hears an intake of breath. "Do you have information again?" Ruth Poole says.

"It's just a hunch."

"You always say it's a 'hunch' but it always happens," Ruth Poole says, filled with admiration. This envy and acknowledgment of Nora's superior knowledge settles Nora down somewhat.

Can knowing the future alter the past?

"Just don't sell the stock," Nora says.

Ruth Poole says "Fine," probably having bought huge chunks of it herself. Her joy makes her overstep the bounds of professionalism. Success makes her imagine a friendlier relationship than exists. She says, like a friend, buddy, pal, confidante, "Nora, do you mind if I ask a personal question?"

"What?"

"You've made so much money . . . you have over $800,000 in your account. Why stay in that old building? You can afford to live somewhere else."

Nora feels the blood draining from her face.

"There are some really beautiful condos going up downtown," Ruth says. "We would buy one, but Ken wants to have a kid, and stay up here."

Nora can only whisper, "How do you know what kind of building I live in?"

Ruth pauses, understanding, too late, that she has presumed too much. She tries to backpedal. "Well, Ken and I drove into the city last Sunday, to see that show *Guys Are Cavemen*, and we were near your street and—"

"You spied on me?"

"We drove down your block, that's all. I matched the address to your account statement. We had to go down the West Side Highway anyway and you're just a block away."

"Get your supervisor!"

"Nora, I didn't mean to upset you. I'm sorry."

But Nora is practically apoplectic. "Who the hell do you think you are, prying into my life? Why do I have to say everything to you twice? *I want your supervisor!*"

And now the supervisor, or whatever you call a boss in a brokerage office, comes on the line. A man, middle-age from the sound of him, deep-voiced, overconfident, smooth-talking and solicitous, asking what's the matter, trying to soothe an $800,000 account.

"I want to switch brokers," Nora demands.

She can tell, from the muffled sound on the line, that the concerned supervisor has covered the receiver with his palm while he talks to Ruth Poole. When he comes back, he dares to suggest that the problem may be a misunderstanding.

"Perhaps if you and Ruth talk about it, it might be smoothed away."

"It'll be smoothed if I transfer my money to Merrill Lynch," Nora says. "How about that?"

"No need! No need to do that," the man says quickly. Ruth has just become history. The supervisor knows just the fellow to take over the account, he says as if he never opposed the idea. One of the best people possible, blah blah blah. Lots of experience. A top-notch person. If Nora can hold a moment, this new, brilliant broker will come on the line.

"Just tell him to stay out of my private life," she snaps, and slams down the phone.

You can't trust anyone. Not one person.

And with that thought, the last barrier to memory drops away and she sees, graphic and unmistakable, in her head, a man, on a floor, bleeding. She sees a knife, rising and falling. She hears a gurgle of pain and sees the spray of blood on the walls.

She says, in the barest whisper, "What have I done?"

The montage continues. She sees herself bending over a sewer at Twenty-ninth and Madison, taking something out of her handbag. A plastic Baggie. Nora drops the thing into the sewer. Nora hears a squeaking below, from rats.

"No."

There are nightmares, she knows, as she backs against the wall, that people suffer—dreams so terrible that they linger even after a sleeper awakes. Dreams where the sleeper sees herself harming a person, killing a person. Sees a loved one, or hated one even, crushed by a car, or bleeding, shot, knifed, dead. Graphic depictions that speed the heart like hers races now.

After this kind of dream, she prays, it can take a while before reality banishes the vision. And now, with her last vestiges of will, she waits for the knowledge that she's only experienced a dream. That today, like yesterday, will have a methodical, rational trajectory of work and simple meals taken alone, perhaps an evening stroll in Riverside Park, along the Hudson promenade, and then an hour or so of mundane television, a sitcom, or detective show, to pass the time.

I killed Paul Anderson.

Twenty minutes later she is still sobbing, crumpled in a corner. The pain balloons out of her, starts in her organs and expands until they might explode. She cannot breathe. She clutches at her windpipe. The images come faster—Paul Anderson, crawling, Paul, gurgling. She even smells the apartment, the lemony furniture polish over the sweetish aroma of blood and leaking life.

Just when she thinks it can't get worse, a new thought comes.

I liked it.

Her hands press over her ears as if to stop thoughts coming.

I liked the way the knife handle felt. I liked not being afraid for once.

Stopstopstopstop.

I never felt that much power, ever.

These thoughts are alive and independent, as if, physically, a new, different person is rising out of her. Someone who Dr. Neiman warned her about. A proud and angry person, filled with more hate than she even knew she possessed.

And this other Nora seems to be saying, *You want to make yourself remember? That part is fine with me.*

You want to feel bad about it?

Tough shit. I liked it.

This pride is too much for her. She forces herself to her feet, totters toward the phone, toward punishment, toward the police, but the phone seems to be getting smaller, as if viewed from the front end of a telescope, which needs, in order to function properly, to be reversed. She sees her tiny hand reaching for the receiver. She sees herself punching in the police emergency number, 911.

"Police!"

She doesn't say anything.

"Hello?"

Nora slams the receiver down.

Do you really want to turn yourself in?

I'm afraid.

Dr. Neiman's voice, in her head, says, *Nora, you're not ready to stop therapy yet. You've built a life for yourself, a start, but you have no friends. This weird job you have isolates you. You keep following people in your files. And you panic when the predictability of your routine is disturbed, even a little.*

Most of all, you should never, ever, drink.

Like a drowning swimmer flailing for a life preserver,

she starts to call Dr. Neiman. She punches in half his phone number when she hangs up again.

He might turn me in.

Nora Clay sinks to the floor, weeping. She is not aware of time passing. At length it starts getting dark in the apartment. She is not hungry, or thirsty. What she needs, she understands, is punishment, but she cannot bear the idea of being locked in a steel cage, unable to get out.

As she dresses again, the sounds of the city outside become nocturnal. She hears a car alarm, and reggae music from an apartment across the alley. She hears footsteps upstairs as the waitress who lives there comes home from work. She smells tomato sauce burning through the air vents that connect, in the old building, all the sixth floor apartments. She hears a dog barking, in anger, or loneliness, or just the need to be free of four walls.

This time she chooses the conservative wardrobe. Light beige cotton skirt, summery and billowy. Bra and button-up white summer blouse with a high collar. Sneakers, high-tops, as unfeminine as possible.

The anonymous look of a New York pedestrian in the night.

Outside, the hot air is heavy with a dreadful sense of too late. She is detached from the lights and people as she treads north on Broadway, past 115th, 123rd, out of the marginal neighborhoods, the yuppie footholds, with their new cafés and Starbucks coffee shops, and into the more ruined section of the city, the darker blocks, the poorer blocks, the blocks filled with funeral parlors and liquor stores, with abandoned buildings and squatters. She is invisible. No one can harm someone who is already dead. Her footfalls are as steady as a shuffling robot's. She feels nothing, not exhaustion, not hunger.

Her body has already died.

And all she sees, the people seeking relief from the heat on their stoops, fanning themselves with *Daily News* editions, the ambulances screaming past, the beggars on the corners, seem to have given up hope.

Once, she pauses in front of an all-night drugstore, with a display of knives in the window. But they are much too bright. Another time she pauses before a stoplight, at Broadway and 131st, a particularly busy street, with cars rushing past. And she thinks, just step into the flow and close your eyes.

Finally, she finds herself on Riverside Drive in Harlem, all the way west, looking down from the aqueduct road at the rushing northbound traffic below on the West Side Highway. It is not a huge drop, only seven stories, but the cars move fast down there, with unforgiving speed, the kind New York drivers achieve when unfettered by a traffic jam. The headlights are the bright eyes of animals. The rushing boxes of steel eat up time and space.

She places both hands on the railing, filled with lassitude now, not peace, but at least acceptance. The frantic energy of the city is gone. She will not let anyone put her in a cell.

Looking down, she inhales the hellish odor of hot exhaust rising.

One foot up on the railing, through a hole in the chain-link fence.

Nora sits perched above traffic, swinging her legs lazily, like an eight-year-old on a summer hammock, on an August night.

No rush. She'll push off in a moment. The whole city seems to have slowed, and drifts by around her, quieter, like the metropolis itself has now become the dream. Below, she sees an old Ford slow in a southbound lane and veer onto the weedy shoulder. A man gets out of the driver's side, and, as he walks across his headlights to inspect the left front tire, a woman carrying an infant gets out the passenger side.

The baby catches Nora's attention, rouses her a little.

You should keep that baby in a car seat, Nora Clay advises the mother, in her mind.

The woman lays the baby on the ground, on a blanket, and joins the man. They appear to be arguing about the tire.

The baby, unnoticed, rolls over and starts crawling, slowly, toward the traffic.

"Hey!" Nora Clay yells, fully aware now. "Your baby!"

But the couple is too busy fighting to pay attention to anything else, and the roar of traffic blocks out Nora's cries.

The baby crawls off the edge of the blanket, into the overgrown weeds. It rolls over on its back, struggles, rights itself, and resumes moving toward traffic again, drawn to noise, or light, or simply fascinated by the brand-new concept of movement.

"The baby!" Nora screams.

She is frantic. She can't stand watching the crawling baby. There is no time to reach it, and her voice is too puny to catch their attention over the rushing cars. She looks for someone to shout with her, but the aqueduct is deserted. The whole city is packed with people, but this street, when she needs help, is isolated and dark.

The baby is three feet from the road.

"Heyyyyyyy!"

Two feet.

Nora is hyperventilating. She has never been so frightened, even this morning. The tragedy she is watching is unbelievably preventable, if only the adults would look up. Nora's practically weeping with helplessness. She runs back and forth, behind the railing of the aqueduct, spots an empty Coke bottle, picks it up.

Arm back, all the way back, like a javelin thrower she saw on TV who won the Olympics.

With all her strength she hurls the bottle out over six lanes of traffic, toward the disabled car in the weeds, hoping to catch the attention of the distracted couple.

But it falls short, on the southbound lanes, twenty feet away from its target. Shattering, it causes a Honda to veer, almost colliding with another car. Both drivers hit their horns. The accident is averted, but the noise, the screeching and honking, finally catches the attention of the man and woman in the weeds.

And now, thank God, the woman spins around, sees that her baby is not on the blanket, and spots the infant inching across the point where weeds and asphalt meet.

She snatches up her baby.

She hugs the child to her body.

She never even sees the joyous figure across the road, jumping up and down, on top of the aqueduct, screaming with happiness.

Watching mother and child, celebrating the baby that has a future again, Nora backs away from the railing, and remembers what she has forgotten all day. It is the reason she followed Paul Anderson in the first place, the terrible thing she knew about him, that put him in her files and on her list.

Nora Clay feels, slowly, a lift begin inside her. A weight is falling off her and she turns away from the drop, at one with her city again. I saved that baby, she thinks, in sync with the rhythms around her, starting the walk south, out of Harlem, toward 108th street, toward home.

I'm hungry. I'm famished.

She stops in a bar on 112th, near Columbia University,

a college bar alive with students and life and music. She orders a hamburger with extra onions and relish and two orders of french fries. The astonished bartender watches the little woman eat a second burger, and a large green salad, and a piece of icing-covered, freshly baked carrot cake after that.

By eleven o'clock, when she lets herself back into her apartment, she's had three gin and tonics to top things off. She feels positively wonderful.

I'll have to work all night to have the results ready for tomorrow.

But at her desk, getting out the tape cassettes, which she ignored all day, her gaze falls on the list beside her computer. On the four names. Paul Anderson. Thomas Jackson. Otto Frederick. Conrad Voort.

She picks up a Magic Marker and draws a line through Anderson.

Let's see which one I'll follow tomorrow night, she thinks.

To hell with you. All of you. I hate you.

I know you.

SIX

Otto Frederick, anthropologist, jungle traveler, university lecturer, unhappy husband, makes his way across the baking concrete expanse of Washington Square Park on the hottest day of the year, the most miserable, polluted, stifling day of the decade. The crazy, dangerous heat makes blood seethe, and has been rising for the last half week.

Frederick is telling himself he has come here to work, to review his latest book manuscript. He is trying to fool himself into believing that he has abandoned an air-conditioned apartment, and comfortable office at NYU, for a change of scenery while he writes.

Bullshit.

He's here to look at women, and collect images to masturbate over tonight. He's hoping that the gorgeous redhead he met three days ago, who actually sought him out to talk to him, will come back.

I haven't been able to stop thinking about her.

Frederick occupies his customary voyeur's bench on the southwest section of the fountain area, which provides an excellent view of women Rollerbladers, Frisbee players, students and druggies in skimpy shorts, halter tops, and skintight summer pullovers that add firmness to the female body, improve upon it, even.

I don't want to sleep with her. I just want to look at her.

But his heart is pounding more than usual on one of these excursions. He's wiping his forehead every few moments, telling himself it's from the heat, not lust. For the last three nights, alone in his apartment, while his wife Nancy is away, the redhead has come to Otto in his mind, removed her clothes, laid in bed with him, sucked his cock, rubbed her breasts against him, filled his fantasies with the smell of perfume and menstruation, turned on the steaming shower to soap him, head to toe.

I've never cheated on my wife, and I certainly won't start today.

"Hi, Dr. Frederick!"

It's her, he thinks, excited. But it's just one of his students, a total looker dressed in black—black jean cutoffs to her lovely black thighs, black lace blouse, black Rollerblades, black hair in one long, luscious braid.

"Doing your homework, Bettina?"

"Ha ha. It's too hot to work!"

But the sight of the girl, which would normally arouse him, doesn't work today. There's no room for other women today. There's only the redhead, Evylyn Noyes. Not even a student but a businesswoman, she'd said. From Chicago. A department store buyer. In New York, all alone, for a week. Beautiful as a model. Actually sitting down next to him, out of some adolescent boy's wet dream, and flirting with him, three days ago.

I'll just read this manuscript and get it ready for the publisher. It's due in five days.

Frederick, holder of the brand-new Benton Chair of Anthropology at NYU, is tall and war-refugee thin, stooped and prematurely emaciated with grayish skin, as if he spends too much time under fluorescent light. His pallor is worsened by a host of diseases he's contracted, at one time or another, after regular research trips to the Amazon; Leshmaniasis, malaria, amoebas, worms. Not to mention the unnamed and apparently unkillable parasites still dozing in his system, periodically waking, and making his life miserable before lapsing back into their comalike state, so their host, Dr. Frederick, will live, enabling them to feed again.

Women never come on to me. They think of me like an uncle, or brother. They've never been interested in me, even when I was young.

He can't believe his luck. Just the thought of Evylyn Noyes makes him so hard he thinks his prick might burst through his pants.

She said she thought my beard was cute.

"Hello, Dr. Frederick."

Oh God! It's her!

"Why, it's Evylyn Noyes," he says calmly. "Isn't that what you said your name was?"

"You remembered," she beams.

She's so gorgeous, more than any woman he's ever spoken to. Fifty, no, a thousand times more lovely than his wife Nancy, who is not bad-looking, but nothing like this. Evylyn's red hair is long, and straight, and it falls all the way down to her small, round ass. The body is petite, and firm, thinner even than Frederick's body, so for once he can dominate a woman in bed, not that he would go to bed with her, he tells himself, even if he had an opportunity.

Not that he would cheat on his wife.

Her eyes are hidden by squarish sunglasses. Her allure is heightened by her soft voice, creamy skin, and by the intoxicating scent of a perfume he has never smelled before.

Even the way she sits, spine arched slightly, face up-turned, attentive, back straight, emanates a kind of fertile, feminine readiness.

"Are you still working on that same manuscript?" she asks, sitting right beside him, on the bench.

"Last chance to correct mistakes," he replies.

Their knees brush. It thrills him. She says, "I lied to you when we met. I'm embarrassed."

"Lied?"

"I knew who you were when I came over. I asked at the school. I wanted to meet the man who wrote *Vanishing Peoples of the Amazon*. I loved it."

Stunned, Frederick does not know what to say. No one ever reads his pitifully ill-distributed books. The world reduces itself to her beautiful face. The heat mixes up the juices of the city, exacerbates the energy in Washington Square Park. It's as if the combined force of all life here—the police patrolling on their dark-colored horses, the marijuana sellers whispering to passersby under the arch, the chess players trying to dominate each other at the concrete tables, the street comedians and guitar players and students—all share one quickening heart.

As she leans toward him, his eyes go down the curve of her breasts. He sees the tip of lace, the top of her bra.

She says, "Studying fertility in the jungle seems so exciting. The dying tribes. The part about the women dancing, in the firelight, in the puberty ceremony, to attract men. It was so . . . powerful."

He remembers being there, the dark figures, whirling, the crackle of wood fire and the howl of monkeys in the forest, in the night.

"The Indians use hallucinogens during the ceremony. It increases their lust," he says.

Why did I tell her that?

"Did you participate?" she says, a perfect stranger asking personal questions.

"I would never do that."

"Because you're loyal to your wife? On the book jacket, it said you had a wife."

"Uh, yes," he says, marveling at her ability to get to the core of things almost instantly. Some people can zero in on the most sensitive topics in a way that makes talking about them seem natural, seem right, at least at the time.

"That's our arrangement," he says. "Nancy's and mine. We're loyal to each other." He feels stupid saying it. Why is it *necessary* to say it? He feels as hypocritical as the church deacon, preaching too loudly as he lusts after the woman in the choir.

Silky white fingers touch his forearm. Skin that, at 98.6 degrees, is cooler than the miserably hot city.

"I admire you," she says, taking off the sunglasses, looking into his eyes, and now he sees himself floating, in the depths of her black pupils. She adds, "And I admire what it takes to do the dangerous work you do. I bet people always want to talk about the romance of traveling to faraway places. But they never pay attention to the difficulty involved."

"That's what I tell Nancy."

Her lips are moist, and parted slightly. "I bet you have to make terrific sacrifices to do your job. I mean, being a scientist . . . you probably have to watch your money all the time."

"That's what I tell my wife."

"You must have to limit how much you spend on apartments and entertainment."

"Yes! Nothing must get in the way of our work! No big apartment. No kids. No pets, even. They're a needless expense when you have important work to do."

"And," she says breathlessly, talking about science the way a rock groupie talks about the Rolling Stones, or a political groupie must gaze at the President, or a literary groupie would regard Ernest Hemingway, with a kind of adoration that Otto Frederick has never, in his life, seen in the eyes of a woman before, "I bet you have to spend months writing those wretched grants, begging the government for just a little money to do your work."

"My God! It's like you're in my head!" he says.

Modestly, she says, "I'm just imagining what it's like. Do you have a picture of your wife?"

"Uh, no," he lies, feeling it in his wallet, where he is crushing it, envisioning Nancy: pretty when he married her, thin but more washboardlike, slightly flabby from not working out, disdaining perfume because it attracts bugs in the forest, wearing those cheap glasses because she saves money on uglier frames, and the same jeans day after day, like he wears, because they decided to use their money for work.

"Is she in New York, now?"

"She's in Brazil. We share a teaching position. I teach fall semester, while she works with the tribe. Then *she* takes the spring. And I go down to visit the tribe."

"You're so lucky to share work with a loved one."

"Yes."

And now, feeling guilty, trying to offset his disloyalty to Nancy, he launches into his standard cocktail party spiel about his terrific "working" marriage, his "functioning" marriage.

"I've decided," he says in his academic, lecture voice, "that anthropologically, it would be interesting to study professional couples, in New York, modern mating patterns, so to speak."

"Really!"

"Yes. More and more, couples meet at the office," he

says, realizing he is speaking of himself, thinking that he is boring her, wishing he would shut up, unable to stop talking. "Our society has weaker religious ties than ever before. And no family ties. Couples meet at work and fool themselves into thinking that their common profession substitutes for a platform on which to build a personal life."

"Let's take a walk," she says.

Why not? Is it so bad, a little walk? he asks himself, moving with her, out of the park, through air that seems thick as water, past his student, and the Mr. Softee ice cream man doing a bumper business on the curb, across from the law school. Heading down Mercer Street toward faculty housing, the high rise where he lives, on Bleecker Street.

Evylyn says, "This heat makes me want to do something crazy. Tear off my clothes and go swimming. Drink too much. *Something*. Does it do that to you too, or are you used to it, working in the jungles?"

He wipes sweat off his face, but it's still dripping down his cheeks, onto his shoulders, out of his armpits. He is frightened of his own emotions.

In fact, her chemical power makes him flash to one of the Karibiana legends, called "First Woman," that he learned in the Amazon. It concerns a female so alluring, so sexual, that any male who goes near her goes crazy wanting to take her to bed. The sun wants to sleep with her, after shining on her face, and together they give birth to daylight. The moon beds her, attracted by the round twin orbs of her ass, and they produce the little stars.

First Woman gives freely of herself to the ocean, the forest, and an entity the Karibiana call "First Animal." Her womb becomes the nurturing place for the birds that fly, the fish and the streams they live in, and the fruitful trees where the Karibiana live.

Finally, in the legend, Frederick remembers, when the earth is populated with plants and animals, First Woman meets First Man, and only he, of all her suitors, is attracted to the total woman, the essence, yin for yang, positive for negative, and that is when human children come to exist.

Nora puts her arm through his.

I will walk with her awhile. Then I will excuse myself and go home.

They turn and stroll north awhile, onto University Place, into an air-conditioned jazz bar named "Arthur's," where they order gin and tonics.

"If I were an anthropologist," she tells him, "you know what I would study? Marriage. Each marriage is like a different country, with its own customs. A couple doesn't realize there might be another way to do things, until they come in contact with an outsider."

Like you, he thinks.

"Two more gin and tonics, please," she says.

"With the Karibiana," he says, trying to ignore the heat growing inside him, eclipsing reason, "every part of the day is ritualized. From what they eat to when they have sex. They don't spend a lot of time making difficult choices."

"But choices can be exciting," she says. "Don't you think?"

Two more gin and tonics, please.

He says, ten minutes later, "Too much freedom destroys people. The average person isn't equipped to make real choices. It's why societies make rules. Excuse me. I'm lecturing."

"No, you're talking and I'm listening and I love it. Do you want another drink? I do."

I'm acting like a schoolboy, he thinks, saying that another drink would be fine. And even when I *was* a schoolboy, I never reacted to a girl like this. The diminishing, rational part of his mind, the disciplined part, is still insisting, like a blind man walking toward a moving train, that she will be a memory, and nothing more, in a few hours. The longer he stays with her, the more sexy images he can store up to masturbate over, when he is by himself in the subsidized, empty apartment tonight, while he and Nancy sleep on opposite ends of a hemisphere.

Evylyn will be a useful memory, like the other young women he sees in Washington Square Park, or the subway or supermarket; in their shorty shorts and halter tops, with their beautiful young breasts spilling out. Girls who, in the jungle, would have been married for five years by now. Girls who would walk around naked, trailed by three kids.

Otto Frederick tells himself that masturbation is a small price to pay for the wonderful opportunity to do research in the jungle. For stability in marriage. For an excellent working arrangement with his wife.

"You want something to eat with the drinks, Otto? I'm feeling happy here. Do you have plans for dinner?"

"I should go home."

"Oh come on. You have to eat," she insists.

He remembers, catching sight of the two of them in the mirror behind the bar—older man and younger woman, gray-haired never-has-been and vibrant female—that early on in his research, he had tried to explain the concept of sexual abstinence to the Karibiana. They'd laughed at him. They'd named him, in their language, "He Who Has Sex with His Hand."

"Two hamburgers," she is telling the attentive waiter, "and a bottle of the Chianti. Otto, can we stay here for the first set of music? It's supposed to be a really great pianist from São Paulo. He plays samba."

"A little while longer," he says, thinking, I can stop this anytime I want.

But the music is terrific, the beat lively, and the air-conditioning cool. To hell with working on the manuscript. Her face, in the light of the flickering candle, grows even more lovely. He remembers lying in his queen-size bed at two A.M., last night, crazy inside, imagining Evylyn with her clothes off. Evylyn writhing beneath him. Evylyn on the beach in Bahia, in Brazil. Evylyn with sand beneath her, taking a bikini off. Evylyn's mouth pressed against his.

"Otto, do you want to come?"

"Excuse me?"

"I said," she laughs, reaching across the table, touching his hand with the lightest, most exquisite brush of fingertips, "that I need to walk a bit again. That I'm light-headed. Maybe we can find a place for one last nightcap, before I go back to my hotel."

Say no, Otto Frederick thinks, thrilled at the illicit sound of that word. Hotel.

"Tomorrow, I have to go back to Chicago," she says.

Nancy would never know, if I did fool around. It would stay secret.

Face it, loser, he thinks, with the brutal clarity that can be provided by alcohol. Even when Nancy is home, I have sex once a month, for a couple of minutes. We argue about money, kids, pets, apartments. Everything except goddamn work.

"I'll come, but I pay," he says, which is strictly against marriage rules, squandering money that could go to research. Pennies add up, he always tells friends. If you simply walk in New York instead of taking the subway, at the end of the year there's enough money saved for a plane ticket.

For all I know, Nancy fools around when I'm abroad. And it doesn't affect the marriage.

And suddenly he understands what this woman's extra power is. Something about her unleashes the natural rage, and urge to dominate, that defines a human male.

He tells himself, standing, steadying himself against his chair, reaching for his wallet, that if he pays, he can stop the evening any time he wants. The payer makes the rules, and the rules will be, he tells himself, no sex tonight.

But would it be so terrible if one time, just one fucking time in my whole life, before I die, I have the kind of experience that other guys have been telling me about for years? If one time I felt like a star in a movie? One fucking lousy time?

"Don't be silly," she says, grabbing the check. "I'll put the tab on my expense account. It's not fair, the way academics have to scrounge for every cent, and business people have expense accounts."

"That's for sure."

"Martinis. First-class air tickets. The best restaurants. Business ought to subsidize science, not the other way around. If it weren't for people like you, people like *me*, the public, wouldn't have vaccines, electricity, everything that makes our life easier. But we never think about that."

"I always say that."

"I bet that book you're writing is brilliant. What did it take, three, four years of work, unappreciated?"

"Three years exactly!"

"And how much did your publisher pay you, if you don't mind my asking? Three, four thousand, max?"

"It's like you're in my head."

"Well," she says as they exit, as the music is cut off by the swinging door, as she takes his arm again, but this time her whole body rubs up against him, as if they are one more amorous couple exiting a late-night jazz joint, "I do feel like I know you, a little."

"What bar should we visit?" he says.

She answers, shyly, "There's a great one at a hotel I know, near here."

SEVEN

Voort is nine years old the day he sees his first murder victim. It is April in New York, a fine, clear Saturday. He is on the roof of the family town house at nine A.M., in the garden, a lean, tanned boy in a wicker chair, studying his fourth-grade textbook. A shadow falls over the lithograph reproduction of *New York City's First Night Watchman, Cornelius Voort.*

"One of the watchman's jobs was to alert the town if Indians attacked," the book says. The picture shows a stocky man with a pigtail and wooden shoes, carrying a lantern and peering into the cobblestone darkness, looking for robbers, murderers, drunken settlers who need help getting home.

"We got a call, pal," Voort's father's voice says.

Voort looks up, filled with excitement and pride.

Lieutenant William Voort, Detective First Grade, stands ready to work in a black-and-white tweed jacket, extra large in the shoulders, crisp white shirt and perfectly knotted maroon tie. Black slacks and shiny penny loafers complete the wardrobe.

Voort says, "You mean I can really come?"

"Mom and I decided. If you become a policeman, you're going to see one of these sooner or later. And if something happens to me before that, I want you to know it's all right to pick another profession. There are already plenty of cops in the family."

"But nothing bad will ever happen to you," the boy says, mistaking hope for certainty. His mother, joining them, wears soft jeans, a flannel shirt of his father's, and carries a potted baby rosebush in her gloved hand, against thorns. She'll be up here all morning, planting.

"If you don't like what you see, take a cab home," she says.

Twenty minutes later Voort is seated in back of an unmarked black Chevy, its siren screaming as they careen south on Second Avenue, the side streets rushing past at a speed that seems so breathtakingly dangerous, considering the packed traffic, that to the boy the rest of the city moves in slow motion. Only police experience life at the proper pace.

The murder turns out to be in Chinatown, on Mott Street, south of Little Italy. It's like another country. The signs over drugstores, vegetable markets, fish stands, jewelry shops, are in Chinese, not even English letters, unreadable to the boy. Voort follows his father through a crowd of gapers outside the entrance to a basement restaurant. The tape blocking off the scene is as thin as confetti at the St. Patrick's Day parade.

A blue tarp covers a man-size lump beneath the awning. From inside the restaurant, men in white aprons peer out, beside cooked chickens hanging in the plate-glass window, to lure diners.

"Stay on the other side of the tape," his dad orders, stepping into the hallowed, marked-off area where only police personnel are allowed.

A boy arriving at work with his revered father. A boy wanting to do the same job when he grows up. All over the city, on this day, nine-year-old boys are going to work with their fathers. They sit in doctors' examination rooms, watching their fathers tell patients to open their mouths, soothing patients while they fill hypodermic needles. They carry toolboxes for their fathers into strangers' bathrooms, where the fathers dismantle toilets, drains, showers, tubs. Boys ride open-air elevators with their fathers at construction sites, making sure the oversized hard hats on their heads don't fly off. Boys in ties and jackets watch, ordered not to fidget, while their fathers cajole juries in courtrooms. They ride ice cream trucks with Good Humor men. They sit backstage on Broadway, during their fathers' rehearsals. They pull a cord on the Staten Island Ferry, which unleashes the bullhorn warning small craft out of the way.

"See what you notice about the scene," William Voort calls back.

Craning to look, nine-year-old Voort watches his father kneel by the tarp, lift the edge slightly, and talk quietly with a uniformed policeman. He pulls a white hand from under the tarp and examines the fingernails.

He looks back to make sure the boy's eyes are trained on the right place, and then quite deliberately, as if his act is necessary for his investigation, which it is not, he slowly unrolls the tarp all the way so the boy sees the full length of the corpse. It looks utterly helpless, more puppet than human. The limbs have contorted at rag doll angles. The legs are tangled, elbows inward, mouth a hole lacking animation. The ash-white face is smeared with red.

Suddenly the fish smell from a nearby store overwhelms Voort. The gasoline odor of the city and the briny aroma from the East River make him gag.

His father covers up the man.

Later, after Voort collects himself, after he watches the questioning of neighbors and the typing of the report back at One Police Plaza, after he sits in the detective pool listening to the men and women talk about something called a "Tong," and something else called "extortion," when the sun is going down, father and the son leave One Police Plaza and take a taxi to the Battery, the Dutch fort that once protected New Amsterdam. They buy banana-flavored ice-cream pops, with almond nuts embedded in the bittersweet chocolate. They sit on a bench overlooking the water, on which the first Voort arrived in the New World with Henry Hudson, almost four centuries back.

"Tell me what you saw," his father says.

"The brick that was lying near the man's head, I guess that's what killed him."

"Good."

"I saw a construction site a block away from the restaurant. If the brick came from there, the killer thought about it, because he had to carry the brick to get to the restaurant."

"How do you know the killer was a man?"

"You mean ladies kill people?"

"Everyone has a temper, pal."

"Death was all twisted," the boy says, as the father watches the ice cream pop Voort is eating. "It looked so . . ." Voort says, searching for the description, grappling for the first time with a concept, finally using a word he learned in school that week. "Permanent."

His father puts his arm around Voort's shoulder, his Old Spice aftershave an odor that Voort will smell the rest of his life, whenever the memory of the man comes up.

"Now tell me the part you're ashamed of, Conrad. That you don't want to say."

"I was, well, glad it wasn't me. Or you or Mom," Voort says, glancing at his father, to make sure these words are allowed.

"Nothing wrong with that. But there's something else, isn't there?"

"I felt terrible."

"I know, but you still aren't there. Tell me, how does the ice cream taste right now?" his father asks. "You're certainly going at it."

Voort is startled that his father knows his secret thoughts. "Delicious," he admits. "Like I'm having it for the first time. And I'm hungry. I felt sick before, at the restaurant. But now I'm super hungry. Is that crazy, after what I saw?"

"No. You should feel sorry for that man, but also understand that everything you experience in life, just the fact that you *can* experience it, makes you lucky. Detectives end up two ways. Some are overwhelmed by the job. They're prepared to see death, but not to feel lucky from it. So they become dark, in here," his father says, touching his chest. "The joy goes out of them. They stop talking to their wives, their family. If you ever feel that, even a little, promise me, if you become a police-man, and the dark gets to you, that you'll quit. I'll be proud if you do."

But Voort doesn't like the idea of quitting. "Is it okay just to promise to think about it?"

His father laughs. "Yeah. But a natural cop, the kind you'll want to be, understands, after he sees death, how precious life is. He stops letting little things get to him."

"Like if I mess up a test at school, I shouldn't feel bad, as long as I tried hard."

"Right."

"Or when your partner Eddie gets angry in traffic, he should enjoy the radio, or the fact that he *can* be driving a car. There's something good in everything."

"You got it, Mr. Detective."

"That's why you brought me today. To test me."

"I want to make sure you understand who you are. That's more important than being a cop, with all your uncles expecting you, all the time, to join the force."

The boy grins, having the gift, even as a child, to make people feel better. "So the point is," he says, "failing homework's not so important anymore, right?"

"Don't even try it, or your ass'll be in a sling."

The two of them make their way from the park, to Church Street, and flag a cab for the two-mile ride up-town, to home.

Three months later Voort's parents die in a plane crash, on their way to Albany to attend a fund-raiser for, ironically, orphans of deceased police.

Did Dad sense this was going to happen? Voort will always wonder. Is that why he rushed the point, taking me with him that day?

He brings the question up, occasionally, when he talks to his parents, in his head, in church. Not that they answer. But Voort believes they hear what he says. He believes in ancestors, and continuity. In family matters, he requires no proof.

And now, two decades later, he is driving with Shari up the Taconic Parkway, upstate, through the Hudson Valley, toward a farm belonging to cousin Matt Voort.

Matt, his wife, and two sons will stay in Voort's town house in New York this weekend.

It's over a week since the Gramercy Park murder, and despite interviews with Paul Anderson's coworkers, girl-friends, investigative targets, Voort has learned nothing of value. Top down on the Jaguar, he cruises twenty miles over the speed limit, in late afternoon.

Cops don't give other cops tickets.

"It's hard to believe," Shari says, "that your family's been on this land three hundred years."

They have not discussed the pregnancy all week. She

is, he knows, still making up her mind what to do about it. But patience is a form of argument, and this weekend will probably decide the question. At least she agreed to come. He wants her to see the solidness of the Voort family.

He says, "Voort trappers killed beaver here, and moose, bear. They sold the hides in New Amsterdam. They built farms near the river."

"They helped the British beat the French."

"Or we'd be speaking another language in New York now." Any subject to avoid the baby. "The British and the colonists drove the French from this valley, during the French and Indian wars."

Mendelssohn's Symphony No. 4 plays on the stereo. Both Voort and Shari wear white; Voort in soft cotton pants and a tennis shirt, Shari in white jeans and matching sleeveless pullover. Voort's black peaked cap says PAL, meaning "Police Athletic League." Shari's, in DayGlo coral, has the logo of Apple Bank, where she is a vice president.

He turns off the Taconic at Route 23, onto a two-lane country highway, and easing off the accelerator, heads west, toward a magnificent lowering sun, through green hills and past farms.

Her hand comes across the gear shift and rests lightly on his. An affectionate touch, but noncommittal.

"Then your family turned against the British," she says. "You can't trust those Voorts."

Voort recalls the leather-bound diaries in his town house library. Heavy pages filled with looping, purple script, in Dutch.

"Most of the farmers around here swarmed north during the Revolution," he says, "to attack British General Burgoyne. He was trying to hack his way south with his army, through the forest near Albany. Trying to reach the Hudson, link up with another British army, and win the war in one glorious campaign."

She says, wryly, "The best-laid plans."

He says, ignoring the tone, "The British weren't used to private citizens carrying firearms." Voort recalls the stories told around his dinner table by his college professor uncle when he was young. "When Burgoyne surrendered at Saratoga, the French government saw we could beat a British army. They sent troops to help win the revolution, and the British suffered one of their worst defeats in history."

Shari gazes out at the long-tamed frontier, a patchwork of farms, diners, homes.

"My ancestors fought the British too, in Pakistan, but we didn't do so well," she says.

"Two great branches of the British Empire, joined," he says. And with those words, the unborn baby is in the car.

I'll need a car with a backseat if we're going to have a baby.

In silence they enter the run-down town of Holland, the warehouse section, with its rickety wooden homes. They turn north, along the wide river.

Shari's hand goes to her flat stomach. "You never asked me to come here before," she says.

"Things changed," he says.

He used to bring Camilla to Matt's farm, he remembers. They cross-country skied or ice-fished in the winter. They sailed Max's twenty-six-foot sloop as far north as Albany in summer, anchored in the brown silty current and made love on deck.

"I changed," he says.

Voort pushes down on the accelerator. Men drive fast when they aren't sure what else to do. Both women, he tells himself, so different, share that mystique of femininity, a core he will never understand, although usually he is happy appreciating it.

"What changed," she corrects him, "is my womb."

"No," he counters, "we changed because of it."

She switches subjects again, to get away from the delicate part, and fill the void as they move. "The commissioner seemed angry on TV, about the Gramercy Park killing."

"More angry at us than the killer," he jokes, remembering the commissioner in his office yesterday, urging him and Mickie to solve the case.

Shari asks, "And Camilla's phone call? The extra information she had?"

"She'd remembered the name of one of Paul's old girlfriends. But it turned out the woman was in Atlantic City the night he was killed."

"Maybe there's another girlfriend who you don't know about."

"We're looking."

"Or maybe someone you talked to lied."

"Someone did," he says, envisioning the dangerous subject of Camilla again; her face, close to his. "The question is, what did that person lie about?"

"And what about that network exec Paul Anderson fought with?"

Voort, surprised, bursts out laughing. "How do you find this stuff out? I don't tell you."

She grins finally. "If you want to learn anything bad about NBC," she says, "turn on CBS."

He thinks, If she won't have the baby, I wonder if it's possible to get a court order to stop an abortion.

But he does not want to fight. He hopes she is softening. It had seemed to him, last week, that she was.

He says, "The exec is returning from a trip to L.A. tonight. I'll talk to him next week."

Cousin Matt's driveway, which they now reach, winds up a hill, through apple, peach, and apricot orchards. The gray stone house, two stories high, and barn and tool shed, overlook a man-made lake. A sorrel mare watches the Jag pull up, from inside a paddock.

She gasps at the beauty. "Who takes care of the horses while Matt is away?"

"Us."

He carries their bags to the house. Inside, the walls are stone, the floors polished planks; the furniture—gigantic kitchen table, cushioned chairs, Dutch ovens, Hudson Valley paintings—are original. The King George couches were plundered from the overloaded supply wagons following ill-fated General Burgoyne.

"The girls would love this," she says as they unpack in the master bedroom, overlooking cousin Matt's woods.

"Then let's bring them next time."

"Right," she says sadly. "Next time."

In the pantry they find the customary "swap gift," between Voorts who exchange residences. A huge wicker basket contains freshly cured ham from the farm, and cheddar cheese, maple syrup, and a bounty of tomatoes, cucumbers, peppers, onions, fresh-baked black bread, and two bottles of Matt's cold white Hudson Valley chardonnay.

"What did you leave for Matt, in New York?"

"Box seats to the Yankees, and second-row seats to the musical *You Kissed My Wife!* A crate of pickles from Essex Street. Plum rolls from Chinatown. And police caps for the kids."

But Shari's not paying attention anymore, and she suddenly says, in a little voice, "Voort, there's no baby."

Voort thinks, She already had the abortion.

Fury fills him. He is surprised how quickly it erupts

and how totally it envelops him. Surprised and a little frightened.

"It isn't that," she says quickly, looking into his face. "Not that. But it turns out I'm the one out of a thousand women that the test isn't accurate for."

Voort feels a hollow ache start in the pit of his stomach. He had not planned a child, but once he'd believed it existed, it had become essential to him.

"You mean you were never pregnant?"

"The gynecologist confirmed it this afternoon. Pretty stupid, huh, to wait to go?"

Voort sits dumbly at the pantry table, inhaling the aroma of life, vegetables so shiny they seem to give off light. He's trying to absorb the news. He wonders if the whole pregnancy claim was a manipulation, a trick. But the embarrassment on Shari's face is too real for that.

Voort realizes he trusts what this woman says, one hundred percent. Unlike Camilla, she would never lie to him.

And that realization, too, surprises him.

"You want to go home?" she says quietly. "We can turn around and go back."

"Why didn't you tell me before?"

She looks away, flushed. "I was afraid you would just walk off. I was chicken, Voort, but I can take it now. Whatever you want. Sorry I made you drive all the way here."

Seeing her agony, he can only say, "Why would we go home? We have a whole weekend here."

She looks up. There seems to be a little more moisture in her eyes than usual.

Voort shoves his hands in his pockets. They are trembling with emotion. He considers how small she seems at the moment. He had not seen, until now, how quietly, how well, she handles adversity, and he has not appreciated the exact depth of her commitment to him. He's been distracted when it came to Shari, and for the last few days, for the first time, he was not distracted at all.

Through Voort's surprise and disappointment, he feels a stirring in his chest that was not there before.

"There's a great spot to have a picnic, while the sun is going down," he says. "Come on."

The basket goes over his arm. Outside, the heat is bad, but the country air soothes them. They pass the paddocks, a horse and a foal nursing, and pick their way through Matt's cherry and apricot orchards to arrive at a bluff overlooking the Hudson. Across the water the sun is huge and crimson, touching the top of the pines.

"I've seen views like this in paintings," Shari says.

Camilla would never eat vegetables without washing them first. Shari reaches for an onion, bites into it as Voort opens the wine. The bitter taste brings tears to her eyes. They tear at the black bread and fresh cucumber. Voort is famished. They drink from the bottle, washing it down.

When they are done the moon is up, white and full. The bluff is bright with reflected light, and the river is silver. There is a vast stillness, as if the earth is a great clock, and the moon, its pendulum, has stopped swinging, suspending time, light, and space.

"I feel stupid about what happened," she says.

Voort kisses her, deeply, and he tastes the yeasty thick bread, sweet onions, and tart wine.

"I'm protected," she says. He is unsure whether her reference to birth control is an enticement, or mere fact of biology.

The kisses grow more ardent. Her hips glide down on the blanket. Voort eases his body down between her legs. He is filled with the kind of gentle expectation that can precede love or signal that it has ended. Her fingers are at his shirt buttons. He lifts her pullover over her head, watches the blue-black hair fall back in place. Her bra is lacy, black, and the act of unhooking it requires that she thrust her small breasts forward. He bites the nipples. Her sweat tastes of wine.

"Oh, Voort."

He slides off her jeans, lean dark legs appearing beneath the fabric. She raises her ass so he can get her panties off. Discarded clothing lies on the overturned empty bottle of Hudson Valley chardonnay.

Voort kisses the rounded top of her shoulder blades. He runs his tongue down her warm, flat rib cage.

"Voort."

She is shuddering all over. Her fingers move into the crack of his ass. She reaches beneath his thighs, caresses his balls, the sides of his penis. Her skin is excruciatingly soft, and he has to stop for a moment, clench his teeth, to keep from coming.

"I want you inside me," she says.

The lovemaking is more intense, gentle, fragile, tonight. They are mourning a child who never existed except in their minds.

She straddles him, her breasts against his outstretched palms. He grasps her tiny waist. They've slid off the blanket, and he feels pebbles in the crook of his back. He sees the trees sideways. Her eyes are closed. He smells the loamy earth, and the moon shines on the round, silent O of her mouth as she throws her head back.

They come together, muscles spasming. Voort spurting into her, semen striking rubber, cells striking poison, as her hips, in perfect sync with his, jerk up and down.

Afterward they lay in each other's arms, as their breathing catches up with them. Her head rests on his belly, his back fits into the cool grass. The air is so hot that there is no need to get dressed again.

An owl hoots in the trees, and from below, the river, comes the hum of an engine.

She says, tracing circles on his breast, "What just happened here is the part, in those arranged marriages, like one you suggested we try, where things get a little lacking, if you know what I mean."

"Maybe passion comes later," he says. "People learn it."

She lifts her head, studies him. "Do we have a little role reversal here? Who's the Pakistani and who's the American? Don't tell me you still want to get married."

"No."

"But something is different, between us."

He says, feeling the warmth of her, "It certainly is."

"I don't need to know what it is. I'm happy. It's crazy how things happen. And by the way, Voort, are the mosquitoes biting you too?"

Naked, they start back the way they came, between the high, dark pines. The air smells of sap and loam. The moon is so bright that the woods glow with the heightened clarity of a superb photographic negative. They step lightly on the grass, city people whose bare feet are unaccustomed to contact with the actual earth.

We can go hiking tomorrow, he says. Or, if you like, antiquing, or sailing. There are so many things to do around here, and I want to show them to you.

"I brought novels to read," she says.

"We can cook a big dinner tomorrow, if you want," he says.

"I wouldn't mind horseback riding."

"There are tennis rackets. And mountain bikes."

They are entering the barnyard, and ahead, from the parked, unlocked Jaguar, Voort's car phone is ringing.

"This is getting to be a habit," Shari remarks as he

opens the door. "Our ménage à trois. You, me, and Bell Telephone."

It's Mickie calling.

"I owe you twenty, Con Man," he says. "You were right. It was a woman. We found pubic hair this time."

"What color?" says Voort, envisioning Camilla's blond hair, holding his breath.

"Black. We got a repeater," Voort's partner says. "A woman repeater. Son of a—excuse me—*daughter* of a goddamn bitch. What's happening to the world? Women are never repeaters."

"Never?" Voort says.

"Look, you won the twenty already. Give me a break. And use the siren. Get back here fast."

EIGHT

The Belham Hotel is small, pricey, and located in SoHo, within walking distance of those art galleries that haven't fled to Chelsea yet. Its clientele is mostly foreign, its decor 1920s, art deco, currently chic in Berlin, where the owners live. From now on, despite the efforts at exclusivity, the lodging will be described in guidebooks as the place "where New York's most notorious lady murderer killed victim number two."

Voort leaves the Jaguar amid the cluster of police cruisers on Elizabeth Street. A *Daily News* photographer recognizes the car, and snaps a photo of Voort kissing Shari good-bye.

"Did Voort tell you what happened here?" the reporters following her to the subway ask. "Are you his girlfriend? Are you related to the victim? Do you have something to do with the killing tonight?"

Meanwhile, Voort flashes his badge to the blue guys at the police tape, ducks inside and catches sight of Mickie, in a tuxedo, exiting the manager's office, near the elevators. The lobby is done in black marble. The palms are potted, the columns mirrored, the fans whirling, despite air-conditioning, and the settees double wing-backed, printed with fawns and nymphs. Mickie's tux, single-breasted, his cummerbund, black suspenders, and bow tie, complete the Roaring Twenties effect.

"You got back in record time," Mickie says.

"I floored it, on the Taconic."

"The desk clerk remembers her," Mickie says, but he looks disgusted rather than happy about it. "Big hat. Giant sunglasses. Somewhere between seventeen and thirty-five years old. She's short and she's white, at least the guy was sure of that. He couldn't describe her face, but he said she was 'sexy.' Killer sexy."

"Her hair?"

"Long and red. We found strands in the bed, but the pubic hair was black. So the red's a dye, or a wig."

"She didn't clean up this time?"

"She may not have thought she had time. The guy in the next room said he heard a scream, but figured it was television. My guess is, she wanted to get out fast after that."

The elevator arrives but seems to take forever reaching the fourth floor.

"Evylyn Noyes," Mickie says, "was the name on the credit card she made the reservation with, by phone. Then she gets here, acts distressed, tells the clerk all her credit cards are in the luggage the airline sent to Pittsburgh. She pays in advance with cash, and leaves a big deposit against damages. The hotel blocks her long distance line, so she doesn't run up a bill. And room service is instructed to take cash from her. We're running the address against the credit card number. Why do I think it's too easy to find her that way?"

"And why go to all that trouble to get the room?"

The elevator doors open. The chief of detectives, a blocky, white-haired man in a cream-colored shirt and brown sport jacket, is standing in the hall.

He says, "We're announcing you're heading the case, Voort." Meaning, Voort will be in trouble, not the chief, if it turns bad. "You'll talk to the press. Don't tell them shit."

When the chief disappears into the elevator, Voort asks his partner, eyeing the tux, "Where were you tonight?"

"Celebrating. Congratulate me, Con Man. My divorce came through today. Syl and I are single again."

Voort stops. He can't believe it. Mickie doesn't even look upset, but he doesn't look like he's joking either. "You're kidding. I thought things were great with you two. This has been in the works for a year?" he says, referring to the minimum time, in New York, required for legal withdrawal from marital commitment, "And you never mentioned it? I'm not sure if I should say I'm sorry or 'gimme a break.' "

"Things with us are better than great," Mickie says as they head down the hallway. "But you know how much extra we were paying in taxes because of that marriage certificate? We don't have kids. We don't want 'em. Now that we're divorced we keep the same house, same life, but save thirty grand a year."

He grins. "That's what politicians mean by Family Values. If you're married, they tax you more."

The banter hides the dread they feel, on a primal level, even though they are professionals, as they approach another mutilation. The city has been preoccupied with the first murder for days. Columnists are calling for the death penalty. Talk shows have run ratings up, with guests including surgeons, psychologists, and criminologists. One radio host, famous for his bad taste, has announced a "find the dick" contest.

"Win a year's supply of salamis," the man announces each morning, then calls the police, on the air, and demands to know why the killer has not been caught.

Religious sermons have zeroed in on the "uncommitted lifestyle." Late-night network comedians have been making cracks about "the modern man with no balls." SURVEY SHOWS MEN IN BARS MORE WARY OF PICKING UP STRANGERS, read yesterday's *Daily News* headline. The accompanying story quoted a prominent feminist:

"I don't condone what this killer did, but it's about time men understand how women feel in an unsafe city."

"This is the safest city in the world," the mayor angrily responded in the next paragraph. "And when our detectives arrest this murderer, we'll be even safer. Visit New York. I love New York."

Now Mickie says, as they reach room 419, "They check in about seven, go right up. They don't call room service. Except for the one scream, they make no noise. At eight-fifteen the maid knocks to turn the bed down. No answer, so she uses the key."

"Anyone see the lady leave?"

"No."

"Shit," Voort says. They've entered the room.

This time the victim never even made it out of bed. This time, from the look of things, Otto Frederick curled up in a ball, unable or unwilling to fight, or too shocked, or in pain, not believing what was happening to him, trying to cover himself up like a kid while the attacker went crazy, stabbing him in the shoulders, torso, breast, legs.

The savagery is remarkable. The throat's been cut. Blood soaks the mattress, and cream-colored pile. It's sprayed onto prisms on the chandelier over the bed, on the digital alarm clock and night table and complimentary fruit basket. Blood dapples the pineapple and white grapes, and drips, in one long, dried-out line, down the front of the minifridge.

Blood's on the wallpaper.

Mickie turns the body over.

He says, trying not to be sick, eyeing the carnage, "Damn."

In the bathroom they find the words *I know you*, in lipstick.

"What the hell does it mean?"

"Maybe they both screwed her over."

"What connects these two guys?"

"Why risk taking him to the hotel? Why have sex first? Why not just kill him, if that's the plan?"

"The wallet," Voort says, hoping some ID Frederick carried will tie him to Paul Anderson. Maybe both victims belonged to the same club, or movie rental store, or church. Maybe they were partners in a business.

"They lived in different parts of town. They worked in different places. They both had MasterCards, like seven zillion other people," Mickie says.

"Did Anderson ever do a show on Frederick? Maybe Frederick was a guest at the network. He was an anthropologist, you said?"

"We're checking the TV angle. And meanwhile," Mickie says, as he pulls a quarter from his pocket and flips it.

"Heads," Voort says.

"It's tails."

Which means Voort will have to notify Otto Frederick's family. He will have to sit with a wife, or kids, and tell them that their darling father and husband, the man they love, who gave them presents on Christmas, who fussed over them when they were sick, was killed in a hotel room where he was having sex with another woman.

Voort hates this part of his job the most. He will never get used to it. But he'd better do it fast, because there are so many reporters outside that he has a feeling one will soon identify the dead man, and the name will go out over the airwaves. As bad as an official notification is, it is worse when the family learns of the death, out of the blue, while they're watching TV, or listening to the radio.

It's after midnight, and he will have to wake people. He uses a phone in an empty, adjacent room and calls the ID Bureau at One Police Plaza. He has the operator search a database of numbers for someone to wake from NYU; a vice president of Public Relations, as it turns out. Voort calls the home number, on the Lower East Side. The man answers on the first ring, instantly professional. His breathing quickens when he hears "police emergency," but he knows enough not to inquire what it is. He double-checks Voort's identity with One Police Plaza, on another line, then rummages for a university phone directory and gives Voort Frederick's address on Bleecker Street and home phone number. He tells Voort that Frederick's wife Nancy is also listed in the directory, as she is another faculty member. At this hour Voort plans to confirm that someone is home, and then visit to make the notification personally.

But when Voort calls, he gets a recorded message saying Nancy is "out of the country" and Otto is "out at the moment."

Voort calls the vice president again, thinking that he prefers to be able to see a family member's face when they get bad news, not only out of compassion, but because that way, if they caused it, they might give themselves away.

Voort waits while the cooperative man gives him more numbers: the Fredericks' neighbors in University Housing, the chairman of the Anthropology Department, and the department secretary, who may know the location of any faculty member out of town.

The secretary, who lives in Staten Island, takes a few minutes to wake up. She sounds older, and competent.

Voort has the impression, from her voice, she has worked at the university a long time.

"You want to talk to Dr. Frederick?" Meaning Mrs. Frederick. "What's wrong?"

"Police business."

"Did something happen to Dr. Frederick?" Meaning Mr. Frederick.

"I need a number for Mrs. Frederick."

Voort prefers not to keep calling both the dead man, and his wife, by the same name.

The secretary senses disaster, which is easy when the police call at 1:45 A.M. "It's complicated," she explains. "Dr. Frederick is working with an isolated tribe, in Brazil. The only way to reach her is by something called a 'ham radio patch.'

"There's a ham radio operator in Brooklyn who helps with the patch. You phone him," the secretary says, "and he radios Brazil. If he manages to reach the Indians he hooks up his ham set to his telephone, and electronically patches the two parties together. That way it's billed as a local call. The Fredericks save money. They're money conscious. Do you want the phone number in Brooklyn? Brazil's close to our time zone. If it's two A.M. here, it's one there."

Unfamiliar with "phone patches," Voort nevertheless wakes up the ham operator now, an elderly sounding man named Don Everly, in Cobble Hill, Brooklyn. Voort apologizes for the lateness of the call, and explains that a police emergency has come up. He must reach Dr. Nancy Frederick right away.

"Who died?"

"I just need to talk to her."

"It wasn't Otto, was it?"

Voort waits on the line, which is filled with static, for twenty minutes, while the stranger in Brooklyn allegedly tries to reach Indians in Brazil, sending a message out into the stratosphere in the middle of the night.

It's magic.

And it's August, in New York, Voort thinks, when thousands of people travel. Clerks, psychologists, even murder suspects take vacations. In the mobile society citizens are uncommitted even to geography. Voort is struck by the number of people he has needed to talk to, over the last few days, who have been out of town.

"Detective?" the old man's voice interrupts.

"I'm still here."

"I've got her on the line. The way this works is, you tell her something, then you have to say 'Over,' so I can throw the switch, and she can talk back to you. It's one-way conversation. You speak only after she says 'Over.' She speaks only after you say 'Over.' If you don't say it, neither of you hear the other. It's just two people talking into a void."

"Are we on a private line?"

The old man laughs. "I'll hear it. Anyone with a ham radio in the world can hear it, if they're on this frequency."

Voort sighs. It can't be helped. He envisions, on the other side of the world, a woman, in a forest, at night, in a dark shack. A woman about to hear that a loved one has been murdered. A woman unattached to her surroundings, hearing the words dreaded by lovers, family, friends.

"Here we go, Detective."

A wavery, female voice, alienlike, almost too high to be human, distorted by the atmosphere, says, "This is Nancy Frederick. Over."

Voort says into the black receiver, a piece of plastic, that he regrets to have to tell her that her husband has been killed. He keeps the hotel out it. When he's finished he says, "Over," feeling ridiculous. From the silence that ensues, he thinks the connection has been severed. But after a moment the alien-high voice says, fighting off grief even through the horrible electronic distortion, "Can you repeat that, please? Over."

More details come out. It is amazing, over a radio, even thousands of miles away, even through static, how crystal clear the woman's agony is, coming through the line. Nancy Frederick tells him that she will get back to New York as soon as possible, over. She will have to arrange for a private plane to pick her up and take her to Manaus, over, and from there, over, she will take a commercial Varig flight to the States. He envisions, from the voice, the tight edge of hysteria, a woman trying to maintain control, trying to act logical in the face of devastating news.

He cannot tell her, must not tell her, all of the details yet. He cannot advertise the mutilation over the radio, even though it is possible, he knows, if she has access to the Internet, that she can call news reports up from Brazil. It is better not to reveal some things until he can watch her face.

It is also impossible to make someone feel better under these circumstances. Voort curses distance; planes, trains, machines that strain love and human connection.

She is saying, "I'll hurry, but if it starts raining, the only way out of here is by boat."

"Over," he says, breaking the connection, frustrated, because if Nancy Frederick knows key information that could help solve her husband's killing, more time will pass before he learns it, time that could enable the murderess to kill again.

A vast clock is ticking out there. He has a bad feeling about these two killings. He is afraid there will be a third.

Voort envisions Dr. Nancy Frederick, thousands of

miles away, trying to radio Manaus and convince a pilot to come pick her up.

My husband died.

"Let's get out of here," Voort tells Mickie when he gets back to the other room. Mickie, in the meantime, has come up with an address for Evylyn Noyes, owner of the credit card used by the killer. She lives on the Upper East Side.

On the way out Voort locates the desk clerk, who is still talking to detectives, readying to leave after a long shift.

"One question," Voort asks the man, a tall, blocky, polite German, sent over by the home office. "You said the woman wore a big hat. Big sunglasses. You couldn't see her face. But you still thought she was sexy. What was it about her, if you couldn't see her, that made you sure she was so sexy?"

The clerk seems surprised, and he frowns, hard, trying to remember.

Voort prompts him. "Her perfume? Her voice? Do you remember her voice? Something about the way she moved? What was it?"

"I don't know. It was all of those things. It is a very good question. I am married, happily, Detective, and very satisfied at home. But when this woman was near me, I was not thinking right, if you know what I mean. I was jealous of the man with her. I wanted to be him."

The clerk glances down, toward his crotch, in the kind of involuntary check that men all over the city, hearing the news, are performing. The maid who found the body has alerted the hotel staff, and through them the news media, of the mutilation. It is going out over the air.

The clerk repeats, shaking his head, "Jealous of that man. Imagine that."

*   *   *

Mickie heads back to One Police Plaza to handle paperwork and wait for lab results. Odds are he'll sleep on the couch, to save himself a two-hour round-trip home to Long Island.

Voort goes uptown to talk to Evylyn Noyes.

At two-thirty A.M., the streets are alive on a Friday night. Released from work, despite the heat, couples are still strolling, dining late, visiting bars, coming home from parties. They think they are safe, Voort knows. They believe they control their own fate. They are looking forward to making love, waking on Saturday morning, reading the paper, relaxing.

Voort scans the streets as he drives, dome light on to clear traffic. The city seems filled with small, dark-haired, sexy women. He spots one wearing an evening gown and high heels, several in baseball caps and jeans, more in shorts and cotton shirts tied at the waist. Any one of them might have murdered a man in the Belham Hotel tonight.

Evylyn Noyes turns out to live on Fifth Avenue, in Alexandria East, one of the most expensive apartment buildings in the city. Granite gargoyles eye Voort from ledges as he leaves the Jaguar in the No Parking zone at the entrance, his police business sign turned out, on his windshield. The doorman, who has a British accent and stiff, formal attitude, strikes Voort more as a butler, and glances, puzzled, from Voort's badge to the sports car out front.

"Excuse me, sir, but are you really a policeman?"

"Yes."

"It's just that policemen, to my knowledge, don't generally arrive in vehicles like this. But Mr. Noyes's friends, who pull practical jokes on him all the time, do."

But when the doorman hears Voort's name, his mouth

drops open. "You were just on the news, sir. About a murder in SoHo."

"Just ring the apartment. I'd like to get to sleep sometime this week."

On the top floor the Noyeses, wakened from slumber, are alarmed at first, fearing that something has happened to one of their college-age children. Voort reassures the attractive couple, as they sit in a gigantic living room. Evylyn Noyes is small, about forty-eight, in a Japanese robe, with sandy blond hair, green eyes, and a page boy haircut. Sexy, Voort thinks, in an average Upper East Side way, from health clubs probably, or a private trainer, massages, facials, and clothes that accentuate the good.

Her husband, Mark, is as big as a football player, straight-backed as a major; bifocals hang on a clip between the lapels of his dark blue terry-cloth robe. The apartment is frigid from air-conditioning, and features floor-to-ceiling windows overlooking the steamy, green expanse of Central Park outside. It's dark as the rain forest out there, except for pools of light where lamps are situated. Light equals safety, or so the municipality believes.

Mark sits protectively against his wife, on the arm of a couch, beside a potted aracaria tree and an original Frederic Remington sculpture, a cowboy riding a bucking bronco, holding on, despite his dangerous perch.

Voort asks politely, "Do you mind if I ask where you were tonight?"

The couple exchange glances.

"At the Waldorf, at a fund-raiser," she says. "The DNC, the Democratic National Committee. From six until eleven-thirty. The vice president spoke."

"Do you mind giving me the names of people who can confirm you were there?"

Mark Noyes says, "Can you give us an idea what this is about?"

Voort doesn't answer and they are clearly disconcerted. But they give him some names.

"Mrs. Noyes," Voort asks, "do you have a Visa credit card?"

She grows more alarmed. "Yes."

"Is it here?"

She disappears, still looking nervous, returns, relieved, holding the card up. The number matches the one that was given at the hotel, over the telephone.

Voort says, "When's the last time you used this?"

"This week. I bought tickets over the phone, from Ticket-Master, to the Big Apple Circus."

"Did you use it to make a reservation at the Belham Hotel?"

Now Mark Noyes stands up, at the mention of the word "hotel." "Look, what is this? It's almost three in the morning."

No, Evylyn says. She never even heard of the Belham Hotel. Nobody borrowed the card recently. None of her children have access to it. The card has been in her possession only, since it was renewed six months ago.

With Voort present, she calls Visa card's twenty-four-hour line and confirms, to her shock, that the card was used, over the phone, to make a reservation at the Belham Hotel yesterday. But there has been no other activity on her account.

"Cancel the card immediately," she says into the phone. "And if new charges come in, they're fraudulent. I haven't used the card."

She frowns, hanging up. "I don't understand. I thought when someone steals one of these things, or gets a number, they run up bills right away, lots of them, before the card can be canceled."

"That's usually how it works."

"But whoever got *my* number obviously used it only once. They had at least a day to buy things with it. It doesn't make sense."

"It'll make sense, in the end," Voort says. "Are you sure you didn't take the card out, leave it on a table maybe, in a restaurant, even for a few seconds, over the last couple days?"

"I'm positive."

"Have you ever met a man named Otto Frederick?" Voort asks, watching carefully.

"No. You, hon?" Evylyn asks Mark.

The husband puts an arm around his frightened wife.

"Or Paul Anderson?" Voort asks.

"That's the man who was killed last week. Oh God. Is this about *that*?"

"Do have any dealings, business or personal, at NBC, or at NYU?"

"Oh God. Oh God, no!"

The questions, the hour, the revelations, have shattered this couple's illusion that they are safe. That this apartment, with its locks, and doormen, and high altitude, can shield them. Voort can see the tension spreading over them. If a stranger had access to one of their credit cards, they are realizing, does that mean someone can reach into their apartment, financial records, business deals?

Voort looks over Evylyn's most recent credit card statements, which she brings out of a desk drawer. He writes down the addresses of a flower shop and a lingerie shop where she used the credit card recently. Perhaps it will turn out that someone at one of the shops, or Ticket-Master, has been stealing credit card numbers.

"You've been very helpful. Thanks."

He leaves his business card, in case they remember something they haven't told him.

Outside, he finds the doorman peering in through the locked windows of his Jaguar.

"Police salaries," the man remarks, wryly, "seem to be getting more in line with the dangerous job you do."

Voort speeds back toward One Police Plaza. It is now past three A.M. Cops all over the country, working on cases, aren't sleeping.

He passes the building where the *Daily News* presses are rolling, and today's morning paper will contain at the very least an article on tonight's murder, and possibly even the photo that the paper's photographer took, of Shari kissing him good-bye as they got out of his car. A photo of his girlfriend, for the whole city to see.

Knowing *Daily News* headlines, he imagines that, in a few hours, a million readers, including the killer, will see something like, MILLIONAIRE COP HEADS MUTILATION CASE.

"Then you'll know me," Voort says out loud, to his invisible opponent, "but I won't know you."

NINE

"**Y**ou're right. It's premature to assume you have a serial killer on your hands, but it was a good idea to call. We have nothing like what you're describing in our files. Women rarely do multiples. My bet is, your perp knew the guys. You just haven't figured out the connection yet."

At nine A.M. the southern-accented voice on the speaker phone belongs to FBI agent Floyd Casey, calling back from the agency's Quantico, Virginia, serial murder unit. Voort and Mickie met the man at a seminar in Washington last year. They'd become friendly, with Casey staying at Voort's town house when he had to speak in New York.

"Guys'll stew for years and then kill strangers," the soft-spoken agent says. He's Voort's age, thirty, from Michigan, a lanky law school graduate, butterfly collector, and former tennis pro who's worked on some of the most gruesome killings in the country. "Bundy. Berkowitz. They saw their victims, and bingo, did them right away. Each perp's unique, but certain factors run across the board. A sad science, eh, Voort, that there are enough of these guys around to make them into a science?

"Anyway, if it turns out you *do* have a serial, your average S.M. was abused as a kid. He usually never fought back. He felt helpless, and carried it, inside him, into adulthood. He needs to get drunk or take drugs to hype himself up, to make himself feel powerful before he does killings. Pop psychology, Oprah Winfrey stuff, but the profile often fits. Gacy drank, in Chicago. Dahmer did. They're paying someone back, some adult abuser, even if they don't realize it. That's why the murders are so furious. When they're doing it, they think they're killing someone else. They start accelerating the process. Less time passes between each death."

"Only eight days passed between murder one and two," Mickie says.

"But you have a woman. It's different with women, at least the profiling. We just don't get a lot of women here. And like I said, I doubt you're dealing with an S.M. I can fax you what little we have, but it won't help."

Voort and Mickie share a private office, unique to the new sex crimes unit. It was decorated by Mickie's professional decorator, who did his house in the Hamptons too. The paint is a soothing terra-cotta color. The sitting chairs are rich brown leather, the desks Mexican pine, the entertainment center made of cedar that fills the room with a pleasant, woodsy smell. There are two big Sony TVs, so the detectives can monitor two networks at a time.

The fold-out couches come from Bloomingdale's, and the fabric design is a geometric southwestern motif, which doesn't exactly go with the original black-and-white Weegee photos—collector's items that Mickie bought—of 1940s police raids. The pictures show cops rousing gamblers, cops herding transvestites into police vans, and they hang above a minifridge stocked with juice, fruit, cold cuts, champagne, hummus, and banana-flavored cupcakes, which Mickie consumes by the box.

"I spend more time here than home," Mickie told

Voort when he got permission to fix the place up. "Is there some law we have to work in a shithole?"

Now the FBI man is saying, "Women perps *we* get are like the ones *you* get. They tend to kill people they know." He sounds as clinical, as professional, as a geologist discussing rock, a hydrologist discussing water. "You got your black widows. They kill husbands, poison 'em usually, for money. Insurance. You got your angels of mercy, nurses mostly, that go after patients in nursing homes. It gives them a feeling like God. Every once in a while a mom gets whacked out. Kills the kids, husband, blames it on some stranger who broke into the house. But we've only had one recent case of a woman killing strangers serially. Aileen Wournos, in Florida a few years back, was a prostitute who did johns on the highway, and robbed them. One woman. You hear me? One. And Voort, you're not dealing with a prostitute, not if she paid for the hotel room herself."

"What about the 'I Know You' on the walls," Mickie says.

"It implies a connection, not a serial situation. Sorry, guys. Hey, Voort, you still dating that blonde, what's her name?"

"Camilla," Voort says.

"Beautiful woman," Floyd Casey says. "How is she?"

"We drifted apart," Voort says, thinking that he may see her today, when he questions one of the executives at NBC. Half the time, she works Saturdays. As usual, when she comes up, he feels a sense of disquiet.

"I liked her. And Voort, don't forget the knife. Women use poison, or guns. Knives are messy, and you have to be strong to use one the right way. A woman'll grab a knife on the spur of the moment," Martin says with certainty, "she won't use a knife if she's planned what's she's going to do."

"But our woman *did* use a knife," Voort says.

"Then maybe she didn't plan," the FBI man says. "Maybe she was spontaneous both times. Good luck."

After they hang up, Mickie pushes back from the table and sighs. "New strides between the sexes. Equality in jobs. Politics. The army. And now homicide."

He's ordered in breakfast from Le Montage. There are fluffy Spanish omelettes and crisp fried potatoes, sesame and poppy seed bagels, marmalade, apple butter, cream cheese, vanilla hazelnut coffee, a basket of pastries, and freshly squeezed orange juice with pulp floating on the top.

"If we're not going to sleep, at least we'll eat," Mickie says.

A corkboard in the room is filled with tacked-up photos of both death scenes. There are two charts on Voort's desk, the one with no food on it. The first chart details the reconstructed whereabouts of the victims, on the days they died, and the day previous to it, as best as the four-person team of detectives can figure. The second chart divides up duties for each detective: who talks to neighbors, who to friends, who to people in the victims' telephone books, who to coworkers.

"Our guys might as well have lived on different planets," Mickie says. "They were never even in the same part of town at the same time. Good luck at the flower shop."

Voort heads out the door, for the store where Evylyn Noyes recently used her Visa card.

Persia Florists turns out to be in her neighborhood, on Sixty-sixth Street, between Madison and Park. It occupies the ground floor of a brick town house with a sign in the second-floor window advertising "Astrology Readings." Across the street is a Korean restaurant, and a private Korean club.

A bell rings above the door as Voort opens it. He is assailed by the sweet heavy odor of too many flowers. They remind him of hospital rooms where he's visited victims. The shop is a riot of heat and color. A swarthy, floridly mustached, elderly man, wearing a vest over his moss-colored shirt, limps with a cane toward Voort from the glassed-in refrigeration unit, where he has been trimming roses. A pair of short, sharp, curved shears jut up from his right hand.

"Welcome to Persia," he says, with a shop owner's smile.

Voort orders two dozen white roses to be delivered to Shari's apartment this afternoon. He writes on the card for her, "Here's to finishing a great weekend soon," and watches as the man jots his Visa card number in a spiral notebook by the cash register.

Only then does Voort identify himself as a detective and explain that he is working on an investigation.

"Do you receive many orders by credit card?" he says.

The man backs a half a step. Alarm replaces the cordial feeling that marked his expression before. "There is nothing illegal here," he says. "I bought this shop in 'eighty-two, after I came from Tehran, when the Ayatollah took over. I love this country. You are policeman? I love police."

Voort assures the man that he is not under investigation. He is just looking into an "incident" that took place in the neighborhood. The man is only slightly reassured, but tells Voort, warily, that yes, the shop does most of its business by credit card, either in person or over the phone.

"And you write each number down in that book?"

"We save the list. A few years ago the FBI investigated many shops in this neighborhood, for money laundering. Now we keep strict records of all sales." The old man shakes his head. "That way we can prove how money comes in here. Those men from the FBI went through all our books."

"Who has access to the list?"

"I, and my son, and his wife," the old man says. "Nobody else. Why?"

"Is your son here?"

"He is in Canada, making a fishing trip."

"Is his wife with him?"

"She is home with his baby."

"Do you have a photo of your son and his wife?" Voort asks, wanting to see if the woman is short, with black hair, or a long red wig.

But the old man becomes panicked at the request. It is clear now that Voort isn't just investigating some vague "incident" that happened in the neighborhood. "Why do you need a photograph? They haven't done anything wrong!"

Voort reminds himself, in the face of the man's terror, that New York is a city of immigrants. This old man fled a police state, and his extreme fright does not imply guilt, as it might in an American. Americans generally have an easygoing relationship with police, at least the white ones do. At worst they show a kind of trivial nervousness in the presence of law enforcement.

Voort assures the man, lying smoothly, that his questions are "standard." Gently, he reiterates the request to see a photo. His visit, he says, "concerns a credit card problem."

The man tremblingly produces a wallet photo taken at a social function, a wedding perhaps, from the tuxedos on the men and the gown on the woman. The color photo shows himself with a younger man, about forty years old, with the same eyes and large nose, and a tall, lovely brunette. The woman has long, raven hair, but she towers over the men.

She is too tall to be a suspect, Voort thinks.

He goes over the list of credit card numbers, matched, purchase by purchase, to the flowers they paid for. A wreath for a cemetery. A bouquet for a wife. A single red rose from an anonymous admirer. A potted palm for someone's new condominium. An arrangement of tulips, azaleas, and daisies for Mother's birthday.

The old man produces a blue folder containing typed sheets of numbers, and says every two months the lists are typed up and stored. Voort and other detectives will painstakingly check the numbers, call the card companies, inquire if any other card here has been reported stolen or used fraudulently.

If there's a pattern, he will return.

The old man keeps pleading as Voort jots down numbers. "My son belongs to the World Wildlife Federation and the Parent/Teachers Association. He would not do a credit card fraud."

"I'm sure you're right," Voort says, sensing nothing wrong. "Do you mind if I use your fax machine to send my office these numbers?"

"Mr. Voort! Use the fax machine. Use the phone. Whatever you want."

"Please make sure my roses are delivered this afternoon," Voort tells the man, remembering Shari walking away from the murder scene yesterday evening, and feeling guilty about the fact that he worked last night until four-thirty A.M. and didn't have a chance to phone.

"Mr. Voort, the flowers are my pleasure, my gift to you! You do not have to make pay for them."

"I do. But thanks for the offer."

I wonder if Camilla will be at NBC, Voort thinks, feeling his heart quicken as he heads for the car.

* * *

Roger Martin, vice president of the news division of NBC, has just returned from a week-long business trip to Los Angeles, and is the only person left at the network, on Voort's list, to talk to about Paul Anderson. A typical TV workaholic, he's at the office on Saturday.

"They had a terrible fight," Camilla had said.

By the time Voort reaches the fifty-second floor at Rockefeller Center, he's spotted at least two dozen small, dark-haired women; on the street, in crosswalks, in the lobby, even on the elevator, where a girl, maybe twenty, in a short skirt, tennis sneakers, and a pullover blouse, carrying Starbucks coffee, had been telling a friend, "That guy killed me. He just killed me."

Only about a quarter of a million dark-haired, pretty women walking around out there today, fitting that clerk's description, Voort thinks.

Now, coming into Roger Martin's sedate, country-style waiting room, Voort realizes that the secretary behind the massive oak desk is *another* small, dark-haired woman, although she does not produce in him the kind of heart-stopping chemical reaction that the desk clerk at the Belham Hotel described.

But one man's beauty is another man's reject.

"Mr. Martin is on a conference call," she says. A name plate on her desk reads, BETH HELMS. "Can I get you coffee while you wait?"

"Please," Voort says, noting the way she averts her eyes, not really wanting a drink but wanting to see how the woman looks without a desk between them.

She walks off in flats. She's petite enough, and her hair is straight, cut very short, Joan of Arc style. She wears a charcoal-colored business suit, and small topaz studs in her ears. He notes, as she hands him his coffee in a real china cup, that her hand has a wedding ring, and that, like the old man's hand half an hour ago, it is trembling.

"Good coffee," Voort says.

"Mr. Martin loves his caffeine. He's an addict."

Behind the desk again, she begins fussing with papers, rummaging in a drawer, staring at her computer screen too long before typing.

"You like working here?" he asks, wanting to get her talking.

"It's great."

She stares at the screen, but her eyes are not moving from left to right. She is not reading. She glances up. "I know why you're here. Are you getting anywhere, looking for the person who killed Mr. Anderson?"

"You knew him?"

"He came here sometimes."

Voort sits back, studies her. "We narrowed it down," he lies, "to someone in Boston."

She relaxes a little. "That wasn't in the papers."

"How often did he come here?" Voort says, having noted her use of the plural "papers," meaning she's been reading *all* the papers, looking for news about Anderson.

"I don't know. Once or twice," she says, pretending to go back to work. "I mean," she adds, "he came to talk to Mr. Martin. They got along well."

Voort glances at his watch, as if he is impatient to see Mr. Martin, which he is not, as if he wants to stop talking to Beth Helms, which he does not, as if he is not cataloging this woman's every reaction.

Still, she senses his scrutiny, and says, "I guess people get nervous when you show up. Being a policeman."

Voort smiles and tells her that happens a lot.

"There's something about policemen," she says. "It's funny, even if a person did nothing wrong, a cop comes in and you feel like you're thirteen again, and your father's watching."

"I know what you mean," Voort says.

"Policemen and dentists," she goes on. "Do you get nervous when you go to the dentist? You're in that chair, and you can't move. He's going to hurt you, no matter what he says."

"Who likes dentists?" Voort says, watching her twist a strand of her hair, by her ear. She realizes he sees it and drops her hands to her lap.

She says, "Once I was getting a tooth drilled and—"

A long, low buzz interrupts them.

"You can go in now," she says. "Take the coffee if you want."

Roger Martin turns out to be an impossibly young-looking man, square-jawed, collegiate, in a dark suit, red tie, suspenders, black hair slicked back from a low, broad forehead. His desk has a phone on it, and nothing else. His shelves have television sets instead of books on them. His immense corner office provides a good view west, down Forty-ninth Street, of Broadway, the Hudson River, the Palisades.

Inside, the room is forest-green, with antique colonial furniture and throw pillows featuring images of pugs, little flat-faced dogs, sitting, eating out of dishes, running. There are Victorian-era lithographs of London on the walls—carriages and horses. Big Ben. A crowd standing outside Buckingham Palace, probably waiting to see the Queen.

Voort is surprised, after the cultured surroundings, to hear Roger Martin's thick Brooklyn accent.

"What a fuckin' way to die," the vice president says. "You're here 'cause he and I didn't get along, right? Half the people you talked to said we had a blowup."

"You argued with him."

"Big-time."

"Tell me."

Roger Martin leans back in his leather swivel chair and grins. He's handsome as a congressman. "I'm a suspect? That's funny. Wait'll Mary hears this. A suspect."

He stands up. He's a compact man, surprisingly small for the power he exudes. He pulls a cheroot from an inside pocket and lights it with a match. The smell of tobacco fills the room, and blue smoke swirls between them.

"It was a terrible way to die, but Paul was a loose cannon. A talented producer, but a guy who brings lawsuits."

Roger Martin puffs, exhales. "Maybe you're one of those people who think, hey, it's the news, for the greater good, so who gives a fuck if the network gets sued for fifty million dollars because of a one minute segment, as long as it's the truth."

Roger Martin pokes the smoking cheroot at Voort. He looks furious. "I give a fuck, that's who."

"So you moved him out of investigations."

"And fast. And he didn't like it. I said to him, Paul, are *you* gonna pay if we lose the suit? Are *you* volunteering to chip in if the court awards those scumbags at Allan Foods our money? Are you even prepared to give up *five* lousy percent of your salary? *Two* percent if we lose?"

Roger Martin shakes his head and puffs on the cigar.

"Not that it would have changed what I did. He wanted us to take the fall for anything he does. Big risk guy. We take the risk. He gets the reward. If we lose in court, big deal, as far as he's concerned. *He* keeps getting paid. *He* keeps doing investigations. *He* couldn't care less about the company. So fine, I figured. Let him produce puff stuff. Celebrities. You know," Roger Martin says, miming a man holding a microphone and dancing. "Michael Jackson."

Voort says, "And he hated it."

Roger Martin nods. "It was torture. Look, did I like the guy? Not particularly. Did I hate him? Who has time? Did I *kill* him? Gimme a break. I don't have to kill people. I fire 'em. I don't even want to think about what that bitch did to him."

"What bitch?"

"His dick, remember? She cut off the guy's dick. We got a lady serial killer loose in the city, Detective. Now she did number two last night. How about letting one of my units follow you around, cover the investigation, you know, step by step."

"No thanks."

"Make you famous. We did it with a cop in Omaha last year. Big murder case. He sold the rights to Paramount. Now he's a consultant in la-la land."

"When's the last time you spoke to Paul?"

"Two months ago. He was right in the chair you're sitting in, yelling at me, calling me an asshole," Roger Martin says, sitting, crossing his legs, protecting his genital region. "Anything else?"

What does your secretary know that she's not telling me? Voort thinks.

Voort hands Roger his card. "You've been helpful."

And now he's leaving the office, going back into the waiting room, feeling that something important remains to be learned here. Beth Helms is watching him, scared, not like the old man in the flower shop was scared, but like a guilty person. And just as he is about to start a conversation, a familiar voice says, from the left, "Hello, Voort."

"Camilla."

She's on the couch. He can't help his physical reaction, the flash of heat that he feels, in his forehead and his throat. Maybe *this* was what the clerk at the hotel was talking about.

The racing sensation spreads to Voort's chest.

She says, "I heard you were up here," and glances at Beth, who was clearly under orders to phone her when Voort arrived.

Ambush.

Camilla's wearing cool beige today, beige pants and short matching toreador jacket, beige high heels. Diamonds, good-sized ones, in her ears, and a diamond bracelet he has not seen before. Little prisms, dancing light.

Is this why Beth Helms looked guilty, or is it something else?

"Roger told me he was going to ask you if we could cover your investigation," Camilla says. "You going to do it?"

"No."

"Why?"

"Is that what you're here for, to persuade me?"

She laughs, oddly flirtatious considering her cooler mood last time they spoke. "Yeah. Mata Hari, that's me," she says. Her laugh is a light, two-note musical sound. It reminds him of the times, in bed, after sex, if they were joking, that he said something amusing to her.

"I'd be the last person able to get you to do something," she says, uncrossing those long legs, straightening that lean body, rising and crossing the taupe-colored pile to kiss him on the cheek, to tease his senses further with perfume.

"And nobody can 'get you' to do a thing anyway. Come on, let's get lunch. I'm famished. We can catch up," she says.

So the game is, Voort sees, I grill you and you grill me. He nods good-bye to Beth Helms, who is inaccessible now, and strides from the office with his old girlfriend, inhaling her aroma, exquisitely aware of every scissored swing of her legs.

And of course the NBC elevator, which is always packed with people, even on a weekend, is empty going down, except for the two of them. And of course the walls of the elevator are shiny copper, so whichever way they look, they see each other, the handsome couple, ex-lovers, who remember every inch of their bodies, except now they are not touching, standing an inch apart.

"I'll just have bottled water," Camilla tells the cashier at the network commissary.

"I thought you were famished."

She pats her tummy. "I am, but who eats?"

"Roast beef on rye, lettuce, tomato, horseradish, french fries," Voort orders. "And Snapple."

"On me," she says, reaching for her bag, but Voort's hand is already at the cash register.

"Maybe I lied a little," she says when they reach the table. All around them, NBC employees gorge on huge lunches for the price of a soup kitchen meal. "You sure I can't persuade you to let our intrepid reporter accompany you on your rounds, protecting our city?"

The roast beef is delicious, and the horseradish makes his eyes water. Voort says, "What didn't you tell me about Paul Anderson? The favor he did for you?"

"Is this a trade?"

"No."

"I *told* you, Voort, it has nothing—"

But he interrupts. "Camilla, a couple years back, we had a dead girl. Nineteen. Just arrived in New York, took an apartment in Inwood. A bloody murder, and I could tell that the neighbor downstairs, a lady, wasn't telling me everything she knew."

"I told you everything relevant about Paul."

Voort holds up his hand. "That's what she said," he says. "I couldn't persuade her to say more. A week goes by, two. The case is about to go into the file cabinet."

"And you talk to her one last time," Camilla says.

"And she tells me the thing that had nothing to do with the crime."

"Well, you're just about killing me with suspense," Camilla says, leaning forward, eyes shining, lips parted, making his groin itch.

"Turns out the woman didn't want to bad-mouth a dead person," Voort says. "Didn't want to speak ill of the dead. The thing she never said was that every night, her new neighbor, the girl, used to turn the TV on extra loud, and watch foreign movies. The lady would go up, bang on the door. No answer. The girl ignored her."

Camilla looks intrigued. "And that was important?"

Voort says, "The dead girl turned out to be deaf. She read the captions. She had no idea the TV was loud."

"Oh."

"We might never have figured it. It was a cash sublet, which she'd arranged by mail, and she'd only been living there a week. No friends yet. No lease. No job. No ID. They'd been taken. The autopsy didn't tell us she was deaf. But once we knew, we checked the deaf schools, the organizations. The guy who did it was deaf too."

"Paul Anderson wasn't deaf, Voort."

"I know he wasn't. I want to know what he was."

She sits back. For a moment her tough producer veneer drops away, and Voort sees she is genuinely troubled. But she shakes her head.

"I can't."

Voort pushes his plate away.

"Don't leave," she says. "We don't have to talk about Paul. Or reporters. Can't we catch up a little? What have you been doing? Don't go yet."

Voort sits down.

"Been kayaking?" she asks, to draw him out.

"A little."

"Me too. Every other evening, after work. And I've been doing volunteer work. I became a Big Sister. I work with this kid from Brooklyn. Tanya. A really great girl."

"You? Volunteer work?"

"Maybe I grew up a little after we split. I got tired of going out, restaurants, theater, me-me-me every night. Tanya's terrific. Really grateful, not like the people I work with, when you do a good job."

"That's wonderful," Voort says.

She beams, as if the compliment really means something. Normally she's uneasy with compliments. She makes fun of the Emmy awards lining her office window-sill, gold statuettes holding up the world like beach balls.

"And your personal life?" she asks. "Seeing anyone?"

"A bit."

She squeezes his hand across the table. "Someone special?"

"It's too early to know for sure."

"The girl who was in the *Daily News* this morning, I bet. The one kissing you."

Voort laughs. "Who's the detective, you or me?"

"I am. Detective First Grade Camilla. When did you start seeing her, you suspect?"

He tells her, and this time she's the one who laughs, like an old pal. "You certainly didn't waste any time after we broke up, did you?"

"It only got more serious recently. How about you? Any news?" Voort asks, not really wanting to know.

She shrugs. "There's no one special. I go out. I have fun. Hey, no rush. Right?"

"Thanks for lunch. I have to go now."

"I'm supposed to thank you. You paid, remember?"

"For what? Bottled water?"

He's thinking, Why do I feel so sad, walking away?

At five o'clock he's back at the network, taking up a vigil by the elevators, watching the flood of employees—even on a weekend—start to leave.

First come the maintenance people, who are on a strict schedule, and whose day shifts end at five. The cafeteria shift is next, and other union people: technicians, sound men and women, makeup people, workers who get paid by the hour.

He spots a couple of local reporters, the weatherman, an anchor for the local evening news, walking in. The anchor is wearing a sport jacket and tie above the waist, where viewers will see him, and ragged, ripped khakis below, where they won't.

At 6:45 Roger Martin's secretary, Beth Helms, exits the elevator.

Voort falls into step beside her as they exit the air-conditioned lobby, into the brutal dusk heat.

"Oh God," she says. "You."

"Buy you an iced coffee?"

"I knew you'd be back." She keeps walking, eyes averted. She stops and sighs. She's well made-up, clearly having freshened up before leaving the office. She says, "How about a vodka instead? And not around here. Everyone from the network drinks around here."

Voort flags a cab and tells the driver to drop them at Knickerbocker's, a piano bar in the Village. "I'll send you home in a cab, don't worry," he tells her.

"That's the least of my problems," she says.

At Knickerbocker's they get a corner table. It's an old-style New York bar, with wooden floors, ceiling fans, and ferns in the corners. The place is half filled, and, at the moment, the baby grand piano stands idle. Voort orders two vodka tonics from the waitress, one more petite woman with dark hair.

"You going to tell me?" he asks Beth. "Or are we going to dance around it awhile?"

"I'm so bad at lying." She takes a pack of Salems from her purse and lights up. "Everybody knows when I do," she says, "except one person."

"Who?"

"My husband."

"Love is blind," Voort says. "I guess the guy loves you a lot."

"He does," Beth Helms says, blowing out a long line of smoke. "Will you keep a secret? Can I trust you?" She peers at him. "You look like I can."

"I'm good for it," Voort says, taking a drink, "unless it turns out to relate to the case." He spreads his arms, and doesn't finish the thought.

"It's not my husband I worry about. Roger will kill me if he knows," she says, meaning her boss. "He'll fire me. He's a family man. You wouldn't know it from the way he talks, like a dockworker. But he's moral. You know, church guy and all that. He won't say he's firing me because I'm married and I slept with a producer. He'll wait, and give me a bad performance record, set up a paper trail, so when he lowers the boom, it'll look like it's related to work. He's thorough."

"Tell me about Paul Anderson."

She sags, and takes a deep drink. But in a way, she seems relieved to talk about it. "He was in the office one day, early on, before he and Roger fought. We started talking. He was nice, and seemed sensitive. I appreciate sensitivity in a man. A lot of men are not sensitive. It's a big thing with me."

"I can see that."

"He told me about some friend of his who died in Bosnia, I still remember the story. It made me cry."

Voort takes a drink.

"After that he used to drop in sometimes. One time he brought flowers. Then, one day, like you, he was waiting at the elevator. It didn't seem wrong to have one drink with him. But we landed up at his apartment. After that, I saw him twice a week."

"Your husband never figured it out?"

"He never figures anything."

"Where were you when Paul died?"

She is really distressed now, wringing her hands, and the waitress, asking if everything is okay, flashes Voort a nasty glance, as if he is responsible for this woman's suffering. People at adjacent tables pretend not to look at them. At least the background music is drowning out, for the neighbors, anything she says.

"I was at a dinner party. With Harold."

"Your husband. You were there at what time?"

"Six till midnight."

"You stayed the whole time."

"Yes."

"Who was the host?"

"Oh God. You can't talk to them!"

"I have to check the story," Voort says. "But I'll tell you what I'll do. I'll send a different detective, and he'll make up a story, ask the host for *his* alibi that night, say he's investigating some other crime. Okay? He'll find out who was at the dinner party. No one will connect you to anything. It's the best I can do."

"You're sensitive too, like Paul," she says. "I like that. Can I have another one of these?" She holds up the glass.

Voort signals the waitress, who puts her arm over Beth Helms's shoulder. "You okay?" she asks, giving Voort another killer look, which says, You are an asshole. You are bothering this woman. She and I are sisters. Go drop dead.

"Feel better?" Voort asks Beth when the waitress leaves.

"Not about Paul."

"What's the rest of the story?" says Voort, the expert on pain, and secrets, and the way lies come out in conversations, a piece at a time, a deception at a time, partial truth by partial truth, until a semblance of a whole tale is in the light.

She says, stubbing out the cigarette, "Why do you think there's more?"

Voort waits.

"It's a secret. You promised."

Voort says nothing. He's already promised, his silence says.

"He got me pregnant," she says, and takes a huge drink, and Voort instantly flashes to Shari, the way she looked yesterday, telling him there was no life inside her, that her pregnancy was a false alarm.

"I had an abortion," Beth says, and seeing the pain in her face, he remembers Shari in her kitchen, torn over the decision, not wanting to abort a child, feeling trapped if she didn't and trapped if she did.

Beth is saying, "He stopped seeing me when I told him. It freaked him out. I shouldn't have let him know."

"It must have been tough," Voort says, feeling the loss of the little life.

"Actually, no. The procedure wasn't tough. But not seeing Paul just about killed me. I'm a sensitive person, like I said. Very sensitive."

In Voort's experience, people who constantly refer to themselves as sensitive, or generous, or kind, are none of those, and are usually the opposite. He is also thinking that he must confirm Beth's husband's whereabouts on the night Paul Anderson was murdered. Maybe the husband found out about Paul. Maybe he did something to Paul. Maybe he was tied in with the woman who killed him.

"Abortion," Beth goes on, lighting another cigarette, "is no big deal. You go in. You pay money. It's over in a minute. But I hated not seeing Paul anymore," she says. "He had a great body. He was the best lover I ever had."

Late-night mass is not for happy people. Happy people go to mass in the morning, to greet the new day, or at lunch, as part of a daily rhythm, or after work, before they go home to loved ones and quiet sleep.

But late-night mass, Voort thinks, standing in St. Patrick's, is for the lonely, the grief-stricken, the souls who wander the streets under artificial light. Sick people come to the newly instituted eleven-thirty mass. Dying people attend. Voort looks over the bent backs, the shabby coats.

A man two pews up is hacking in a way that indicates deep pain, trouble in his lungs.

A woman two feet to Voort's left is on her knees, sobbing.

A teenager behind him is muttering, to the air, "Poppy, are you there?"

It's been a fruitless day at work. The lab found no match-up for the fingerprints in Otto Frederick's hotel room. The DNA tests on the killer's pubic hairs didn't come up with a match either. The wig hairs belonged to a generic brand, not a specialty shop. Frederick's neighbors and coworkers reported him a loyal husband, a shy man, who they never dreamed would end up with another woman, in a hotel room.

No enemies. No bad business deals. No fights at work. "Nada," Mickie said.

"I'm sorry, Poppy," the teenager behind Voort says, then slips from the pew, lost in private torment, and is gone.

Sometimes it is hard for Voort to remember his father's advice, twenty-one years ago.

"If the dark gets to you, promise me, you'll quit."

You have to work at it, like love. You have to work at living, Voort says, under his breath, "God, thank you for life, for light, for sound, for Shari, for the ability to feel happiness. Thank you for taste. Thank you for health. Thank you for the parents I had, and for letting me know them before they died."

If he hadn't worked so late, he would have visited Shari tonight.

God, let me do right by her, he thinks, and as he does so, remembers, with slight guilt, that when he used to include Camilla in his prayers, he would say, *Let me make her as happy as she makes me.*

Well, that's over.

Voort remembers the words of the FBI man this morning. "It probably isn't a serial killer. You just haven't seen the connection between your two killings yet."

But Voort shakes his head. He doesn't believe it. There was something in the violence at the death scenes, something in the lack of connection between Paul Anderson and Otto Frederick, that tells him the FBI expert may be wrong.

Like the business about women not using knives.

She went for the neck first, the kill zone. She planned it. She just went after the rest of the body after.

Voort stands to leave, sleepy now, feeling the pain emanating off the half-dozen supplicants remaining in the brightly lit church. Reaching for a couple of hundred-dollar bills to put in the poor box, he tries to squeeze past the woman beside him, and sees she is still crying, silently now. He is touched by the helpless way her shoulders shake, the way her hands are up, covering her face, as if, by blocking her eyes, she will shut out whatever image fills her mind.

"Excuse me," he says.

She goes on crying.

"Excuse me."

She looks up, a small woman, the five hundredth he has seen today. Blond hair. Green eyes. Tears streaking her heart-shaped face, dripping down to her plain cotton frock, a faded yellow sundress on a thirty-year-old woman.

"I'm sorry to bother you, but you seem distressed. If you want to be alone, I'll go. But I was wondering if there is anything I can do to help."

She catches her breath. She has to wipe her nose, which was dripping.

She tries a grateful smile, but only manages a wretched mockery of it.

"My mother died."

"I'm sorry," Voort says, sitting down, remembering when he got the news, years ago: a boy on a softball field, a boy watching his uncle walk toward him, a boy, frightened, seeing the look on the oncoming face.

"I got a letter," she says. "She was only fifty-two."

"I hope it was painless," Voort says.

She touches Voort's hand, looks into his eyes.

"You are kind," Nora Clay tells Voort.

TEN

"**I** am not imagining things," Nora Clay announces. "I am changing, becoming more powerful. The phoenix rises from the ashes. Synapse by synapse, I metamorphose into something new."

She paces, naked.

"You think I'm unbalanced? Then you don't understand anything. My happiness cannot be imagination. I am experiencing actual chemical evolution. A laboratory, testing my blood, would find it altered. It would be redder, thicker. It would pump faster. The clumsy pupa becomes the butterfly. The earthbound worm takes to the sky."

Nora throws her arms wide and pirouettes, giddy with delight. She has never felt so high, so filled with utter, druggish happiness.

"No one ever paid attention to me before. Now I am all they talk about."

Alone, she is talking to her tape recorder again, readying to go out into the city again, two weeks after meeting Voort.

"I never dreamed I could feel so free."

At eight P.M. she has left off the air-conditioning and opened the window wide. The new Nora does not fear things anymore, not heat, or fate, or commitment. She wants to let in the vast, anonymous rage outside. The heavy air strengthens her, does not debilitate her.

"Once I stopped fighting the city, I merged into its energy. Do you understand what I am trying to say? I am trying to explain this power to you. And I am not going to destroy my diary tapes anymore. I will collect them. Someday, they will help people understand what I did."

The city noise—cabs, car alarms, sirens—wash in with the glow from the street.

"And I am getting smarter. I am planning more, not leaving things to luck."

Humming, like a girl readying for a date, she lays out new clothing, just purchased, on her bed.

"For my new man."

First comes the curly white-blond wig, Marilyn Monroe style, with a flip in front. It was quite expensive. A snap-up case for colored contact lenses and pleated green plaid skirt come after that. Matching kneesocks. Shiny penny Loafers. White, button-up blouse, crisp and ironed in its clear plastic wrapping.

"I know what you want, Thomas Jackson. I know what you dream of."

Nora adjusts the wig on her head, an inch forward, then back. She eyes it appraisingly in the long mirror on the closet door.

"Been fantasizing about me, Thomas? Of course you have."

She fixes a red barrette to her hair, peers at the pleasant way the shiny plastic reflects overhead light.

"I look just like that girl you met in high school. The one you saw at a bus stop, for Catholic school students. The one you picked up and brought, in your father's Chevrolet, to your driveway. Then you pawed her. Put your hands under her skirt. Cigarettes smoldered in the ashtray, and the windows fogged. You've never stopped thinking about that girl. I heard all about it. All about you."

On the computer screen, which is on, and humming, Thomas Jackson's expression seems to quiver, actually respond to her mockery, as if Nora's new power can animate electronics; metal, and chips made of plastic. Thomas Jackson has a lean face, older than Paul Anderson's and Otto Frederick's, hatchet-shaped but not unattractive, considering the money he's put into it.

"I know every dime."

His tan comes from weekly sessions under lights at Tantrific. His black eyes, and 20/20 vision, are courtesy of laser surgery. His hair is full and dyed black, no plugs showing after last year's painful and costly transplants. Nose by Dr. Klein. Heart valve by Dr. Wackenhut. Bunions gone thanks to Dr. Ross. Tummy by suction, not sit-ups, not sweat.

"Are you waiting for me, Thomas? Our date doesn't start until ten-thirty."

With a flourish, like a queen waving a wand, she banishes him from the screen. The face is sucked back into the guts of the system.

"Dear diary, Dr. Neiman lied to me," she remarks to her own reflection. "He said no harm could come from imagining anger. But if a person only imagines it, she can never have the satisfaction of releasing it."

Nora shuts the computer, checks her watch, finds she has a few extra minutes. She reaches up, to the shelf above the computer table, and extracts a single manila file, her printed-out version, from the alphabetized selection.

"Hello, Voort."

But opening it and seeing that smiling face, blond hair, blue eyes, she frowns, vaguely unsettled.

He's attractive.

So?

You struck up the conversation with him in church two weeks ago. And when you saw those eyes . . .

She furiously banishes this kind of thought.

But Dr. Neiman's voice is in her head now, allowed in by her lapse. And he is trying to drag her down, as always, saying, Well, Nora. All these men you've told me about, how they fall for you. Wouldn't it be funny if this time it's the other way around?

Shut up.

He adds, "If this time everything reversed itself?"

I am too powerful for that to happen.

Nora begins turning pages in Voort's file. First comes the latest piece of information, a *Daily News* clipping, showing Shari, on her tiptoes, planting a kiss on his cheek, in front of the Belham Hotel two Friday nights ago. Shari's right hand wraps the bottom of Voort's left bicep, and she cradles a picnic basket with the other hand, as if the couple left a midnight dinner to drive to the murder scene.

"Shari lives in Brooklyn," the article reads. "And works at Apple Bank headquarters, where she is a vice president."

"I got your address from the phone book," Nora says to the picture.

Nora finds another photo, several months old, of Voort with another woman, blond this time.

In the clipping, Camilla lies in a hospital bed, head bandaged, and even in this painful setting, her glamorous quality comes through.

HERO COP SAVES GIRLFRIEND FROM KILLER IN SERIAL SLAYINGS.

As she turns pages, Nora changes who she addresses in her mind. Sometimes it is Dr. Neiman, sometimes Shari, and now it is Voort. "My family came from Holland too," she recites, practicing.

She shakes her head. She sounds too eager. When she sees him again, she'll have to slow it down.

"My family came from Holland too."

Better!

But the great mood is still gone. Normally her files, the knowledge they contain, accentuates her power.

But now Dr. Neiman's voice, in her head, that naggy whine that comes in seconds of doubt and can wreck the best, finest moments, is back. *You were going to kill yourself three weeks ago, Nora. Do you really feel as strong as you pretend?*

I'm not pretending. I am changed.

It looks more to me like you're swinging from one emotional extreme to the other.

"That detective doesn't bother me," she says out loud.

"He doesn't bother me," the voice in her head mocks. *"He doesn't bother me." Is that why you want a drink? Is that why you're going to the sideboard and pouring a gin again, to fortify yourself, if Voort doesn't bother you?*

Nora pours a half glass of straight gin, takes today's tape from the recorder, labels it, and places it in a small, black, velvet-covered box, which is labeled "My Diary."

She carefully removes her wig and folds it, neatly, with the new clothing, into a small embroidered canvas overnight bag.

"I must concentrate on Thomas Jackson now."

She takes another sip of the gin.

The good mood is coming back.

But the doctor *still isn't gone in her head*, even with the tape recorder off.

Voort has been on your list from the beginning, he says.

So?

He is looking for you too.

She claps her hands over her ears.

That's no coincidence, he says. Your mother used to say everything happens for a reason. It's like a message. It means what you are doing is wrong.

A message? Some kind of cosmic message from heaven? Is that what you're saying? Don't make me laugh! Are you a real doctor or a witch doctor? A scientist or a shaman? You just want me in your office so you can try to get into my pants again.

In her head, the doctor has no answer to this, and he falls silent, embarrassed by his lapse. She presses her advantage.

Of course Voort's looking for me. He works in sex crimes, doesn't he? The police classify what I do, not understanding them as punishments, as sex crimes. And sex crimes is the natural place for someone with his history.

Dr. Neiman just sits there, trying his last weapon, the power of a psychologist's silence.

Nora is sweating, in this contest of wills. She can even imagine the skinny little asshole, in his oversized leather swivel chair, in his office, with his glasses accentuating the size of his ridiculously baby-bald head.

As if he is saying, what if everything you are doing is wrong?

It isn't.

Then why are we having this conversation, since you make it up? And why don't you make these men wear condoms when you fuck them? Why don't you worry about catching AIDS? Because you don't care what happens to you, that's why.

No, it is because I am strong and that strength protects me.

You should have jumped off that overlook the other night, and saved everyone a problem.

Nora takes a longer drink. The alcohol spreads through

her system, and after several moments the image of the doctor begins fading.

But still he manages to get out, You are a suicide waiting to happen.

"If it's such a sign," she says out loud, her anger back now, strong and clear, "let's see who gets to whom first."

And finally the doctor is gone. But during the argument, she sees, she knocked Voort's file off the table. Papers lay scattered from the window to the rug. Naked, she gets on her knees, gathers sheets and clippings and puts them back in order. First comes the original piece of information she'd received, which got her interested in him. The information she learned at her job. Then comes supporting material she's gathered: a *Daily News* article and photo of Voort, after he solved the Bainbridge case last year; a glossy three-page spread from *House Beautiful* magazine on his "fabulous $4.5 million town house, with it's prize-winning roof garden." The article specifically names pieces of artwork in the house, and provides photos and background on his old Dutch family.

"My mother loved flowers," Voort is quoted as saying. "She used to work at the flower market."

Nora flashes back, as she replaces the final sheet in the folder, "Personal Observation," to a day she stood outside One Police Plaza, *Daily News* photo in hand, and spotted Voort as he left work. She sees herself behind him, on the 6 train, rocking north, following him into the Village and a jazz bar on University Place. She remembers sidling over to the friend whom Voort talked to in the bar, after Voort left.

Nora had asked the man breathlessly, "Wasn't that the cop who was in the *Daily News?*"

The man's eyes, traveling down her body, had brightened with desire.

"You got it. That was Conrad Voort, a good friend of mine," he bragged.

Nora sees herself acting interested instead of repulsed. "Does he come here a lot?"

"Whenever there's a good saxophone player. He loves jazz."

"I bet women are all over him."

"He's with one lady at a time, and he's got a girlfriend now. A banker. From Pakistan. I, on the other hand, am unattached. Buy you a drink?"

"Sorry. I have to go."

Now, back in the present, Nora thinks, I'm late. I better hurry.

She finishes the gin, goes into the bathroom, and brushes her teeth.

She dons the outfit she will leave the apartment in tonight, which she must wear in her neighborhood, where people recognize her. Now that the police seek clues about her, she must be extra careful to appear shy, as always. She must not go out in sexy, garish clothes anymore. Neighbors must not relate her appearance to reports they see on the news.

She slips on new red lacy underwear, which only Thomas Jackson will see, which comes from Victoria's Secret, the kind models flaunt on glossy pages. Thomas Jackson, her impeccable source informed her, loves this sort of undergarment. She slips on matching panties, thonged ones, because Jackson is turned on, big-time, by the twin moon shape of a small woman's ass. She dabs on a touch of Chanel No. 5, his scent of choice, behind her ears, and on her crotch.

The episode of uncertainty is over. Her spirits are as high as the mercury in the thermometer near the window.

Nora Clay completes her image by pulling on a plain

brown dress and olive cotton shirt, short-sleeved, as noticeable, as colorful, as a janitor's old uniform.

What a wonderfully drab picture I make.

A small but sharp knife, and the white plastic bag of newer clothes, go into her overnight bag. She turns the light off, and the glow of the city saturates the studio apartment. The noises from outside seem louder. She steps into the hallway and locks her door as a woman's voice behind her says, "Going out?"

She whirls, and recognizes her next door neighbor of nine years, but her heart is pounding.

"Just taking a walk, Mrs. Knox," she tells the eighty-year-old, who stands in a slip, sweating, a Virginia Slims cigarette smoldering in her hand.

Nora asks, "Can I bring you anything from the store?"

"You are so considerate," Mrs. Knox says, fanning herself with her free hand, her skinny legs outlined beneath the much-washed fabric. Mrs. Knox's cheap wig is clipped on. She is an apparition of feminine deterioration, a sexless thing waiting to be released from life by emphysema, from the sound of her cough.

"Why, you look radiant, Nora! Your face is glowing!"

"I flourish in the heat."

The woman pokes a tobacco-stained finger at Nora's chest. "I bet there's a man in your life, finally. Isn't there?"

Nora says, "Several, actually."

"It's about time they realized what a gem they had. Because that's what you are, Nora. A ruby. A topaz."

"Take care of yourself, Mrs. Knox. At least try a brand of cigarette with less nicotine."

"Too late for that, honeycake. I send more smoke into this city than Con Edison." The old woman breaks into harsh coughs.

And now Nora is heading out, down the steps, away from the apartment building, along Riverside Drive, with its leafy trees, and then up toward busy Broadway.

At nine-fifteen P.M. it is almost 100 degrees outside. The city air looks like gray steam in a bottle. The heat has permeated Manhattan with a physical languor, a drained quality, which can erupt, at any time, into violence. Teenage boys, young animals to Nora, sit on stoops she passes, hiding their cheap beer in paper bags, as if even a moron could not guess what they have in there. Who hides a Coke?

They play music about violence, about death, on boom boxes. Usually they croon to Nora when she passes, "Hey sweetie, baby, honey, love pie. Suck me. I make you happy! I make you my sex slave who wants it all the time!"

But tonight she turns to them, just stares at them when they start up with her. She can't help it. She is too powerful to take abuse anymore. The new fire in her will not allow her to stroll past these beasts without reacting. They fall silent. Do they sense the change? Do they understand, like a herd of zebras, that the she-lion is in the grass?

The subway takes her south, the air-conditioning in the car whining, turned high, despite Con Edison's warnings of a power failure. For the Transit Authority, the consequences of uncontrolled heat in the subways are too violent to contemplate. The transit cops leaning against the doors seem bored. They'd prefer to abandon any pretense of working. Passengers squashed against each other read newspapers made soggy by the heat.

MEN PAY MORE ATTENTION TO GIRLFRIENDS AND WIVES, IN WAKE OF KILLINGS she reads, over the shoulder of one woman, in the Style section of New York's secular Bible, the *New York Times*.

I have changed the city.

Nora gets off at the southernmost stop in Manhattan, South Ferry.

She hurries toward the Staten Island Ferry terminal, makes her way to one of the long benches that line the vast upper-deck cabin. At ten, the boat is half filled with late commuters. Manhattanites rarely travel to Staten Island for an evening. Passengers wilt, on the hard wooden benches, close their eyes, try to block out the city.

The horn sends them chugging into the harbor for the fifteen-minute trip.

Nora walks out on the deck.

The evening stirs the stew of chemicals over Jersey City: diesel exhaust, refinery smoke, auto fumes from hundreds of thousands of vehicles. On both sides of the river, steel, tar, and concrete emit back the heat they have absorbed all day.

Manhattan's towers disappear into the thick mist. Nora makes her way to the ladies' room and changes out of her plain cotton dress into the clothing she brought in her overnight bag.

She stays in the bathroom, ignoring angry banging on the door, until she feels the ferry slowing, maneuvering for docking. The banging stops. A woman outside curses her in another language. The deck reverberates with the impact of hull bumping terminal.

She dons sunglasses and joins the crowd spewing from the boat, trudging up the ramp leading to Richmond Terrace, the shoreline drive. New York's fifth borough is an aberration, a piece of New Jersey that got sucked into the metropolitan charter. It has been trying to secede from New York for years. It has a factory town feel. She sees small shops up there, Borough Hall, and courthouses. A herd of cars has arrived to rendezvous with commuters. Housewives and househusbands and screaming babies in car seats observe the daily ritual of commitment, rendezvousing in their automobiles.

How was your day at the office, honey?

By the time Nora reaches Bay Street, she sees that half the commuters around her are soaked with perspiration. But the heat does not bother her. She is fresh with purpose. Her sense of well being is strong. She is focused and excited.

"Vanessa!" Thomas Jackson's voice cries from the waiting throng ahead.

There he is. By a green Seville, waving.

"Van-essa!"

People turn to look at her. They see a blond woman. A thirty-year-old dressed like a pom-pom girl. They will remember the outfit, the sunglasses, not the face. They will remember nothing useful.

His skinny arm waves back and forth. His Cadillac is shiny as a new knife. He hurries toward her, down the incline, with all the eagerness of a fifty-four-year-old man in his second childhood, and takes her bag. He practically stumbles on the way back to the Caddy. Nora can almost feel the heat generated inside him pouring out.

"You look gorgeous, Vanessa."

"You too, Tommy!" She makes a small mirthful sound in her throat. "Well, men don't like to hear that they're gorgeous. So I'll say handsome."

He straightens, preens. He dresses, she thinks, like an old man in Miami. The cream-colored pullover shirt, buttons open, shows the V-shape of middle-aged rib cage. The matching pleated trousers and low-heeled lightweight shoes plead silently that he be taken as sexily as an Italian film actor, not an urban hick. The Rolex looks out of place on him. The sunglasses on top of the man's transplanted hair are too oval, the wrong shape for Thomas Jackson.

"Hungry?" he says, practically salivating at her schoolgirl clothes, trying to keep his eyes from bursting out of his head. His look keeps traveling down her skirt, legs, kneesocks.

"Come in the car, it's so hot out." He opens the passenger door as if it is a five-star hotel in there, the Villa d'Este, as if it smells of the Alps in there, not factory air freshener. "All cool. Isn't that better?"

"You're considerate, Tommy."

"How was the art world today? Sell a million-dollar painting at that SoHo gallery of yours?"

Back to her, he's looking into a compartment inside his door.

"We sold a Scott Burton chair, just a concrete chair, to a collector from Kansas," she says as he half listens, breathing audibly, rummaging in the compartment. She says, "He paid $200,000 for a chair made of concrete, can you beat that? But I don't get any money from it. I just manage the place."

He turns to her, hand outstretched, a small black box in his open palm. He says, "This made me think of you, because it is so beautiful. I hope you don't mind that I got it for you."

It's a bracelet. With little emeralds on a gold band.

"Those are real jewels, honey," Thomas Jackson says. "They go with your eyes and your nice little outfit."

Of course, she knows from his file, as she coos with delight, that the odds are Thomas Jackson never bought this object. Odds are, he stole it from one of the estates he sells, but she allows him to persuade her to put it on.

Thomas Jackson, crooked estate auctioneer, probably walked around some dead person's home today, allegedly cataloging items to be sold, and slipped, as he's prone to do in unobserved circumstances, small objects into his pocket.

If anyone misses them later, they will be put down as "lost."

Anyway, the bracelet's probably worth five, six hundred, tops, she knows. He sells the really good stuff. He only gives girls the flawed ones.

"Tommy, I've never seen anything so beautiful in my life."

"I have, honey," he says, "and it's you." The Caddy lurches to life as he adjusts his skinny butt on the pillow he keeps on the front seat, adjusts the climate control, electric seat, volume on the cassette stereo, which happens to be playing a romantic Sinatra tune.

He does not say where they are going, which is fine with her. She hopes it will be private.

"When you walked into my auction gallery two weeks ago, and knew so much about the business," he says, "I could tell you worked in the art world too."

"You're smart," she says, noticing a bulge in his shirt pocket, the size of a plastic pill vial. "I'd love to come to one of your auctions sometime, and watch you work."

How soon does he have to take his Viagra before sex, she wonders, for the drug to work?

"I'll set it up, sweetie. Meanwhile, I bet you're starving. Trust me on the place?"

No. I have to be smart now and avoid public places, if I can help it.

Nora looks down, as if shy, and too embarrassed, after receiving such a thoughtful, generous gift, to question even his most mundane suggestions.

"It's so nice out tonight, Tommy," she says, sweeping her arm at the shoreline going by, the panorama of ruined harbor and pollution. The slopes of the distant Verrazano Bridge choke the harbor neck. The emerald-green lights on the span are half obscured by the atmospheric haze.

"Would you mind if we ate outside? Get a picnic? Sandwiches, bottle of wine. Eat on the beach, or in the car. I've been cooped up in that gallery all day."

"Great idea!"

"Are you *sure*?" she says, laying her hand briefly, on his thigh.

His voice grows hoarser.

"Leave it to me." He pulls into a strip mall a few moments later, up to a deli. "Whaddaya think of these murders?" he says, turning the engine off.

She jerks. "Murders?"

"Those guys," he says, and for a chilling instant she thinks, He knows.

"Oh, Tommy. Are you afraid of me?"

"Terrified." But he's grinning.

She giggles. "Oh you."

"I'll get the food. Sandwiches, you said? You like chicken salad?"

"My favorite," she says as his hand unconsciously touches the bulge in his shirt pocket. His Viagra pills, again.

And minutes later they are cruising along the Atlantic, southwest, toward the scimitar-shaped tip of the island. He rejects a couple of overlooks where other cars are parked. He pulls into a small gravel bluff, shielded by maple trees, with a slat-railed fence blocking a twenty-foot drop to a dirty beach, a railed stairway leading down there, and a fairly good view, at the moment, of a monstrously white cruise ship inserting itself into a fog bank offshore.

"Want to eat on the beach?" he asks.

She snuggles closer. "In the car," she answers.

"With air-conditioning," he says, and opens the bag, takes out two smoked turkeys on pita, one bottle of California pinot noir, napkins, brownies, plastic champagne flutes, and a corkscrew.

A Ford pickup truck pulls in beside them, with another couple.

Shit.

She feels the cool wine go down, hit her belly, spread, sweetly, though her system. The sandwich tastes extra wonderful, but she wishes the pickup would leave. She pretends to look the other way when Tommy discreetly reaches into the breast pocket, extracts the pill box, and pops a pill in his mouth.

Instant hard-on.

The other car leaves. It is dark outside now. The air smells of salt. They have finished eating.

She is so excited. Wet with anticipation.

"Were you ever married?" she says.

He laughs. "Once or twice."

"You have a kind of generosity I associate with men who were married."

"I like pampering women, if that's what you mean."

She moves closer. Their hips touch now. She sees the bulge in his pants. She can already feel what he will be like, inside her. "What went wrong, exactly, between you and your wife?" she says, rubbing his arm, smiling, knowing *exactly* what happened, that the little white pill awakened this failure's long-dormant dick, which sent him sniffing around other women like a fourteen-year-old, which resulted in his catching the clap, and his wife filing for divorce.

"You grow apart," says Thomas Jackson, the bad actor. "But she and I are still friends."

Nora Clay wants to bray with laughter at the lie.

But instead she tosses the ball of waxed paper that held her sandwich onto the backseat. She says, "You are one sexy guy, you know that?" These are the exact words that the Catholic school girl, the girl he dated once and never forgot, said, so many years ago. She slides her hand teasingly up the ridge of his leg. The girl did that too. After a moment Nora turns her face to him, sees the shiny uncontrolled look of lust.

"You are so beautiful," he says, the mantra she has heard all her life.

The four-word vocabulary of the stalking male.

The lapping of water down on the beach sounds like slow, steady breathing. His arm comes around her. He is surprisingly powerful, and his belly, when she moves her hand under his shirt, is soft for such a lean man. She is not used to fifty-year-old bodies. He emits the faint odor of decay, or age, or incipient failure. But the dick is young, and big, inside his trousers.

She says, "Oh, should I take him out? The poor thing is all caged up."

This is fun. Enormous fun. She feels the dirtiness of his hands moving on her legs, up her thighs, between her thighs, slipping beneath the lace panties. The windows are fogging. The steering wheel is in the way.

"You crazy broad," he says in delight. "You got the little girl clothing and you're crazy, aren't you?"

"Do you mind?"

"Touch me again."

"Like this?"

"Yes."

"And this?"

"Oh, man."

"And how about this?"

"Ahhhhh. I'm going to come if you don't stop."

"We can't have that, not yet, not without a little more audience participation."

His dick is huge, the biggest one yet, hard as a baseball bat. The drug is really working, or perhaps the effect is fueled by her. The sense of power she had earlier is cresting. She knows that no one will see her tonight, stumble on this place, witness what is about to happen. It is certain. She is protected. It is a cosmic fact.

She just *knows* she has time.

She straddles him, legs wide, reaches down and sits on him, but she does not put him inside her yet. She teases him. She guides the side of his dick against the bottom of her legs, and the rim of her ass, and the thonged panties.

"That feels great, Vanessa."

He tries to get his fingers inside her. She says, "Not yet." She kisses him. His disgusting tongue is inside her. "Just one more minute. What's the rush, Thomas?" she says.

He's groaning. He's crazy with desire.

She lowers herself onto him now.

"Ahhhhh. Agggggggghh. You're so hot inside," the auctioneer, the nonstop talker, says. "So wet inside. Oh man," he says, breathing hot air on her neck, thrusting his tongue in her ear, squeezing her breasts, her nipples. "Oh yeah. Oh, that's it. That's definitely it."

The windows are so fogged she cannot see outside anymore.

And now she feels he is going to come. His balls are getting harder, more compressed, in her hand, and he is trembling, getting ready to erupt from his drug-induced horniness. She slows. She reaches, to the side, to the seat, making sure his eyes are closed, and her hands slip into the overnight bag. He is probably seeing, beneath his closed lids, the Catholic girl in his father's car thirty-five years ago.

The knife comes out of the bottom of the bag. She can see, in the rearview mirror, one of his eyes closed, and the right half of her own face, glazed and looking dispassionately back, and a bit of wooden handle of the knife.

He is saying, "Faster now. Pleasssssse."

He starts to come.

She plunges the knife into his neck artery.

But he surprises her. He is so old, and skinny, and weak looking, but he starts to fight. He has enormous power, more than she would have thought possible in circumstances like this.

Thomas Jackson moves fast, screams in pain but throws her sideways, instinctively knowing not to waste movement, shoving a hand to the spurting wound in his neck. The knife is stuck. The blood is spraying.

He strikes her, hard, with his fist, punches her in the chest and drives the back of her head sideways, against the rolled-up window.

"*You're* the one," he says in a guttural approximation of speech, a gasp of prehistoric fury that probably drove his ancestors to keep fighting against bigger animals, stronger men, more powerful diseases.

"I'll kill you," he says, and she feels herself struck again, in the belly this time. She doubles over, heaving.

Things are not supposed to be like this. She is protected. How can this be happening? Everything is going wrong. She can't breathe. She must reach the knife again. But Thomas Jackson is choking her. He has her down, half off the seat, and his hands are around her throat, crushing her larynx, her esophagus.

"Fucking woman," the auctioneer says.

Flailing, she hits glass, the dashboard, his face, his skinny, bony chest, which cannot possibly have this much power, but he does.

That force is waning, just a little, but not enough.

A fine red spray shoots all over the car.

And she is holding something, blacking out. *It is the knife*, which somehow she has extracted from his neck. It is in her hand.

She begins striking at him, over and over.

Too late. Nora Clay is dying.

She cannot see anymore.

I am going to die in this car.

And then suddenly his hands slip and fall away.

She can breathe again.

Thomas Jackson is motionless, on top of her. He stinks, having voided himself, and her throat burns. Each gasp of air sends knives of pain down her esophagus.

She pushes his body off.

He slumps, one arm over her chest, one over the seat. His head tilts toward her, eyes open. He looks as if, in death, he has lost some hearing and must come closer to properly make out her words. His skin is torn on the lips and near the eyes. Wounds shred the formerly cream-colored shirt at the shoulders, chest, stomach.

Nora Clay grips the knife.

Now it is *her* eyes that have glazed.

And she starts, again, even though she knows he is dead, to stab.

Ten minutes later she stumbles from the car. The overlook is deserted. Below, the dark surf roils, and she sees red running lights on the port side of a tanker heading for the Verrazano Narrows. Her breathing returns, slowly, to a semblance of normal. She is soaked with his blood, and the interior of the Seville is as red and wet as a meat factory.

She smears the blood on the driver's side window, with her finger, into letters.

I know you, she writes.

She turns away, sick finally, heaving up the sandwiches and wine. His violent resistance terrified her.

Nora Clay retrieves her overnight bag from the backseat, reaching gingerly past him, as if he might return to life. Inside, dry and clean, are the clothes she arrived in, neatly folded into a plastic bag, with a terry-cloth towel, a hairbrush, makeup, a scarf.

What to do?

She goes down to the beach. Gradually, the rolling, whispering surf calms her.

Naked, she wades into the ocean. It is tepid, but cooler than the air, and it is slightly oily. She begins to scrub; her arms, her vagina, her hair, her legs. The moon is yellow and small dull clouds hang motionless. The water is soupy, and after a moment she realizes it is filled with bobbing, floating objects. Tiny little walnut-shaped sacs, brushing, comfortingly, against her legs, her belly.

They are jellyfish, the nonpoisonous kind, washing in toward the beach. Touching her, emitting soft green light, they are little sacs of life, and she feels as if they are playing with her, loving her.

Something lower down, something more actively alive, brushes the top of her feet. She moves away.

Scrubbing. Salt scraping away blood.

I am protected. I am owed this protection.

There will be bruises on her neck, though. What to do about them?

A thousand people will suffer injuries tonight, in the city. There's no big deal about a couple of black-and-blue marks, as long as no one associates me with this spot.

One hour later, and a mile away, head lowered, collar up around her neck, scarf wrapped around her face, a small woman in a brown dress boards the municipal bus to the ferry terminal. The driver has other things on his mind besides this passenger. The other people on the bus read, or doze, or listen to music over headphones that block out the world.

Nora sits, alone in back. She opens a magazine in front

of her face, just like she will do on the ferry, returning to Manhattan.

No one notices the mark on her neck.

She is thinking, I never bled in the car. So the police won't know he struck me. They won't be looking for someone with bruises.

She tells herself, a moment later, *Voort's the last one left on my list.*

ELEVEN

"**I** want to tell you about commitment," Mickie says. "For two people, it almost never hits at the same time. One person has to risk everything. Has to wait for the other to come around."

"Any particular reason you're telling me this?" Shari asks as they dance.

Mickie taps his forehead. "My brain is like President Reagan's. A thought comes into it and out my mouth the same time. No lag time. Also," he says, swinging her around, "I'm your fan."

They are in Flushing Meadows Park, in Queens, in a sea of police officers and their wives, husbands, significant others. Four frustrating days after the murder of Thomas Jackson, they're attending Police Athletic League Night, a celebration of volunteers among New York's finest.

Mickie and Shari dance beneath the gigantic silvery Unisphere, on the plaza, all that remains of the 1964 World's Fair. Beyond the expansive lawn are the Long Island Rail Road tracks, the elevated IRT line, and, farther off, the neon sculptures adorning the sides of Shea Stadium.

The city has donated the space. Restaurants have provided the steak, lobster, clams, beer, wine. The NYU Orchestra volunteered an evening of music.

Cops surround the Continents—Antarctica and Asia and Africa. Dancing police shield the whole world, for a moment, from harm.

A few feet off, Voort glides past with Mickie's wife, Syl, in his arms. Shari's daughters are gyrating, giggling, and whirling to the tune of "New York, New York."

An NYU vocal student sings about "making it" in New York.

"Parisians celebrate love," Mickie says, dipping Shari. "Romans love food. New Yorkers," he says, "sing about obstacles."

"Let's talk about something else, like how you and Voort met."

The sky is purplish in the west, over Manhattan, and Prussian blue overhead, as the moon rises and the sun sets.

Mickie wears a beige lightweight suit from Barneys, of Venetian cotton. Shari's in white pants and a V-necked blue-and-white-striped cotton shirt that shows off her petite frame. Voort, coming into view between whirling couples, is in khakis and a seersucker jacket, with a solid dark blue tie. The music switches to another Sinatra favorite, "In the Wee Small Hours of the Morning."

Mickie's smile fades. His dancing, lively until now, slows.

"It's not a happy story," he says bluntly, "I didn't come from money, like Voort. My mother was a prostitute. An addict in Hell's Kitchen. I never met her, but I read her records later. And my father," he says, shrugging, "who knows?"

"You don't have to tell me this."

"Why not? Plenty of people have it worse. The foster home wasn't bad. And growing up, when I got wild, and did things I shouldn't have, which," he adds, winking, "was a lot, I was lucky because nobody ever found out about them. After a while I got smart enough to straighten out, went into the Marines, and after that into the Academy. And about that time, I fell in love."

"With Syl."

"I'm talking about my first wife. I was twenty-two years old and I came home one day from the Academy to see her sitting by the window, in the dark, crying. She says, 'You're not going to believe this. I have cancer.' "

"Oh God."

"Twenty-year-olds don't get cancer. And pancreatic's the worst."

Mickie and Shari stop dancing.

"I wanted to quit and take care of her, but we would have lost the health insurance. So I had to stay in the Academy."

Shari takes Mickie's hand. They walk off Unisphere Plaza, onto the grass.

"I'm sorry."

"Yeah, well, we're talking about love, aren't we? And commitment. I was top guy in the Academy until then, but I stopped caring about it. I still went to class all day, listened to instructors talking about law, justice. But all I could think was, what kind of justice is there in my wife dying before she gets to live?

"Nights I'd go to Mt. Sinai, where she was in a double room, always with other dying roommates. Women waking in the middle of the night, screaming. Begging for help. Gardner, my wife, was terrified enough without that. And it got worse. Half the time the nurses couldn't get her intravenous lines in. She had delicate veins. They'd keep sticking those needles in, missing, apologizing, going at it again."

"I'm so sorry, Mickie."

"She was the only person I ever trusted, until then. I didn't know there could be others."

Mickie is sweating, from memory. They sit on a bench as Voort and Syl dance past and wave.

"One day I get to the hospital and she's not in her room. I panic. The desk nurse tells me she's been moved to a private room. But we can't pay for that. The nurse says, that's taken care of.

"Taken care of? By whom? And when I get to the room, there's a *private* nurse there, and she's slipping the intravenous line in, and for Christ sake, the things you thank God for, like a needle going in without pain. The nurse tells us she's going to be there all the time now.

"And I say, who sent you?

"And she says, 'The guys at the Academy chipped in.'"

"That's great," Shari says, wiping a tear.

"Except," Mickie says, nodding, "when I get to the Academy, nobody knows what I'm talking about. I didn't even know Voort then. He was in the class, but we never talked. Years later he told me he couldn't stand watching the way I was deteriorating. He said he knew I'd flunk out. After a couple weeks I began suspecting it might be him, who paid for the room and nurse, because he was the only person I even vaguely knew who had money. And because he never asked about her, like everyone else did. It was like he knew if he asked, he'd give himself away. And also, I think, to Con Man, it was respectful not to ask."

"Did your wife get better?"

"She died a month later, but it was a hell of a lot better with Voort's help."

"That's a terrible story, and a great one too."

"But it's only half the story. Every good story has two parts, and that was the first. Remember, Voort never acknowledged helping. Eight months later, after we graduated, when we were cops, I *still* had never gotten to thank him. I'd see him every once in a while, but we weren't friends. We'd nod hello. That's all.

"The thing is, you gotta understand that Voort, in this department, is royalty. He's a Kennedy. Having him around is like, in England, when the prince goes into the military, and he's supposed to be just one more air force pilot, or sailor, but everyone there knows he's the prince."

"Voort the prince," she says.

"Think about it. There are plenty of cop families where guys have been on the force for generations. But not millionaire families who go back so far. Every cop in New York knows who Voort is. He's the head of that family, even though he's young. He owns the house. He's the one the uncles go to if they're in trouble. He's the Godfather of the Voorts. And he makes it look easy. He's smart and competent, and every once in a while some cop hates him for that. So it's months later, in Brooklyn, right? I'm in this bar—"

Another voice, a woman, interrupts them. "Mickie! How the hell are you?"

He has to stop the story as a *Daily News* reporter comes up, a chubby blonde with a big smile, holding beers for Mickie and Shari; a trick, so she can ask questions.

"You're not supposed to be here tonight," Mickie says.

"Yeah, well, my brother-in-law the cop invited me. Mickie, do me a favor. Give me something I can write, anything, on the 'Jackie' case. We're calling her 'Jackie the Ripper.' New York's first lady serial murderer. Whaddaya think?"

"New lows in taste," Mickie says.

The reporter wedges one leg between Shari and Mickie, her expression as concerned as her body language is aggressive. It's been days since Thomas Jackson was found in Staten Island, lying in a gravel overlook, outside his blood-smeared car, and there are no leads. Police got an anonymous call from whoever found him and, in a well-meaning attempt to revive him, pulled him from the Cadillac, messing the interior up.

After that, for whatever reason, the caller fled.

"What could connect a TV producer, an anthropology professor, and a Staten Island auctioneer?" the reporter asks.

"They all hated the *Daily News*."

"If you can't give me anything new, can you at least confirm what I learned? That Jackson's friends told police he'd been bragging, for a week before he died, about some woman he'd met? Someone named Vanessa, in her twenties, petite, dressed like a kid, worked in an art gallery, had the same interests he did. Is that right?"

"I'll call the *Post* instead of you next time something good happens," Mickie says. "Try to explain to your editor why you don't get any stories from me anymore."

"I'm only trying to do my job," the reporter says, sulking and turning away.

The reporter's information is right, Mickie thinks, but a discreet check of art galleries so far has revealed no "Vanessa."

Now Shari says, "Finish what you were saying. You were talking about months later, in a bar, in Brooklyn."

"I'm there with a friend," Mickie says. "I was drinking too much after she died, and I see three cops hassling Voort, at the bar. He's there with a date. And those three," Mickie says, shaking his head, "are bad news. Two were in the Academy with us, bottom of the barrel. The third's a veteran, in trouble at the time. He liked to use his fists too much. He was a boxing champion, Golden Gloves, and never should have been a cop, not after the year 1800."

"Hassling Voort how?" Shari says. "It's hard to imagine anyone getting to him."

"At first they didn't. It was stupid stuff. He's a rich kid, they said. Richie Rich, they kept calling him. They said he got through the Academy because the instructors were afraid to fail him, which was actually the opposite of the truth. Voorts make sure instructors give other Voorts an extra hard time.

"But these guys are loud, and they start on Voort's father, who was dead then, an ex-lieutenant. They're saying he was crooked, that he was on the take."

Shari looks furious.

"When Voort and his date move away, the three amigos follow them. By now they're embarrassed that, in front of the whole place, they can't rile Voort. So the jokes get cruder. They zero in on Voort's date. Finally, the boxing champ touches her, runs his little finger along her jaw. Calls her 'darling.'

"Voort pushes off the bar and says, 'Outside. Now. All of you.' "

"Three of them? Didn't anyone stop it?"

"You ever try to stop Voort from doing something? All we could do was make sure that only one went outside with him at a time. Golden Gloves went first. Ten minutes later, when he came back in, without Voort, I could see Voort had done damage. His eye was cut. His mouth was bleeding. But now the *second* guy went to fight Voort."

"This is making me sick," Shari says.

"I'll stop the story."

"You should have stopped the fight," Shari says in a harder voice.

"I shouldn't have stopped anything," Mickie responds. "Cops come with a whole set of personal rules, ways you see the world that civilians appreciate when they need help. You can't shut a sense of justice on and off. It's inside you all the time. Voort made his rules for his problems."

"Rules," Shari says.

"Yes. Rules. The second cop goes outside, and fifteen minutes go by and neither of them come in, so a bunch of us go out. They're across the street, in Prospect Park. They're a mess. Exhausted. Lying there. And as we're standing there, the *third* guy goes up to Voort, 'My turn,' he says, which was finally too much for me. I tell the guy, no way, and Voort gets up, pushes himself up against a tree and wobbles over to me. He's bleeding like a pig. His clothes are ripped. He says, 'Stay out of it, or I'll pound your ass too.' "

Mickie issues a low laugh.

"My ass, can you beat that?"

"They actually fought?"

Mickie nods. "And the third guy beats the shit out of Voort. Voort has no juice left by now. But Voort keeps coming at him. Keeps getting up. Charging the guy. And after a while, even the other two assholes can't stand it, and they stop it. They all drive off, congratulating themselves."

Now it is Voort himself who interrupts the story, coming up to them, his arm linked with Syl, a tall, lean redhead with curly hair and creamy skin. Syl's a surgeon at Mt. Sinai, where she met Mickie when his first wife was sick, although they did not start dating for two years after that.

"War stories again," Syl says.

"He's telling me how he met Voort," Shari says.

"I finished the Prospect Park part," Mickie says.

Voort's beeper is going off.

Voort claps his partner on the back in a rare show of physical affection.

"No need to talk about that, Mickie."

But Mickie continues. "Voort's doubled over. He looks up. He sees me. He knows I've been trying to figure out how to thank him for the nurse, and my wife. He says, 'Can you drive a stick? I'm seeing double here.' So I drive him home. And that's the story."

"No, that's not the story," Voort says. "Because two weeks later I find out that Mickie went after all three of those guys, one by one. He found one in a bar. One in Central Park. He actually went to one's apartment. And Mickie is ferocious when aroused."

"Ferocious," Mickie repeats, grinning, and suddenly Shari can see the animal inside, the beast.

Voort says, "He put two of them in the hospital."

"Wait a minute," Shari says. "You didn't help Voort when you could have stopped the fight, and *later* you went after those guys?"

"Don't try to figure it out," Syl says. She shakes her head, in tolerant and amused disgust. Lightly, she taps her breasts with both hands, like a gorilla. "It's the code," she says.

"Of three-year-olds," Shari says.

"True," Syl says, squeezing Mickie's powerful arm, "but with great thirty-year-old bodies."

They laugh, and the music is playing, and Voort excuses himself, hoping the beeper going off means a break in the case. He prefers to take calls out of the girls' earshot, and he never uses a cellular phone for sensitive calls.

The number he is to phone back, he sees, is at One Police Plaza.

He returns the call from his "hub person," the member of his detective team responsible for coordinating field information.

His trepidation grows as he waits for the hub person to come on the line. Has there been another killing?

He does not see, behind him, the way Shari excuses herself from Mickie and Syl and goes off to the refreshment stand. A blond woman gets in line behind her, strikes up a conversation with her, says that her "date" is "drunk and getting worse by the second."

"Which one's yours?" the blonde, Nora Clay, asks as forty feet away Voort's thinking that the murders will not stop until he has made an arrest.

"What's *your* boyfriend like?" the blonde asks Shari as Voort, impatient at the delay in the phone call, feels something extra about these particular crimes. There is something in them, the savagery and repetition, that rips at the overall fabric of the community. There is always violence in the city, it has always been part of life, but these murders have heightened the malevolent element.

Every once in a while a particular crime can alter the consciousness of a whole population: make citizens look twice when they enter stores, walk down darker streets, or receive phone calls from strangers, acts they never felt nervous about before.

Voort remembers that last night he even dreamed he was a victim. In the dream, he lay in the Staten Island parking lot, on gravel, by his Jaguar, doors open, and he was unable to roll away from a knife coming down at him. He was moving in slow motion. He could not see the face of the woman above him. He awoke just before the blade cut flesh.

Safe, in his town house, but wet with sweat.

Finally, the hub detective, Cathy Ramsey, is on the line. She tells Voort, "Professor Frederick just called from Kennedy Airport. She's back from Brazil, about to go through Customs. She couldn't get a plane from the jungle because the landing strip was too muddy. She had to take a boat out. She says she'll get a cab to her apartment on Bleecker Street. Meet her there if you want."

Minutes later Voort is explaining, to Mickie, Syl, and Shari, who is back from the refreshment stand, that he must go, that he has someone to interview.

"And it's the opposite way from Park Slope again, I bet," Shari remarks wryly. Voort's appreciation of her easygoing nature goes up another notch. She's no pushover, but she understands things.

"I guess I'll take the girls home in a cab," she says. "I met another woman who may want to go with us. She lives a couple of blocks from me, and her date's acting like a jerk, she said."

"Cab schmab," Syl says. "Mickie and I will drop you and the kids. Voort, you have a great lady here."

Shari scans the edge of the crowd, for the blond woman, to offer her a ride, but the woman is gone.

Voort kisses her. "I'll call you later," he says.

Syl says, "What if she," meaning, they all know, the killer, "did everything right? And left no clues?"

"Then she'd be the first one in history who didn't make a mistake. But what if I missed it?"

"You haven't," Shari says.

"I keep wondering," Syl says, "who's next?"

They fall silent. They hear the band playing; music, party noises, laughter.

Voort, Mickie, and Shari are worried about the same thing.

Voort is surprised as he reaches his car. A cold front sweeps into the park, dropping the temperature a steep thirty degrees, reinforcing the notion of reversal in the natural order of things.

There is the sense, at the moment, that even the weather has gone schizophrenic.

People caught outside at the dance scurry toward cars, home, bars, restaurants.

A brisk wind shakes the trees, stop signs, and traffic lights as Voort drives the Jaguar toward the Queensboro Bridge. In 1909, when it opened, it required tolls on sheep and donkeys. Now the vehicles have changed, but the pace is still that of a mule.

On this evening, however, spurred by the crisp weather, cars move more briskly over the bridge's two levels. Or is it that the drivers do not trust the solidness of the span shielding them from the drop?

Voort turns left off the bridge and takes Second Avenue to Greenwich Village, and Houston Street to the NYU housing complexes. They are United Nations–tower-shaped high rises near the sprawling school. Since faculty do not earn enough to afford pricey Manhattan housing, the university subsidizes them. Voort leaves the Jaguar, police visor down, in a private driveway ten feet outside the entrance. He fixes the "Club," a lock against theft, across the steering wheel, and makes sure the electric alarm system is on.

On the thirteenth floor, Dr. Nancy Frederick opens the door to what turns out to be a large, cookie-cutter-style apartment, where Voort recognizes the artful use of third world artifacts for decoration: items purchased overseas, inexpensive tribal masks, spears, drums, and musical instruments, affixed to the white plaster walls. Potted ferns line the window, which faces south, toward Tribeca. The furniture is padded wicker. Squarish woven baskets act as end tables.

"Want a rum?" Dr. Frederick asks as Voort sits on the sofa. "I need one. I have the powerful stuff, from Brazil."

She is small and lean in a stringy, muscular way. She looks exhausted, red-eyed, after days on boats and airplanes. She is surprisingly pale for someone just back from the tropics. Her mid-length black hair, with gray strands in it, is tied back with a yellow rubber band. Her thonged sandals flip-flop across the parquet floor, beneath the frayed hem of old jeans as she disappears into the kitchen. Her plain tortoiseshell glasses make her brown eyes slightly wider, more watery, as she comes back. Good breasts. Good hips. Good natural feminine sway as she deposits a tray on which sits a tall, clear bottle, sugar bowl, lemon peels, and two glass tumblers clicking with ice, on the wicker coffee table.

"The rum's cachaca. You mix it with lemon and sugar. It's destroyed half the tribes in the Amazon," she says. "I can use some destruction tonight."

"Just a little for me," Voort says.

"That's what everybody says at first. It's addictive."

Voort puts a spoonful of white sugar in the glass, adds a lemon peel, and two shot glasses worth of the clear cane drink. The stuff is powerful, all right. Nancy crosses her legs, watches from the wicker couch, and takes a big sip.

"I have to go to the morgue in the morning, to confirm the ID," she says.

Voort can feel her dread. "You don't have to look at the whole body," he says, "just the face."

As if that will make her feel better. Still, she looks a little relieved.

He says, "Do you have someone to go with you?"

"A friend from the university."

"Do you want me to come too?"

She looks surprised, and grateful, but Voort's motives are not solely humanitarian. He prefers to watch family members, always potential suspects, when they view the remains of the deceased. It's possible that Dr. Nancy Frederick paid someone to harm her husband. Not probable, but conceivable, and who knows, maybe watching her ID the body will give her guilt away, or spur a memory of hers that he can use.

"I can handle it," Nancy says. "But I can't believe it. A *hotel* room." She breaks down.

Voort lets her cry. He moves to the couch, when she seems to need more comfort. He puts his arm around her. They sit there, the woman weeping. Voort says nothing.

"What am I going to do?" she finally says.

Which is not a question that requires an answer. At length the sobs subside, and she sniffles, looks up, and excuses herself to wash her face, which gives Voort a chance to walk into the kitchen and scan the knife array. They are all there. He examines the size of the blades, re- membering the size of the wounds in the body.

Frederick was not killed with one of these particular knives.

When Voort comes back, she's on the couch again.

She says, "What do you want to know?"

He starts with the standard stuff. When was the last time she heard from Otto? Was there trouble in their marriage? Did he have a girlfriend? Was she aware if he ever fooled around?

"Him? No. But now I wonder, maybe he was fooling around the whole time."

Voort asks if Otto had any enemies. If there was any- thing about him, sexually, some proclivity, that might be useful to the police.

"What kind of proclivity?" she asks, annoyed.

"Some habit he had. Some need."

"We were a plain old boring married couple, if that's what you're asking. And we did plain old boring married things. Is this relevant?"

"I have no idea, to tell you the truth. We've had three killings and we're trying to find a connection."

She finishes her drink, reaches for the sugar bowl, the lemon peels.

He doesn't even know what he is looking for, isn't even sure, if he stumbles on something important, that he will recognize it as useful. She allows him to go through the dead man's possessions: notes, phone books, even pockets. It is a sad and sordid task. Voort finds himself in a closet smelling of mothballs, pulling tissues and crumpled slips of paper and gum wrappers from shirts, jackets, and trousers.

"Send in grant application. Buy toilet paper. Fix faucet," the notes say.

Voort asks her, as she sits on the bed as he works, "Did any of the tribes he visit conduct ritual mutilation?"

"That's offensive. Just because they're different from you doesn't mean they're animals."

"Sorry."

An hour later Voort is clicking through Otto Frederick's computer, in the home office, calling up file after file, with her help, scanning notes on tribal fertility rites, age tables, linguistics.

"Did he ever mention a woman named Evylyn Noyes?"

"No."

"How about Paul Anderson? Thomas Jackson?"

She shakes her head.

"What about old girlfriends, from before the marriage? Did he ever have any problems with them?"

"He never *had* old girlfriends."

She breaks out crying again.

Voort gives up, for the present, at least. By now he's heard about how Nancy met Otto, at school, after she moved to New York from the University of Montana. He's heard about their working honeymoon in the jungle. He's heard a hundred disconnected facts, stories, conjectures. The time Otto broke his leg while replacing a lightbulb. The time he almost bought a beagle, but decided against it, because feeding and paying for it would take money from research.

Voort asks her the last question he always poses in interviews.

"Do you want to ask me anything?" He has found, questioning people, that when both sides can make inquiries, the mood becomes friendlier. A source who senses a connection is more likely to phone Voort later, if a useful thought occurs.

"Why did this happen?" is all she can say.

"Do you have someone to stay with tonight?" Voort asks. Although she is exhausted from travel, and from downing three of the powerful rums, she does not look like she will sleep.

"I'll be fine," she says, lying.

"How about if I stay? I can sleep on the couch."

"You don't have to."

"I'm tired," says Voort, who would rather be home, but who knows that this woman could use company, and also that, if by some remote chance she had anything to do with her husband's murder, tonight will be one of his better opportunities to learn things from her, as she is tired and disoriented and therefore more likely to make a mistake.

He says, "I can lie on the couch here. We don't have to talk anymore."

"Thank you. I'm grateful."

She turns off the lights. He lies in the stranger's living room, a dead man's living room, surrounded by the dead man's things, a room away from the dead man's wife. The apartment is so high up there are no buildings opposite, and consequently no curtains on the window, so the anonymous urban glow shines in.

He thinks, have I missed something? He thinks, what an awful thing to come home to. He thinks, I will take Shari away next weekend, to some place beautiful. To a beach. To a cabin.

He is dropping off to sleep.

"Excuse me."

She's back, in an ugly purple bathrobe and faded blue cotton pajamas. She seems smaller without the protection of clothes. She's holding a photo from her wedding day.

"This was in the drawer."

Voort gets up, having a feeling that the photo isn't important. She just needs an excuse to talk some more. He asks her to sit at the kitchen table, and rummages in the cabinets, among the cheap dishes, finds a World Trade Center souvenir mug, and boils water. He locates a cardboard box of bags of chamomile tea.

"Usually, when one of us comes back from a trip," she says, in a small voice, watching him work, allowing him to assume control over her domestic rhythms, "we have a little ritual. We drink the cachaca. We show photos and tell stories about what happened while we were apart. No matter how tired we are, we catch up."

"That's a good routine," Voort says.

"Now we won't do it anymore."

"I'm sorry."

"I can't believe he's gone."

"I know."

"Now I don't have him. I don't have the twins. I don't have anyone."

Voort, at the stove, measuring in sugar, stops.

"What twins?" he says.

She really breaks out crying now. Voort knows that this is what her life will be like, at least in the near future.

Short bursts of activity. Long hours of incapacitation, sleeplessness, nightmares, regrets.

"We never really had the twins. He didn't want children."

Voort's heart starts beating faster. "Go on."

"We talked it over when I got pregnant. I wanted them, but he said, 'What about the expense?' He said, 'Who will take care of them? Not me.' He said, 'I go to Brazil twice a year, and I'm not going to stop.' "

Voort's heart is pounding. "You aborted them."

"I went to the clinic," she says. "I gave them the check. It was a nice place, with music, classical selections, strings, not Muzak. There were magazines on the environment. I read an article about Siberian tiger cubs being kept alive at a zoo. While my own twins were going to be torn out. And there was a social worker who came out and explained to the women there—he used a little wooden model—how you got pregnant. How to avoid it. As if we didn't know."

"Twins." Voort's throat is dry.

She says, "I would have had two boys and now I have no one."

Voort carries the tea to Nancy Frederick. He puts the tea on the brown wicker table. He stirs in the sugar. He holds her hand.

"What was the name of the clinic?"

"Lieb-Young," she says, in a small, agonized voice, "on the East Side."

Five minutes later Voort is in the study, out of Nancy's earshot, looking for the number for Beth Helms in his electronic directory. The phone number for the NBC secretary comes up in digital numbers, led by a 718 area code, meaning she lives in Brooklyn, Queens, or the Bronx. Voort punches in the number.

Never mind that the clock reads 2:45 A.M.

"Hello?" It is a man's voice, drenched with sleep, annoyed, as if he suspects a wrong number.

Voort identifies himself and apologizes for calling at such a late hour. He asks to speak to Beth, and there is a muffled sound. The man has covered the receiver with his hand.

Hurry.

Now the secretary is on the line, voice a little shaky. Voort envisions her in bed, in the dark, with a man eyeing her with curiosity or suspicion. He envisions her gathering her senses. She must be terrified by this call, that her husband will find out about her affair with Paul Anderson, but her voice, when it comes, only trembles a little. "Detective Voort? Hello?"

"I need to ask a question."

"I told you that information at the office," she lies, for her husband the cuckold's benefit. "I don't know if I have it here. Don't you people take notes when you interview someone?"

She sighs. Not bad as an actress, Voort thinks. Her voice is gathering strength. She tells him, "It's possible I have what you need downstairs, in the den."

And then he hears, "Honey, hold the phone and hang up when I call to you, okay?"

Voort waits. He hears a rustling noise, and receding footsteps. He hears a man breathing, then a phone receiver being picked up, and her voice.

"You can hang up, Harold."

The man doesn't hang up, though. The breathing continues. Voort thinks, wryly, So he never suspects a thing, huh?

"Harold, you can hang up."

Click.

Voort feels bad fooling the guy, but he promised to keep Beth's secret.

"Are you crazy calling me at home?" she hisses, as if *he* is the lover, as if *he* is the one who screwed her in Paul Anderson's apartment in Gramercy Park.

"What was the name of the clinic where you had your abortion?" Voort asks.

No answer. She is listening, before she speaks, to make absolutely, one thousand percent sure that no one else is on the line.

Then she says, "What do you need that information for? You said you'd keep my secret."

"Just tell me the name."

"I don't see—"

"Or I can drive over and knock on the door, and ask in front of your husband."

"I thought I could trust you," she snaps. "I thought you were sensitive." She sighs. "Lieb-Young Clinic, if you have to know. On the East Side," she says. "Christ, what will I tell Harold, about why you called?"

"Make up something," Voort tells her. "You seem pretty good at that."

TWELVE

The thirteen-year-old girl, who will one day change her name to Nora Clay, and become a murderess, who will alter a whole city's rhythms and affect the way New York explores love, plays with the children. She adores them. She looks over the towheaded boy playing with glass marbles. The redheaded two-year-old girl on the swing. The O'Brien twins, fighting again. The Pack girl, coloring a book.

All Nora's Saturday wards—the quiet ones, the boisterous ones, the ones who cry when their mamas drop them off in the morning—*all* of them have something special to offer: looks, or intelligence, or simply *freshness* in the way they see their little world, that wins Nora's heart.

"You are a natural mother," her mama says, watching her work.

It is the afternoon Nora's life will change forever, the pivot point that will send her plunging in the wrong direction. It is the last two hours she will ever experience anything approaching normal joy.

Her mother says, "One day you'll have your own kids. That's the purpose of a woman, to be a mother. You are *my* purpose. The reason I am alive."

Their day care center is in New Thames, Massachusetts, fifteen minutes off even the secondary roads, in the northwest corner of the state. Once a mill town on the Housatonic River, it lies too far from the turnpike to lure tourists in appreciable numbers. It is too unskilled in labor to attract new industry. It offers too little, in fact, of anything desirable to the outside world to exist as anything more than a satellite for more important locations.

New Thames supplies the cheaply paid shop clerks to the outlet mall in Lenox, the cleaning women who scrub the toilets in summer homes in Adams, the laborers who hammer nails into the dormitories at Williams College.

The day care center serves the children of the wealthy who live fifteen to thirty minutes away.

And Edith Shay, Nora's mother, stands on the front porch of their rambling, crumbling Victorian, at three, on an August day, as parents arrive to pick up their kids. She says, "Nora, are you meeting your friend Harriet at the pond?"

"As soon as this place is clear."

"Watch out for rocks underwater."

"You worry too much."

"Here comes the last father now."

A new blue Volvo rolls to a stop on the dirt driveway of the three-story building. Upstairs is the apartment shared by mother and daughter. Downstairs is the center.

Nora, off from middle school, helps every day. It saves money.

"The roof is broken again," says Edith, a heavy, round-faced woman, with tufts of blond hair on her cheeks, and the muscular arms of someone who cleans other peoples' floors.

"I know. It rained in my room last night."

"Why didn't you tell me?"

The girl looks up adoringly. Her dad died when she was seven, and Mom works hard, extra hard, not only at the day care center, but she also polishes floors for condo owners at the Jiminy Peak resort. The money she earns flows away continually, replacing rotten gutters, rusty pipes, sagging steps, frayed wiring. Soon their battered fourteen-year-old Chevy Nova will need to be replaced too.

Nora says, "I didn't want to worry you. I caught the drops in a pot."

The last child to go home today, Carl Spires, kisses Nora on the cheek, and toddles down the steps into the arms of his lawyer father.

"Was Carl good?" he asks, but his eyes travel to Nora's chest, to the breasts that have budded prematurely and rise to push up her I LOVE MASSACHUSETTS T-shirt.

"Carl's my little man," Nora says, as the chubby three-year-old preens.

"Nora'll be a looker," Mr. Spires tells Edith, smiling in a way that seems more than friendly, that seems thirsty.

"Don't I know it," Edith says.

Mr. Spires turns red.

"Boys'll be climbing the windows," he says.

"Then we'll just push 'em off," Edith says, polite, meaning, Go away now.

"You ought to take her to New York sometime, Mrs. Shay, enroll Nora in one of those schools for models. A kid with her looks can make thousands, not to mention her acting ability. She was great in *Glass Menagerie* in school this year. I read a piece in the *Berkshire Eagle* about a girl from Lee, only fourteen years old, and now she's earning twice as much in modeling as the senior partner in my firm."

"New York," Edith says, "is a cesspool. The last place I want my little girl. There's plenty of time to act when she grows up."

The Volvo leaves in a cloud of dust, and the air is still. There is the buzz of summer insects and the heat is moist but friendly. The house occupies a heavily mortgaged lot half a mile from town, on a road of steamrolled dirt and gravel. The nearest neighbors are Richie's Package Store, on the town side, and, on the other, a quarter mile downwind, usually, the dump.

Edith has Nora's blue eyes, but never, even as a girl, had the figure.

"Okay, my perfect daughter," she says. "You've been working since eight. Go have fun."

Nora retrieves her balloon-tired Huffy three-speed bike from the garage. In her lime-green rucksack she puts sunblock, a plastic water bottle, a blanket, a pack of almond M&M's. She's wearing a two-piece Kmart bathing suit underneath her shorts and T-shirt. No cars appear as she pedals toward the pond. She passes pasture and woods, and glimpses gray rock walls in thick copses of pine or oak, which two hundred years ago bounded the farms covering this part of Massachusetts.

At a sign saying REVERE STATE PARK, she turns onto a narrower paved road that terminates at a small lake, which at first she thinks is deserted. Her friend's bike is not here. Harriet must be late.

Then Nora hears voices.

They are boys' voices, nearby. Older, teenage voices. And now, laughing harder than the boys, she also hears a girl's voice, high and excited.

They're having a party, Nora thinks.

Curious, she leans the bike against an oak and pushes through the brush along the shore, ignoring nettles and no-see-ums, hungry biting bugs.

The girl's voice, closer now, is saying, "I *bet* you want me to take off my clothes!"

And a pleading reply, from a boy. "You said you would."

"I changed my mind. Is there a law against that?"

Nora sees them now, as she peers through a gap in the wild blueberry bushes. Four boys and the girl, all in bathing suits. She even recognizes them. The two taller boys play on the regional high school basketball team. Joshua Low and Roger Trumbull are local stars, and although she has never spoken to them, their names roll across the gymnasium during games, over loudspeakers, and in chants from the stands.

A shorter boy with glasses, Will Green, is the son of the high school principal. And dark-haired, wide-shouldered Curt Maze, an angry kid, is the son of the deputy chief of police, and is often in trouble.

Will and Joshua. Roger and Curt.

Nora recognizes the girl, too, although she is from another town. She is the lead cheerleader of the "Rockets," a blonde whom Nora has seen in front of the football stands during fall afternoons, and in the regional gym in winter, when the basketball team plays.

She holds her breath. An ugly tension is building. The boys are passing a liquor bottle around, drinking directly from it. The cheerleader uses a plastic cup.

The cheerleader spits her drink out. She wears a tiny two-piece bathing suit that accentuates more than it hides. She has a face as angelic as any Nora sees on television. But her voice is not the happy one she uses at football games. To Nora it seems cruel, as she calls Joshua "skinny" and Roger "weird."

"Curt, you probably have a teenie weenie," she says.

Nora is embarrassed for them, and also puzzled. The boys are clearly stronger, and there are more of them. Yet it is the girl wielding power here. Her taunts grow worse, make the boys look ineffective. In a gym, bouncing balls, they seem so sure of themselves. But under the barrage of female scrutiny, they wilt.

They laugh along with her, at each other, but it is clear they are pretending, so as not to look hurt.

"You're four horny assholes. You guys should be on TV."

Nora is so embarrassed by their humiliation that she creeps away, and when Harriet does not arrive, decides to go swimming alone, as long as she's here. She strips from her shorts and T-shirt, wades into the cool pond and swims with expert strokes to a raft. Climbing up, she unclips the top of her bikini, the way she saw older girls do, sunbathers in the *National Geographic*, in Europe.

"Secretaries in Monaco lie by the Mediterranean during lunch break, and get an even tan," the caption in the article said.

The heat lulls her. There is a pleasant lapping sound, of water rolling against oil can drums that, filled with air, support the raft. She falls asleep after a bit, and wakes suddenly, realizing she is not alone anymore.

The boys are on the raft too.

Will Green, the principal's son, seems to be yanking his hand out of his bathing suit.

The sun is lower. The air is cooler.

The girl who was taunting them, the cheerleader, is gone.

"Have a nice sleep?" Joshua Low, the taller basketball player, says.

His voice is neutral but the surprise makes her sit up so suddenly her bikini top falls away. She is mortified. Her fingers tremble with nervousness and she is unable to clip it back.

Curt says, "Need help?"

The boys erupt with laughter.

It is not friendly laughter. It is ugly, the kind they absorbed from the cheerleader. Laughter that substitutes for things better left unsaid.

Surrounding her, they seem enormous, elongated like only high school boys can be, alive with hormones, acne, muscles rippling beneath their skin. Together, they have merged into a different entity, a single consciousness that is strangely, threateningly, male.

She cannot fasten the stupid clip.

"You sure you don't need help, Nora?"

"You know my name?" It has not occurred to the thirteen-year-old that sixteen-year-olds might pay attention to her. They have better things to do, she has always thought—play ball, date older girls. Prettier, smarter girls who are surely more interesting, athletic, fun.

These boys hang out with kids with cars. Nora's friends ride bicycles and never travel farther from home than the Dunkin' Donuts across from the volunteer ambulance service.

"Every guy knows you, Nora," says Joshua, the leader, smiling with his mouth only. Standing, he towers over her, and makes the raft rock, and he's looking down into the top of her suit, which at least is clipped back in place now.

"Like you don't know it," Curt says. "Like you don't know guys follow your every move."

And now she sees the empty rye bottle on the raft, rocking with each movement as the boys shift stance. Glass clinking against wood.

"The beauty queen of middle school. Wanna go out with me?" Will asks, his words slurred.

"I'm not allowed."

The boys howl at this. She is simply not adept, like the cheerleader, at handling them. "She's not allowed," Will mimics. "Hell, Nora, we won't tell. It'll be our secret."

There is a rising cocky drunkenness in them, which is looking for an excuse to erupt.

She says, "I have to go."

When she stands, she is afraid, for a moment, that they will block her. The moon is rising even though it is still dusk. The swallows are out, swooping and eating mosquitoes, snapping prey the instant they detect flight. She dives off the raft, and underwater hears the four boys leaping in behind her.

And now she is swimming, jerkily, because her nervousness has crystallized into fear. They swim beside her, big limbs rising and falling, thrashing water, as they whoop and clown, and Will's voice is calling, "Help me, Nora, I'm drowning!"

But of course he is not drowning. He is on the swimming team. He can do the butterfly stroke and cross a pool in seconds. He can move in water like a fish.

When she reaches shore there is a brief moment of relief, until she realizes she cannot see her clothes on the rock where she left them.

"Lose something?" Roger says, dripping, standing up.

"A bicycle, maybe?" Joshua says, behind him.

"Say please, and we might help you find it."

"Oh ease up, you guys. It's in the trees, over there," Curt says, pointing, and she is so pathetically grateful for this small bit of hope that she says "Thank you," and walks into the trees, except once she gets there, she can't find any bicycle, or clothes.

"Didn't your mom tell you, never believe a stranger," Curt says from behind.

"She told me if anyone bothers me, to call the police."

Silence.

"So you just get out of my way," she says. "Or that's what I'll do when I get home."

It is getting harder to see them in the dark. They shuffle a little, and then magically part, and she walks through them, back toward the clear area around shore, thinking, All you have to do is be strong with them, except that is when a hand grabs her, spins her around.

"The police, huh? You're going to call the goddamn police?"

Curt's face is close now, and she can smell the alcohol, and terrified, she has not even realized that her right hand has balled into a fist. She is so panicked it comes up, hard. It strikes him right in the mouth.

"She hit me!" he cries.

And with those words, the night goes out of control.

Later, she will remember charging him, pushing him and fleeing, the rush of bushes and rocks, and she'll remember that just as she sees her bicycle, lying in the dirt, someone pushes her from behind, and she will remember hitting the ground, and the way the fists rain down on her, in a retribution she had not, before now, imagined possible in her generally peaceful world.

She'll remember the way they turn her over, and that, when she starts to scream, Will's hot, dirty hand presses against her mouth.

"She bit me!"

The way his fist looks, hurtling toward her face.

For years she will not remember the exact sequence of events after that, the way they roll her over, the way they handle her like an opposing tackle in a football game, the way their faces change, in the moonlight, glaze over when they see her body, pale, against the floor of the forest. The way they seem to merge into one another, when her bikini top is ripped off.

"You like it, don't you?"

"Girls tease you but they want it!"

For a long time she will wake with the face of the boy Joshua imprinted in her mind, inches from her own, and the stench of his rye-soaked breath, and the sweat on his chest, covering her, and she will never forget the pain when something shoves into her, from below, as two of the boys argue, saying, "I'm next," while the fourth, Roger, frantic, tries to pull them off.

"What are you doing?!"

But he will not pull anyone off. She will remember that when she tries to scream, there is the shiny tip of a hunting knife, a bowie knife, pressed, almost tenderly, against the skin of her cheek, below her eyelid.

"I will cut you," Joshua is saying. "I will slice off bits of you. Ears. Eyes. Lay still."

She will remember that, when they are finished, Roger is crying, as if *he* is the one who was attacked. There is enormous pain inside her. She will remember their slurred logic and panic as they argue, waking from lust, as the full impact of their acts hits them.

"We can't let her tell!"

"She liked it!"

"Oh God, what did we do?"

Kill me, she will remember thinking, and she will remember the knife back against her face, and Curt, whispering, next to her ear, you better not tell. You better promise. Curt saying, "If you tell we'll get you. And we'll get your mom. We'll burn that house. Don't think we won't. We'll find you wherever you go. We'll cut off your fingers. We'll cut off your mom's tits."

"Let her up," Roger says, crying.

"Not until she promises."

"I promise," she moans.

"You're just saying it. You don't mean it. I'm telling you," Curt is telling the other boys, "if we let her go, we're going to regret it." They hesitate. And she shrieks, with all her survival instinct and life force, *"I promise! Don't hurt my mama!"*

That plea, the real anguish, and the notion it gives

them, that they still have some power over her, makes them step back.

She will not remember stumbling to the bike, righting it, will not remember, for years, until Dr. Neiman brings it back, the wave of agony sweeping up, into her, knife-like, when she makes contact with the seat.

She careens, on the Huffy three-speed, over the dark country highway in the moonlight, an old woman now, not a child anymore, rushing, as if speed might erase fact.

Edith is on the porch, hands on hips, looking out toward the road when Nora finally turns into the driveway.

"There you are!"

I promised not to tell or they'll hurt her.

But as the child collapses in the mother's arms, sobbing hysterically, the story comes out right away.

Now it is years later, nine-thirty A.M. in New York, and Voort and Mickie wait in the black Caprice two blocks from the Lieb-Young abortion clinic on Madison and Fifty-fourth Street. The police visor is down. They are in a no parking zone in front of a construction site. They must not show themselves at the clinic before it opens, at ten, must not frighten away the murderer, if, by good fortune, she is on her way to work there right now.

The window is rolled down, and there is a paper bag of egg sandwiches between them. The day is unseasonably cold and gray.

"There's something funny about this whole setup," Mickie says, handing Voort a sandwich from a waxed paper bag, and a sugared coffee.

"What's that?"

"Don't you think it's a little perverted that we're about to raid a place where they kill babies, to arrest a woman who kills adults?"

Voort's in a two-button blue jacket, khakis, light blue shirt and maroon tie. Mickie's in a charcoal Armani jacket from Barneys, pleated gray slacks, and Bruno Magli shoes.

"'A woman's choice,'" Mickie says, turning the slogan over. "It's simple when you say it, but so is 'A baby's choice.' Some things," Mickie says, "should not be a choice."

"I didn't know you felt so strongly about it."

"Who says it's legal to suck a fetus out if it's less than five months old? And then, if twenty-four more hours pass, the kid counts as a person? So on August ninth you can pay a doctor to do it. August tenth, one day later, it's a crime. That make sense to you?"

Voort is thinking of Shari, and the choice they faced a few days ago. He'd been surprised by the vehemence of the longing he felt, to keep his baby, when Shari announced she was pregnant. Had been surprised by the intensity of his rage when he thought, for a mistaken moment, that she'd aborted it. He simply cannot conceive of aborting a child he fathered, but he is also not comfortable with telling other people what to do.

Only minutes to go now.

They are angry, he and Mickie. After all the frustration on this case. Now that they have a lead, their ire spreads out, makes the whole city seem more irritable, more impersonal.

On the seat beside them lie police artist sketches: of a woman in sunglasses and big hat. Another of a woman with long red hair. There are variations too, conjecture sketches by the artist. The redhead with short hair. The woman wearing oval rather than rectangular sunglasses.

Wild guesses. But Voort hopes one may be right.

"Let's go," he says into the hand radio as the digital clock hits ten to ten. Chilly wind hits them as they leave the car. Fighting the urge to hurry, which might alert the perp, they merge into the stream of pedestrians—the ones with enviable work schedules—due at their jobs at the luxurious hour of ten. Publishers. Music agents. Clerks opening expensive boutiques, computer stores, specialty shops.

The clinic occupies the ground floor, as it turns out, of a town house, wedged between a Turkish restaurant and a glass office building. As the detectives walk up, a well-dressed woman, maybe a patient, is disappearing inside. Two more women, detectives on Voort's team, stroll toward them from the opposite direction.

Voort tells the group, "I go in with Cathy. Mickie, Rhonda, watch the front and back. No one leaves."

And now Voort and detective Cathy Ramsey, a quiet, attractive, diligent brunette, whom he has never worked with before, mount the steps, ring the bell, and eye the closed-circuit camera aimed down at them. Voort hopes that whoever is watching will believe a patient and her escort have arrived.

"Yes?" a woman's voice says over the intercom, pleasant, professional.

"My wife and I want to make an appointment."

If Voort's ploy does not work, he will identify himself, but he prefers to get inside first. There is a pause, as if the person inside is considering if they're anti-abortion activists. If they're carrying weapons.

Then a bell rings and they enter a foyer, and are buzzed a second time into the waiting room. At first it looks to him like the waiting room of any general practitioner, internist, dentist. A receptionist is busy writing in an appointment book, behind glass. Cushioned chairs line two walls, half of them filled with fairly prosperous-looking patients. *Glamour*, *Smithsonian*, and *Cosmopolitan* magazines lie on a glass coffee table.

No windows. A soft, New Age string melody plays over hidden speakers.

But now Voort sees the difference between this and other doctors' offices. The patients here lack the pallid or feverish look of the sick. Several glance away rather than making eye contact. They are not bored or curious, like patients he's used to seeing in his own doctor's office. He realizes he is in a place for more than simple medical help. It is a place some people use for an exercise in expediency, for withdrawal from commitment.

Also, visitors here seem to require armed security. He catches a glimpse, beyond a vase of fresh tulips on a side table, down a hall, of a guard, a woman in a business suit, but the look of scrutiny she is giving him is unmistakable, as is the small bulge beneath her tailored jacket. She is pretending to drink from a fountain, when actually she is checking Voort out.

"Can I help you?"

The receptionist, a small, dark woman, who fits the description of the murderess, is looking at them with a mixture of helpfulness and wariness. Perhaps customers don't stroll unannounced into this place.

Voort produces his badge, and watches the receptionist's smile die when he asks to talk to whoever is in charge.

"You're a detective?" she says much too loudly.

Voort hears a gasp behind him.

One of the women in the waiting room is running for the door.

The line of cars arrives at the New Thames Day Care Center three hours after the doctor leaves. The chief of the New Thames police has already interviewed the hysterical, weeping girl, and departed. The doctor has taken blood and semen samples, and given her a shot to calm her down.

From her top floor window Nora sees that the town's only police cruiser is back, leading four civilian cars. The Honda Civic, she knows, belongs to the high school principal, Will Green's father. The red Dodge Ram pickup belongs to the parents of Curt Maze.

The vehicles seem like beasts, growling, in front of her porch.

What do they want?

One by one the parents get out of the cars. They are dressed in their Sunday best, subdued cotton print dresses, and Kmart jackets for the men. The police chief—a lean ex-army sergeant with a limp—a man who normally deals with nothing worse than speeding tickets, and leaves big cases for the state troopers, leads the group, disappearing from Nora's line of vision, tromping up to the porch.

The two-note chime of the front doorbell, normally cheery, makes her jump.

She sinks to the floor, crawls to the corner. Moonlight illuminates the rag dolls on the girl's rocking chair, and magazine photos of teenage boys, movie stars, taped to the lemon-yellow walls.

Nora is trembling. She is polluted inside. No one must have contact with her, especially *these* parents, who spawned those boys. In her mind she keeps seeing their sons approaching. She sees a bit of Joshua's chest, smooth, hairless, sweaty. She sees her bicycle lying on the ground, near her face.

Downstairs, voices are arguing.

And now Nora hears footsteps coming up the stairs. She pushes against the wall, as if to merge with it. As if to disappear.

A knock.

"It's Mom. Can I come in?"

"No."

But the door opens anyway. From out of the light, Edith advances in, scoops her up, cradles her. Everything will be "all right," Edith assures her. The boys are "caught."

But who cares if they are caught? The damage is done. And the parents are still down there. They want something, or they would not have come.

At length, when Nora's breathing slows, Edith explains that the boys admitted everything. Their parents and the police chief have come to see Nora, to speak with her.

"Why?"

Edith rocks her. "To talk to you about what to do."

"But you said the boys are arrested."

"I mean, what to do next."

"They go to jail, right?"

The girl breaks out sobbing, and Edith says, "Shoosh. Shoosh. I'll tell them to go." And minutes later the cars leave, giving Nora the barest feeling of marginal control in life. But the next morning they come back.

Again she hides in the room. And Edith makes the pilgrimage upstairs to tell her, as the parents wait, "They promise to leave if you want. They're torn up about what happened. They just want a couple of minutes of your time. Baby, I told them, that if you want," Edith sighs, "I'll make them go again. But I think you might want us to talk to them. You and me."

Nora doesn't even want to deal with the question of whether to go downstairs. She is unaccustomed to turning down requests, and she hardly ever turns down Mama.

Edith says, "If we talk with them a few minutes, I believe they will never come back, if that's what you want."

So Nora allows herself to be dressed. Jeans hide her leg

bruises, a blouse shields the marks on her arms, back, breasts.

"My face is ugly, Mama."

"No, it's the most beautiful face in the world."

Shirt tucked, sneakers tied by Mom, hair brushed by Mom, Nora, the debutante of violation, descends the stairs toward the half-dozen upturned faces, expressions knotted with a kind of misery that was never there before. Nora recognizes the adults, even though she does not know them well. The principal is a friend of Mama's cousin. The deputy chief of police's wife was a cheerleader, with Mama, in high school. Dad's bowling team used to go up against Joshua Low's father. Nora saw the man at the local lanes.

Hands in laps, jaws tight, they sit in the living room, balancing Edith's filled teacups on their laps. Now that Nora has joined them, they are unsure how to start. A dog barks outside. A breeze washes in through the open windows, bringing a smell that will forever terrify Nora. Pine.

The chief finally speaks. He is balding but handsome in an athletic way, despite the limp. He grew up as Mom's next-door neighbor, one town over. "Those boys are in custody," he begins.

Nora stares at the pattern on the woven carpet, the oval threads making up lines of crimson, azure, emerald, black.

"I beat the crap out of Josh," interrupts his father. Mr. Low smacks his fist into his palm.

The chief flashes Mr. Low a look, meaning, Let me talk. He asks Nora, "Can I come closer?"

But he's already doing that.

"Can I sit on the other side of the sofa with you?"

He speaks as if soothing a dog.

"Nora, what happened is terrible, unforgivable. You

don't have to say anything if you don't want. We just want you to listen. Because what happens next, to the boys, is up to you. It is *your choice*, so we just want to talk about the options. I have their confessions. Their fingerprints are on your bicycle. And they, uh, tested out in other ways. The second we bring in the state police they will go away for a long time, until they are as old as I am. They will never bother you, or your mother, again. I promise."

Mrs. Green is crying, twisting a handkerchief in her lap.

"Why not come with me to the window," the chief coaxes, "and you'll see they're out in the squad car, in back."

Nora is filled with panic. "You brought them here?"

She flinches when the sheriff's hand moves toward her, and he pulls it away. "Just take a look, Nora, for a second. Stand behind the curtains. They won't know you're there. It will make you feel better. You'll see, they're locked up."

She is weak, and it is as if she is dreaming. She goes to the window with him, anything to make these people leave. The police car is right up beside the porch, and in back, she sees, quite clearly, from the side, that the face nearest hers, all beaten up, red and pulpy, is Joshua's.

One of the other boys, Roger Trumbull, turns to Joshua. His face is also bandaged, and there is a patch over his eye.

"That kid," Roger's father says. "Wait till I get my hands on him again."

All four boys seem smaller, at this distance, and younger than she remembers. Was it only yesterday that the terrible thing happened?

"Like I said, we'll do whatever you want," the chief repeats. "We will enforce the law. But there are different kinds of laws, Nora," the chief says, standing behind her, at the window. "There's the good law of the Commonwealth of Massachusetts, a fine set of rules for strangers, family, friends. That law comes with TV cameras and reporters at *your* door. And the whole state knowing what happened to you."

He pauses, as if picking the right words. As if this is some crucial part. "And there's justice between people who need each other, live together."

Roger's mother says, "He is talking about us."

The chief says, "What will happen now will be Nora's law, Nora's justice. *Your* say, not some strangers in Boston. That's why we're talking to you before we bring in the state. Once that happens, this town is finished, and you will never have privacy again. The whole country will know every detail of what happened to you. But there's another way. And I promise those boys will get hell either way. We will support you, whatever you do."

"What is he talking about, Mama?" Nora asks.

The parents are staring at her, needy.

"Darling, let him talk," Edith says.

As the adults look on, the chief explains to Nora another kind of justice, the kind, he says, that will "protect her." That will "shield her." That will "keep her safe."

Seventeen years later, at the Lieb-Young Clinic, Voort occupies a swivel chair in the office of Dr. Martin Lieb, director and managing partner. The room is sunny and comfortable, with lots of potted ferns, books on built-in shelves, and a colorful abstract painting, a Koontz, over the working fireplace.

The nineteen-year-old on the couch is the woman who bolted from the waiting room when Voort identified himself.

"Please don't tell my parents I was here," she says. "They'd kill me."

She is small enough to match the height of the murderess, attractive, in a subdued way, full-figured, with curly auburn hair, a dark pants suit, an expensive diamond-studded silver bracelet, and a pair of squarish sunglasses perched on top of her head. She does not look pregnant.

"I won't tell your parents," Voort says. "But maybe they'd understand."

"No way."

Behind the girl the door opens and detective Cathy Ramsey flashes Voort a thumbs-down signal. It means the girl's alibi for the night of Otto Frederick's murder, which is that she was at school at Wesleyan, in Connecticut, has just checked out over the phone.

"You can go," Voort says. He never thought she was going to turn out to be guilty. He just had to check, after the way she tried to flee.

As she walks out, Dr. Lieb enters. He is a compact man in his late fifties, bald on top, with a brushy white mustache, a maroon shirt, French pleated trousers, and a white medical jacket half unbuttoned over his dark tie. Reading glasses hang, on a cord, around his neck. He has a concerned but cooperative, avuncular air.

"I've canceled all procedures for this morning, and told the staff to stay, as you requested."

Actually, Voort ordered this, but there is little point in saying it.

"I recognize you from TV. You're Detective Voort, aren't you? You're working on those murders."

He's not surprised to see me here, Voort thinks as he waves the man onto his own couch.

"Doctor, two of the men who were killed impregnated women who had abortions here."

The doctor jerks and squeezes his eyes shut. "Two?"

he says in a soft voice after a moment. "Oh God. I thought you were here about that man in Staten Island."

Voort keeps his expression neutral but his pulse speeds up. Thomas Jackson is *not* who he meant. Jackson has not, until this very second, with the doctor's words, been linked to this clinic.

Lieb, distressed, says, "I didn't realize he'd really been here until you showed up today. When his photo was in the *Times*, one of the nurses said she recognized him. She said he'd been in, with a patient, a few months ago."

The look changes to embarrassment. "We all pooh-poohed it. She's the kind of person who watches *America's Most Wanted* and thinks she sees the suspect in her supermarket. But she insisted. She said he was flashy. He stayed in her mind."

"Why didn't she phone us?"

"We made so much fun of her she decided she must be wrong," the doctor says. "Now I feel terrible. And you're saying . . . you're saying *two* of the men were here? Oh God."

"Actually," Voort says, watching carefully, "Thomas Jackson was *not* one of the men I meant."

The import of Voort's words hit the doctor. "But that means all *three* of the guys . . . *all* of them . . . You're saying someone here is responsible."

"I need to see your records on these men."

"We don't have any. Fathers, if they were the fathers, aren't *in* our records."

"Never?"

The doctor has gone white. "We only keep records on patients, unless the man paid by check, and it bounced. But we still wouldn't know if he was the father."

"Check the billing records. And check some dates of procedures for me, please." Voort gives the doctor the name, and Social Security number, of Nancy Frederick and Beth Helms.

Dr. Lieb frowns, and looks uncertain. "I'm not allowed to show you medical records unless the patient permits it."

"Just the dates. We'll worry about records later."

"Technically," the doctor says, rising, "dates are records." But he goes to a Dell computer on his glass-topped desk and taps in questions. A moment later he says, squinting at the screen through reading glasses, "Helms came in last November."

He types more, and lets out a deep breath.

"Frederick was here the same week."

Voort feels himself closing in on some key point. "Did anything go wrong with their procedures? Can you tell me that much? Did anything special happen at the clinic that week? Think. Anything to tie them together?"

The doctor scans the screen. "Nothing went wrong on this one. But if you want to look yourself, you'll have to get a court order, or the patients can sue me. I'm sorry."

"Did the same doctor do both abortions?"

Lieb sighs. "Me."

"Were the same nurses present? The same personnel at the clinic on those days?"

"Some of them are here now. Your detectives are talking with them. I can give you the names of the others. I can't imagine that anyone here would be guilty of these things." He shakes his head. He seems shocked and sincere. He says, "Another doctor switches with me in the afternoons, sometimes. She's not coming in today, and she wasn't here those two days."

"Was anything special going on at the clinic last November, in general, that you remember? Try to remember. Problems with workers, outside contractors? Anything, even if it seems minor."

Lieb shuts his eyes again. At first Voort thinks the man is grieving over his business, the consequences that public exposure will have to his clinic. But then he sees that Lieb's left hand has involuntarily gone to his thigh, near his groin. Lieb is mourning the murder victims.

"No problems. We had construction on the roof, and there was some banging, but that was it. Do you know how many abortions we did last November? Is someone going after the fathers? Oh God."

Voort has already thought of this. "What about anti-abortion activists. Any incidents? Protesters trying to block the place? Threatening phone calls?"

"Not for a couple of years, and we got a court order against those two."

Voort says quickly. "What two?"

"A couple from Lancaster, Pennsylvania. They used to double-park outside, with loudspeakers on their car. They had placards in their windows. 'Baby killers.' That kind of thing."

"What did they look like?"

"Elderly. In their seventies, I'd guess. I think the man had a heart attack, and they stopped coming because of that, not the court order. They didn't care about courts."

Voort gets the names of the couple, and a copy of the court order, with their address in Pennsylvania. He will call their local police later, and inquire if the couple belongs to a larger anti-abortion group, which might have targeted people in this clinic, or if they have a daughter, relative, or friend who fits the description of a small, dark woman, who might have blamed the stress over the abortion issue for causing the man's heart attack.

Lieb is slumped on the couch, shaking his head. "I don't understand it," he says. "If someone had a gripe against us, wouldn't they strike at the clinic? Or me? Why the fathers?"

He bolts up. "My God! We better warn all the patients who came in around that time. It'll cause a panic."

"I'd rather my detective did that," says Voort, who has already planned it, "in case one of your patients is the woman we're looking for. I don't want to frighten her off."

"But you're talking about a hundred and fifty patients just for that month!"

"We'll have to talk to all of them anyway," he says, thinking, So many abortions. "I'll put my people on it. They work fast. Meanwhile, let's talk about your staff."

The doctor explains that the clinic uses the two rotating doctors, and four nurses.

"Our receptionist has been with us five years. We also have a social worker, available for counseling any patient. The service is included in the price. Some of the women who come to us," Lieb says, clearly sympathetic to them, "are pretty upset."

"I can imagine."

"There are all kinds of potential psychological consequences, for a mother to give up a child."

Voort says nothing.

Slightly cooler, the doctor says, "You're wondering, then, why do I do it, right?"

"That's your business."

"When I was in med school, I saw two girls die after improper abortions. Butchered. I never forgot it."

Voort nods. He likes this man, and now, together, they go through each staff member's history, addresses, family, record, anything that might tie them to the dead men.

Voort learns nothing useful.

Yet the answer must be here.

It's driving him crazy. And the doctor's words, "You're talking about one hundred and fifty patients," makes the threat more dire. Somewhere in this building, perhaps in this very office, or chair, something started that ended in the death of three men. Some act, or conversation. Some pain given. Some agony that has not died.

Dr. Lieb says, at length, "Anything else I can do for you?" It is now two P.M., but he is not in a rush. He seems agonized that his clinic was the starting point for the murders. He is just asking a question.

Voort has had Lieb distribute the addresses of staff members who are not present to detectives Cathy Ramsey and Rhonda Grey. He also provided Mickie with a computer printout of patients who were in last November. Detectives are already starting to spread around the city, contacting employees and patients.

The problem is, Voort knows, that with this kind of high profile case, someone will probably alert the media too. By tonight, especially with the abortion angle, the killer will make, again, every news show in the country.

And she might run, knowing that we're closing in.

One hundred and fifty procedures.

Someone knocks on the door.

All Voort can say, to combat the frustration, the sense of violence building, the tidal wave of rage about to crash down on him, is, "I want to talk to everybody here again, even if my people spoke to them."

Mickie opens the door, says, "Excuse me," to the doctor, and "Conrad," to Voort. Bad sign. Mickie never calls him Conrad.

"Got a minute?" Mickie says.

Voort excuses himself, filled with foreboding. In the hallway outside, Mickie, for once in his life, has trouble beginning whatever he is about to say.

"We've been going over the list of patients, assigning names."

"Someone else has been killed?"

"No, but one of them will be someone you'll want to

talk to. Camilla was here last November." Mickie looks embarrassed. "Maybe you already know about this."

Meaning, Weren't you two going out with each other last November?

"According to the records," Mickie says, "Camilla had an abortion two days after Beth Helms."

The new boiler arrives at Nora's house a week after the attack, paid for and installed, free of charge, by the company president himself, Joshua's uncle.

The painters come Wednesday, the roofers Friday. The men drive up, ignoring the girl at the upstairs window. Slavishly grateful to be working for free, to be helping their sons, or nephews, or cousins avoid prison. They exterminate the carpenter ants in the second floor gable, dehumidify the basement walls, redo moldings, and over the next few weeks, replace a fence, the washing machine, the master bedroom floor, the rusty gutters.

The boys have been released from jail in their parents' care. They never leave their houses and the rumor around town is that, nightly, their fathers beat the shit out of them.

"The house looks much better," Edith says, eyeing the improvements. "Doesn't it, Nora?"

Roger's second cousin builds an entertainment center in the den. Will's older brother comes back from Vermont one day with a truckload of new cherrywood flooring.

"For your bedroom, Nora," Edith says.

A fine, new, copper rooster weathervane crowns the roof.

"You don't have to go along with this," Edith says. "You can press charges any time. But you have to admit, darling, the place has never looked better!"

The boys have been told that they will be suspended,

when the term starts, from the basketball team for "fighting." Roger's younger sister starts bicycling over on afternoons, to help with the children. By the fourth week the boys themselves begin showing up at the day care center, only when Nora is gone, of course. They mow the lawn, scrub the windows, floors, kitchen, oven. They get jobs in nearby towns; in Pizza Huts, or gas stations, earning cash so if Nora goes into any store, or to the movies, or bowling, or if she wants clothes, the boys pay.

"They'd be working in prison, making stop signs for the whole state, if you weren't so good to them," Edith remarks. "But this way let the injured party benefit, without putting you through a circus. Darling, someday your college will be paid for by these people."

But it feels wrong. And one day a state policeman comes to the house, asks to speak to Nora, says someone phoned the barracks and said she had been attacked.

"Were you attacked?" asks the cop, a tall, kind-looking man in a brown sport jacket. "Did four boys attack you?"

Nora says nothing.

"My God, Nora," Edith says, looking terrified. "That is an awful story! Tell your mother what happened."

It is clear what Edith wants.

"No," Nora tells the policeman, her gut hurting.

The officer stares at her, nods thoughtfully, shifts his gaze from Nora to Edith.

"Are you sure?"

In a toneless voice, Nora says, "Yes."

"Mrs. Shay, here's my card. If she changes her mind, please phone."

"Oh, that call must have come from a prankster."

The weeks go on. At least, as long as summer vacation lasts, Nora does not have to pass the boys in the halls.

But in September, when she starts high school, she sees them every day.

By now the smile that used to brighten her face is gone. She slumps when she walks. She has nightmares she cannot remember, but Edith assures her they will go away.

"Trust your mom, hon."

Nora dreads going to school. She is sure everyone knows what happened, even though no one mentions it. She fears passing the boys in the hall. Hates the way they look down, or away. They'll be talking with someone, laughing, and catch sight of her, and everyone, all of them, boys and girls, or even teachers, will shut up.

In late September she arrives home to see a brand-new fire-engine-red Jeep Cherokee in the driveway.

"Isn't it a beaut?" Edith says. "It's got air-conditioning and a stereo. Eddie Trumbull's brother-in-law is a dealer, in Pittsfield. Let's take a ride!"

"I don't feel well, Mama. You go."

Another time she comes home to find boxes, gifts from Bloomingdale's, delivered by parcel post, from New York.

"A little information about people isn't a bad thing," Edith says, trying on a shearling coat. "No, not a bit. I've been thinking, wouldn't it be nice to go to Boston, this weekend? Stay in a hotel? See a show?"

Nora feels dirty going, guilty somehow, but Edith loves the trip.

And I want my mama to be happy, Nora thinks miserably.

"Why don't we go to the Caribbean this Christmas," Edith says, back from Boston, spreading out brochures. "Or would you rather take a cruise? I've *always*, my whole life, wanted to go on a cruise."

"But I thought you don't trust other people to take care of the children."

"Oh pooh. Some very reliable people have volunteered to work for us if we go away."

Edith is sipping a cherry cider on the porch, as they have this conversation, and it is late October, unseasonably warm. Edith has put on weight, especially in her arms, from the free pies, cakes, steak dinners sent over almost daily from the restaurant, with mashed potatoes, heaps of asparagus or corn, hot breads, puddings, bottles of wine.

She is changing. She always wants things, Nora thinks.

When Edith sees Nora's stricken face, she puts down the glass.

"Oh, honey, my main wish is that none of this happened. Do you want to change your mind? Are those boys bothering you? You are my life, and your desire is mine. Do you want to press charges?"

Nora thinks, I should have done that right away.

Edith's eyes grow wet with emotion. "I don't care if I grew up with those people, if their families include my best, only friends. If they are innocent of the terrible thing their boys did. I'll phone the police this very minute."

But she stays in the chair.

"Yes, that is what I will do," she says after a moment. "The statute of limitations is still valid. My poor girl."

"Maybe you *should* call," Nora says, and watches her mother's face fall with disappointment.

Nora's stomach is hurting. It always hurts these days. She wishes her father were here, to talk to, to get advice from, but he is dead. She says, "I guess it won't be so terrible if we try this a little longer, Mama."

At least Edith's approving smile is back.

"Okay, but only if you're happy," Edith says, picking up her cider again. "Because nothing else is important if my darling daughter is not happy. And you know what? If we took the boys to court, it would break us. They would fight us. The whole town would fight us. They would say you tempted them, not that you did."

"I didn't!"

Edith nods. "I know you didn't. I'm just telling you what they would say. They might even win. And of course the whole thing would be on TV, and the radio. *Everyone* in the state would know what happened to you. People would probably drive here, to the house, just park and wait to see you, take pictures of you. Not that something like that should keep you from doing what is right."

"Yes, Mama."

"Those parents, who did nothing, would be destroyed. I'm just mentioning it."

"I know."

"Those parents never hurt anyone," Edith repeats, dabbing a handkerchief at her eye. "But this way those boys will work for us every week. They will never stop being your servants, Nora. If you know information about people, those people have to do what you want."

Nora throws up.

"Don't get upset, baby."

"I've been sick every morning"

Edith gets out of the chair. Her drink spills.

"I've been dizzy, and my ankles are swollen. Something is wrong inside," Nora says.

Edith has gone pale. She says, "Let's take a ride to Dr. Trumbull," who is Roger's uncle.

They take the brand-new Cherokee.

"Did you miss your period?" the doctor says, at his office, probing at her secret places with steel implements.

"I never had any period, ever," Nora says.

"Pregnant," Trumbull announces, when the tests come back. "I'll schedule the procedure as quick as possible. It'll be quick, Nora. It'll be over one, two, three."

"What procedure?" Nora says.

I will have my own child, Nora thinks. I will have my own little baby. I will love it. And no one will hurt it. At least one good thing came from that horrible day at the pond.

"Are you crazy?" Edith says.

"You said the purpose of a woman is to have a child."

"But you are not a woman."

"Then how come I can have a baby?"

"Oh, Nora," Edith says, sitting beside her on her bed, stroking her hair, "You've had a terrible time. You're not thinking right. You quit the acting club. You don't go out. But if you thought about the problem rationally—"

"I love my baby. I feel her inside me," Nora says, holding her hand to the flat of her stomach. She is a natural mother, a bearer of life.

She says, having a feeling of rightness about her pregnancy, if nothing else, "I can't help how she got inside me, but killing her would be like killing one of the kids in the day care center."

"Stop saying 'her.' It's not a child."

"I'll never let anyone hurt her. I'll protect her."

Edith snaps, tired of the argument. "You couldn't even protect you."

Nora runs upstairs, to the redone attic, with its new wood paneling, new couch, new TV, new minifridge by the new picture window. She is crying. And Edith, bursting in behind her, is furious.

"You think in the real world you can run into a room and get away from things? Are you listening?"

"No!"

"You think you can protect a baby? Then tell me, what if you have it and one of those boys wants to take it away?"

Nora looks up, terrified.

"Didn't think of that, did you? But one of them is the father, isn't he? He could go to court to get that baby. Or his family could, even if he's in jail. And if the court said so, then that boy, or his parents, *your baby's grand-parents*, could *take away that baby*. And even if they failed, they would be here *all the time*. Because a court allows a father to visit his baby. That boy, *and his family*, would come here on Christmas. And even if the boy was in jail, he might still have legal rights, and—"

Nora is crying, holding her stomach, as if to clap her hands over the baby's ears.

"Nora, honey, I know what's best for you. You are my jewel. You are the only thing I love in life. Don't you think that, if this was a good idea, don't you *think*, if there was even the tiniest bit of sense to it, having this baby, who would be *my grandchild*, that I would love it as much as I love you?"

"Then why are you saying these things?"

Edith stands.

"Because I know what can happen. I hate that you have to learn this at your age, but that's life. How would you feel if the police came one day and *took away* that baby and *gave* it to that boy?" Edith says. "Because when outsiders get involved in things, like you appar-ently want, when *judges* and *lawyers* and *people we never even met* get the power of life or death over us—"

Nora is crying harder.

Edith presses her strength, her advantage. "That thing inside you came from rape. Not from love. Not from a husband. You will have a husband who loves you one day. I promise. It will be easier to find him if you *do not have a rape child*. And that thing in you will even look like one of those boys. Maybe it will have Joshua's face, and it will say 'Daddy' when it sees Joshua. How would you like that?"

"*Get out of here!*"

"Why don't you just take one of these pills that Dr. Trumbull gave you, to calm you down. Take the pill. Wash it down. Good. You are my good, beautiful, wonderful girl and I love you, and I think that maybe, right now, you should even take a second pill, just this one time, to make you feel better."

Nora is sobbing.

Edith says, "I wish the whole thing never happened too. I wish we could erase all the evidence. One day, years from now, you *will* have a baby. *Your* baby, that came from love. And that baby will grow into *your* child, *your* loving child, and every sight of it, every glimpse of it, will give you good, happy memories, and you will have a loving man with you. Trust me. Believe what I am saying. It is for the best."

At length, Nora, half drugged, allows herself to be persuaded to go to the doctor. The procedure is quick, and legal, just like Dr. Trumbull said. It takes place in another town.

"You'll feel better soon," Edith says on the way home.

"I don't care."

"How about a steak dinner? We'll go to Beef House and order the best, how about that?"

"Whatever you want," Nora says, broken, in the corner of the Cherokee, still feeling the steel probe, and the vacuum, inside her. The worst part is, she does not yet feel any pain, and she knows she should.

"We can go to the movies in Pittsfield, honey. We could get a sundae after that, hot fudge, at Ben & Jerry's."

As the days pass, and autumn advances, as the leaves turn colors, her posture becomes even more slumped, and she stops caring for the way she looks. In school she barely hands in homework.

The state police detective comes to the house one more time, but Nora refuses to see him.

Sometimes she breaks into tears when she sees the children arriving at the day care center.

"Hell, we can close the place," Edith says, worried finally. "With so much money coming from other things. I'll get a job somewhere. If you don't want to see the kids, you don't have to see the kids."

So the day care center closes. Roger Trumbull's family moves away, to California, and Curt Maze's family moves down South somewhere, but checks keep coming. Nora never stops thinking about the lost baby. She dreams she is holding a baby. Sometimes she feels nauseous, as if she still carries the baby, but the doctor says the symptoms are in her head.

Two years later, at age fifteen, she still breaks into tears sometimes, if she sees a picture of a baby in a magazine, or on television. And in town, the gratefulness that people felt toward her, for not going to the state police, has turned to resentment. They don't like having to work on the house all the time. They don't like the way Edith wants more of everything. They don't like feeling trapped.

They start to make fun of the girl. One day Nora hears younger boys, thirteen-year-olds, in the middle school-yard, singing:

Nora Shay. What a lay.
Fuck her all day
But you'll pay
Forever and a day.

That afternoon she makes her way to the principal's office; Will's father is startled to see her. None of the parents ever like seeing her. He has not spoken to her for two years. He is unsure whether to treat her as a student, or friend, or woman, or anything except a threat.

Principal Edward Green would be happier if she were dead, Nora thinks. Everyone would.

Nora explains that she is going to leave school and go away, and that she wants to complete, by mail, her high school diploma. She says he will never see her again after today.

"That's not allowed," he tells her officiously. "We can't give diplomas by mail. And your grades have been dropping."

For the first time since the rape, Nora sits up straight, looks at him, hard. She actually stares at him. She lets the threat hang there. She acts the way her mother acts. She sends out her will, and lets him feel the power that is welling in her heart, the fury, against his son, and him, and everyone here, a rage that wants to come screaming out and ruin every single person in New Thames.

"Actually," he says, cracking his knuckles, "perhaps, for you, we can make an exception."

That night she is on the Peter Pan bus, out of New Thames, heading south. And a bare three hours later the bus reaches New York, another country, as far away as Bangkok, as far as Nora is concerned.

Looking out the window, eyeing the steel-and-concrete towers, she understands that she is inserting herself into a different kind of womb, a cold one, where you take care of yourself, where there is no nurturing fluid. A landscape which, with its absence of trees, or smiles, or any semblance of public gentleness, represents the true state of the earth.

New York, she thinks, is where I will change my name, and who I am.

I've hit bottom. Things can't get worse.

But instead of finding comfort in the notion, she is weighed down by a premonition that she is wrong, again, and that even her own certainty will betray her in the end.

THIRTEEN

Voort must concentrate on what the social worker, Alec H. Mitchell, is telling him. But he can't. It is impossible. He keeps going back to Mickie's words, in the hallway outside Mitchell's office a few minutes ago.

Camilla was a patient in this clinic last November.

"I told the other detective everything," Mitchell says. "Why do I have to talk to you?"

"Just a few more questions."

Was I the father?

Mitchell sighs theatrically. He is in his late twenties, Voort guesses, athletic-looking in a fitted dark brown shirt and tie. His small, round mouth imparts a slight air of petulance. His curly hair sets off his soft eyes. His upper body is almost too powerful for his legs. The man probably uses steroids, or works out obsessively.

Mitchell's office is small but neat, painted beige, with wooden slat blinds at the window. On the walls are paintings of a sunset, lilies in a field, the Alps, bison on the prairie; images designed to soothe visitors who wish they could be transported far away.

"I *told* the other man, not all patients talk with me," Mitchell says. "It's optional. The first consultation is free. If they come back, we work out a fee. I try to be thorough."

Or was the father of Camilla's child Paul Anderson?

The furniture is brushed leather, the glassed-in shelves behind the social worker's swivel chair are filled with files in blue folders.

Voort notices a softball mitt, cleated athletic shoes, and an aluminum bat on the floor, by the closet. There is a neatly folded lime-green softball team shirt on the couch.

"Big game at six-thirty, against Mt. Sinai," Mitchell boasts, more like an excited boy than a medical professional. "We're playing for the league championship."

Voort makes himself concentrate. "Do your files include the name of the babies' fathers?"

"We don't refer to fetuses as babies here," Mitchell says. "And I told the other man, there's no set procedure. If a patient mentions a father's name, I might jot it down. I don't want to ask again. I look like I'm not paying attention if I do. But if a woman is reluctant to name names, I don't press it. Some of them aren't even sure who the father is."

"I'd like to see if names are mentioned in three specific files."

Mitchell sits back, webs his fingers, more like a movie doctor than a real doctor, which he is not. Maybe, Voort thinks, because the man doesn't have the higher degree, he compensates with attitude. "I *told* the other detective, I'd like to help, but I can't produce records without written permission. Otherwise I can be sued, unless you're showing me a court order. I know the law."

"That might take hours."

"So you want to take a shortcut."

"Look, three men have been murdered," Voort says impatiently. "All of them impregnated women who got abortions here. There's no other link so far. No record of the men in the billing department, or in the notes describing the procedures. No employee admits to talking to the victims. For the moment, that leaves your files as the possible connection."

Mitchell shakes his head. "Only I see my files, even if the names *are* there. You can read them yourself the second I have permission *from the patients*. I'm a stickler for detail. The right way may take longer, but that's why it is the right way."

Voort stands. "I'll have to ask you to stay here, while I make some calls."

"But what about the softball game?"

"The right way," Voort repeats, "takes time."

Voort asks to use a private line, then calls Nancy Frederick and Beth Helms. He's fortunate enough to reach both. He asks if they would give permission for him to see their medical records.

"I'll fax permission over now," Nancy Frederick says.

But Beth Helms grows nervous. "You don't need to see my files. I told you what you ought to know."

"You're forcing me to get a court order."

He hears her muttered curse.

Voort coaxes her. "I told you I'd protect you. But if this clinic is where everything started, you'll be dragged into it in the end. And if I go to a judge, you'll be in it right now. A court order puts you in the public record, where reporters can find it."

Beth Helms agrees to fax permission for Voort to see her files.

And now he must make the last call, the one he dreads. He hesitates. He would rather see Camilla's face when they have this conversation. He cannot believe she would abort his child, and not even tell him if she was pregnant.

But Voort does not have the luxury of time.

Even while his finger approaches the phone, he knows the clock is ticking. He envisions a small, dark-haired woman, with a knife in her purse, someone who was once a patient at this clinic, or knew a doctor here, or talked to this social worker.

One hundred and fifty women came to this clinic last November.

Voort punches in, from memory, Camilla's office number. She is "in a meeting," a secretary says. Voort tells the woman to get her out. Now.

His mind jumps to images of Camilla. He sees her at the Hudson River fund-raiser where he first met her, and in the boathouse, where they kept their kayaks. He remembers the way, out of the blue, she broke up with him.

"I guess I'm not over my old boyfriend, Voort."

Maybe he was the father.

And now her voice is on the line. "What happened?" she says breathlessly. "They got me out of a meeting."

"I'm at the Lieb-Young Clinic, on Madison and Fifty-fourth," Voort says.

A gasp. "Oh God."

"I need to see your file, Camilla. There's a link between the murders and this place. I need you to fax the social worker, now, and give written permission for me to get into that file."

"How could there be a link?"

"I'm not going to explain."

"I'll come over. I'll look at the file with you."

"No."

"We have to talk about this, Voort."

"Yes we do. But right now, will you fax it? Yes or no?"

She takes the fax number and says, in a little voice, "When can I see you?"

"Later," Voort says, and hangs up, angry, disgusted. Already the receptionist is coming in with the first two faxes. Alec H. Mitchell hands over the first two files, which are surprisingly thick. Clearly the man does pay attention to detail.

Maybe Camilla was sleeping with that boyfriend at the same time she was seeing me.

Voort opens the Frederick file. It is clear, he sees, that she was upset on the day she came in here. She did not want to have the abortion, Mitchell wrote. She wanted to give birth to twins.

"The husband, Otto, is author of *Vanishing Peoples of the Amazon*," the social worker wrote, along with notations like "cheap" and "complains about low book advances" and other comments on the man's envy of people who get paid more for their jobs.

So! Otto's name is in the file.

Voort turns to Beth Helms, where the extensive notes say, "She misses Paul Anderson, the father, an ABC producer who suggested she use this clinic. She was hurt to learn from another of Anderson's exes that he works from a 'script' with women, tells them stories about a friend who died in Bosnia, to get sympathy, then invites them back to his big Gramercy Park apartment, talks about commitment when he wants to turn the subject to birth control."

And now Voort holds the blue folder containing Camilla's secret thoughts and fears on the day she visited this place. The day she lay on a table here, on a cotton sheet, and got anesthesia, and opened her legs for a doctor, not a lover. For extraction, not insertion. Camilla came here to consummate the ultimate act of noncommitment.

"Patient is reticent to talk to me and only did so because a friend suggested that she may be 'blocking' emotion. She will not discuss the father, but I recognize her face from a photo in the *Post*. She dates a policeman, the millionaire cop who won the suit against the city. Voort."

And now it strikes Voort.

I am a potential victim.

He feels as if his balls are shriveling.

"Find anything?" Alec H. Mitchell says, looking on from the couch, more cooperative now that he is not legally responsible for Voort's eyeballing the files.

"You're sure nobody else sees these besides you?" Voort says.

"I take the notes. I write them up. I lock the files away."

"In these shelves," Voort says, glancing at the glassed-in cabinets behind the desk.

Mitchell glances at his watch. He had struck Voort at first as immature, in his desire to play a game rather than help an investigation. Now Voort wonders if there is something more here. Is he nervous?

Voort rises and walks to the cabinets. They are locked, all right. He takes a paper clip off the desk, twists it until it breaks, inserts both pieces into the lock, and maneuvers them.

"What are you doing?" Alec H. Mitchell protests.

Voort swings open the door. "Pretty secure, all right," he says.

"They were never broken into."

"You're sure of that."

"You're the first one. If the lock is broken, you'll pay!"

Voort sits back down. Alec *is* nervous, rubbing his index finger, unconsciously, against the leather arm of the sitting chair. Voort can even hear the mild scratching sound.

"How about cleaning people? Do they come at night, to this room?" Voort asks.

"*Someone* has to clean up, don't they? They don't read the files."

"But they're here, alone."

"You don't expect me to stand over them, watching, do you? Do you oversee people who clean your office?"

"I notice there's a new paint job," Voort says, pushing the man now, watching a bead of moisture appear on the left side of his forehead. "When the place was painted, did you move the files?"

"Into the basement. But it's secure down there."

"How long were they there?" says Voort, who is experiencing a sense of déjà vu, that something here reminds him of some other place, some important place. But where?

"The basement was locked," Alec Mitchell says. "Can I go now?"

"Anything else you want to tell me?" Voort says. "How about the computer. Are you tied into the Internet? Could hackers have gotten into your files?"

"The way you talk, it's like these files are sitting on the street outside and anyone can get to them. I protect them. You're saying I don't do my job."

"Is that what you think I'm saying?"

"You're implying it."

"I'm sorry you feel that way. How about a glass of water. You thirsty?"

"No."

"I am," Voort says, and excuses himself. When he comes back, Alec H. Mitchell is peering at the lock in his wooden shelf, in a fearful way.

"You really think someone got into my files?"

Voort sips water. Let him stew a moment. Let him ask the questions. Let him reveal the thing he is hiding.

"But who would do that?" Alec says.

"How's your social life?" Voort says.

"Why is that important?"

"Got a girlfriend? Fiancée? You're not wearing a wedding ring."

"I've been dating a very wonderful woman. She's a model."

"Pretty, huh?"

"Beautiful. And very smart."

"What does she look like?"

"Dark hair. Dark eyes."

"Tall? Most models are fairly tall."

"No. She's small. Tiny."

"Got a picture?"

Alec Mitchell seems relieved to be talking about anything beside his files. He produces his wallet, flips it open and shows a photo of a very good-looking woman, with short dark hair, the right age, right size, in a bathing suit, on a beach.

"Sexy woman," Voort says, trying to rile him, wanting to see what happens. "I bet guys come on to her all the time."

Alec Mitchell says defensively, "She doesn't go with anyone else. Why are you saying these things?"

"Is she threatened by your work, the way you spend days talking to women about their sex life? I bet a lot of women would be jealous of that."

"Lucy is very secure."

"Can I have her number?"

"I wasn't anywhere near those men when they were killed. You're checking on me, aren't you?"

"Do you have a problem with that?"

Alec Mitchell says, "It's just these Gestapo questions, that's all. Anyone would get a little riled at your attitude."

"My attitude," Voort repeats quietly.

"Like this is the Inquisition or something. Give some people a badge and they turn into Mussolini."

"I'm sorry you feel that way. But," Voort says, every alarm inside him roaring, screaming now, telling him he has found the right place, "I have to check the alibis of anyone who comes to our attention. So where were you those nights?"

Alec Mitchell looks terrified.

"I'll find out in the end," Voort says. "And then it'll be in *my* files. Police files. Unless," he says, letting the deal sit there, "it turns out not to be relevant."

"You'll keep it between us?"

"If it has nothing to do with the murder, sure."

"Don't tell Lucy," Alec Mitchell whispers.

Voort says nothing and the silence drags out.

"I have had one or two gay experiences, but that doesn't make me gay. A lot of people go both ways," Alec says.

"I need to check," Voort says.

Alec names a bar in Greenwich Village, which Voort knows well from his sex crimes job. It is a leather bar. A bar where people start with drinks and end with pain. A bar that only men visit. A bar with a sign outside showing an anvil and a hammer.

"The bartender knows me."

"I'll need Lucy's phone number, and address," Voort says. "But I'll keep away from the gay part, for now."

Mitchell recites a phone number for the cute little brunette, starting with area code 702.

"Where's that?" Voort says.

"Nevada. I visit her there. She hates New York, never comes here."

Shit. But he will check.

Mitchell says, shakily, wanting to leave, "If you're finished, can I go to the park now? The game starts at six-thirty. They need me in left field."

As the social worker walks out, Voort cannot, for the life of him, think of more questions. But he has a feeling he has missed something. Maybe it will occur to him later, tonight, when he's with Shari, or driving in his car, or getting ready for bed.

Voort leaves the clinic, hails a cab and tells the driver

to take him to NBC studios. It is time to confront Camilla and learn the story that she would not tell him before, that was "not related" to his investigation.

As the cab threads Midtown traffic, going west, he closes his eyes to concentrate, goes over everything that happened at the clinic just now.

Again comes the feeling that something in the social worker's office reminded him of something else, but what?

To try to see the connection, Voort switches to the other people he's interviewed. Paul Anderson's girl-friends. The man in the flower shop. Otto Frederick's neighbors.

Suddenly he opens his eyes. The taxi is in a traffic jam, on Fifth Avenue. He'd been concentrating so hard, he didn't even hear honking.

"The flower shop," he says out loud.

The driver says, "Did you say something?"

Voort orders the man to turn around, to get him to Central Park, where the social worker better be playing softball. Better be reachable.

Voort sees the link and it amazes him.

"Hurry," he says, and he reaches to alert Mickie on his phone.

"That new associate has the hots for you," the other secretaries tell Nora Clay.

"No he doesn't."

The secretaries giggle at the way she blushes. They are at her desk, outside the thirty-seventh-floor office of the senior partner of the New York law firm of Jayne, Low, Borelli and Stephens. It is four years since Nora moved to New York, and three since her graduation, first in her class, from secretarial school. She has worked her way up in the firm, enjoying its sense of solidness, security, wealth.

"Admit it, Nora," a secretary named Diana says, "Morgan Cooper keeps finding reasons to pass your desk. He can't take his eyes off you. We heard he's rich. He played fullback at the University of Tennessee. He's as good-looking as Brad Pitt. Talk to the guy."

"I have to work," Nora says.

They are Nora's friends, the secretaries. Diana and Loretta and Ruth—all young, her age. All single. They eat brown-bag lunches together, and go to movies on Thursday nights. They shoot pool in the firm's lounge, after the lawyers are finished each night.

The other girls starve themselves to better afford tight dresses, silk stockings, good leather high-heeled shoes, perfume that will turn a man's head.

"How come you never go on dates?" Diana, smartest of the three, asks Nora when the other two go back to their desks.

"I haven't met anyone I like."

"Half the men in the office want to go out with you."

"I have a good life by myself," Nora Clay says.

Diana makes a mocking sound in her throat. "Right! Watching TV every night."

One May day, when Nora takes her brown-bagged tuna on wheat into the thirty-seventh-floor elevator, she finds the new associate, Morgan Cooper, there already, on his way down from thirty-eight. He's carrying a brown bag too.

"Know any good places to eat out there?" he asks.

Despite her straight-ahead stare, heat crawls up her neck, into her cheeks. The elevator is so tiny.

"There are lots of places, Mr. Cooper. You'll find one, I'm sure."

He is impeccably polite, always groomed, in a conservative suit and white shirt today, suspenders, and a muted tie. He reeks of masculinity.

He says, with a polite Tennessee accent, "There are always choices, but only good ones count."

"Try Sixth Avenue," she says, hurrying the other way when the doors open, to merge into the crowd.

When she turns around, a block later, he is gone.

My clothes are soaked with sweat. I better take a cab home and change.

Back at the office after lunch, he doesn't try to talk to her. He doesn't walk past her desk the rest of the afternoon, and she considers the possibility that all he wanted, after all, was directions.

But a week later Nora arrives at work one day to find a wrapped package on her desk, with no note. It is a book: Diane Ackerman's *The Moon by Whale Light*. It has a beautiful blue cover, showing a silvery whale rising from the sea. The essays inside depict animals, creatures so endangered that, at night, reading in her single bed, Nora weeps for the whales. The penguins. The wide variety of life threatened by men.

Three weeks later she finds another volume, this time Peter Matthiessen's *The Snow Leopard* on her desk, about a man whose wife has died, who seeks solace by trekking through the mountains of Nepal, looking for the rare, magnificent, big cat who shuns man.

Who is leaving the books? she wonders, although, deep inside, she suspects.

"I heard Morgan Cooper broke up with his girlfriend in Nashville," Diana announces.

"I want his ass," Ruth jokes.

Yet even when Morgan is working late, and one of the girls lets him know, with a smile, that she is available, he never takes up the invitation.

"Maybe he doesn't like girls," says Ruth, brashest of

the four. "There are no photos of women on his desk. Women never phone him."

And then, in the elevator, at lunchtime, Morgan is there again, with a brown-bag lunch again, and a book.

The Moon by Whale Light.

"My favorite," he says.

"I read it," she says.

"I don't suppose," he says, "that you might consider spending twenty torturous minutes eating a sandwich with me. I'm new in town."

And astounded at her own answer, feeling the sweat break out again, Nora actually hears herself say, in a toneless voice, "One place is as good as another, I guess."

He laughs. "This is where we left off. There's always a best choice."

They bring their smoked ham with mustard, for him, and avocado with tomato slices, for her, to the fountain garden at MOMA, the Museum of Modern Art. It is pleasant to be surrounded by Picasso sculptures. Bubbling water cools the shady garden, making a soothing noise as it falls.

A week later he asks her out again, this time proposing a bench picnic in the park behind the Fifth Avenue Library. "There's a lunchtime concert. A string trio from Juilliard," Morgan tells her. "I read about it in the *Times*."

"Fine."

"Did you grow up in New York?" he asks when they get there, trying conversation while the music plays.

"No."

"Have you ever gone to these concerts before?"

"No."

He does not touch her. He does not flirt. He does not, like other men, whistle at her, or call to her, or pretend that they experience, in any way, the vaguest possibility of physical intimacy. He does not "accidentally" brush against her elbow. He does not ask her to a movie. He is quietly polite, yet he does not seem shy.

They start to eat lunch together once or twice a week after that, talking, as they dine, about neutral subjects. The office. The city. She deflects questions about her past.

"I bet he's gay," Ruth says one day, in the office pool room, where they are shooting a rack after work. Ruth is angry because she stayed late last night, wore her sexiest dress, and volunteered to bring Morgan Mexican food while he wrote his brief on the Shanghai account.

"He didn't even notice."

"I think," Diana says, knocking the eight ball into a corner pocket, grinning lasciviously at Nora, "that Morgan Cooper has someone else on his mind."

A month of lunches later, Morgan asks Nora if she would like, on a Saturday afternoon, a safe, public time in the city, to accompany him back to MOMA, for an early film.

"I'm not doing anything else that day," she says. "But I have plans that night. I'll have to leave early."

"Me too. A friend is coming into town."

Nora is surprised by a stab of jealousy. What friend? she thinks.

The film turns out to be a World War II story from Holland, about hiding Jews in basements, from invading Germans. But when she tries to remember it, alone, that night, watching TV, all she can think of is the way Morgan's arm felt beside hers. All that muscle and bulk.

"How about a movie Friday? After work," he suggests two weeks later. "Or do you think I turn into a vampire when the sun goes down?" His grin is irresistible. He forms his hands into claws. "Dracula," he says.

"If we get back early," she says, "I'd love to go."

"Do you like baseball? I have box seats to the Mets on Sunday night," he says the week after that.

"I've never been to a baseball game."

To get there, they have to take the subway, where the boisterous, pennant-hungry crowd pushes them up against each other. It is the first time they touch for any extended period of time. The contact is inescapable. His mouth is six inches from hers as they speak, and his hand, on the overhead rail, brushes her fingers. She feels a warm, liquid sensation between her legs, a weakness in her knees, but tells herself it is from the rocking of the subway.

When the doors open at Shea Stadium, spilling the crowd onto the platform, she is relieved, but also disappointed that the contact has stopped.

That night, for the first time, he takes her home, in a cab, all the way back to 108th Street. It is June, clean and cool, and the stars are out. The city is at its best. Broadway is alive with strollers, shoppers going in and out of the bagel and ice cream shops, the coffee shops. They pass Columbia University students, and concert-goers coming home from the Cathedral of St. John the Divine.

"Everyone back in Nashville is asleep by now," Morgan says. "This place is just getting started."

At the door to her building he stops. He stands a few feet away. His smile is lovely, and she wonders, fears, yet also hopes, that he might try to kiss her. But he keeps his hands in his pockets.

"Ever go to FAO Schwarz?" he says.

"What's that?"

He laughs. "For an alleged New Yorker, you don't take advantage of your own city. It's a toy store," he says, "on Fifth Avenue. The best in the world. They let you play with the toys. I'm going to pick up a chess game for my nephew on Wednesday. Want to come?"

And Nora hears herself say, feeling like she is falling, like ice is breaking in a pond, like the water is closing over her head, "I can cook dinner after that, if you'd like."

She is overwhelmed suddenly by the feeling she had in the forest, back home, years ago. She is trapped. She cannot breathe. She sees the boys walking toward her. She manages to kiss Morgan good-bye on the cheek. But when she gets inside the apartment, she is shaking.

She dreams of the boys that night and wakes bathed in sweat.

In the office, later, she confesses to Diana, "I'm afraid."

"That man likes you."

"I'm going to drive him away. I'm going to ruin things. I know it. I can't help it."

"Ever consider seeing a psychologist?"

Nora breaks out laughing.

Diana leans close, whispering. At Jayne, Low, Borelli and Stephens, you don't speak in loud voices about psychologists. "I mean it," she says. "A lot of people see one. I do. He's right in your neighborhood. Dr. Neiman."

"What happens when you go?" Nora asks, frightened by the notion of sharing thoughts. "Do you sit on a couch? Talk about your parents?"

"He helped me," Diana says. "I had this intimacy problem. I threw myself at guys who weren't interested. I ran away from guys who were. I ended up with musicians. Married guys. Guys on drugs. I told myself there was something wrong with *men*, but Neiman showed me I didn't really want to be with someone. I was afraid I'd be overwhelmed."

"You wouldn't have figured this stuff out yourself?"

Diana holds up her left hand, and ring finger, which as of this week showcases the smallest diamond. "Why do you think I was able to say yes to Dennis finally? Dr. Neiman helps you learn about yourself. If you don't like him," Diana says, jotting his number down, "don't go back."

Nora throws the paper out, but the next week, when Morgan tries to kiss her on the mouth and she stops him, and then breaks into tears after he leaves, she makes the appointment.

"You have a lot of rage against the boys who hurt you, and your mom," Neiman says, as they sit in his little room, which she will come to know well, as he radiates concern. A young/old man who seems sexless.

Nora shakes her head. "I don't have any 'rage' toward Mom," she says, feeling the kind of shortness of breath that always comes upon her when memories of her old town pop up. "I mean, I don't agree with what she did, but she was trying to protect me. She had my best interests at heart."

"Your best interests," Dr. Neiman says, in that maddening way she will find he has of repeating things.

"Look, you didn't grow up there," she says. "You don't know what it was like for her, alone, trying to bring me up. The house busted all the time. My dad dead. She never had anything herself, any enjoyment, until . . ."

"Until what?"

In a tiny voice Nora says, "Until after I got raped."

"You haven't visited your mom in years," Dr. Neiman points out. "You haven't called her, or written. Why?"

"I just wanted to cut off all connection with that place, that's all. I don't want to talk about her."

Dr. Neiman says, "Then what about the boys? Did you ever try to find them? To prosecute or confront them? What's the statute of limitations on rape in Massachusetts anyway?"

"That's stupid, after all this time." Nora is trembling. "I'd be a freak, in the papers. Like Mama said."

"Are you scared to talk to them?"

"They aren't worth thinking about."

"Would you say, off the top of your head, that the kind of fear you feel when Morgan is close is the same way you felt when you used to see those boys, in school?"

"No."

He says nothing for a long time.

"Maybe a little," she admits.

At length Dr. Neiman convinces her to try to contact the boys and "confront them," whatever that means. At first she can't do it. But then one night Morgan tries, while they are kissing, to touch her breast. As soon as his fingers make contact with her dress, she stands up.

"You have to leave."

An hour later, on the phone, she is saying, "It's Nora, Mom."

She hears crying on the other end.

"Oh, Nora, I can't believe it. I'm so happy to hear you. I thought something happened to you. I've been trying to find you."

"Why? So you can get your house fixed for free again? So you can threaten people?" Nora is terrified at the rage pouring from her. It seems to be growing so fast she can barely speak.

Edith is weeping. "I miss you."

Nora stops this kind of talk right away. "Are the two boys who stayed there still around?"

Edith is silent. Then she says, almost desperate, "There's no need to talk about that. That happened a long time ago. Are you married? Do you have children? You always wanted children," Edith says. "Why, if you had children, I'd be a grandmother. I could visit. Let's talk about something nice."

"*Where are they?*"

But all the boys are gone now. Will and Joshua were killed in an auto accident, Edith says, two years ago. They were drunk, went out of control on Route 8 and smashed into a tree. Curt Maze, the violent one, she heard, joined the army and died in Saudi Arabia, in some hushed-up military incident. Roger Trumbull "disappeared from California, like you did from here. No one knows where he went."

Nora can hardly breathe. "I'm going to hang up now, Mom."

"At least give me your address. I'm so lonely. Let me write you. I love you."

She tells Dr. Neiman the next week, "I left her my address if she wants to write, but I told her not to visit, or expect an answer. I'll never get to tell the boys how I feel now."

"Then write it down. Or say it into a tape recorder. Pretend you are talking to them, that they are only a few feet away. Let the rage out. It's safe. It's only imagination. Let yourself go. Imagine anything you want, killing them even, knifing them like they threatened to do to you. *You have to get this out.* Saying it might be a start."

"But it seems so silly, walking around, talking to myself. Is that the best you can come up with?"

"Therapy isn't magic, Nora. I can't give you a pill to erase your memories. I can't cut them out of your brain with a scalpel. All I can try to do is make them real to you, and give you the opportunity to deal them in a different way. Right now, when you see Morgan, part of you is thinking it's *them* with you, *them* trying to kiss you."

So Nora tries the tape recorder. She knows that, if she doesn't do something, fast, she will drive Morgan away. And she is amazed at the rage that pours from her, night after night, as she paces the apartment, muttering, over and over, like a crazy woman, "I hate you. I want to kill you." Sobbing. Falling asleep in a chair.

In her head, at night, at two A.M., while the rest of the building is sleeping, *she* is the one holding the knife on the boys. *She* is the one making threats. *She* is the one digging the blade into their skin, threatening to cut them to pieces.

"Do it a hundred times, until the image is boring to you," Dr. Neiman says. "Until you don't want to do it anymore."

It's ridiculous, she thinks, but she trusts the doctor. She tries what the doctor says. She has no other alternative. And a few weeks later, when Morgan tries to touch her, she finds herself kissing him back hotly. She feels her body responding.

It is a miracle, and she starts to cry.

Morgan pulls back. They are in his apartment, on Fifty-first Street.

"Don't stop," Nora says.

And when he touches her again, it feels different than when the boys did. Morgan is gentle. He undresses her slowly, kissing her on the neck, shoulders, belly, pulling back, controlling himself, saying, "Is it okay? Do you want me to stop?"

"No."

"Nora, I can tell something horrible happened to you. It's okay if this is as far as we go today."

"I don't want to stop."

A blessing from God, and from Dr. Neiman. She has been in a dark tunnel, but visible, finally, is the smallest flicker of light. She feels Morgan's hands, *Morgan's* and not the boys, on her breasts, belly, thighs, knees.

She is twenty-one years old now and has never been touched this way. Her nerve endings come alive with pleasure. She is moaning. They are naked now. He is white as marble, and he lies on top of her.

There comes one horrible moment, when he penetrates her, when she flashes back to the pond, and sees, clear as fact, the flushed and drunken face of Joshua above her, and she starts to push Joshua off, except Morgan's voice says, "It's all right. We've done enough for today. I love you."

Her vision clears. It's *not* Joshua.

"Come back here," she says.

Afterward she says, "I have to tell you a story," and the truth comes out. All of it. About Mom. The boys. The town. The arrangement. Emptying herself, she feels exhausted, not even caring, in a way, if Morgan will leave. Dr. Neiman was right, she realizes. Talking isn't as good as revenge, but it can accomplish things. Words can make you feel better, if they are the right ones, said at the right time, and if the listener is the right person.

Morgan makes love to her again.

Even if he leaves me now, I'm getting better.

He gets up, goes to a dresser, and when he comes back, in his glorious male nakedness, he holds a small black box in his hand, a box covered with black velvet.

"Nora?"

It's a ring. A diamond ring.

She cannot believe it. Mama said this would happen one day, but she thought it impossible.

Seeing her face, the lack of expression, Morgan takes a step back. "Maybe I took it out too soon," he says, and with those words, she bursts out laughing, really whooping.

"Any more time and we would have died of old age," she says.

Morgan, she finally believes, is a real, true magician. He can rearrange molecules. He can turn dark into light. He can take drab New York buildings and give them color. He can add beat to music, make jokes funny, add spice to food, and he even has power over time itself, to make it faster, to make days pass quicker as they get wedding rings, a blood test, pick out an art gallery, to hold their wedding. They register at Bloomingdale's and Tiffany's for gifts. They fly to Nashville to meet his family.

"Lucky you," the girls at the office say.

She starts to see what life is like in the upper echelons of the law firm. Now she uses car services instead of subways, eats at French restaurants instead of McDonald's, spends weekends in the Hamptons instead of the Sony Theater. Even the doctors are different. They take more time with her, examining her, because now, thanks to Morgan's legal machinations, she is in a better health plan, not a cheap, money-saving HMO.

"Your blood pressure is fine, cholesterol fine. You're a healthy woman, a healthy couple," the doctor tells her, after the exam that Morgan suggested they both go through.

"Thank you."

"But you can't have children."

Nora sits in the man's ground floor Fifth Avenue office, and believes that the traffic noise has just twisted his words, made them inaudible, so that she heard him say something he did not.

The doctor moves his chair closer, frowning. "Your insides are damaged."

Nora feels Morgan's hand grip hers.

"Whoever did the abortion," the doctor says, shaking

his head, "I'm sorry to say, messed it up. It's better off for you if you don't even get pregnant."

Morgan the Magician cannot rearrange the broken atoms of her womb.

Outside, afterward, knowing how she feels, how, for Nora, the whole city is whirling and she feels dirty inside, polluted, dead inside, he tells her, "I still love you."

"You do?"

"We'll adopt a baby."

"Really?"

He repeats, smiling, yes, adopt it, and we will love it. And it will love us. Morgan is handsome, and gallant, and he has never, he says, been more sure of anything in his life.

Except if he is so sure, she thinks a few days later, why has his ardor in bed dropped off a little? Why is he tired at night? Why is he suddenly working late, telling her to "go out with the girls" instead of hurrying back to her.

There will be a logical reason. I'll just be patient.

The reason is contained in a note she finds, on his dresser, the next week, when she wakes on a Friday morning and he is gone.

Nora, love, I don't know how to say this. They teach us in law school to confront, and argue. But with you, I'm a coward. I can't marry you. I want a baby. I want to be a father. I know, if I tried to pretend otherwise, that it would eat at me, and I would stop loving you. We would have a bitter marriage, not a happy one.

You probably don't believe that I am heartbroken. But it will take months for me to get over this. That's why I've agreed to work on the Shanghai case, to be liaison over there. I'll be en route when you read this. I'll phone from China when I land.

She is rolled up in a ball, in his apartment.

She starts breaking things.

No baby.

No Morgan.

That night, in her apartment, she starts to drink.

At two A.M. her neighbors hear her screaming about knifing boys, and killing Morgan, and they call the police, who find her oven on, the gas flowing, and a half-unconscious woman on the tiled floor of her kitchen.

"We have to report a suicide attempt," the cop who responds to the call says.

"Please don't. I was starting dinner and drank too much and forgot to light the oven. I swear it. It wasn't suicide," she says.

"Give her a break," the neighbors say.

So no charges are filed. No fingerprints are taken. There is no record in the city of New York of the fingerprints of Nora Clay.

Her work, at the office, diminishes in quality. She starts drinking at night, going to bars, taking men home.

"Perhaps, Nora," the senior partner tells her, firmly but gently, a month later, "you might want to work somewhere else now, considering the bad memories here. The truth is, we have to cut back on staff, and you're the one who's been here the shortest. I'd be glad to give you an excellent severance package and terrific recommendations."

"They're just firing you because of Morgan. Fight them in court. Win a bundle," Diana says that night, in a bar, where the two of them are on their third gin and tonic.

"Who cares," Nora says.

"We'll all testify for you," Diana says. "Well—*I'll* testify at least. Fight them."

But Nora is broken. She doesn't want to see these

people anymore. Not the lawyers. Not the secretaries. Not even the damn building elevator, where she and Morgan first met. She doesn't want to even leave her apartment anymore. But at least Dr. Neiman, bless him, when she calls to cancel, suggests that he come to her apartment for their sessions, for a while. And he says that until she is "on her feet," he will waive a fee.

"Please don't drink so much, Nora," he says.

She cuts down on alcohol and stays at home as much as possible. She lives on her savings, depleting them. If she walks to the store, just the simple energy required drains her, and she breaks into tears when she sees babies on the street, or in photos while turning pages of magazines. She shuts off the television if a baby appears on screen, cooing, crying, playing in a diaper commercial.

I don't deserve to live.

Morgan calls for a while, but there is nothing to say, and he stops.

Diana phones. "You'll need money, Nora."

"I don't care."

"You need a job."

"I don't want to go outside anymore."

Just the thought of people looking at her in the street makes her want to throw up.

Diana's voice drops to a whisper. She is at the office, so she must appear to be working. "Listen, I can help you. I know a special job that is perfectly suited for you. A strange job that I had before I came here. You can do it at home. No one will see you. A package comes once a day and you send one back. And you learn things. Oh, do you learn things. Want the phone number?"

And that is how Nora gets the position she still has eight years later, when the murders occur, when Voort is in a taxi, and has just ordered the driver to take get to Central Park, fast.

* * *

The heat is back. The cold front is gone, and the damp, oppressive air has returned, thick and hellish. "Don't jog. Don't go for a bicycle ride. Just breathing out there is dangerous," says the weatherman on the radio as Voort's taxi drops him off at Central Park West and Eighty-first Street, close to the entry point for the Great Lawn, and its softball fields.

Voort starts running—across the bridle path and past the Delacorte Theater, Belvedere Castle, the park's weather station, past cyclists and Rollerbladers and the hardier or crazier joggers venturing out, past tourists on vacation and nannies wheeling babies. He charges through an entrance in a chain-link fence and onto the Great Lawn, a wide, long complex of softball fields—a gigantic meadow filled with activity, where at least a half-dozen games are in progress.

Under the blazing dusk sun, men and women round bases, shield their eyes in the outfield, jeer at umpires, drink soft drinks on the sidelines.

Voort has no idea which game the social worker is playing in, but he remembers that one team in his game, the man said, was "Mt. Sinai Hospital," and that the team shirt on Alec Mitchell's couch was lime-green. Three teams visible across the complex of fields sport that color.

Voort runs to the nearest backstop, gasping in the hot air, asking if this is the Mt. Sinai game. It turns out to be a Restaurant League game, the wrong game.

But a girl in a wheelchair, a coach, from the looks of the clipboard in her hand, points to the far backstop on the meadow. The fielders in that game wear green shirts too.

As Voort cuts across the other games, players yell at him. "Hey! There's a game in progress! Go around!"

He reaches the last field, his chest hurting from the

dirty, hot air. He stops, heaving, as a voice yells, "Time!" meaning the game should stop for a moment. All the players are turning to him.

"Get off the field, man!"

"Can't you see we're in the middle of a game?"

But Voort fixes on the left fielder, who has turned, who is staring at him, frozen, hands at his sides, fielder's mitt against his thigh. Alec Mitchell's eyes are wide with fear under his black-brimmed hat, and as Voort comes up to him, he seems to wilt, to shrink.

"A stickler for the rules, huh?" Voort says.

Mitchell says nothing.

"No one else sees the files except you, huh?" he says, remembering the man's office, the rows of blue folders containing his typed notes, and the identical blue folder that contained the credit card records in the Persia flower shop.

Voort actually pokes the man in the chest. He is filled with rage. For all Voort knows, another victim might have died while Mitchell pretended to know nothing.

"You were too lazy to type your own files, asshole. Tell me," Voort says, "who the goddamn typist was. Tell me who typed your files."

FOURTEEN

"All over the city, tape recorders are spinning. Capturing your every secret, every lie. Go ahead. Lock your door. Do you really think no one knows what you're saying? Do you believe, for a second, you can block out listeners? Maybe in the past only God heard the falsehoods uttered in your bedroom, or the privacy of your automobile. Now the IRS is present, and a private detective, a business spy.

"After a while, I'm there too."

Nora Clay is putting the finishing touches on her new, fabulous, Nora Clay Museum.

"Isn't technology wonderful? Instead of inventing a cure for cancer, scientists provide snoopers with microphones so tiny, almost invisible, that one can be right in front of you, in a button, and you don't even see it."

Clip clip, go the long shears in her right hand. The article she separates from the op-ed page of the *Times*, entitled "Speculations on New York's Serial Murderess," was written by a Yale sociologist. "We can assume," the professor writes, "that our killer was abused as a child."

Our killer, Nora thinks.

I belong to everyone now.

Her once bare walls are jammed with articles and police sketches. She loves looking at them. Adores reading them. She spends hours poring over photos of the men she killed.

FBI TO AID FEMALE SERIAL MURDER CASE, reads a headline from the *Wall Street Journal*, beside a two-page spread from *Newsweek* and a front-page article from the *Washington Post*. The third paragraph in the article says, "New York City detective Conrad Voort will continue to head the investigation. The FBI will participate and observe, said a Bureau spokesman in Washington."

"'After all,' the spokesman said, 'Voort identified these murders as serial before we did, and the truth is the FBI has little experience with female killers of this kind, so we'll all play on the same team.'"

She says, "How do I know so much about people?" She casts back, in her head, to a cramped, sloppy apartment smelling of cats and the East River, a living room alive with traffic noise from the Brooklyn Bridge outside. She is at the job interview she took eight years ago, for the position she occupies now. She sees herself on a lumpy couch, talking with a surprisingly fit and athletic-looking middle-age man, a hiker and climber, judging from the photos on the walls, showing him mountaineering in Nepal.

"If you join our company, Executive Home Secretary, you'll work from home," he tells her, over hot tea. "You'll get a delivery each day of tapes to transcribe. You'll send them back by messenger when you're through. Then we bind the transcripts into our nice blue folders, for the client, and you'll get paid by the page."

"I did plenty of transcribing at the law firm."

"You got a superb recommendation," the man nods. "Truth is, most people, at one time or another, could use a professional secretary. They need something typed. A business meeting transcript. A dictated legal brief or book manuscript. All kinds of things. But they don't *have* their own secretary, so they flip open their handy yellow pages, to 'Typing Services,' see our ad, and call. You'll enjoy the range of work here. One day you'll be transcribing a scientific paper. The next day, a medical referral, containing intimate details of a patient's medical history."

"Isn't the legal work confidential?"

"Sometimes." The man slides a legal form toward Nora. "You'll have to sign confidentially agreements, like this one," he tells her, as if a scrawled signature on a slip of paper constitutes an ironclad guarantee to clients that their secrets will never be misused.

"Nora, you'll never meet your clients. You'll probably never even see me again. But it's a very efficient system. We have people freelancing for us in all five boroughs. A lot of them are new moms who need work while they watch a baby. Or girls just out of secretarial school, looking for a more permanent job. College students. Artists. Actually, it's unusual—our good luck—to hire such a highly recommended person as yourself."

He gives her a look of speculation, the male glance of animal appraisal she has come to loathe.

"You don't look pregnant, Nora. So I bet you just had a baby, right?"

"Yes."

"Congratulations," he says, his eyes losing their predatory sheen, sliding to the stack of books on trekking in the Himalayas, on a bookshelf over a big TV. He wants her to leave now that the interview is finished and that a baby has somehow made her undesirable to him. "Good luck."

Now Nora remembers the first delivery of tapes, two days later. Boring stuff at first. A medical transcript, a dermatologist referral. A speech at a neighborhood block association meeting, protesting a new zoning law. A term paper on "The Glass Ceiling in Business for Women," in which the author, apparently a grad student at Columbia University, simply dictated her work into a tape.

Then, on the third week, Nora sits down at her computer one morning, gratefully numbed by the parade of anonymous, uninteresting jobs, and is shocked to hear a different kind of tape. Against a scratchy background comes the sound of a man and woman, whispering.

MAN: You know what I couldn't stop thinking about all morning? Your ass.

WOMAN: You're so romantic.

MAN: I brought roses, didn't I? Come here.

WOMAN: I'm thinking about it.

MAN: (kissing noises) Touch me. Oh yeah. My wife won't do that, won't even think about it.

WOMAN: Mmmmmm. Tasty.

Nora shuts the recorder, falls back in the chair, her heart pounding. She doesn't want to hear any more. Who would make a sick tape like this?

"Who do you think?" says Diana, the secretary from her old firm, when Nora phones. "A private detective, I bet, or the guy's wife, getting ready to ram it to him in court. Honey, you wouldn't believe all the places microphones are hidden in this city."

Diana laughs. "I bet if scientists put all the effort into medical research that they do into snooping technology, they would have cured cancer by now. Once I had this tape of a city councilman, a married guy, with an exotic dancer, and—"

"But it's not legal to record those things," Nora says.

"Not your problem," Diana says. "You're not breaking a law. You get a tape. You don't know who made it.

For all you know, it could be a playwright trying out new dialogue, or actors practicing."

"But it's not that."

"Have fun," Diana says. "Wait till you hear some of the really good tapes. I got the whole transcript of a grand jury hearing once, on a big bribery case. Someone must have hidden the mike in the room. I have no idea who. Maybe a jury member, doing it for amusement. But at night I'd read about the case in the *Daily News*. The paper had no idea what was really going on. Nora," she says, chuckling, "anyone can buy directional microphones, pencil microphones, even mikes that look like buttons, in a hundred spy stores and catalogs. And," she adds, "people do. They really do."

"I won't type this kind of thing."

"Sure you will. You need the money. You'll start to enjoy the good stuff, look forward to it. And even use what you learn."

"Use it how?"

A pause. "It'll be a nice surprise."

And the surprise happens two weeks later, after a series of transcribed fifth-rate short stories, a college application essay, medical notes on plastic surgery patients, a tape someone made in an AA meeting, and several dozen badly worded business letters. Nora puts on the earphones one morning, in her robe, with Mozart playing on her stereo, and from the tape hears the sharp scratch of wooden chairs against a hard floor.

MAN ONE: I need the divorce finalized by January third.

MAN TWO: Why?

MAN ONE: I'll tell you fucking why. Because two days after that, only the biggest damn drug company in the country is going to announce it's purchased my research lab, and the value of

> my stock in Calmer Medicines is gonna qua-
> druple, minimum. That's why. And I don't
> want that bitch getting half of it. I already paid
> her with half of my life.

MAN TWO: You're sure of this deal?

MAN ONE: The agreement is signed, Sammy. They're just
> holding off the announcement for two weeks.
> I'd buy stock if I were you.

Nora stops typing. It is Christmas week, and snow is
falling outside the barred window. She hears her breath
quicken. She stares at the word "quadruple," and at the
phrase "the agreement's been signed."

How do I buy stock, anyway? she thinks.

She rummages in her desk drawer, finds her last bank
statement and sees the figure $7,500 under savings. In
New York, that's nothing. Just her rent-controlled studio
costs $1,300 a month. In New York, an apple can cost a
dollar.

*I read something about a good stockbroker in one of
the other tapes.*

Nora crosses the room to the day's transcripts, and
picks out one that came in, from a couple therapist, in
Connecticut. She finds the medical notes on someone
named Ruth Poole, a PaineWebber broker, and her husband, Kenneth.

"Ruth is a highly successful, talented broker, yet she is
insecure at home," the doctor remarks.

Nora locates the thus-recommended broker in Connecticut, through directory assistance, and tells Ruth
Poole that a "friend" recommended her. She feels more
control over her life when she knows things about the
person she's dealing with.

"I'd like to buy stock in a small company called
Calmer Medicines," she says.

"I never heard of it," Ruth Poole says. "But I have some very attractive technical stocks that I'm recommending."

"No. Calmer Medicines," Nora insists, and wires five thousand dollars, most of her savings, to buy a stock selling at two dollars a share.

Two weeks later Ruth Poole calls up.

"Calmer Medicines is being merged into Global Pharmaceuticals," she says. "Your two dollars a share just went to fifteen dollars. That's a $32,000 profit in a couple of weeks. How'd you know to buy it?"

"I had a hunch."

Later, come more tips in the tapes; references to deals in board meeting transcripts and separation agreements and lawyers notes and partners' breakups. Ruth Poole buys, for Nora, shares in a company that has just patented a new antibaldness drug, and then a company that sells computers by phone instead of in stores, and later a European consortium that buys up water rights in the American West.

"You're the smartest client I have," the broker tells Nora.

And now, years later, in her apartment, Nora shakes herself back to the present. She says, "Shall I tell you more about the cesspool of information, the parade of disgusting revelation, that clients pay me, their anonymous typist, to write up every day?

"A defense attorney hides his recorder under a table at the Assistant D.A.'s office, as he plea-bargains a psychotic client down from assault with a deadly weapon to breaking and entering. A former star in one of the city's top public relations firms is writing a kiss-and-tell book detailing cases where the company provided drugs and prostitutes for famous singers.

"The list of my clients is as endless as transgression. I am the human cog necessary to complete their dirty acts.

I listen as workmen discuss phony injuries, to fool their compensation boards. To a tape an insurance investigator made of a couple admitting burning down their own house."

Nora decides to attach her newest clipped article, on "Jackie the Ripper," to the last available inch of free space on the wall, by the computer desk. "We are looking at a new kind of predator," says the head of Christians Against Violence in Media, in the piece "I Blame TV."

Next to this article is a *New York Post* guest column by a medium claiming to have had premonitions about where Nora will strike next.

I love the sex. I love it when they're inside me, and I have power. I only wish the feeling could last longer. It passes so quickly, and then it is done.

On her desk are stacks of cash, bound with red rubber bands, that she has withdrawn from her bank. "A precaution if I need to flee."

She will store the money, a hundred thousand dollars worth, in a strongbox she has rented, under the name Sheryl Lande, in a storefront facility and mail drop that a blind man runs, in the Bronx.

There is also, on the desk, a new velvet-topped box, filled with her diary tapes. "I no longer throw them out each day, after recording them." Now that she has stopped merely fantasizing about violence, she has found that listening to the tapes can help her relive the thrill.

"Of course the majority of my jobs are innocent. And clients are never identified in the manifest that comes to me each morning. But often it's easy to figure out who they are. The material is filled with references. People call each other by name. They mention companies, phone numbers, addresses, or even investigations I can look up on the Internet.

"I remember," she says, leaning back, "the first time that I followed someone I'd heard about in a tape."

She casts back, as she tells the story, to an April week, six years ago, nothing special about it, except that it was the week when the accumulated weight of her years of isolation changed her behavior pattern. When television shows, her usual distraction, irritated her, with their banal jokes and happy, unreal families. When her books made her more aware, not less, that she was living only half a life.

And the notion of seeking out someone on a tape started with a funny case, not a tragic one. It was a tape that epitomized one of those quirky legal fights that can only happen in a city where residents are packed like animals in a zoo, where type A workaholics, crammed into expensive cubicles in high rises, have no time for anything except work, and pay strangers to buy their clothes, choose their furniture, wash their laundry, and even baby-sit pets.

A dog walker, Nora thinks now. It started with a professional dog walker. She remembers the tape vividly: the request for a restraining order by a woman against a dog walker, another woman who, every night at nine P.M., stopped outside the complainant's building with fifteen dogs on leashes, so the animals could shit on a strip of public grass. The dog walker would then, the complaint read, pick up the droppings "while the creatures' howling causes grievous mental distress to my client, who seeks only a normal level of quiet."

That building is only a few minutes from my apartment, Nora remembers thinking.

So one night, when Nora quit work at the customary hour of eight-thirty, she decided to walk over to the scene of the daily complaint.

It was a pleasant spring evening, cool, with a breeze

blowing off the Hudson, and Nora, with about a hundred thousand other New Yorkers, went for a stroll. At nine she found herself on a bench, at Riverside and Ninetieth, across from a high-rise, red brick prewar building. The address on the awning matched the one on the complaint. She could see, across the street, an intense-looking woman in a red cashmere turtleneck, on a second floor Juliet balcony, irritably looking south, as if anticipating trouble.

Sure enough, five minutes later the dog walker appeared, half controlling, half pulled forward by a dozen canines. A German shepherd. An Irish wolfhound. A beagle. Poodles. A collie. All panting and straining while the young woman crooned, "Whaddaya smell, a squirrel?"

This is great, Nora thought.

Spotting the dog walker, the woman on the balcony stepped back into her apartment and slammed the window shut. Through the double-paned, double-strength, "city quiet"-made pane, Nora watched her get on the phone, gesticulating while the younger woman arrived at the strip of grass right by Nora's bench.

"A lot of dogs," Nora said.

"You gotta love 'em," the woman said. "Hey! Napoleon! Leave Svetlana alone!"

"People ever complain about the noise?"

The young woman rolled her eyes. She was a hippie type, dressed in farmer's overalls, with a red kerchief over her bangs. "There's one asshole across the street," she said, bending and picking up after her wards. "She must have been bitten by dogs in a former life or something. She actually hired a lawyer, can you believe it, to try to keep me from coming here. Fuck her. Now I come here on purpose, right, babies?"

The dogs barked and leaped in delighted response.

Across the street, the woman on the phone shook her fist, through the window.

Back home an hour later, typing again, Nora experienced a delicous feeling of satisfaction, far more fulfilling than reading books or watching TV. She was finally seeing the real, live people she wrote about.

"That's a funny story," Dr. Neiman said when she related it to him the following Tuesday, "but you might want to think about making real friends, putting together a circle of acquaintances for yourself."

Two weeks later Nora again went out to track down one of her subjects, this time a sadder case, a secretary, like she used to be, who was fired when she made a sexual harassment complaint against her boss at her law firm.

The allegations had been clear in the transcript. A senior partner had followed the woman into the ladies' room, making lewd suggestions. At the Christmas party, he had shoved her against a wall and put his hand on her groin.

Nora, enraged, got the girl's address off the legal brief. She took the subway to Astoria, found the one-family home where the girl, unemployed now, lived with her parents. She waited until the girl went out to shop, and trailed her to a drugstore and a butcher. They never spoke.

"You started a file on the girl?" Dr. Neiman said, frowning, the following Tuesday. "Why?"

"I feel like I know her."

"Nora, she's a person. She's not entertainment."

"Maybe, someday, I can help her."

And now, back in the present, she says, to her tape recorder, "Since then, each time I've gotten an interesting job, I've done extra research on it. I've matched names to voices. I've gone into the city, at night, and found the subjects. I've watched them. At first it was a game, but now I understand, with my library of sin on my shelves, that, as my mother used to say, everything has a purpose. That I was destined to use my files for good."

"Ma . . . ma," interrupts a voice, almost on cue, a small, pure, unsullied baby voice from above, from a vent near the kitchen alcove. New neighbors have moved in upstairs. Afternoons, Nora can hear their baby gurgling to itself, happy and safe. And that winning and helpless sound drops her back into memory . . . to the morning five months ago when she put on the headphones, switched on a tape, settled into her padded black leather chair, humming, contented, and heard a man's voice say, formally, "This tape was made at the Lieb-Young Clinic, November twenty-first. The patient's name is Nancy Frederick. Her procedure will commence in an hour."

Nora's typing slowed as she realized what she was hearing. She missed keys. She shut the recorder off and stood up so fast she forgot her earphones were still attached to her Sony. The recorder flew toward her face at the same time the earplugs dropped out.

Trembling, she put on her coat and took a long walk in Riverside Park, by the Hudson.

I won't listen to it. I'll send it back.

But when she came back, hours later, when she tried to slip the tape back into its envelope, she couldn't do it. She couldn't stay away from the tape. She had to hear it. Shaking, she put the earphones back in, and heard:

"Nancy Frederick complained that all her husband thinks about is money. He insisted she abort the fetus. He threatened to break up their marraige if she did not."

Nora realized that tears were running down her cheeks.

The next segment, from a different day, concerned

someone named Beth Helms. "She says her boyfriend, a prominent producer at NBC, quote, 'Cares more about the suit against him by Allan Foods than about me.' She accused him of seducing her by, quote, 'script.' Quote. 'First he got me drunk. Then he appealed to my sympathy by telling me about a friend of his who died. Then he invited me back to his Gramercy Park apartment, showed me his terrace, and, after we had sex, started talking about commitment as a way of bringing up birth control.' Beth says she spoke to other women Paul slept with, and the scenario is always the same."

Animal, Nora Clay thought.

But she typed the tapes, her rage growing. A new kind of curiosity had seized her. She wanted to see the men who hurt these women, and two other women mentioned on another tape. She studied the Beth Helms segment for clues, and called up, on the Internet, anything she could find on the NBC–Allan Foods lawsuit. And there, on the screen, she saw a smiling photo of a blond man, NBC producer Paul Anderson.

That night, when Paul left Rockefeller Center, Nora was behind him as he walked down Fifth Avenue, as he visited Barnes & Noble, as he stopped into Tiffany's, where he bought a woman's watch and had it gift-wrapped.

"For a loved one?" the sales clerk asked.

Paul Anderson laughed. "Call it a gift of lust," he said.

And now, months later, in her apartment, Nora Clay says, into her tape recorder, "I never got another shipment from that clinic, but I kept copies of the tapes and transcripts. I reread them. They broke my heart."

Upstairs, the little voice coos again, audible thanks to the idiosyncratic marvels of New York apartment acoustics. Nora stops work, goes to the vent, and listens to the baby. She gets a pleased, glazed look in her eye.

Nora sings back softly, lullaby lips pressed against the

iron grating over the vent, as if the cool metal is the downy head of a baby.

"Information is power. And I must use all my power against Mr. Conrad Voort, tonight."

You were right, Mama. I am a natural mother. I am the mother of all babies that need protection. I cannot carry them in my womb, but I can save them. It is the reason I did not kill myself.

When I stood in the sea after punishing Thomas Jackson, in the warm dark water, and the jellyfish rubbed against me, like birth matter, placentas, I realized I was in a womb, being thanked by unborn babies, the little souls, even the individual eggs that have not yet been fertilized. I am the mother of these not-yet conceived babies. I must protect them. There is a reason I cannot have a child, and it is that I am now focused on the innocents.

And the little voice, from the vent, cries out in infant wails, trying to articulate a need which, hopefully, a loving adult will fulfill.

Nora has a few more tasks to perform before leaving to find Mr. Conrad Voort tonight.

Humming, from her files she extracts a manila folder labeled ID CARDS, and flips it open. Inside is a single sheet of paper, a form she designed herself, giving, efficiently, information she has collected on STAMATY, ROLAND, as the typed name in the upper left-hand box reads.

The form gives an address in Williamsburg, Brooklyn, Social Security number and phone number, all gleaned from the tape that she originally transcribed on the man. Under "Usefulness," she has typed, "Provider of false ID cards for hire. Phony license, passports, Social Security cards, etc.

"Informer for police as part of a plea bargain agreement. Vegetarian. Collects baseball cards. Terrified of prison."

Under "Physical Description," filled out after she followed Stamaty, the sheet says, "Short, dark, thick glasses, bad dresser. Lives alone. Smokes a pipe."

Now, as she punches in the number, which begins ringing in Brooklyn, she envisions the ramshackle clapboard house that she once watched him leave, months ago.

A hoarse, smoker's, cancer-ridden voice croaks, "Yeah?"

"It's Sheryl Lande."

No answer. Just breathing.

"Did you do what I asked? Did you make up the driver's license and other ID cards?"

"Who are you? Where did you get my number?" the gruff, nervous voice asks.

Nora relishes the power that comes so easily now that she is unafraid. "I told you before. I know you make IDs for illegal immigrants, for criminals. I know you're a stoolie for the police too. Have you mailed the IDs to that postal box? Or shall I call the *Daily News* and tell them about your business?"

What she does not tell the man is that a detective recorded a meeting with him because, with the officer's retirement approaching, he'd taken to verifying everything interesting, to write a book on police life, which he has signed a contract to produce.

Stamaty says, "Yeah, I mailed them. Pretty smart, the way the photos you sent were fuzzy. I'd bet someone would have to look four times before they realized it was you. I bet if I passed you on the street, I wouldn't even know it."

"You wouldn't," she says, and hangs up.

"Even animals," she explains to her tape recorder, as she goes to the files again, for REALTY, "provide their dens with escape routes. Even moles and weasels are shrewd enough to know that one day the hunter might be at their door. They might need to flee out back."

The number she punches in with a second file in front of her causes a phone to ring in Riverdale, and she envisions the banker there—a white-haired, strikingly handsome man—whose participation in a red-lining scam, a civil rights violation punishable by prison, was recorded by a resentful bank employee, who used the tape and transcript to get a better severance package.

"Good afternoon, Mr. Milhouse," she says to the man. "This is Sheryl Lande. Did you do what I asked? Did you find me a furnished apartment among the foreclosed properties managed by your office?"

"You promised you wouldn't tell the newspapers about me if I did."

"Don't worry."

"I'm sixty years old. If it were in the papers, it would kill my wife."

"I said I wouldn't tell."

"I express-mailed your leases to your P.O. box two days ago, like you asked. And I changed our records to show you as legal occupant."

"There's furniture there?"

"Like you asked. The former owners just vacated, left when they couldn't pay their bills."

"And food? The people using it will come at night, from far away. I want it to be stocked, with canned stuff, not fresh food."

"I don't want to know who they are. But how did you find out about the list of properties? Do you work at this bank?"

"I know everything you do."

Her acts, tapes, and clippings, in the end, will comprise her legacy. They will form her warning. They will, when Voort is dead tonight, punished for the death he caused, become the altar on which she celebrates her metamorphosis.

"I was a nobody, but everyone is talking about me now. I'm famous. I don't even think I'll need to drink gin anymore for courage to carry out my punishments."

She goes to the window, looks out on the city, the pulsating life.

"I understand now what I always wanted, and it was to be somebody else, not Nora. Somebody good and strong. Somebody who no one would dare try to hurt."

She relishes the sense of life-achieving satiation. The final number she punches in is for Executive Home Secretary. Even after six P.M., odds are that someone is there. And the fact that she hears a recorded message, instead of a human, doesn't mean the office is unoccupied. Executive Home Secretary is so busy that the exhausted owner usually keeps the machine on, whether he's there or not.

"It's Nora. Thanks for the work you sent my way over the years. But I'm moving away, to Minnesota," she lies, because after all, she's saved so much money, and from now on she will devote all her time to being a protector. Planning well takes time.

"Don't send me tapes anymore. I'll write you when I land and tell you where to send the last check."

Another lie.

"I am amazed," she says, hanging up, "that once I was afraid to leave this apartment. That once these walls were my whole world."

I always knew the secrets, the insides of other people, the dark that lives in them.

At last I know myself.

* * *

At the same time, a few miles away, squad cars quietly block both ends of Front Street, a narrow cobblestone lane near the Fulton Fish Market. One block north, the Brooklyn Bridge rises, its heavy ramps vibrating from traffic. To the east is FDR Drive, alive with more cars.

Voort and Mickie lead half a dozen detectives and one visiting FBI agent to the street level door of a five-story converted warehouse with a red brick facade.

The heat is back.

Behind Voort, as he looks over the nameplates by the apartment buzzers, stand a trio of flak-jacketed cops from Police Emergency Services, carrying lock picks and a sledgehammer.

EXECUTIVE HOME SECRETARY, reads a handwritten slip of paper beside the third-floor bell.

Voort remembers the words of the social worker, Alec Mitchell.

"I don't know the name of the typist. Just the service. I send tapes to them, and they farm the work out. I just get a bill."

Mickie says, "Let her be here."

"Maybe the office manager did it, or the owner of the business, anyone with access to the transcripts," the FBI agent, Raymond Boone, had argued on the way over.

"No. The typist," Voort had said. "Because all the victims were mentioned in the same batch of transcripts. *The same mailing of tapes.* If you figure there are lots of typists working for the service, and they never know whose tapes they're going to get, I'm guessing our typist got one shipment, covering the social worker's interviews over one particular period. That's why all the victims are clustered around the same time."

"If someone back at the office did it, they would have dozens of shipments to choose from. Alec Mitchell's been sending tapes to Executive Home Secretary for months. The guys getting killed would have impregnated women visiting the clinic over a longer period of time."

Boone had said, "Don't assume."

Voort had gotten Executive Home Secretary's address from Alec Mitchell, and the name of the owner from the computer girls at One Police Plaza, who checked municipal tax rolls and came up with James L. Houk within minutes of Voort's call. They told Voort that Executive Home Secretary is a home business.

Now nobody answers the buzzer, so Voort tries a neighbor. Forceful entry is to be used, the department directive goes, only in cases of emergency, and if there's no other way inside.

Whoever lives in 5B just buzzes them in, without asking who is it.

Mickie says, disgusted, "They never learn."

Voort leads the team up three flights. It's a clean building, newly painted white, the wooden railings smelling of lemon polish, the new gray carpet fresh from the factory. There's only one apartment on the third-floor landing, with an empty umbrella stand outside and a couple of color photos of mountains, covered with snow, decorating the hallway. No one answers the buzzer, which is loud enough for Voort to hear from the hall.

He knocks, hard.

"Mr. Houk?"

"Can I help you?" interrupts a voice from above, from the stairway. A white man of about forty stands there, unsure whether to go up or down. He's probably the resident who buzzed them in, and now he's checking, belatedly, the identification of his visitors.

He wears a blue-and-white-striped silk bathrobe, and slippers. "My God!" he says, staring at the array of armor. "You're not Eddie. I thought you were Eddie."

"We're looking for Mr. Houk."

"He's out of the country," the man says, taking a tentative step closer. "What's going on?"

"Out of the country where?" Mickie demands, holding up his ID.

"Unreachable, in Tibet. He always goes trekking in August. His phone never stops ringing, so he never leaves a number when he goes away."

"I can't believe this," Mickie groans.

"Did he do something wrong?"

Voort says, "Executive Home Secretary. Is it closed in August, when he leaves?"

Now the man comes down to the landing. He is slight, and dark, and his graying rib cage shows under the lapels of the bathrobe. He is cooperative in a wide-eyed way. He is in thrall. "A woman comes every morning to run the service for James."

"What's her name?"

A shrug.

"What does she look like?" Voort hopes the description will match.

"Black. Tall. Maybe fifty."

"Shit," Mickie says.

"Are you the owner of the building?" Voort produces an official-looking paper. "This is a search warrant."

"What did James do?"

"I didn't say he did anything."

"The landlord lives in Bay Ridge," the man says. "I have his number upstairs."

Realizing that the bathrobe is loosening, he pulls the belt tighter. "Or are you looking for one of James's clients? They send him crazy stuff. You ought to hear his stories."

"Does someone here have a key to this apartment?"

"There's no super. And James is finicky about who

goes in. I think it's because he's a slob. Only that woman has a key, and she won't be here until nine tomorrow."

"Well?" Mickie asks Voort, meaning, Do we save time and bust in, or waste it waiting for the owner to arrive, which could take an hour, during which another murder could be taking place?

Voort orders Emergency Services, "Get us in."

Minutes later the door is open, in splinters. The city will buy James Houk a new one, from "Hardware Supply," which has, in an obscure clause of its municipal contract, the exclusive job of replacing doors that cops or firemen break down.

"Stay here," Voort tells the man, as well as two more neighbors, young women who have joined them on the landing after hearing the noise.

The detectives flow inside, guns drawn, just in case. They spread through the apartment.

No one is there.

"He runs a business here? It's a total shithole," Mickie mutters, disgusted, eyeing a cat bolting under an afghan, half hanging from an armchair that has been shredded by claws.

The place is a mess. It looks like one of those apartments old ladies live in, after thirty years of collecting junk, and feeding cats, and not throwing out kitty litter in time.

"What a stink."

The living room/office is a mass of rickety-looking tables piled with newspapers, magazines, pencils, tapes, and blue folders like the ones Voort saw at the clinic and at the flower shop.

There are transcripts everywhere, fat unbound ones on chairs, shelves, on the top of the refrigerator, and piled, four high, on the double bed, beside two more curled-up cats.

There are two phones and two answering machines.

"Let's see who called," Mickie says. "Maybe it was Jackie."

"Stop calling her that," Detective Cathy Ramsey says.

The cats are darting under the bed, around the refrigerator, onto windowsills, under tables. Voort notices, in various stages of panic or feline defiance, one calico, one auburn tom, two tailless Egyptians, and a half-dozen mixed breeds. A white Persian sits on the rug, looking stupidly at him, the only cat not running.

It rolls over, begging to be rubbed.

"The names of the typists have to be here somewhere," Voort says.

But the detectives cannot locate the names. Opening file cabinets, they find a climbing ax in the "New Business" drawer, and boxes of cat food under "Old Business." Probably, files have been computerized recently, because each drawer—"Taxes," "Payroll," "Miscellaneous"—reveals, instead of paperwork, rubber lace-up boots, plastic trash bags. And a teak salad bowl with tongs, and smaller bowls.

Voort does not find the typists among the piles of invoices by the window, which only name clients, or in more transcripts on the floor, or on the TV, with the empty box of Cheerios, or on the chaise lounge, where a panicked cat has thrown up.

"Maybe that woman, who runs the office, took it with her."

"Why would she do that?"

"Where are the names, then?"

Detectives go through the bedroom drawers, closet shelves, kitchen pot racks. Voort returns to the neighbors, who now include an Asian couple holding a baby, and a second man from upstairs, wearing a bathrobe matching the make and color of the one worn by his friend.

"Anybody recognize this sketch?" Voort asks, holding up a police drawing.

"I saw that in the *Post*!" the Asian woman says. "Is that one of James's typists? He's always interviewing them."

"Do you know how many typists he works with?"

"He once told me he went through forty of them in one year."

Damn.

Not to mention that the typist in question could have quit the transcription service by now.

The first man in a bathrobe says, "Wait'll Tony hears about this!"

"Who's Tony?"

"Our friend who just got a job on the news, on Channel One."

"Do the city a favor," Voort says. "Don't tell Tony, okay?"

"We won't," says the man, but he doesn't sound convincing.

Voort controls his fear that these people will alert the television news. He seats himself on the landing in order to seem less official, more like a neighbor, or a winning friend.

He says, "I know how much you want to share what you know, with your buddy. But if you do, we could lose an opportunity. This woman could kill someone else. Do you want responsibility for that? There'll be plenty of time to talk later. We'll give you credit, in the news, for keeping quiet, for helping to catch her."

The neighbors look at each other.

"We'll shut up," the first man says, embarrassed. "And we don't need any credit."

When Voort gets back inside, Mickie's at the answering machine. "Most of the messages are from clients, but two are from typists. One from someone named "Annie," and another from "Nora," who's quitting.

Voort's brow goes up.

"Did she say why?"

"She's moving to Minnesota. At least that's what she says."

"When?"

"She doesn't say."

"She sound nervous?"

"The machine is half busted, like everything else around here. It's staticky and you can't tell anything about the voice."

Through their frustration, the detectives look at each other. They are wondering, Do we get the phone numbers of the two who left messages, from Bell Atlantic, and visit them tonight? Or try to locate the woman who runs the office and get more names? Or do we wait until morning, to get a whole list, so detectives can talk to all the typists at the same time. That way, there's less chance of one typist phoning the others, maybe spooking the guilty one away.

A time gamble. Voort looks at his watch. If the neighbor was right, an office manager will be here in the morning.

Fourteen hours to go.

"I'll get the numbers," Mickie says, "and pay a visit. I'll do a Vallella," he says, referring to a detective strategy, ruled legal after a 1971 case, to make up a bullshit story, just to get a look at a suspect and try to match a description.

Just in case "Nora" or "Annie" is who they are looking for.

Mickie adds, "If the typists are freelance, they probably don't even know each other."

"I got into the computer," Cathy Ramsey interrupts, coming up.

Their spirits rise. Cathy leads them to the computer, in the living room.

"It's an old model, a soft drive," she says. "I can't find payroll files. I think those records," she indicates a couple of index-card-sized boxes, "should be with the other disks, in there. But they aren't. Maybe someone took them home, to work on them tonight. Also, apparently the main office of Executive Home Secretary is in Albany. This is a franchise. Could be the employment records are there. I can't tell."

"Or maybe someone swiped them. Or called from the clinic and warned someone here to erase records," Mickie says.

"You could hide the Statue of Liberty in this junk pile," says Ramsey, eyeing the mess.

"Keep looking," says Voort, wiping sweat away. "Maybe it's here."

Ninety minutes later, when the detectives have left the apartment, leaving a guard, in case someone shows up tonight, Voort exits a taxi in a small parking area off the West Side Highway, at Hubert Street, in Tribeca.

Mickie is off to try to find "Nora." Her address was easy enough to find. All he had to do was match the time of her call to a list a phone company source accessed, of Executive Home Secretary's incoming numbers. The source then consulted a reverse phone listing, which matches numbers to addresses. A minute later Mickie knew where Nora lived, on West 108th Street. He also knew her full name. Nora Clay.

If he learns anything interesting, he'll call Voort on his cellular phone.

Cathy Ramsey is off to find the other typist, Annie, who left a message on the machine.

Voort is following a third thread.

Filled with trepidation, he crosses the Hudson River promenade, toward the chain-link fence protecting the boathouse. He does not want to talk to Camilla, does not want to learn about her abortion. He does not want to know if he was the father.

Voort fears what he might do, if he was.

The boathouse is tin-roofed, single story, and cinder block. It is usually open on summer evenings, staffed by volunteers who loan kayaks to anyone wanting to try them. Camilla is a champion racer. After the boathouse closes, she often sticks around, doing repairs.

In Voort's mind it is winter at the boathouse, and it is snowing so hard he cannot see the river.

Voort knocks on the wooden door. Only half a year ago, his heart would race when he met her here.

In his mind, he is in a kayak, in a blizzard, yelling her name, hearing, from the whirling whiteout, a gunshot.

He saved her life that night, when Ian Bainbridge tried to kill her.

Now, carrying her abortion clinic file, Voort watches the door open. Camilla's wearing paint-smeared denim cutoffs and a gray T-shirt dabbed with white. She's barefoot on the wooden plank floor. She's messy, but her beauty is so great that she looks like a model in a paint commercial.

Half a dozen fans are blasting, ineffectually blowing hot air around inside.

"Hi, Voort."

She holds a terry-cloth rag that smells of kayak polish. Behind her, Voort sees her little one-person Mad

River racer, on sawhorses. More kayaks line the wall, in squarish berths, shiny under the artificial light. They quiver each time Pier 26 vibrates with the gentle movement of the Hudson.

"Voort, I wanted to tell you about what happened at that clinic."

He walks past her, pushing away his personal questions. He tells himself this is a professional call.

"Did you ever hear of Executive Home Secretary?" he asks, turning back.

"Executive what? No." Her face is open, vulnerable, and her voice low against the whirling fans. "You want to sit down?"

But Voort does not feel like making himself comfortable. "Camilla, on the day you went to that clinic, did anything happen, that you remember, out of the ordinary? A fight? A protest? Someone staring at you? Think back. Even a weird conversation."

He has already asked Nancy Frederick and Beth Helms the same thing. Although police are concentrating on the typists, the team must still follow up the old leads. They have not yet specifically linked a typist to the crimes.

Camilla shakes her head. "Aren't you going to ask about you and me?"

"Did you discuss the clinic with Beth Helms?"

Camilla looks confused. "Why her?"

"Did you ever meet Nancy Frederick?"

"I would have told you if I did. I would have known that was important."

"What was the favor that Paul Anderson did for you?" Voort asks, which of course brings them to the personal part.

He feels his breathing slowing, and from the river outside, the sound of a tugboat horn, and lapping water.

"Paul referred me to the clinic. He'd sent girlfriends there. He came with me when I went, and spent time with me, afterward. You may not believe it, but he advised me to tell you everything. Before I got the procedure done, and afterward too."

Voort feels his heart close up, like a steel door slamming shut inside him. "It wasn't a 'procedure,'" he says. "It was an abortion."

"I got pregnant the first time we slept together. The condom must have been broken. I assumed you didn't want a baby. No," she says, shaking her head. "That's not right. I didn't want one, so I let myself assume you felt the same way."

Voort is unaware of exactly how much time passes. From the bike path he hears the slapping sound of sneakers, joggers approaching.

The sneakers recede as Voort says, "I would have wanted it."

"Even if we didn't stay together?"

"What does one thing have to do with the other?"

Camilla's regret is etched in the lined immobility of her face.

And now Voort opens her blue folder, the file that he has taken, with her permission, from Alec Mitchell. The light is poor, from a single bulb, but bright enough to make out the neatly typed words.

In Beth Helms's file he'd read about Paul Anderson, how the man took her back to his apartment, and talked about commitment, and started backing away as soon as she got interested.

In Nancy Frederick's file, he'd read about her husband's obsession with his work, and his cheapness, and how all he ever talked about was an Indian tribe in the Amazon.

Now he reads, out loud, "Question. Have you consulted the father about your decision to have an abortion? Answer. He doesn't want a baby."

"I might have said that," she says, reddening. "I don't remember."

"Question. You're sure you talked about it with the father? Answer. He's hard to talk to. Can we move on?"

"It was none of his business. Paul thought I should talk to him, but he kept asking about you."

Shifting stance, she conveys the sense that if she does not move, her blood vessels will, on their own, explode from tension. She says, "I thought at the time we would just go on seeing each other. Later, if things worked out, when we were ready. . . ."

"When *you* were ready."

"That maybe we could try again."

"We'd already conceived a child."

Her voice is as unanimated, as dead, as time that has passed. "When I left you, I thought I was doing it to go back to Kenny. I couldn't admit the real reason was that my secret got bigger. Eating at me. Nothing like twenty-twenty hindsight to make you feel like a fool."

Voort closes the file.

"Want to hear something stupid, Voort?"

"I just did."

She takes a step closer. "You wait for the right time to tell somebody something, and then you have to say it at the worst. I keep thinking about you. And not from guilt. I miss you. I liked the things we used to do. I liked the way we could talk about anything. I was afraid that everything was so good between us, that it had to be phony. That it would blow up.

"Paul always said I should have stayed with you. He would have liked it that I brought you into the investigation. My job doesn't seem so satisfying as it used to. Maybe that's why I started to do volunteer work. I wasn't committed to anything except myself. And this woman you're seeing," she says, with a kind of hopelessness, "seems nice. In that photo, in the paper, her eyes were shining when you kissed her. She seemed to know what she wanted, when she had it, not later, when it was gone."

"I like her," he says.

"That's good," she says.

Camilla goes back to her kayak, and doesn't look at Voort, as if he's already gone.

The rag squeaks as she polishes her racing kayak. Her hand goes around, in circles.

"I don't suppose you missed me too."

"I did miss you," he says.

"I don't suppose there's any chance of having coffee sometime or—" Camilla says, and stops, and turns to look at him. "Something."

"No chance," Voort says, and leaves.

Outside, in the moonlight, accentuated by the vastness of the river, its lonely swishing, he can feel a huge emptiness inside. It is sour, with tangible substance. It forms, inside him, into a rock-hard ball.

He has never been so disappointed in a person in his life.

He thinks, *I don't know what I ever saw in her.*

At eleven P.M., thirteen hours before Executive Home Secretary opens, Voort is in the third pew at St. Patrick's, head bowed. There is no cemetery he can visit, to stand over a stone commemorating a child who was never born. There is no object he can touch to aid memory: a pair of little trousers, a tricycle, a soccer ball, a doll.

He must grieve in his imagination, conjure the deceased at the same time he says good-bye. He is grieving, too, for Camilla.

"God, I'm feeling the dark my father warned me about. Help me remember good things too. Keep me from becoming bitter. Let me appreciate the blessings you give."

There is no answer in the cavernous atrium. No blast of light. No feeling of celestial weightlessness, elevating him.

The pews are silent. The statues look away. The stained glass windows are impersonal depictions. The buttresses are mighty tree trunks, in a concrete forest in which Voort has become lost.

"Hello."

It is the woman from last week again. The small blonde who was upset because her mother died. Voort has been so preoccupied with grief that he did not hear her slip up beside him.

Tonight she wears a black cotton skirt and blouse, an appropriate lightweight garb of hot weather mourning. Her collar is oddly high, cutting off the view of her lower neck. Her hair is tied back, her skin smooth and healthy, although pale. Lacking makeup, she nonetheless emanates an intense feminine quality, a soft, winning liquidity, in the pools of her eyes, in the gentle movements, in the way, neck arced, she conveys vulnerability, and pain.

Voort says, "I was thinking about you."

"Why?" She looks not directly at him, but shyly, to the side, so he only has a good look at her profile.

Well, he thinks, help comes in odd doses. He is grateful to have someone else's troubles to take his mind off his own. "I was wondering how you were," he says, pushing away Camilla, remembering how, eight days ago, he sat on the cathedral steps with this woman, and she tearfully related to him the story of her mother's death . . . a freak fall in a bathtub, a head hitting the porcelain sink. A rush of blood, an hour later, in a restaurant, from the ears.

"I was hoping you weren't having too bad a time with it," Voort says.

"Thank you." But as she turns slightly, Voort frowns, spotting, from this new angle, inside the barely open V of her blouse, the edge of an ugly bruise, a deep purple wound that comes from blood vessels broken not only at the surface, but also far beneath.

He has seen this sort of wound on a woman before, in the sex crimes unit, and the sight of the ruined capillaries never fails to bring a rush of anger.

"If you don't mind my asking," he says, "what happened to your neck?"

"I thought I covered it. I fell."

"You fell," Voort repeats, in a noncommittal voice, as the beat of his heart gets louder.

"I was getting dishes out of the cabinet, and I stood on the stool and it tipped."

The notion that, on top of her grief, this woman has to deal with physical abuse is intolerable. Voort extends a finger and says, "Do you mind?" as he barely parts the collar, and sees finger marks at the base of her throat.

"Who did this?" he says.

Her voice thickens with anguish. "My boyfriend. Ralph. He didn't mean to. He was mad."

Voort envisions a man, bigger than this woman. But any man would be bigger than her, stronger.

"Ralph had trouble at work. I made him angry."

"And what is the terrible thing you did to poor Ralph?"

Voort takes her arm, steers her out of the pew, does not want to have this conversation in a whisper, in public, where anyone can slide over and listen to them.

Her smallness makes the assault more monstrous, especially in light of the way he is sensitized to pain tonight.

Voort gets her outside, to the steps leading down to Fifth Avenue.

"I didn't tell you before, but I'm a detective," Voort says, and shows her his shield.

She looks terrified.

"Don't do anything to Ralph."

He has heard these lines before, and they always enrage him. Why is it, he asks himself, that the abused, twisted by self-hatred, protect the giver of pain? The weak shield the strong. The delicate lie down before the mighty, and they are trampled, and left bleeding and, always, blaming themselves.

He says, "I won't do anything unless you let me. But I'm going to try to convince you to let me. Your boyfriend had to apply serious pressure to make marks this bad."

He is thinking, I am with one more woman whose self-image is so abysmal, all she can commit herself to is pain.

At least Julia, as this woman called herself the other night, has relaxed. "You don't want to hear my troubles," she says. "If you're in church this late, you must have your own."

"Just talk," Voort says, seating himself beside her, on the cool marble steps.

And of course the story comes out, like it usually does. Ralph, Julia says, has a "hard" job, and "needs attention." He became enraged over all the time she spent weeping over her mother. Ralph felt ignored, and, as he is prone to, went to his favorite bar, the Watering Hole and drank too much, and coming home, hit her "once" when she asked how much he drank.

"Did he try a little choking too?"

"He didn't mean it."

Actually, she says, pathetically, Ralph has a good side too, the way he brings her roses, and cries after he hits her, and begs forgiveness. The way he promises not to drink, and for weeks afterward doesn't even take a sip of beer.

Like a goddamn script, Voort thinks. *I've heard this so often. But each person is special. To each victim the process is unique.*

Julia starts to cry.

She says, "I wasn't even going to leave the apartment tonight. I was afraid someone would see the bruises. But I wanted to go to church."

Voort is exhausted. He needs to sleep. He's been out for the last nineteen hours, working. It's hard to think. In the morning, detectives will be back at Executive Home Secretary, and hopefully learn the name of the typist he seeks.

If things go well, he might make an arrest.

But right now Julia needs help. He can't just walk off, so he offers to buy her coffee. He's got to try to convince her to talk to someone at Social Services. Or at least to get away from Ralph.

For her to have to deal with that asshole while she's grieving her mother is an abomination.

Julia thanks him, but shakes her head. "It's too lit in a restaurant. I don't want people to see my neck."

He hears the rumble of thunder, and a moment later feels one fat warm drop of rain hit his cheek.

"Then how about a quiet bar? It's dark," he says. "Nobody will get a look at you. I can't just leave you on the steps."

"I can't stand people to see me like this."

Voort feels a second drop, and a third.

"Look, Julia, it's starting to rain. This isn't a come-on. I have a girlfriend. I was going to go home and make coffee anyway. It's just as easy to make two cups as one. And believe me, I'd feel better, *I* would, if we talked a little. I'll put you in a cab when we're through. Don't worry about the hour."

She looks up, teary with undisguised gratefulness. "Don't go to the trouble."

Voort helps her up and over to the curb, waving for a taxi. The rain falls harder. The drops seem silvery in the headlights of the cab that draws up.

Inside, she presses against him, like a little girl, not a woman. There is nothing sexual in it. It is human comfort that she seeks.

"If you can't trust a policeman, who can you trust?" she says as the driver hits the accelerator.

"What's your last name, anyway?" Voort asks.

"DeGraff."

"A Dutch name?"

"My great-great-grandparents came here from Utrecht."

"See that? I'm Dutch too," Voort says. "Maybe we came from the same village."

Julia DeGraff pulls her black bag closer, on the seat.

She says, smiling, "I knew there was a reason I liked you right off."

FIFTEEN

Ninety minutes earlier, while Voort talks with Camilla, Detective Second Grade Mickie Connor pulls the unmarked black Chevy Caprice into a parking space on 108th Street, half a block west of Nora Clay's apartment.

The night is thick, hot and oppressive. The block is inhabited by a mix of pre-stock-market-boom residents—poorer blacks or Hispanics in run-down brownstones, and a single men's residence—and postboom arrivals—young brokers or attorneys who occupy finely maintained prewar buildings, where two-bedroom apartments sell for more than Tudor homes on the North Shore of Long Island.

Signs on lampposts warn that a private security firm patrols the block at night.

Nora Clay's building has no doorman. Under a flickering bulb in the foyer, Mickie presses the buzzer for apartment 6E.

No answer.

He checks his watch. Ten o'clock, but in New York, especially for a freelance worker, it's still early to be out.

Mickie returns to the car, shoos away teenagers on the hood, and watches, for the next half hour, as people go in and out of Nora's building. None of them matches the description of a petite, pretty, black-haired woman.

At ten-thirty he tries again, in case Nora might have been visiting a neighbor, or doing laundry in the basement.

Nothing.

What if she already moved to Minnesota?

Wait much longer, Mickie knows, and it will be too late to ring the other bells, to check on her.

So Mickie tries the buzzer for Nora's neighbor, 6F. Moments later an elderly voice, too hoarse to be identifiable as a man or woman, barks over the intercom, "Timmy Roth, if you don't take your finger off that bell I'll cut it off!"

"Police," Mickie says, explaining that he's going door-to-door with a sketch of a rapist. "There have been attacks in the neighborhood. We're checking if anyone saw the guy. Sorry to bother you."

And actually, Mickie stopped by the local precinct before coming here, for a sketch of a real suspect. Detectives there will cover for him if someone calls to check.

"Cops, huh?" the voice says. "Wait."

A minute goes by. Then five. Then Mickie sees, through the glass and wrought-iron front door, a bent old woman in a housedress, a skeleton of a woman, shuffling toward him through the dimly lit tiled lobby. She sticks her face against the glass and shouts, like someone hard of hearing, "Show me your badge!"

He holds it up.

"And a photo ID! I know that phony stuff!"

He does so, liking her.

"What's your name?"

"Mickie Connor."

"I called the precinct," she yells, unlocking the door. "They said you were going around."

The lobby smells of lemon polish, and beneath that, something more sour, mildew, from the heat, or the housedress. The woman's shoulders are bent, her face is fragile as a bird's, gray hair thinning, bones forming knobs beneath her cheeks and jaw. But her voice is as harsh as a stevedore's. Mickie figures over half a century of cigarette smoke has toasted her larynx raw.

"If you're talking to everyone in the building, why start with me? With the sixth floor? I called my friend on five. You were never there."

"Ma'am, we knocked on doors earlier. Now I'm talking to people we missed."

The woman peers up at him, frowning. "No one knocked at my door."

"Maybe you went out then."

She seems to remember a trip somewhere, to a doctor, or a store.

"Lemme see the sketch," she says, peers at the portrait of a man in a stocking cap, with oval sunglasses. "I've seen this on the light poles outside. Who'd he rape?"

Mickie tells the truth, that the victims were three women, over the last few weeks, between Ninety-seventh Street and 109th.

"Why'd you wait till after three rapes to go door-to-door? Why not do it right away?" the old woman barks, not letting up.

"Manpower shortage."

She makes a derisive sound in her throat. "You could have posted the sketch in the lobby."

"I will. I'm also trying to reach the tenant in . . ." Mickie says, and pauses as if he cannot remember the next apartment on his list, "6E."

"Nora?"

"She doesn't answer her bell."

The old woman grins. "At eleven o'clock, what young person does? Where do you think you are, Iowa City?"

she says, with a Manhattanite's disdain for any place between the West Side Highway and Wilshire Boulevard.

Mickie tells the woman that the rapist has targeted young women, petite, attractive women, between nineteen and thirty years of age.

"Nora's petite, all right. The little thing. And she's that age. Don't scare me."

"He likes black-haired women," Mickie says. "With straight hair, mid-length."

The old woman looks more uncomfortable. "That's her."

"Someone in the building told me Nora's moving away, to Wisconsin, or Minnesota."

"Really?" The woman looks surprised. "I don't know anything about that. Who wants to live in Minnesota anyway? What the hell's there? Lakes?"

"I think I'll go up and knock, in case her bell was broken." And then, as they ride up in the elevator, he asks, "She have a boyfriend?"

"Quite a few," the old woman brags, as if she deserves credit for Nora's social life, warmer now that Mickie has passed the New York test. He's coolly weathered suspicion and abuse.

"She used to be shy. I used to tell her, go out, enjoy yourself. But she stayed home."

"Then how'd she meet the boyfriends?"

"Mister, if you ever saw the way men look at Nora, even in those schlumpy clothes, you'd know she wouldn't have to go out of her way to meet anybody. She just finally took advantage of the offers."

"That good-looking?"

"Moths to the flame," the old woman nods. "Just watch Nora walk down a street sometime and you'll remember all the good times you ever had, when your body could still enjoy them."

Mickie laughs. But, tired, he's failed to realize he has just been given a description that, in a man, would fit the FBI profile of a serial killer. To Mickie, a shy, lonely man is angry, waiting to explode. But a shy, lonely woman is meek.

"The rapist picks victims who wear sexy clothes," he tells the old woman, as the elevator door opens on six. The hallway smells of Chinese food, and he hears bits of a television cop show, a Mozart concert from PBS, and the hard, metallic beat of rock and roll.

"Nora never dresses like that. She downplays her looks," the woman says. "I always say, 'Nora, get a short skirt. You have a beautiful body.' "

She waits while Mickie knocks on Nora's door, having no idea he is standing two feet away from the news clips taped to Nora's walls. The photos of the dead men. The editorials on serial murderers. There's even a picture of him and Voort.

The old woman says, "Want a shot of Irish whiskey while you wait? I have Bushmill's."

"How about cold water." He hopes she might have a photo of Nora in her apartment, but to ask would arouse suspicion.

The woman's laughter turns into hacking. "Water? There'll be plenty of time for water when your insides rot, in twenty years, and you're not allowed to drink anything else. I'm eighty years old and I didn't get here drinking water. People don't know how to enjoy themselves anymore. Who's the old lady? You or me?"

For Nora Clay, the delicious feeling of anticipation— part fear, part thrill—begins as the taxi stops outside Voort's Thirteenth Street town house.

It starts with a prickly sensation in her toes and fingertips, as if her blood has stopped circulating, when in fact it is probably flowing faster now, as her heart speeds up. The pleasurable buzz spreads and becomes a heightened awareness of everything around her: the way Voort smells, the veins on his hands as he stuffs dollar bills through the opening in the driver's bulletproof seat divider, the staccato attack of rain on the roof, even the running colors, the red brake lights of traffic smeared by water sloshing, in heavy streams, down the windshield.

"Ready to run?" Voort says.

I am shielded from being caught because I am no longer afraid.

The storm has cleared the street of people. Nora runs with Voort through the downpour, up the walk to his big carved oaken door, and she sees, up close for the first time, the detail in his eight-hundred-dollar antique greyhound head knocker, featured in *House Beautiful*. When he closes the door behind them the street noise cuts off abruptly. She watches him punch in the number shutting off his burglar alarm.

Seven, one, one, two.

"We better get you something else to wear," Voort says, water dripping from his blond hair.

It is cool in here from central air-conditioning, quiet and even more comfortable than *House Beautiful* described it. To the right, from the front hall, she admires the living room, with its polished teak floor, shiny as a clipper ship's deck, it's antique woven rugs and gigantic Dutch fireplace and Hudson River oils hanging above colonial era original furniture. The baby grand piano sits by the lace curtains. *House Beautiful* said that Voort's mother used to play each day when she came home from work at New York's flower market.

"Don't tell me this is an original LeClerc," she says, knowing, from the magazine, the exact age and pedigree of the cushioned rocking chair.

"You know furniture?"

"My uncle worked at Christie's. He used to teach me about the items to be sold each month," she lies.

To the left is Voort's formal dining room, with its original Shaker table, where *House Beautiful* said he entertained politicians, musicians, cops, at huge dinners, "holding court for some of the city's most interesting people."

"I've got one or two women's shirts upstairs that should fit you," he says, unbuttoning his jacket. She sees the gun pressed against his sopping shirt.

"Be right back," he says.

He's handsome.

I don't care.

His eyes are beautiful.

And now he is coming back down the stairs, holding, on a hanger, an expensive-looking maroon-colored blouse, slightly long for her, but right in the shoulders. "My girl-friend's," he says, as if reminding her he is not coming on to her, except that since he is a man, this is a lie.

In the end, they all want the same thing.

His guile makes her angrier.

Everything they do is a lie, she thinks. Every smile. Every paid check in a restaurant. Every gift of a music box, bouquet, front row Broadway ticket.

Oh, let me pretend to be sensitive, she knows Voort is thinking. Let me act as if I am your friend. I will use phony sympathy to get your clothes off, to fuck you, to plant a seed for a baby, which I will have a doctor cut out afterward, when I've branded you, and made you useless.

I know you, Voort.

Changing shirts, in the downstairs bathroom, Nora makes sure not to dry off entirely, so the moisture will dampen the blouse's fabric and make it cling. She removes her bra, and leaves the top two buttons of the blouse open.

"How about something to drink?" Voort says when she comes out.

"Whatever you're having."

"Cider? Coffee? Come in the kitchen. I told you. I'm having some myself," he says. "My metabolism is crazy. Coffee puts me to sleep."

He has taken his gun off and changed into a dry shirt while she was in the bathroom. The gun is gone, upstairs, she hopes. Or out of reach. She follows him, watching the confident sway of his shoulders, the concave space between the blades. She makes admiring conversation, praises his art, which she's read about, surprising him by knowing painters and dates.

"I loved those Sundays, at Christie's, with my uncle," she says. "He was from Amsterdam."

In the huge Dutch kitchen, she sits at a butcher block table, on a stool, below hanging copper pots, as he grinds coffee. The smell of hazelnut fills the room. She has spotted, by the Mr. Coffee, the finest display of kitchen knives she has ever seen; a row of bone handles protruding from a wooden block.

"I like to cook too," she says, sliding out the longest blade.

The knives, she read, come from Dresden. They were made at a factory that once produced the finest guns. Their blades are so sharp, the *House Beautiful* reporter wrote, "that they might scratch diamonds."

"How do you know I cook?" Voort says.

"It would be a waste of this great room if you didn't." She slides the knife back. "And you really didn't need to bring me here," she tells him.

"I told you. I'm selfish. I'll feel better if we talk." He smiles.

Of all the men she has punished so far, she is the least familiar with Voort's method of seduction. Camilla, his loyal girlfriend, refused, at her abortion clinic, to provide details about him, other than saying how much he didn't want a child.

Nora says, "Being a policeman must be exciting. Do you have a specialty? I read an article about cigarette smugglers, how they drive up from Carolina. Did you ever work on that?"

Will he try to kiss me in this kitchen? she wonders. Or suggest a tour of the house, like Paul Anderson? Will he give me a present, like Thomas Jackson?

"Let's go out back," Voort says. "The greenhouse is nice in the rain."

Her hand trails along the counter, an inch from the knives. He unlocks a dead bolt at the rear of the kitchen and they walk directly into his greenhouse, where two redwood lawn chairs and a matching table sit amid a riot of flowers.

She says. "I love this! Azaleas. Bougainvilleas. And this is a rosy periwinkle, isn't it?"

Rain pounds, diligent but unable to reach them, on the glass roof.

"You know flowers too?"

"I work at the flower market."

Don't overdo it.

But Voort beams. "My mom worked there, a long time ago."

"Is she still alive?"

"No."

"I'm sorry," Nora says. "Then you know what it's like to lose a parent."

Her eyes lock on his as she sips his sweet hot coffee. She's been told, over the years, how beautiful her eyes are, how they draw in men.

His act, his phony concern, is good, she thinks. She wonders if this is how he lured poor Camilla to bed, got *her* clothes off, put his dick in *her*.

I am the sister of all women who have been screwed over.

Did he take Camilla to the greenhouse, brew her coffee? Ask about her troubles too? Ask about her sick sister, or father, or trouble at work?

Actor against actor. Nora slumps her shoulders, the way she used to do in high school, when she had all those students in the audience sobbing. Back then, in acting class, the teacher told them, "If you want to create an emotion inside, think of something, in your own life, that caused it to happen."

So now she summons up her dead baby, forces herself to picture a little glob of mucus and blood, folded into a towel, like garbage, and dumped in the trash.

It is killing her, but Nora bursts into real tears.

They killed her.

"Ralph kicked me and I lost a baby," she says, and wants to laugh as phony protective rage leaps into his face. He really looks like he cares! The asshole ought to be in movies.

"Ralph didn't mean it. He was aiming for my leg, but I was curled up, for protection."

Her tears are like strings pulling Voort closer. He slides his chair beside her.

And now he will say, "You have to do something about Ralph," she thinks. Or something like that. Go ahead, speak the words.

"You ought to think about changing things with Ralph."

Let me help you.

"There are people who can help."

I know it's hard.

But he doesn't say it.

She thinks, Now touch me. Put your arms around me. Pretend to comfort me.

But Voort doesn't do it. He keeps talking, not making his move too fast, superbly controlling his act, voice filled with indignation as he tells her that nothing can make up for the loss of a child, and it's even worse to suffer through such a blow at the same time as grieving a parent!

Telling her that his own parents died years ago, but not a day passes that, in some way, even for a fraction of a second, he does not think of them.

Blah blah blah.

She turns her face to his. His lips are close. She can see the shine of moisture on them. She will make it easy for him. She is getting tired of the acting. She wants to get to the deed.

"You're nice," she says.

She puts one hand to his chest, to the left side of his bicep. She glides it, slowly, a caressing motion, light physical contact. She imagines his skin under there. She feels the heat coming off him.

"If Ralph doesn't stay away, you can get a court order," Voort is saying.

"I feel safe with you," she says, letting him see how much she wants him to kiss her, how she wants to feel his tongue inside her, his dick inside her. She is wet now. She wants Voort too.

"Julia, you may not believe it, but you can feel safe all the time, if you let Social Services help you."

She lays her head on his chest. He doesn't fool her for a second. His heart is galloping.

Voort says, as phony as the chief of police back in New Thames, Massachusetts, "After you talk to them, if you don't want to file a complaint, you can go back to Ralph."

Voort pulls away, reaches for coffee.

What the hell is wrong with this guy? she thinks, annoyed. He can't be missing my signals?

"More coffee?" Voort says.

He's not gay because he made Camilla pregnant, and there was that photo in the paper of Shari, the girl he's probably screwing over now. From the happy look on her face when Nora talked to her at the Police Athletic League dance, Shari didn't seem to be hurting, sexwise, not from the shiny look in her eye.

Maybe he's not attracted to me.

That's never happened.

Maybe he actually invited me here just to talk.

She starts to get nervous.

"The guy hit you, Julia. It wasn't an accident. And it wasn't the first time, was it?"

"No," she says, thinking, Don't you dare try to pretend I don't know you!

The rain suddenly falls harder, making the little greenhouse, with its flowers, its cloying smells, its harsh humidity, more intimate.

She has not yet punished a man without sleeping with him. The trigger has been the act.

Voort is saying, "Let me give you the name of a woman. Just talk to her."

"I feel so alone," she says, trying again, putting all her effort into it, the truth of it, and finally Voort puts his arms around her.

She turns her face up.

She opens her lips.

His eyes are so blue, and close, and she can now feel his undeniable attraction to her. It is not her imagination. Cells are heating up in him too. Her power is back. She'd suffered a moment of doubt, that's all. She urges him, in her mind, feel my body. Feel my hands on your chest. Put your hand inside my blouse. Put your lips on mine.

Reveal the animal.

Finally, *finally,* Voort bends close.

Nora Clay's fire escape, Mickie sees, dangles ten feet above the alley. Her window is dark up there.

It is now midnight, and he is back on the street again. The old woman is upstairs, sleeping, and Nora still has not come home.

"She's probably staying at a boyfriend's," the woman had said, kicking him out. "More power to her."

And Mickie tells himself, *Come back tomorrow. There's nothing to do here now.*

But, reluctant to abandon a job, he scans the trash-strewn alley and sees, twenty feet off, chained to the building, a garbage Dumpster.

You've been up seventeen hours. Go home and sleep.

Mickie gazes down at his tailored clothes and says, out loud, "There better not be rats in there." He returns to the car and leaves, hanging there, his Armani jacket, Armani tie, and neatly folded white shirt. He doesn't mind getting his undershirt dirty, but not the dress shirt.

The rain has stopped, but the inside of the Dumpster will be sopping.

"If I see one goddamn rat, that's it," he says.

Back at the Dumpster, he leans against the warm, wet steel, trying to roll it under the fire escape. In this heat, the garbage smell is awful.

For what? To look in a window?

The Dumpster doesn't move, so he pushes harder. Mickie is a powerful man.

The Dumpster slides three feet to the left. It is now under the fire escape.

Reaching, he hauls himself into the Dumpster.

"Yeah, Mickie. Be a cop. See the world."

From this new vantage point, Mickie manages to wrap his fingers around the lowest rung of the ladder. He strains, hauling himself up.

"All I had to do was wait eight hours for morning. She's probably getting laid, that's all."

Hot, wet, miserable, Mickie climbs toward her window.

I can't believe it! Voort didn't kiss me.

Voort pulls away from Nora, steps back, in the greenhouse. It is clear, from the patronizing look on his face, that he never *intended* to kiss her. He's *hugged* her, like a brother, or friend, or five-year-old. Like the big strong man soothing a small agitated dog.

Nora says, trying to control her rising anger, "Got anything stronger to drink? Gin?"

He looks surprised. "Sure."

She follows him back into the house, away from the glass ceilings, the prying eyes of neighbors. *He was supposed to kiss me. They always want to kiss me.* She feels the air getting hotter in the house, and there's a ticking in her chest. Her breathing becomes quicker. She panics when people do not do what they are supposed to.

Control yourself.

He hands her the drink, in the living room. She downs it quickly, and asks for more.

You're going to blow it.

Nora knows she's not acting right, but she can't help it. She's too rattled. In the living room, all those Voort cop portraits are looking down at her.

Say something or he'll get suspicious.

And then suddenly, *right here,* for Christ sake, in *Voort's living room,* Dr. Neiman is back in her head, with his droning, probing voice. A vulture feeding on doubt, saying, Maybe you were wrong about Voort.

That's impossible.

Maybe he's not like other men.

They're the same. Only the tactics change.

But Dr. Neiman just nods, in that maddeningly superior way. He says, I told you it was never about men in general. It's always been about the boys in Massachusetts.

Stopstopstopstop.

Look how Voort is staring at you. He's figuring it out. You're losing your equilibrium. Your power is draining away. It was only imagination all along.

"My head!" she says out loud.

"Want an aspirin?" Voort asks.

She downs the gin, feels the beginning of numbness spreading, but it is not enough.

And as if Voort knows exactly how much his false sympathy is getting to her, as if he is some kind of sadist pushing her, enjoying it, making it worse, he says, in the same touchy, feely, bullshit way, "Look, if it bothers you to talk about Ralph, we can discuss something else. Tell me about your job, at the flower market?"

"Stop pretending you know about me," Nora snaps. She knows she's losing it, but she can't stop herself now. She is confused and angry. And panicking. "You and your easy life. You just met me. You don't care. You can't have the slightest idea what I'm going through."

"Even a stranger can care."

Nora lets the anger build. "I know what you really care about," she says. "This whole conversation is all just words to you. Did *you* ever lose a baby? Do you have the slightest idea what it's like?"

"What are you talking about?"

"What does a man know? A man knows nothing. No baby can grow in you."

And Voort's face changes, goes pale.

In a sad voice he says, "But I do know."

"Give me a break. You? Happy in your four-and-a-half-million-dollar house? *Tell* me what you know. Tell me the horrible thing that happened to *you*, that *you* can never change, that makes you think you can ever understand me."

And Voort says, "I also lost a child."

Nora stops, riveted, blood draining from her face.

"I don't talk about things usually," he says as if considering whether to go on. "Not personal things. But I was in church, mourning that child, when you showed up. If I tell you what happened, if just a little you think I have an idea what you're going through, will you talk to the social worker?"

"What is this, a deal?" she says, terrified.

"Are you afraid to talk to her?"

Pick up the bag. Get the knife.

"I said," Voort says, as Nora understands that *he* has become the powerful one here, *he* is absorbing strength, "will you talk to the social worker then?"

She does not want to hear his story.

"No deals."

But Voort just smiles. "Okay," he says, and the story comes out.

She cannot move, cannot leave. She cannot tear herself away from the man on the couch, going on about a "girl-friend" who he loved, who left him.

That's Camilla, Nora thinks.

He tells her that only tonight, this very evening, he learned that, without his knowledge, she aborted a baby they conceived.

"She never told me she was pregnant," he says.

He's making it up to get sympathy, to sleep with me.

But he could have slept with me already.

He says, "I would have wanted it."

Nonononono!

Her headache is monumental. Spikes of hot pain are driving, between her eyes, into her brain. And then the worst thought of all slips through that pain, past her guard.

What if I don't know him at all?

"So then I left the boathouse," Voort is saying, "and went to church . . ."

Her brain is broiling, as if synapses are burning up, cells are blistering and popping. Beneath her skin, she feels veins twisting and coiling like snakes.

He really did want that baby. A man wanted it.

She turns, running, makes it to the bathroom and throws the bowl open and then she is throwing up not only the food she ate this evening, pasta, salad, gin, but her stomach feels like it is being wrenched out too. Her pancreas, intestines, heart, trachea—spewed into the white bowl to be churned away like shit.

Which is what I am. Shit.

The retching mixes with the babble of voices, in her head. Voort's, Dr. Neiman's, Nora's, Mom's.

He would have been a good father.

Everything has a purpose, darling.

You never knew any of the men you killed. Your files were illusions.

All the last voice can say, over and over, through the cacophony, is, *Stop him from talking. Get the knife from your bag. Shut him up.*

By the time Mickie reaches the sixth floor, he's drenched in sweat. The window is open, but set back from the iron bars, in the brick wall. He can barely reach Nora's curtain and push it aside to peer into the dark.

What am I looking for anyway?

Who knows? But he climbed up here on the long shot that he might learn anything of value. The gods of flukiness rule is, Keep trying, hope you'll get a break.

I hope she doesn't have a dog.

Mickie squints, trying to make out, through the jungle of hanging plants, anything inside.

No growling, but he is ready, at the slightest hint of breathing, or the rush of paws, to pull his hands out.

So dark in there.

Mickie makes out, vaguely, a single bed, which strikes him as oddly childish, a table, and lots of rectangular shapes, newspaper or magazine articles, on the wall opposite. It's too dark to make out headlines or words.

There's a pen flashlight in my pocket, in my key ring.

As Mickie gropes for the a light, he hears, from across the alley, a woman shouting.

"You on that fire escape!"

Great.

"Hey! Get off of there!"

Mickie shines the tiny light into the blackness. It penetrates five feet of gloom, illuminating a bit of computer screen, a desk, and blue folders—transcripts, he knows.

Big deal. She's a typist so she has transcripts.

The voice is shouting, "Pervert! I'm calling the police!"

Mickie sighs. He's supposed to keep a low profile tonight. *What's he supposed to do, scream, in an alley, I'm a cop, and the tenant here is a suspect?*

Mickie looks up. At least five people are looking at him from open windows now.

He climbs down from the fire escape, listening for sirens. *Wait till Voort hears this ridiculous story.* He drops onto the trash Dumpster and cuts his hand as he swings down to the ground.

Mickie hurries to the car. Blood is flowing from his

hand, from one of those small stinging wounds that bleed all over the place.

As he wraps a handkerchief around the hand, he hears a siren.

At least I learned she hasn't moved away yet. I'll talk to her in the morning.

As he drives off, he thinks, Call Voort? Tell him Nora's description matched, in a general way, the girl we're looking for?

Nah.

Because it's after midnight. Because the city is still alive, packed, and Nora Clay, like ten thousand young single women in Manhattan tonight, is probably out carousing, or in a boyfriend's bed, or one of a thousand restaurants that don't close until two.

Let him sleep.

Mickie heads crosstown, through the park, and then downtown, toward the Midtown Tunnel. He thinks, if I hurry, I can get five hours of sleep tonight, before I have to come in again. I'll leave my own car downtown.

He's not supposed to take a city car home, to Long Island. It's against the rules.

Kiss my ass, he tells the chief of detectives, in his head.

Nora stumbles from the bathroom. Voort is just standing there, concerned, handsome, sympathetic. She can't stand it. The whole house is spinning. She knows what she must do.

"Why not lie down," he says.

"Upstairs?" Maybe, finally, he is making his move now.

"No. On the couch."

His kindness is prying her open, like a can opener, slicing through her medulla, into the protective synapses of her brain.

Voort helps her lie down as Dr. Neiman's voice says, in her head, I warned you to stop.

"I'll get you water," Voort tells her.

When he leaves the room, she gets up from the couch.

She opens the bag.

Inside, finally, she touches the knife.

SIXTEEN

"**W**ant to go hunting tomorrow with Uncle Billy and me?" Voort's father asks, one November Saturday, when Voort is nine. In his room, the boy looks up from relacing his football cleats, readying for a peewee game between St. Ignatius and St. Patrick's.

"I didn't know you hunt, Dad."

"I don't. So why am I asking?"

"Another police lesson?"

His father forms his hand into a gun, and the thumb strikes the index finger, like a hammer.

"We leave before sunup, at four."

Next morning, with Bill at their table, Voort's mom serves them heaps of pancakes, a pot of coffee for the men, milk for the boy, and the three guys head up the Taconic Parkway, in Uncle Bill's Ford station wagon. It's a perfect fall sunup, bright and golden, and the leaves are crisp, and filled with sugar this time of year. Peak time for death in the New England forest.

All around them, on the road, other cars, filled with men, and guns, head north too.

"What are we after?"

"Deer. Bill skins them, and cuts up venison steaks."

"Did you ever shoot a deer, Dad?"

Uncle Bill says, steering, "He only shoots guys."

"That's enough," says Voort's father, the older of the brothers.

At Route 90 they turn east, leaving the low hills of eastern New York, entering the gently rising ones of the Berkshires. They pass exits for New Lebanon and West Stockbridge. They turn off the highway by Lee and continue east, on Route 20, and soon after, before eight, Bill turns onto a dirt road, through forest, and parks in a copse of oaks.

"Put on this orange hat, pal. And stay close to us. Don't talk unless Bill gives permission."

Bill, a lieutenant in the police in Staten Island, gets a rifle with a telescopic sight from the car.

"Hey, Conrad. Lemme put this paint on your face. You'll look like a jungle fighter."

Then, in single file, as Voort's heart thumps in anticipation, Bill leads them into the woods, through a fern-shrouded forest floor, over fallen logs and gray New England rocks, down steep hills to the edge of a swamp with dead trunks rising from the dark water.

Voort almost misses the weathered, dilapidated lean-to, of gray wood, at the edge of the water, not far from the hump of a beaver dam.

Bill whispers, "In you go, butch."

Other than that, they don't speak. Voort relishes the intimate silence of male companionship. They drink coffee together. The steam rises, and drifts away from the swamp.

After an hour they see a black bear, drinking.

Bill whispers, "Not in season."

Then they see, rising from the water, something green detach itself from the reeds and cattails. Bill raises the gun, puts it down.

"It's a hunter," Voort whispers. "With a crossbow."

The man disappears silently into the brush. Time passes,

but Voort just sits, knowing there is a police lesson in this, somewhere, marveling at the way, as it becomes more familiar, even an unmoving landscape can offer greater detail. The whole breaks into smaller pieces. A mass of green becomes individual cattails. A smudge of brown moves after a while, and Voort sees the deer.

The sound of the shot explodes beside him. Geese, honking in fear, take to the blue sky, fleeing.

The deer lies on its side when they reach it. It is a big stag, still breathing. The hole in its flank rises and falls with each labored breath. Voort wants to cry. The animal's eyes roll with pain and fear. The legs jerk back and forth, as if the brain is saying "Run" but the muscles cannot respond. Red froth bubbles from the hole the bullet has made.

"Get back," his father orders.

There's another shot.

"That's our venison for the year," Bill says.

The carcass is incredibly heavy, robbed of elegance, and blood drips on the boy's new camouflage jacket. They strap the deer to the station wagon and bring it back across the state line, to the farm that Cousin Matt will one day inherit, and where they will sleep tonight.

After dinner, when Voort is on the porch, relishing the country, Dad comes out, carrying two tumblers of scotch, one filled to the top, with ice. One showing just the merest sliver of amber, on the bottom.

"Want to try it?"

"Egh."

"You'll probably grow to like it. When you reach a certain age, anything that's bad for you is usually fun to eat or drink," Dad says.

They sit on rockers, two-hundred-year-old thin, sturdy Shaker models, of New England oak, that have been in the family since just after the Revolution. Form fitting function. Beauty from simplicity.

"Tell me," Dad says. "What did you learn?"

Voort's been thinking about it all day, trying to understand the lesson.

"That shooting causes pain."

"Keep going."

"That you never want to do that to a person, unless you have to."

"The deer," his father prompts gently, rocking. "Tell me about that. Someday, if you decide to be a detective, you will hunt prey in a different kind of forest. By watching that deer, what did you learn about the people you may one day hunt?"

"That they blend in with the place where they live?"

His father sits back, rocks, smiles, tussles his hair, says, "Connie, you're a natural. Some fathers get natural baseball players. Me," he says, so Conrad feels the male love flowing down through him, "I get a natural cop. Someday, if you're a detective, you're going to have to rely on more than facts to find people you're looking for. A murderer is like a deer. He needs to fit in to survive. He pretends to be part of the greater landscape. But sooner or later, because of who he is, because he's *not* like other people, he breaks the pattern. You have to be ready to see it when he does."

"The pattern," the boy repeats, looking out from the porch at the patchwork of fields, a barn, a velvety fall night sky. Up there, he notices a change in the pattern of unmoving pinprick lights. One light moves differently. It is an airplane. But at first it looked like a star.

"Someday," Voort's father says, "you'll probably even meet your prey before you realize who he is, talk to him, interview him, and he'll smile at you, like an innocent person, and joke with you, or even get angry that you're asking him questions. All the while that murderer will be pretending to fit in with other suspects. *Be ready when he breaks the pattern.* It might be just a little thing when he does. A weird look. An action out of place."

And now it is years later. Voort's beloved father is dead, and Voort stands in his huge kitchen, running the faucet, putting ice in a tumbler, filling a glass for "Julia DeGraff," who, to his knowledge, is still lying in the other room, out of sight, on the couch.

He frowns.

Something is not right.

He can almost hear his father, his first police instructor, and the best of all of them, tell him, "Never ignore your feelings. Always figure them out."

So what is it?

Voort sees that the thing bothering him is the extremity of Julia's reaction a few minutes ago, when he rejected her advances. Oh, he knew she was coming on to him. It happens once and a while with a victim—a weak-willed person, a person who gravitates to authority figures, or needs a savior, or is simply attracted to him.

Voort gently repels the advances, and they subside generally, then the interview with the woman goes on.

But this is the first time someone got angry, and actually *ill*, when he turned her down.

Keep figuring, his father's voice says. *You're not done.*

Voort shuts the water, leans against the lip of the sink, frowning. Her pattern is wrong. First she's weak, gentle, and then, a moment later, furious.

And even ill.

And once the woman has become suspicious to Voort, like any good detective, he runs back over his entire experience with her. It comes as a series of quick images.

He sees her in church, in the demure clothes, which don't go with her violent reaction later. He remembers her passiveness in the face of her boyfriend's violence. He hears her telling him that she is Dutch, like him, that she works at the flower market, like his mother did. He hears her identifying the exact artists who made the antique furniture in his house, by name.

She has so much in common with me.

In fact, he realizes, every single thing she has told him about herself directly ties into his life, *into pieces of it that were published in a magazine*. Half her references were in *House Beautiful* last year.

And then another thought hits him. *Four and a half million dollars*. She knew the exact value of this house as it was printed in *House Beautiful*, but the reporter made a mistake. She had the wrong number, the *exact* wrong number, from that magazine.

Not to mention she barely asked details about my job. Everyone asks about that.

Shit.

Voort flashes, heart quickening, to the detective report he'd read, after Cathy Ramsey finished interviewing Thomas Jackson's friends on Staten Island. He zeroes in on one paragraph on the ink-stained official municipal form.

Jackson told his friends that his new girlfriend's appeal was more than just intensely physical. She understood his business, and hobbies, and they even shared fantasies. He felt like he'd met a sex bomb who had everything in common with him.

And now Voort hears Mickie's warning.

If Camilla got an abortion at that clinic, you could be on the list too.

But I met her by accident, in church, because she . . .

. . . because she walked into my pew, where I go every night. And then she just happened to be a sex crimes victim.

His head is pounding.

A small, pretty, sexy woman. A woman who got Otto Frederick to trust her so much that he went to a hotel with her, and Paul Anderson to invite her to his apartment. A woman who won the trust of bigger, stronger men, by learning about them first.

The phone is ringing, but Voort ignores it. He takes the glass of water back into the living room, but Julia isn't there.

"Julia?"

No answer.

Voort puts down the glass. His gun, he realizes, is upstairs.

"Julia?"

The phone keeps ringing.

Voort stands and listens, but over the phone he can't hear footsteps, or a toilet flushing, or a door slamming.

Shit.

Voort checks the bathroom. Maybe she got sick again. But the door is wide-open. She is not there.

The ringing stops.

He goes to the front door. It is closed, but unlocked, and Voort remembers locking it when they got here.

The house is so quiet, he can hear himself breathing. Keeping his senses alert, for any creak or hint of movement, he forces himself to think. Everything makes sense, he knows, once you figure it out, and there will be a rational reason for her sudden absence.

Did she flee? Did she come into the kitchen behind me? Did she watch me and sense that I was figuring it out?

Am I getting alarmed about nothing? No. Trust your instincts, his father drilled into him, year after year.

The portraits looking down on him in the front hallway, the Voort police ancestors, seem to be wanting to warn him about something.

He thinks, Does she need the victim to sleep with her before she can hurt him? Maybe I rattled her so much when I turned her down that she left.

Voort remembers the way Julia, or whatever her name is, handled that knife in his kitchen. He freezes at a slight creak from upstairs. It's the kind of noise he hears regularly in the house. It may be the sound of a two-hundred-year-old structure, settling. Or it may not.

Or does she want me to think she left? That way I'll undress, shower, go to bed, turn off the light.

And then she'll come at me.

Voort sees Thomas Jackson's body, bloody and sliced up. He sees the crater in Otto Frederick's groin.

His house, his haven, has become a trap.

I need the gun.

He knows, gliding up the stairs, keeping to the wall, so they will creak less, that there are a hundred hiding places in this huge town house. Hide and Seek had been his favorite game—the way he and his cousins had spent whole days when he was a boy. They'd clutch imaginary daggers and leap out from closets at one another and scream, "You're dead!"

There are three floors' worth of hiding places, plus a finished basement and an attic packed with boxes. There are libraries and studies and guest bedrooms and a pantry. There are closets filled with clothing. There are armoires big enough for a small woman. There is a laundry room. There is the garage.

Leave the house, and turn the alarm on. That way, if she even moves around a little, it will go off.

But he thinks, furious now, She won't chase me out of my own house. Not to mention, he thinks, that she may be smart enough, if I try to trick her that way, to stay hidden until I come back.

It's no game now. The house seems to breathe with

him. In his bedroom, where she wanted him to take her, all seems quiet, undisturbed. The big old bed is neatly made. The double closet door is shut. The portrait of his great grandfather Nicholas Voort, a mounted policeman, advises him, with its alert visage, not to turn his back on the closet as he opens the night table and retrieves his gun.

He feels better with the blued steel in his hand.

From the closet comes the faintest, almost inaudible creak.

Voort rips the door open.

Nothing.

Voort starts on the third floor, the guest floor. He goes from room to room. He tries the nursery, unused since he was a boy. The toys on the shelves, antique wooden cutout "soldiers," three large handmade "steamships" from the Ossining line, are all museum quality. The Forbes family tried to buy them at one time, for Malcolm's collection.

He can't stand that she may still be in *his home*, that he just invited her in, like Paul Anderson did. Even knowing what type of person he was looking for, he turned out to be no better, no cleverer, than the victims he sees every day.

She's not in the smoking room, or piano room.

A faint scratching spins him left, in the hallway. It comes from the windowsill. Pigeon out there.

Or is she moving around behind me, changing to hiding places I've already checked? That's the way we used to do it when we were kids.

He knows the only solution to this question, and hates it. But he has no choice. One man is simply not enough to thoroughly check this house.

Voort phones the local precinct and lies to the officer who answers. "Mauricio, I got home and my alarm was off, my door unlocked. The place is too big to check myself. Send a couple guys over, will you? We can go through all three floors at the same time."

The squad car pulls up five minutes later, with two blue guys inside. They all split up, in the house.

"Empty," says the driver, a big black officer, coming down from the attic, twenty minutes later. The white guy finds nothing in the basement.

"Voort, you must have scared them off when you got home. Anything missing?"

"Not that I can see."

"This place is big as a hotel. See you, Voort."

Voort watches the squad car leave, then goes into the kitchen, gets a plastic Baggie and carefully, with the tips of his fingers, empties the glass she drank from into the sink. He brings the glass, in the Baggie, to One Police Plaza. The lab is open twenty-four hours a day; a long, wide room, smelling of chemicals, bright as a hospital, with marble-topped lab tables which Voort, age five, used to sit on, feet swinging, as the technicians explained to him what they did.

"Whaddaya got, Dutchman?" the ex-hippie running the place says, as he takes the glass in rubber-gloved hands. He's a fifty-year-old with hair as long as Veronica Lake's, gray and thinning and slicked back in a ponytail, so his skull shows. He's worked here so long he knew Voort's dad. His computer chess game is set up at his station, by his microscope, chemicals and magnifying glasses and volumes on DNA, blood types, fingerprints. There's a boom box playing an oldies station. Voort hears an Emerson, Lake and Palmer tune as dated as the Woodstock T-shirt the technician wears.

"This just in," says a voice on the boom box, the voice of a young news announcer hoping to rise from the wee hours, when only the sleepless listen to him, to a position of auditory prominence in the city. A kid's voice now. A first-job-in-radio voice, but excited, as if it has something truly interesting to impart.

"There's a break in the Jackie the Ripper case that has stymied police for the last month. Just tonight, the *Daily News* has learned, detectives narrowed the list of suspects to a transcription service that works out of a home office on Front Street."

Uh-oh.

"Detectives believe that the murderer works for the service."

I don't believe this.

"They will be raiding the service in the morning, when it opens, for a list of employees. We'll tell you more as soon as we know."

Voort slumps as the music switches to "Heard It on the Grapevine." As if whoever chooses selections tonight picks tunes that mock the police. The technician looks up from his microscope, gray from working late hours, his gap-toothed smile huge.

"The fingerprints match!" he says. "Congratulations! Who is she? Where did you get the glass?"

And Voort, filled with rage and humiliation, as he envisions the firestorm of trouble about to break over him, can only say, "In my house."

SEVENTEEN

Nora Clay sits in the last seat on the 9 train, in the corner, at three A.M., as it hurtles north, on the elevated tracks. She is in a panic. She is afraid that if she simply moves, unlocks her muscles, she will start screaming out loud.

At this hour the subway, that great worm burrowing its way through the guts of New York, hosts a smattering of passengers, drunk or lonely or simply needing movement to keep themselves occupied, as the metropolis creeps toward one more bleak dawn.

To Nora, their faces seem detached from their bodies. The car breaks into pieces; a bit of seat, an empty Coke bottle rolling on the floor. The world is fracturing; the very atoms that hold matter together, released from commitment to the laws of physics—separate and tear asunder the fabric of the air.

Outside, tenements crowd up toward the tracks, half of them abandoned by paying tenants, yet occupied by rats, squatters, dogs. The devastated part of the city flowing by doesn't even begin to approximate, in its misery, the devastation ripping her apart.

Voort was innocent.

Nora stares down at a *Daily News* on the floor, its pages scattered, black huge bombshell headline staring up at her.

KILLER WORKS FOR TRANSCRIPTION SERVICE.

"Police expect to learn the name of the murderess today," the lead paragraph says.

Inside the car the light flickers, as fickle as the city. The ads opposite her address the poor, and marginal, luring them to cheap dental clinics, or injury attorneys if they've fallen or been hit by a car. If they've suffered from a botched medical procedure and can no longer walk, speak, think, listen.

In her head Nora keeps seeing the sight that propelled her out of Voort's town house. It is Voort himself, at his sink, back to her, slumped. Voort staring into a glass of water. Conveying, in his intensity, that he has figured things out.

I panicked.

I could have attacked him. He was only a few feet away.

Perhaps, she tells herself, if he had tried to kiss her, or even looked at her with that hungry gaze she has come to associate with men—if he had shown the slightest sexual interest, she would have had the strength to finish what she'd started.

But he hadn't.

I never knew him.

And how could she punish him for something that, clearly, he never did?

He wanted that baby.

She remembers fleeing from his house, terrified by more than fear of being caught, into the rain.

The worst part is, if I would have met someone like him, years ago, if I had known a man like that could exist . . .

She cannot permit herself to go any further with that kind of thought.

"I said, got a quarter?" A voice slices into her. A man

in brown rags, stinking of bodily functions, a swaying urban apparition, stands before her, his dirty palm out.

Nora Clay stares up at the man. His face goes in and out of focus. Is he actually talking to her?

He sways off, muttering, accustomed to being ignored, his leg muscles attuned to the rocking car, functioning without thought.

And now the train stops and everyone is getting off. But the doors are not closing.

"Lady? It's the end of the line!"

A conductor, yawning, gestures from the far end of the car. He wants to go home.

It is hard to move, but she manages to rise and shuffle onto the elevated platform. The widening vista, the choices in direction, terrify her.

RIVERDALE, a sign says. Clutching the railing, claustrophobic in a public place, she exhibits some last talents at self-preservation. She wobbles down a long stairway to the commercial street beneath the elevated platform. She is on a dark block of one-story-high shops; closed, locked, grated.

Why am I here?

Now she remembers.

MAILBOXES AND LOCKERS FOR RENT, blinks the yellow sign, half a block ahead, through the mist and drizzle, beyond bums sleeping in a liquor store doorway.

OPEN 24 HOURS A DAY.

She tries her old mantra of control to give herself strength enough to function. She tells herself, as a big old Buick growls past, *I know those drivers.*

But the truth is, she knows nobody. She never did.

Maybe the men I killed were innocent. Maybe they wanted babies too. Maybe their girlfriends lied at the clinic, like Camilla.

A wave of remorse makes her knees buckle. She sits

down on the curb. She does not care that she is getting wet. She cannot rise.

If they catch me they will jail me.

In a few hours, Nora knows, when the sun comes up, her picture will be on television. The whole country will see it. People in New Thames will see it, and they will call Detective Conrad Voort, and millions of people will learn about the brutalized thirteen-year-old, Nora Shay.

Get inside, she tells herself, where it is dry, and where, at least, you can think.

I don't deserve to live.

But now another voice is in her head, a soft male voice, Dr. Neiman, saying, *Let me help*. He is at his best when she is weak. He loves when she needs him. He is only critical when she's strong.

Go away, she thinks.

Call me or you will hurt yourself.

She has drifted, she sees, into the otherwise empty and starkly lit commercial mailbox establishment. Inside box number 4497, rented a week ago, when she was confident, when she believed she could control fate, she finds the plastic shopping bag she left, a Medeco key, and two brown wrapped packages, addressed to Sheryl Lande, mailed here by the men she telephoned earlier today.

She leaves her old ID in the locker.

Nora Clay walked into the service.

But Sheryl Lande walks out.

Just step into traffic. It's easy. It's raining. The road is slick and drivers will not be able to stop.

No, a stronger part of her says, take the phony ID, and use the disguises in the bag, and find a bus, or plane. You can do it. You can bury yourself among the millions. You can get another typing job somewhere, using your new name, and then you will have access to information again. Information is power. It can help you survive.

Consulting a little map that has come in her envelope, she walks off the main drag, and up a hill lined with Tudor-style apartment houses. This part of the Bronx, its northernmost extremity, more resembles gentrified Westchester than the barrios and tenements to the south. There are trees dripping with rain. And newer cars on the street, not even dented ones, with alarms, and throbbing red lights warning away thieves on their dashboards. In the playgrounds the swings have not been vandalized. The paddleball courts are unmarred by graffiti. She hears the growl of a garbage truck a few blocks away, masticating residue, crushing trash.

At length Nora stands outside the double glass doors leading into an apartment building. The brass key from her envelope fits the outside door, and the one to the foyer too. The lobby smells of floor polish. The elevator is quiet, and dry, and it lets her off on the ninth floor, where the note in her envelope directed her to 902.

She leaves wet footprints, already diminishing on the vacuumed hall runner, as if she has never passed.

The shiny round Medeco key smoothly clicks in the lock of apartment 902.

She closes the door behind her.

She sinks to the floor.

The rain, outside, has picked up again, and washes down a large living room window. In the semidark, Nora sees the lumps of a couch and wall unit. The place smells lived-in, of dust, wool, Lysol, fish. Perhaps some cruel joke has been played on her and 902 is still occupied. Perhaps the owners will momentarily return.

Get up. Go back out. Choose the way you leave the world, before the police catch you.

She is assaulted, suddenly, by images that, over the last few weeks, she has been savoring. She sees a knife thrusting downward, and Paul Anderson, Otto Frederick, Thomas Jackson trying to scream, holding their throats, or sides, trying to crawl away from her on the floor.

She begins weeping finally. Rolling, crying, moaning.

She says, out loud, "What have I done?"

She says, an hour after that, "I will make it right."

EIGHTEEN

"**W**hat you're telling me, then, is that you had her in your living room, right there, and you let her walk out."

"Yes."

"And *you*, Mickie, went to Nora's apartment, saw she wasn't home in the middle of the night, and just drove home and went to sleep."

"Call me crazy. After seventeen hours up, I was tired."

The office of New York City Chief of Detectives Hugh Addonizio is on the thirteenth floor of One Police Plaza, a corner room filled with awards, plaques, and photos of the chief with famous people: the governor, a New York Yankee pitcher, an Italian tenor, and the chief's pet rottweiler, Ernie. The sunny, spacious room faces east, so, if Addonizio turns around, he has a million-dollar view of the river, Brooklyn Bridge, and South Street Seaport, streets he first patrolled as a beat cop, forty-one years ago.

Addonizio is sixty now, white-haired, in a white shirt and black tie, sleeves rolled up to reveal hairy, muscled forearms. He still lifts weights at least an hour a day. His power comes from hitting and lifting as much as intellectual exercise, from consumption of food and drink, not abstention. His acumen results from natural cunning, honed by years of using it.

And his anger, on this morning after Voort let Nora go, derives from today's page one article in the *New York Times*.

"Should we have broken into her apartment?" Voort says.

"No," Addonizio says with an angry flick of his right hand, with its Detective Endowment Association pinky ring with a "chief" shield on it. "You did a good job. You tracked her down. You ever hear that quote about Napoleon? He had to pick a new field marshal. One of his generals was lobbying for a friend, saying, choose Pierre. He's smart. He's good. And Napoleon said, 'I know he's good. Is he lucky?' "

"You're taking us off the job," Voort says.

"Yep. You didn't tell me you were personally involved. You should have taken yourself out of it as soon as you learned of your girlfriend's abortion. Can you tell me one hundred percent that you went to talk to her, and not with Mickie, to Nora's apartment, because it was the right thing to do?"

"Yes."

Addonizio sips hot coffee from a china cup so delicate that, in his big hand, it seems like it will shatter. But contrary to his appearance, he has a light touch.

"I believe you. But," he says, shrugging at the paper, "we gotta feed the lions."

"Cathy Ramsey'll run things. Anyway, thanks to you, we ID'd Clay. We have her photo, that the transcription service gave us. Give Internal Affairs a couple days to clear you, and you'll be back on the job. No problem. But next time, tell me things. I hate surprises."

"Hugh—"

"It's a final decision. Meanwhile, go up to the country or something. You have overtime coming. Bring me back some fresh trout."

The *Daily News*, also on Addonizio's desk, is open to page five. There's a photo of a tall woman, hand over her face, ducking into Rockefeller Center.

COP'S GIRLFRIEND ABORTED BABY. VOORT WAS ON 'MURDER LIST' AS NUMBER FOUR.

"When I find out who's leaking this stuff, I'll kill him," Addonizio says. "Meanwhile," he adds, looking at his watch, "I gotta go tell the mayor I chewed you out, but he said be gentle."

Addonizio grins.

"Maybe I'll donate money to him myself sometime."

Outside, in the hallway, after they leave, Mickie says, "Watch yourself, Con Man. She'll be back."

"She won't come after me."

Mickie just stares.

"I don't know how to explain it," Voort says. "In a funny way, I felt a kinship with her."

"You never know about a nut, buddy. Keep your gun close. Meanwhile, as long as we're on paid vacation, let's drive to my place, get beers. The blues are running. Normally they don't come until later. But like everything else this summer, they're out of whack."

"No thanks."

"You did a good job, Con Man."

"She was in my house."

"You're lucky that's as far as she got. And remember, you figured out who she is. If it weren't for you, everyone would still be running around with their heads up their ass."

"Yeah."

Voort watches Mickie retreat. When he gets outside, on the plaza, it's ten o'clock, brutally hot. The stagnant air has come back. He pulls out his cell phone and punches in Shari's work number by memory.

"Ms. Khan's office," the secretary says.

"Is she there?"

"Oh," the voice says, recognizing him, and in her pause, Voort feels the receptionist, who he has met once, wanting to ask him what happened last night, wanting to say, *What were you doing with another woman besides my boss in your house?*

"Yes?" Shari's voice says.

"You have any time off coming?"

"You mean, like, leave now? With twenty minutes notice?"

"Ten minutes notice," Voort says, understanding, from the pleasure in Shari's voice, that she trusts him, that if she has any questions about what happened last night, they will come out later, in normal conversation.

Shari says, "What do you have in mind?"

"Finishing that trip we started, to the country."

"You mean that beautiful place, with the river, the sunset? And horses? The cool place with the terrific smell, instead of the garbagy stink of the city? Why on earth would I want to go there?"

"I don't know what got into me," Voort says, grinning. "Forget I brought it up."

"Let's see." He hears pages turning, envisions her checking a calendar. "It's Thursday," she says. "I can take tomorrow off. But I can't leave until six, and Zia has the kids starting tonight, so it'll just be us, mister."

"I'll meet you at the bank, take you home. You can pack and we'll leave from there."

"Voort?"

"What?"

"I'm glad you didn't get hurt."

He makes his way toward the subway. The plaza is filled with people, hurrying to jobs, to eat, to make phone calls, to take meetings. He remembers the FBI observer on the Nora Clay case saying, when they first met,

"My first impression of New York came from an old movie. It was a man in a pencil mustache, yelling, into a phone, 'I'll be there in twenty minutes!' "

"That sums it up," Mickie said back.

In the subway several people glance at him, recognizing, probably from the papers, the city's sacrificial offering this week, in its perpetual fifteen-minutes-of-fame sweepstakes. The car is packed. He's wedged beside teenagers wearing knapsacks and Mets caps, a couple speaking Russian, and a small, red-haired woman, back turned, gazing up at the ads for the new thriller novel, *Early Death*.

He exits at Fourteenth Street and strolls, killing time, to his town house. He locks the door behind him and calls Matt, up in the Hudson Valley. Matt tells him the farm is vacant this weekend. The family will be in Boston.

At five, having read all day—the diaries of Nathaniel Voort, a colonial fur trapper in southern Canada—and having periodically checked with Cathy Ramsey to see if Nora Clay had been located, he goes downstairs to the garage, carrying a duffel bag filled with weekend clothes.

The Jaguar is in top condition. Air conditioner running, he maneuvers through traffic to Apple Bank headquarters, at Forty-seventh and Park. Shari is waiting on the curb, lovely in a long charcoal-gray dress, with a slit up the front, and matching lightweight summer wool jacket. She carries her small leather briefcase. Business dress, Voort finds, heightens the femininity in a woman, by trying to suppress it.

She slides into the car. She kisses him on the lips. She lets her tongue slide into his mouth. Despite the heat her skin feels cool. Her perfume is heady.

"Maybe suspension isn't so bad after all," Voort says.

"I'm not going to be able to leave tonight. I have to

finish up some work at home. Is it okay if you stay over in Brooklyn, and we get going in the morning? I'll make dinner."

"Things are getting better by the second."

"This is nothing compared to what happens next."

NINETEEN

Oddly enough, Nora sleeps pleasantly. In her dreams she travels back to the best vacation her mother and she ever took. They drove in their old Pontiac, east from New Thames, to Cape Cod and the Atlantic. They stayed in a rooming house run by a woman named Mrs. Ives, paying fall rates. They rode rented bicycles every day to the beach, carrying peanut butter and jelly sandwiches, and a thermos filled with iced tea. They ate picnic lunches and, in the evening, sunburned and happy, riding toward the rooming house, they would sing, as they pedaled, "Oh, Mrs. Ives. Mrs. Iiiiiives."

Nora opens her eyes.

She blinks. The smell of salt, of Cape Cod, is fading. She looks around a new room, a strange apartment. She has not slept in any bed besides her own in eight years.

"Oh," she says as it all comes back.

She squeezes her eyes shut, seeking a last few moments of sanctuary. It is late for her to rise, ten A.M., and the light slanting in through half-open blinds is still benevolent, more morning orange, less noon white.

Nora gets up. She did not inspect the apartment last night, but does so now.

It's not her style, but who cares? The walls are mossgreen, the closets smell moldy, of old clothes and mothballs. Photos of strangers are arrayed, in glass frames, on cheap pine shelves, dressers, and end tables. In one picture an old man sits in a rowboat. Twin girls grin beneath a sign reading "Camp Tomahawk." A man and woman, in matching red parkas, wave, from the deck of the Empire State Building.

Other lives.

Whoever lived here just walked away, she knows, when the bank closed in. Urban Okies, they left their wall hangings and cutesy knickknacks: embroidered pillows showing Huck Finn carrying a fishing pole, ceramic cats swiping at ceramic birds, on a maple base. A music box plays "Tara's Song." The refrigerator magnets hold down notices for a senior citizens meeting, a zoning board meeting, an appointment with a cardiologist.

"Police announced yesterday morning that Nora Clay's real name is Nora Shay," an announcer says over the rolling black and white television, when she switches it on.

Yesterday? That means I slept more than a whole day. She watches, fascinated.

"Shay grew up in Massachusetts, according to Detective Cathy Ramsey, now in charge of the case. Ramsey received a call from police in Massachusetts after the nationwide alert was released at eight-thirty yesterday."

For Nora, there is no rush. Time has slowed. As the heat rises she turns on fans around the apartment. They stir motes of dust, columns of gray, that swirl in sunbeams slanting and striking a saggy couch and an old record turntable, drifting down on an Adirondack woven rug on the scuffed parquet floor.

In the kitchen, she decides she must eat. She is not hungry, even though she has not fed herself, but she'll need strength for what she must do today, the thing she decided on before she fell asleep. Nora finds cooking oil, pancake mix, canned tuna. There are Rice Krispies, which she spoons from a bowl with water, raisins, and dried apricots that lost their last bits of moisture a long time ago.

The banker who arranged for this place did a good job. And it is ironic, she thinks, eating, that it was only thanks to Dr. Neiman coming on to her, three months ago, that she took the final step in her metamorphosis into the information queen, moved beyond mere facts in her files and gleaned from transcripts, and beyond personal surveillance, to blackmail.

She remembers the day she returned home from her last visit to the doctor's office, crazy with rage, remembers thinking that she wanted to know more about Dr. Neiman, the liar, the trickster. She remembers going to her files, finding, in a legal agreement she'd transcribed, a suit settled out of court, a dispute between a former husband and a private detective who had violated the man's privacy, gone beyond legal limits in learning information about him for his wife-at-the-time.

Nora had phoned the detective from an untraceable pay phone and told him she wanted to learn "everything possible" about Dr. Neiman. She'd given him Neiman's address and phone number.

"Lady, you'd be amazed what I can learn. Come in and we'll draw up a contract."

"No contract. No fee." Nora had then listed charges against the detective—privacy law violations, breaking and entering, illegal surveillance—which, if made public, would bring him to the attention of the police and end his business.

He never even argued. He just sighed. "Fine. No contract. How do I get the information to you?"

"Post it on the Internet," Nora remembers telling him, choosing a public chat room she could access from home. "And change Neiman's name, call him William

Thames. Get the facts right. List the name wrong. I don't want him discovering that someone's investigated him."

"And you'll, eh, keep my stuff private?" the detective said, his fright boosting her confidence.

"I said I would. And while you're at it, look up someone named Louis Vale. He works for a messenger service."

Two weeks later she had a file on both men. The wall around her, the protective shield of knowledge, was complete. She told herself that she would never deal with any man again, never trust even a doctor or business acquaintance without learning all she could about them first.

And now, her breakfast finished, Nora leaves the dishes in the sink. She will leave no diary, no tape recording, today. Her heart does not race with anticipation, or even fear, as she dresses and watches her own face on TV.

"This photo was provided by the transcription service where Nora worked. If you see her, call police."

Nora adjusts the last wig in her repertoire, from the locker; a brown thing, streaked with gray, making her look at least five years older. A sexless flip, above the shoulders, preferred by women who guard their allure from strangers—women who ride fine horses, who clench their jaws when they speak, whose first names sound like last names, whose great-grandfathers owned coal mines or clipper ships that paid for town houses on the East Side.

In the bedroom, before a full-length mirror, Nora slips in green contact lenses and dons wire-rimmed glasses with clear lenses. She slides bite-size bits of rubber, purchased at a costume store, to the rear of her mouth, between teeth and cheeks.

Her face looks rounder now.

She ties on Doc Martens boots, one size too big, stuffed with pieces of yesterday's *Post*, to make her two inches taller.

The radio is saying, "From now on police will release all relevant information in the case to the public. 'We were too secretive before,' Detective Ramsey said. 'The average person can help catch Nora now.' "

The great clock of inevitability is ticking. The sluggishness of the morning is wearing off.

Eight million people are watching for me now.

Nora puts on a daisy-colored dress, loose fitting, to hide her figure. She reaches for the last bit of her disguise.

"Police have distributed photos in subways, stores, at airports, and the Port Authority."

She sees that the thing that New Thames feared long ago, publicity, has come to them. She allows herself to wonder what life might have been like had she grown up here instead of there, in a city where the police would have gone after those boys. It's a thought she has never had, until now, but it is useless.

No answer comes. What occurs to her instead is a phrase she typed a year ago, while transcribing a tape of a business meeting, a legitimate recording made by a stockholder. On the tape, a board member told the audience that a particular sales strategy had reached the "point of no return."

"That's the point when you can't go back," the man had said. "The distance to the end is closer than to the beginning. You have no choice. You hope and proceed."

Her dressing finished, she goes to the phone and punches in Voort's home number. She remembers it from the sticker on his receiver, the other night.

His recording says, "Please leave a message."

She tries the girlfriend's number, in Brooklyn, and this time a woman answers. "Hello?"

In the background a radio is blaring.

The woman tells someone in her apartment, "Conrad, turn that down, will you, please?"

Nora puts down the phone.

The TV says, "Over a thousand police in the tristate area search for Nora Shay."

She closes her eyes and inhales deeply, the way she used to do, in middle school, before walking out on stage and being blinded by floodlights.

She is not nervous. She has passed, she knows, in this particular life, her point of no return. The knife she had at Voort's house is still in her bag. Unlocking the apartment door, moving into the hallway is like walking onto the stage. She makes it all the way to the lobby before she sees anyone, in this case a young woman entering the building, lugging two heavy shopping bags.

Will she recognize me?

The woman looks into Nora's face. Her eyes widen.

The eyes travel down Nora's body.

"How many months till you have your baby?" she asks.

"Two." Nora pats the round shape beneath her dress. "The first three months were just awful."

"Don't I know it." The woman rolls her eyes. "You just move in?"

"Couple of days ago."

"I'm Helen Ravenel, 8A. Boy or girl?"

"Boy. Bill Jr.'s dad's working at the store this morning."

Nora waddles from the building, into the heat, the direct light. She is unaccustomed to being out during the day. The air is gritty, the sky cloudless yet gray. She tells herself to move more slowly than usual. Everyone looks at her but no one really sees her. Every half block she pauses, like a pregnant woman, and holds her belly, as if trying to catch her breath.

"Lady?"

She turns toward the boy's voice.

"Can I help you up to the subway platform? My aunt just had a baby. She had trouble with stairs."

At the top she finds herself in a crowd of late commuters, half of them reading newspapers which feature, on the front page, photos of her.

Two hundred Noras flow through the sliding doors, into the arriving subway train.

"Ma'am, take my seat."

"You are so kind," she tells the man.

I thought I knew them.

The train jerks to a start.

As it rushes into Manhattan, heart of the city, she hears snatches of conversation. The people are talking about her, about Nora.

Her black bag, on her lap, shifts so that she feels the hard bone handle of the knife through the leather bottom.

"I hope the cops shoot that bitch," a woman to her right, on the seat, tells her friend.

Voort and Shari take their time. They rise late, go out for breakfast. They find a restaurant and order blueberry pancakes, sausage links, pulpy fresh orange juice, and hot coffee.

Shari says, "No rush. I'm glad we didn't drive up last night. I was exhausted."

Voort pays the bill, and they stroll along Seventh Avenue, Park Slope's commercial strip. It feels odd to him, but not unpleasant, to not be working on a Friday.

"I'll buy treats for the ride," she says.

"It's only two and a half hours."

"You don't like fresh pears? Or smoked turkey?"

"You talked me into it," Voort says, and she takes

him three blocks down, to a shop called the Strolling Gourmet.

There's a crowd here, artists or writers in this neighborhood. They are buying goodies for upcoming weekends in Fire Island, the Berkshires, Bucks County, southern Vermont. Voort takes a number as customers order carrot cakes and hams to give to their country hosts. They ask for fresh scones, cherry Danish, Kenyan coffee beans.

They will be roughing it in the country, city style.

"I can't go without Danish for three whole days," a man says.

". . . A pound of goat cheese. And cornichon pickles. And calamata olives, no, make that cracked Sicilians," says a woman in front of them, looking as serious as a district attorney discussing a crime bill. "No, Ed hates Sicilians. Would you mind putting *back* the Sicilians and giving me Greeks instead?"

They spend thirty-five minutes in the shop, and when they reach her apartment the phone is ringing. Shari's oldest daughter, Aya, is calling.

"I cut my knee," she tells Voort.

"Are you okay?"

"Daddy washed it, and kept me home from school. But it still hurts."

"How about some phone magic to make it better? Hocus-pocus and manohkis," Voort recites, remembering the rhyme his great-aunt used to recite when he was seven. "Take the pain and make it plain."

"It didn't work."

"I'm a bad magician."

At eleven he walks back to Seventh Avenue to get the Jaguar from the garage, where the automatic door has jammed, so he must wait another quarter of an hour while a repairman fixes it. At eleven-thirty he finds a parking space in front of the brownstone and rings Shari's bell. She does not come down.

He tries again.

No answer.

Sighing, he goes upstairs and uses his key. Nothing takes longer, he thinks, remembering Camilla at the start of trips, than getting a woman out of her apartment for a two-day journey.

"I'm in the bathroom," Shari calls.

He carries down her bag and the cooler she's packed with sandwiches. He turns on the radio, to a phone-in show, as he waits in the car.

A caller is saying, "That detective screwed up by not taking himself out of it. He should have taken himself out when he learned his girlfriend had an abortion."

"Call us with *your* opinion on *Love Is Blind*," the hostess says. "Did Detective Voort let his heart get the better of him? Or would you *prefer* to have a law enforcement officer have a personal involvement in a case, and work harder?"

Voort switches stations.

"Nora Clay's apartment was filled with photos of her victims," the all-news announcer is saying.

Voort shuts off the radio. As Shari appears on the brownstone steps, he glimpses, in the rearview mirror, a small, heavy-looking woman coming up the street. Pregnant, from the way she is swaying.

Shari gets in. "Don't pull out yet."

She checks her makeup in the mirror.

The woman coming up the block stops to catch her breath.

Shari says, "Go."

He takes Eighth Avenue to the Prospect Expressway to

the Brooklyn Queens Expressway to the Battery Tunnel.
Traffic is stalled on the West Side Highway, first as they
approach the turnoff for the Holland Tunnel, then by the
turnoff for the Lincoln Tunnel, then on the Upper West
Side, as they approach the entrance ramp to the George
Washington Bridge.

"Last time we went to the country," Shari says,
opening the L'il Oscar, handing Voort a pear, "you didn't
wear your gun. You're afraid she's coming, aren't you?"

"It's a precaution," Voort says as they break free of
the jam. "I wouldn't bring you if I thought it was dangerous. But if you're nervous, we can go back."

"After all the preparation? No thanks. But," she says,
and hesitates, "I didn't talk about her last night, since I
knew you had a bad day. And we don't have to talk
about her this weekend. But can we discuss her a little
now? I've been listening to everyone else on the subject.
It seems ridiculous not to bring it up."

"What do you want to know?"

"She was in your house and she just left?"

"Yep," Voort says, blowing out air.

"But why?"

Voort feels the smooth, powerful engine, and a sense
of control, in driving, that his professional life, of late,
has lacked. "Actually, in a weird way, I think it's because
there was a kind of connection between us."

She puts her hand on his knee as she echoes, puzzled,
"Connection?"

"I guess if the situation is right, you can feel a connection with anyone. You meet a stranger. Get in a conversation. I'm sure it's happened to you too. Maybe it's the
subject, or mood. But for a moment, that stranger feels
like an old friend, or like they might become a new one.
You might even tell them a secret. It's safe. I told her
about Camilla's abortion."

"You had Nora in your house, and you were talking about Camilla," Shari repeats in a flat voice.

"We were talking about abortions," Voort corrects. "I was trying to convince her to talk to a Social Services counselor. She had bruises on her neck. She'd told me her boyfriend hit her. That she'd lost a baby. I'd just talked to Camilla and abortion was on my mind. By sharing the story, I thought I might get her to listen."

Shari rubs his leg. "It must have been painful for you."

They are on the bridge, heading west, avoiding heavy construction on the Sawmill River Parkway and taking a longer but quicker route since the Taconic is undergoing repaving. For once the traffic jam is on the other side of the road.

"The reason she left my house, I think," Voort says, "is that each guy she killed, in her mind, caused an abortion. She never blamed the woman. It was the *man* who needed to be punished. When she realized that wasn't the case this time—"

Voort stops talking.

He hears Mickie, in his mind, say, *Watch your back.*

"What's wrong?" Shari says.

He tells Shari, as he looks for a place to turn around, "Get the phone. You have to make a call. I need both hands to drive, because of the stick shift."

Voort slams the car through a temporary gap in the road divider, into the inbound lanes.

"Look out for that car!"

He hits the brakes. Now they're stuck in traffic, on the eastbound side. He reaches for the police light, the portable turret light. But the cars ahead are wedged into every inch of available space, and there is no shoulder here.

"Voort, what are you doing?"

"She's going after Camilla," Voort says.

* * *

Camilla Ryan, successful TV producer, Emmy winner, a woman on top of her professional world, who has been devastated in love, sits in the control room of her weekly investigative magazine show, *Target!*, overseeing final editing for tomorrow's seven P.M. broadcast.

"Can we cut the credits?" the director says as they monitor a tape showing a dying man on a New York street, being worked on by ambulance attendants. The man lies half buried by construction debris after scaffolding on a Midtown high rise fell on him. "It was sabotage," the director says. "Our union source admits it. If we cut the credits we get twenty more seconds for interviews. When we win a Polk award we'll get credit enough then. Whaddaya say?"

"Cut the credits," Camilla orders the technicians.

The room consists of two rows of cushioned seats, opposite a wall of TV screens, all showing different segments of the upcoming program. The union source, his face blacked out. The builder who fired his workers. The wife of the dead man. The mayor making a speech after the scaffolding fell.

The bottom row of seats, below Camilla and the director, is filled with technicians and a twelve-year-old blond girl with a pigtail. The girl wears a T-shirt, blue jeans, and a black sweater borrowed from Camilla, against the raging air-conditioning.

She is Tanya, Camilla's "little sister" in the volunteer program in which she participates. Once a week, for the last four months, Camilla has spent a day with the motherless girl, taking her to movies, helping with homework, going to museums, or zoos, or just eating out.

"You are so cool, Camilla," Tanya says when they are through and threading the maze of hallways back toward Camilla's office. She adds, "I want to work in TV too."

"You'll be good in it. You're smart, and you don't take no for an answer."

"I'll be a producer like you."

Camilla smiles. In the office, she gives the girl treats; freebies that came in this week from PR people trying to get their clients, or new products, on TV. A pound of Belgian chocolates. A board game called Cranium. A half-dozen hard-back novels from publishers, which Tanya consumes nonstop.

Tanya is Russian, from Brighton Beach; an A student whose mom died of a heart attack last year. Dad's an engineer with the Con Edison power company. During hot summers he practically lives at the plant, making sure the equipment doesn't blow out from heavy use.

"Can you get me a job as an intern here, Camilla?"

"In a few years. You have to be in college."

"Everybody loves you. You're perfect."

Camilla says, trailing off, "Actually, that's far from the truth."

"You mean that stuff on the news. I saw it. It's your business what happened, not anybody else's. You were right to do what you did. Those press people should leave you alone."

"I thought you wanted to *be* a press person."

"I won't bother people about their personal life."

"Then good luck getting a job, Tanya."

"You looked sad on TV. You like that detective, don't you? But every guy we pass looks at you. Go out with one of them instead."

"I got bored with that."

"My father says there's millions of guys."

"Numerically," Camilla says, "he's right."

"Why not talk to Voort, tell him how you feel. You always tell me to do that if I have a problem with people."

"Why not get ready to go home, Miss Nosy, and see your father for a change," Camilla says, "instead of me. Be glad he managed to get off work today."

"You're not mad that he made new plans? That I'm canceling on you? Do you have something else to do?"

"Tanya . . ." Camilla smiles, filled with affection. "When you have my job, and there's nothing to do, that's called vacation."

They take the elevator to the lobby. On Saturday morning Rockefeller Center is quiet.

"Dad says he wants to meet you," Tanya says. "He's handsome. Maybe you can go out with him."

"Have fun at the beach. And wear sunblock. You get red."

Tanya waves and ambles off with her plastic bag of treats, confident, an urban rat disappearing into the familiar subway. Once, Camilla tried to ride home with her, worried about letting her travel alone, and the girl became offended. "What do you think I am, five?" she said.

Now Camilla sighs and goes back upstairs, to the local news division, a warren of desks and cubicles on the fourth floor. She finds the executive producer in his office, feet up, poring through the morning's *Wall Street Journal*.

He grimaces when he sees Camilla. "I figured out how to predict the stock market, and it has nothing to do with economics. If I buy a stock, it goes down."

"Did you do what I asked?" she says.

"It's a waste of manpower."

"I didn't ask your opinion," she says. "That woman's going to try for Voort again. I know it. She failed the first time, and I want someone keeping an eye on him twenty-four hours a day, even if it drives him crazy. At his house. Outside his office."

"And what's our guy supposed to do if he sees her coming?"

"I *want* her to see, and stay away."

"That's the police's job."

"They're not doing it."

"What if our guy gets hurt?"

"Are you planning on calling our correspondents back from the Mideast too?"

The producer sighs, sits up and puts down the paper. "Camilla, you're not responsible for what happened yesterday."

Camilla steps all the way into the office and shuts the door behind her. She folds her arms. When angered, her fury is legendary.

"I asked a favor, not to have to justify myself. If you don't want to do it, say so."

"I did it. I just think it's a waste of—"

"I know. Manpower. And you think I'm not responsible," she says, stepping closer. "But I got pregnant and didn't tell him. I lied about Paul. I lied to that social worker, and Nora heard those lies and went after Voort. If I could, *I'd* stand outside his house every night, watching. *I'd* follow him, but he'd spot me. He'd stop me."

She's so angry, she is practically crying.

She snaps, "So if I'm not responsible, *who the hell is?*"

"Gus Mobley's been assigned to it."

"Why couldn't you say so in the first place?"

She storms out.

In her office, calming herself, she gathers up her things. She'd cleared the day for Tanya, and so has no more work to do. She'd been planning on taking the girl on a Circle Line cruise around Manhattan. Then to a blues concert in Battery Park. Then maybe catch an early movie, by Disney, the new animated film, getting raves, about Anne Frank hiding from the Nazis during World War II.

Camilla leaves the building and heads for the subway. It's filled with tourists, riding south. She hears snatches of German, Italian, Korean, Portuguese.

She exits at Franklin Street, comes up out of the earth, into the inferno of heat-absorbing concrete and tar. She decides to buy food, go home, read in the roof garden, make a quiet dinner.

Rent a movie, maybe. She could use a good romance.

One more Saturday night without Voort, in front of the television.

Now she ducks into Gourmet Kitchen, to buy food for this evening and the rest of the week. Dietary treats to substitute for companionship. Or maybe she'll buy one of those purebred dogs, she thinks, Hungarian hunting hounds or Norwegian minihuskies, currently the rage among singles in Manhattan. Commit yourself to designer pets if you can't find a mate.

She buys Spanish Castellano cheese, dill shrimp, eggplant salad, raspberry chicken cutlets. She buys salad greens and pita bread and sourdough ficelles, fuji apples, Irish salmon, summer melon mint soup, Guylian Belgian chocolates, and a half pound of babaganoush. She buys an Australian chardonnay, two bottles.

All the stuff Voort likes, Camilla thinks. I am one lovesick puppy.

Forty hours till Monday.

At least a reporter should be tailing him, maybe protecting him. Bugging the hell out of him.

Forty hours.

Then I can go back to work, at least.

Voort even has me praying.

God, keep him safe.

* * *

The George Washington Bridge, built in 1934, is a 3,500-foot suspension span linking 179th Street in Manhattan with the city of Fort Lee. Its four million tons of steel, asphalt, and steel cable, PR spokesmen bragged, when it was completed, would "ease the life of the tired commuter."

At least that's what the Port Authority said.

At the moment, traffic is moving at a tortoise pace as Voort yells into his car phone, "Listen to me, Cathy! She's going after Camilla!"

The portable turret light—red and spinning—is on, but traffic can't move out of the way, so it is useless. Shari sits staring at him, expressionless, while on his left a passenger in a Plymouth van is holding up the *Daily News*, toward Voort, pointing to the photo and mouthing, "Is this you?"

Staticky, but clear, Voort hears Detective Second Grade Cathy Ramsey, now in charge of *his* investigation. She's at One Police Plaza, coordinating the search for Nora Clay.

"Voort, your personal life is getting in the way of your thinking. Nora doesn't hurt women."

"She's changed."

"You can't let an argument with your girlfriend screw things up."

"She's not my girlfriend," Voort says, aware that Shari has jerked at the words.

"I'd watch out for myself, if I were you. You're the one on the list we found at her apartment. You're the one whose photo was on her wall."

"You're not listening."

"I'm listening. I'm just not agreeing."

Voort tries to push away the urgency in his voice, make it sound reasonable. Cathy has always listened to reason before. "I'm telling you, if you saw the way she reacted when I told her about the abortion, if you saw the way she looked—"

But Cathy cuts him off. "I'm sorry. You're just not in charge anymore, and I have the FBI here. I don't have time to stay on the line with you."

"Then send someone to watch Camilla as a favor."

"A favor?" A pause. "You want me to do you a favor. Look, rich boy," Cathy snaps, surprising him. She has always been polite and professional with him. He had no idea she resented his wealth. "Maybe it's time someone who came up the hard way got a chance around here. Someone who doesn't give money to the mayor to get ahead."

Voort hits the brakes to avoid inching into the fender of a VW Beetle in front of him.

"You're the one who leaked that stuff about me to the press," he says. "Weren't you?"

"I don't know what you're talking about. I have to go," Cathy says.

The phone clicks off.

Traffic jerks and stops, inches forward. The speedometer isn't even moving. Voort hands the phone to Shari and recites Camilla's office number from memory. When she hesitates, he says, "Don't give me a hard time too."

"Target!" the receptionist says at NBC.

Voort asks for Camilla, hears static, then nothing, then static again.

"Sorry," the receptionist says, coming back on the line. "She left for the day."

He tries Camilla's home number.

"It's me," the answering machine says, as if the whole world should know who "me" is. "I'm not home. Leave your name, and the time you called."

"Camilla, it's Voort. Pick up. It's an emergency," he

says, struck by the ludicrous fact that seven months after saving her in the Bainbridge incident, he is racing to reach her again. Or was Cathy right? Is he imagining things?

"She's after you," he says. "Don't open the door for anyone. If you get this message, call my car phone. Don't go home. Don't go to the office. Stay in a public place."

"Try her beeper," Voort tells Shari, reciting the number from memory as he pulls around a Mr. Softee truck and hits the brakes again.

She punches in Camilla's number quickly, but her face registers that he recalled it without hesitation.

On the dashboard the digital clock turns over, indicating the passage of another minute. They have been stuck over the river for almost a half hour.

Shari leaves Voort's phone number on Camilla's beeper.

"Look," Voort says, "I remember everybody's phone number. I'm good with phone numbers."

They break free of traffic finally. Voort floors the accelerator, toward the ramp leading south, and the West Side Highway.

"It's the expression on your face, whenever she comes up," Shari says. "But that's not important now. Just get to her before Nora does. We can talk about other things after that."

TWENTY

Camilla finishes shopping at Gourmet Kitchen, gives her address to the checkout girl, so her order can be delivered, and takes her time heading home to her new apartment, a loft co-op she purchased a month ago finally opting for the permanence of owning a place over a temporary lifestyle of paying rent.

She strolls into a small, favorite jewelry shop featuring original silverwork, tries on earrings, but rejects them. She stops in Marty's Books and picks out three volumes, a Eugene Linden predicting widespread instability in the new century, a Terry Tempest Williams on environmental problems in the Great Salt Lake, a Toni Morrison novel about a woman with a hard life.

Outside the bookstore she helps two women, lost tourists, find the subway. "I'll take you there," she says.

Ten blocks to home.

This part of Tribeca is still in transition from industrial to residential neighborhood. Converted warehouses stand beside functioning ones, all, from the outside, looking the same, their huge windows overlooking narrow or charming cobblestone streets, depending on your point of view.

Camilla loves the neighborhood, the rough edge of it, the privacy at night, when it is semideserted, the fact that she can walk from home, anytime she wants, to her beloved boathouse.

She turns her corner and sees, ahead, that the only person visible on the block is a short, slightly heavy woman beneath the green awning of her own building. The woman is pressing her finger against a bell, trying to get inside.

As Camilla gets closer, the woman sees her and gives up on the buzzer. She turns to Camilla.

She's pregnant, Camilla thinks as she comes up, and pulls her key ring from her bag. They are both beneath the awning.

"Can you let me in?" the pregnant stranger asks.

Camilla looks down into impossibly green eyes, too green to be real. They must be contact lenses. The woman's hair is ugly, a brown flip streaked with gray. Her cheeks are swollen as if she's had mouth surgery. There's a welt on her neck, accentuating Camilla's feeling sorry her, especially in the heat.

The belly beneath the woman's yellow dress is so huge it seems like any second it will burst open, expelling the life she has been nurturing inside.

"My feet," the sweating woman says, "are killing me."

"Who are you here to see?"

"Fred Ostermann," comes the prompt reply. Camilla envisions the man, whom she met once, at a meeting of the co-op board. He's a *U.S. News & World Report* reporter, if she remembers correctly. The woman says, "Fred said to come directly here from the train. He's supposed to be here."

Camilla, embarrassed to refuse, nevertheless must follow the rules of the co-op—drummed into her by the board when they approved her application for residency, three months back.

Never let *anyone* in the building who you don't know.

Even a child, or old lady, or pregnant woman, because there have been incidents. *No strangers allowed*. If you can't stand the rules, don't move in.

"Sorry," Camilla says, feeling ridiculously insensitive, turning down a pregnant woman. "But there was a mugging in the hallway a few months ago."

The visitor wipes her brow. She's sweating like an athlete. "I'll wait for Fred in the foyer," she pleads. "I won't bother anyone. What do you think I have in my bag? A gun?"

Camilla considers asking the woman up to her own apartment, to wait, but the truth is, in the last few hours the city has drained an edge off her compassion. She's been helping people since early this morning. There were the interns at work who needed advice on their love life. The director who needed professional help, and Tanya, and the man in the subway she'd given two dollars, and the one outside the market who'd followed her for twenty feet, until she handed him money too. There were the needy tourists.

All she wants to do at the moment is be alone.

"I can't. But the restaurant across the street is air-conditioned. Why not wait for Fred there?"

Camilla turns her back, finishes unlocking the door, and, as she pushes against the pane with her shoulder, to open it, feels a punch in her right side, and a hot slithering intrusion, an actual physical presence, in her side. She gasps. The woman has stumbled against her, she thinks at first, as their legs tangle, as they fall through the door into the air-conditioned foyer.

Two women toppling onto the polished gray stone floor.

The pain is terrible, in Camilla's knees, where they struck the floor, and in her side, from where Camilla watches the woman withdraw something long and silvery.

Oh God.

The woman, breathing heavily, sits on the floor, blocking the exit to the outside.

"You killed Voort's baby," she says.

The pain is exploding in Camilla, as if the cut is getting bigger, and her insides are ripping along the lines of the thrust. The other woman's dress has risen up, exposing not a swollen stomach but a mass of white linen taped to her belly. This vision of false pregnancy is somehow more terrifying than the knife.

I recognize that face now.

The woman says, "You don't deserve him."

One of the woman's contact lenses has fallen out. The eye beneath, blue instead of green, is wide and glassier than the false lens. Camilla tells herself to get up, to run, but her body is not responding. Her legs lay straight out, shaking. She has no power over them.

I'm going into shock.

As the woman straightens, her hairpiece slides left, showing black hair beneath. She looks, with the wig half on, with the contact lens out, mad.

"I know who you are," Camilla gasps.

The pain has reached the back of her throat. It is everywhere. She feels a rush of wetness soaking her clothes.

The two women are not moving. They're a foot apart. Time has stopped.

Outside, on the street, someone walks by, not even glancing into the foyer. Just a flicker of movement, and it is gone.

"I'll stab you again if you try something," Nora says, gliding toward Camilla, eyes locked on Camilla's. When Camilla doesn't move, even her arms, Nora frowns, and glances down at the trembling legs.

"You *can't* move, can you?" she says. "Or is it a trick?"

Camilla is bigger, athletic, and she works out. Normally she would be stronger.

Nora is so close now that Camilla feels the warm edge of her breath. She is close as a lover, the blade hovering so near that Camilla understands that even if she *could* move, it's too late to block a thrust.

The door has shut, rendering the street unreal, bright as a knife, distant as escape. The green-walled lobby is silent, sealed by triple-strength glass and the white noise hum of central air-conditioning. There are English prints: jockeys on horses, and men and women, in nineteenth century top hats and hoop dresses, strolling in a park.

Camilla looks into the face of this insane instrument of retribution. She watches her own spreading life seeping into her cotton blouse, spreading.

At least she won't hurt Voort.

"Now you know what it felt like for your baby," Nora says, maneuvering herself behind Camilla, sliding between body and wall, until she cradles the helpless producer. "Your baby couldn't get away either, when the doctor came to kill it. Do you think it knew, at the end, what was about to happen?"

"I don't know."

She squeezes Camilla's shoulder, hard, with her free hand.

"Of course your baby understood nothing logically, but human beings sense things. Do you think it sensed the forceps coming?"

"I hope not."

"Now you say that, but you didn't care then," Nora says, forearm over Camilla's shoulder, blade touching the side of her neck. "You know, last night I was filled with so much despair," Nora says, "that I questioned what I've been doing. I thought I'd been wrong. But then, at the worst moment, when I was about to give up, the blackest time, it was like Voort was talking to me. And he wasn't trying to tell me I was wrong. He was letting me know I had to *expand* my mission, and admit to myself that a women might want to kill a baby too."

Attacker and victim are reflected in the mirrored north wall of the foyer. Camilla watches Nora spit something from her mouth, into her free hand, and toss it onto the floor.

Rubber.

Nora says, "That's what Neiman was trying to tell me too. It wasn't just those boys. It was *her*."

"Who?"

"She died and sent me a note, you know. It said, 'You were right.' Can you beat that? She knew it all along. *She* didn't want me to have that baby."

"Yes," Camilla agrees, barely whispering, thinking, Figure out who she's talking about. Calm her. "It must have been terrible for you."

"That man ripped my insides up. She could have stopped it."

Nora snaps her mouth shut, surprised for an instant to find herself conversing with Camilla.

She yanks Camilla closer, arm around neck, cutting off air. "You haven't the slightest idea what I'm talking about."

"Then . . . tell . . . me."

The elevator suddenly comes to life, with a grinding of gears and the electric sound of moving pulleys. The door opens, only feet away. A woman starts to get out.

"Oh my God!" the woman says.

Camilla watches sandaled feet retreat back into the elevator. The door closes.

She is losing vision, and sensation. That much, at least, is a gift. Little bursts of black flower and ebb in front of Camilla's face.

And now in this slowed-up time there comes to her the sound of banging, on glass, as if far away, and following Nora's gaze, she makes out two adults, silhouetted, outside, trying to get in.

"Go away," Nora cries.

The glass shatters.

And Voort's voice is saying, close by, "Nora. I lied."

Dreamy now, Camilla sees that Voort has busted the glass with his gun. His hand is coming past the hanging shards, the glass stalactites. And Nora is saying, through Camilla's pain, "Get away! I'll hurt her again."

Nora clutching Camilla, as if the producer is supposed to protect *her*. Camilla feels the prick of the blade against her artery.

Camilla thinking, I'm going to pass out.

Voort halts, unsure what to do, inside the foyer. His gun is out, but he has no clear shot. Nora has pulled Camilla close, on her lap, so that Camilla shields Nora's belly, chest, crotch.

I have a four-inch-wide target and my hand is shaking

"I lied to you last night," Voort repeats, forcing his eyes from her knife to Nora's face. The hostage instructors always used to say, *Keep eye contact.*

He says, "I wanted to sleep with you. That abortion story, I made it up to get sympathy. You weren't supposed to leave the house. You were supposed to do the wild thing with me."

"You're just trying to help her."

"Absolutely," Voort says, inching right, hoping it will

ive him a better shot, which it does not. "My job's to elp her, but I'm still telling the truth."

"How can you even stand her, after what she did to ou?" Nora says. "You can't fake the hatred I felt in you ast night when you talked about her."

Camilla shudders, down her whole body. Voort can-ot tell if she can hear them or not. Sweat has run into is left eye, blurring his vision. When he closes the eye, to ry to clear it, the four-inch target seems to glide left.

"We're not talking about *her*. We're talking about 1e," he says, using the modulated, I'm-your-buddy tone e'd learned in hostage class.

"We're talking," he continues, "about how I fooled ou. That abortion story was bullshit. Camilla *wanted* a aby. I made her go to the clinic. Didn't you read her le?"

Now Voort senses Shari coming into the foyer too, be-ind him, stepping carefully through the glass.

He tells Shari, "I told you to stay out of here."

But nobody is paying attention to him today. *Control he scenario,* the hostage instructor always said. Well, he whole fucking scenario is way out of control, he hinks.

"Remember me?" Shari asks Nora, from the side, and 'oort is amazed at how calm she sounds, how friendly.

Nora squints at her. "From the police dance. You're is girlfriend."

"You asked me questions about him."

"What are you doing here?"

"I wanted to tell you, one woman to another, I heard vhat he just said and he's telling the truth. He used the ame line on me, when I met him, told me how Camilla urt him, how she got pregnant. Only later, after we slept ogether, he told me it was a game, to get sympathy."

"Go away."

"I don't have any power over what you're going to do," Shari says, "but if you're going to hurt that woman at least know the facts."

"How could you stay with him, if you knew he was like that?"

"Nora? Is that your name?"

"Don't try to be nice."

"Nora. He's a good-looking guy. I get horny, too."

Nora groans.

Shari says, inching closer, "He gets you to feel sorry for him. Then he fucks you. But he's good."

Voort hears sirens now, not necessarily a good thing under the circumstances.

"I didn't know," Voort says, picking up the thread, watching the eyes shift from Shari back to him. "You were such a good actress I bought everything you said about your boyfriend. Loving him. How did I know you wanted me to come on to you? Hell, if I knew it, I would have done it.

"And now, the funny thing is," he adds, as the siren gets closer, "now maybe you've ruined Camilla's chance to have a child."

The knife wavers, but remains at the neck.

Voort says, "But who wants a kid, anyway? A whiny baby that keeps you from having fun."

"Shut up."

"No way would I want any little brat, all that snot and piss. Who can sleep with a kid around? That's what I told Camilla. I said, 'Camilla, if you want that kid, I'm leaving and—' "

"I said stop!"

" '—and no way will I even help.' Face it, Nora. A pregnant woman gets fat. Waddling around. Who wants to look at that? You should have seen her *after* the aborion. Crying all the time. She drove me crazy. I told her, what's the big deal about getting rid of—"

"*Stopstopstopstop!*"

"You can always have another kid."

The siren is on this block now. Voort hears the screech of tires on asphalt. And then running footsteps. A couple of blue guys are about to rush in here, guns drawn, and see a man holding a gun on two women. He hopes the call they received told them they'd be helping an officer on the scene. But that would only have happened if Cathy Ramsey sent them here, not a call from a bystander.

He can't even shout, "I'm a detective!" because that will break the mood.

And if I shoot now, I may not hit a target that small.

"Police! Freeze!"

But Voort doesn't freeze. He keeps talking, not wanting to break eye contact, not wanting whatever influence he is exercising over her to snap. He says, loud enough for the blue guys behind him to hear, emphasizing her name and hoping the blue guys understand, "Nora Shay, that's why I'm a good cop. I know how to manipulate people."

Camilla slumps. Her eyes roll up, and her lids, which he used to watch when she was sleeping, which she used to use to "butterfly kiss" him, bending close, fluttering the lashes, letting the briefest, most delicate, most tickish contact occur, are closed.

"You think *you're* a good actor, Nora? I'm better."

The blue guys, thank God, say nothing. Maybe they recognize him. He's been on the news enough. Or maybe they're simply confused, or Shari's giving them some kind of signal.

"You know why I could manipulate you so well?" Voort says.

I don't know whose hand is shaking harder, her, or mine.

"Why?"

"Because *I know you.*"

Her expression goes blank.

There's the briefest relaxation of the knife, away from Camilla.

But then she says, "You're lying to me. You love her."

The knife moves fast, and Voort fires, sees paint fly off the wall to Nora's left. He hears a ricochet and thinks, *I missed,* because Nora has completed the movement, finished the thrust.

Oh God.

The blue guys rush her.

Cops pulling Nora to her feet, by both arms. She is not even fighting.

Camilla, lying there.

And Nora, saying, in a little voice, "It hurts."

He tears his eyes from Camilla. He sees, disbelieving, what the blue guys have not noticed yet, that the bone handle is protruding from Nora's belly.

From the ultimate intended target of Nora's attack.

Nora. Not Camilla. *Nora.*

The cops see it now. As they let her down, she slides to her right, to the floor.

"Please," she whispers to Voort, looking down at herself, "help." She's gathering herself for another thrust. She does not want him to save her. Voort rushes forward, but she reaches, quick, with both hands, and grunting, yanks the knife across her belly.

Shari is screaming, "What's happening? What's happening?"

Voort pulls Nora's hands off the handle. She has gutted herself. She is convulsing, to the sound, through the smashed door, of a crowd outside, and the too-late wail of the ambulance.

Voort's hands are slick with blood.

Nora is trying to tell him something.

He leans close. She is dying.

"Did you really lie to me?" Nora whispers, meaning, Did you really make up the story about the abortion? Did you really make *her* have the abortion? Were you really responsible for that fetus not being born?

And Voort says, "I lied. You did the right thing. I lied."

TWENTY-ONE

Two days later Voort sits in the office of New York
City Chief of Detectives Hugh Addonizio, just the
two of them, high above the river, a blue sky outside for
a change, and two airplanes up there that seem to be
heading toward collision, trailing white condensation
that dissipates, becomes less distinct as they safely pass.

"What's this?" Addonizio says, eyeing the shield and
gun Voort has deposited on his desk.

"My father told me, a long time ago, if I ever got to
this point, quit."

"He was a great guy," Addonizio says, standing and
walking to the window, eyeing the metropolis outside,
the little tugs on the river, the helicopter coming in from
La Guardia to the riverside helipad. A barge. The tram to
Roosevelt Island. The perpetual movement which, in all
directions, is a fixed feature of any view.

"He was my boss," Addonizio says, "when I started as
a detective. What are you going to do?"

"It's not like there aren't choices."

"Yeah." Addonizio says, coming back, putting Voort's
gun in a drawer. "You know what I wanted to be, before
I was a cop? A mailman. I thought it would be great,
being outside all the time, in the sun, even the rain.
That's an outdoor job in a city. A cowboy? Nah. A
mailman! No boss looking over you. And I told my fa-

ther about it and he hit me, right here," Addonizio says, touching, with his cigar hand, the white-haired top of his head. He said, 'Hughie, are you out of your mind? Do you know how bad that union is?' "

Voort laughs.

"Do me a favor," Addonizio says. "I have a problem. One last job for me. It's easy. You'll like it. I'll even keep the badge and gun while you help me out. Nothing difficult. Get out on the river. Take that kayak of yours—two, three weeks on the water. Go north. All the authorities are supposed to be cooperating, Water Marine cops, Westchester guys, making a sweep out there. Bunch of assholes have been getting drunk, hassling women in boats."

"Boats," Voort says.

"Boats." Addonizio nods. "Problem is, on the water, they see cops coming. They quiet down. In a kayak, you can get their license. Frankly, it's not important enough to assign regulars to it, but since you're leaving anyway, what do you say?"

"Hugh, did you just make that up or have you been saving it? That's the stupidest thing I ever heard."

"I know. But I tried."

"How did you know I was planning to take the kayak up the Hudson anyway?"

"Two of your uncles were in this morning, to warn me. All I'm saying is, take time. Think about it. If you want to be out, you're out. It's not like you have to quit this second."

"I won't change my mind."

"Then consider the time a gift," Addonizio says, holding up his hands. "More pay. Even rich guys like you can use money for incidentals, like maybe two weeks salary will take care of one month's payment on that car of yours."

"Thanks."

Voort gets up, leaves the office, passes, on his way out, the empty desk formerly occupied by Detective Cathy Ramsey, suspended for leaking information to the newspapers. Detectives in the pool nod to him, as if none of them know, which they obviously do, that he just told Addonizio he quit.

Outside, on the plaza, the day is warm, but cooler than it has been. The worst of the heat wave is over. The city basks in the kind of summer that advertising people depict when they want their customers to long for August. The air is clean. The girls look pretty. Starlings chirp in the trees. Summer days were probably this nice during Peter Stuyvesant's time, when Voorts were the city's night watchmen.

The easterly breeze smells of saltwater, not pollution. Outside One Police Plaza, people lounge on benches. Voort sees tourists with cameras, and workers loitering before they go back to their civil servant desks.

Voort crosses Broadway to reach the small, shaded park surrounding, on three sides, City Hall. Shari is waiting on one of the benches, beneath an old oak. Pigeons scatter at his approach. An old woman nearby is throwing them bread crumbs.

Shari looks up, takes off reading glasses, closes a blue manila folder, but not the kind Nora's company used.

"Hi, Voort."

He sits down, but he does not kiss her.

She says, "Did you visit Camilla today?"

"I will, later. But she's getting better. She was even working yesterday, from bed."

"I can only stay a few minutes," Shari says, glancing at her thin little ladies' watch, on her lovely feminine wrist. "I have a meeting at ten."

"Okay then, what did you want to ask me?"

"A favor. Don't call the house for a while. The girls are attached to you. They ask about you. It makes it harder for them if they're talking to you, now that we've broken off. Let a couple months go, then, if things are right, when they're used to it, come over one night for a friendly dinner."

"That would be good."

"For them too," Shari says. "They need to see that guys, even if a relationship doesn't work out, don't just disappear."

"I'm not going back with Camilla."

"That's up to you," Shari says, getting up. "The problem was never how you treated me. It was the way you looked whenever she came up, the expression on your face when we were rushing to reach her. It was obvious, Voort. There's nothing to discuss. You have to give things time, and you need to be alone while you do. Anyway, I gotta go. The city of Camden wants a big loan and we're considering giving it to them."

She pecks him on the cheek. His skin tingles as she pulls off, sways off, the movement of her lean body drawing glances from the sanitation worker sweeping the park, the men reading papers, the two teenage boys on skateboards.

When he can't see her anymore he finds a cab to New York Hospital, buys flowers in the lobby, and takes the elevator to the fourth floor.

"I've been counting my trophies that come from knowing you," Camilla says, sitting up in bed, in a hospital gown. She's gorgeous, as always, but pale. She'll be a lovely old lady, he thinks, years from now. She's favoring her left, uninjured side.

Her speech is slow, from drugs, but she is alert, even smiling. The overhead TV is tuned, of course, to NBC.

She touches her hospital gown, in the chest, with her index finger. "Bainbridge shot me here," she says.

She tilts her head toward her right side, which, Voort sees through a gap in the gown, is swathed in bandages. "And here's Nora's contribution. You're a dangerous guy to know."

"Where do you want the flowers?"

"On the windowsill," she says as the phone rings. She says, eyeing it, "Those shitheads at the network. You're not going to believe this, but one of the doctors told me, when I was under and they were operating, someone actually called from *Target!* and asked the receptionist if I was under anesthesia or alert. He needed to find the tapes of the Princess Diana wedding. He actually asked the receptionist if I could talk, during the damn operation."

Voort laughs. "He'll go far."

"With that attitude, he'll be network president."

On the TV, the midday news announcer is saying, "Services for Nora Clay were held today in the town of New Thames, Massachusetts. Tune in tonight for a one-hour special on New York's first serial murderess. Now a word from Hyundai, the big value car at the amazing low price."

"That girlfriend of yours," Camilla says, "had guts, coming into the building with you like that."

"She's special."

"I'm happy for you, Voort. Looks like maybe you have a future there."

"Yeah."

A pause. With the main issue out of the way, they chat awkwardly, about her condition, the hospital food, the nurse running the ward. But they have shared an intensity of emotion in the past that makes anything less feel insubstantial. This is the kind of conversation conducted by people getting to know each other, not by people who know each other well.

At length he says, for lack of a better way to end things, "Take care of yourself."

She says, with a wave, as he leaves, "You too."

Outside again, he returns home, picks up the knapsack he's packed, and takes the cab to the boathouse. He carries his fourteen-and-a-half-foot Perception-model kayak to the water. It's a new beauty, silver-colored, with a rudder for greater control. He lowers it in after making sure his supplies—tent, food, water—are sealed in the forward, lockable compartment.

Voort paddles the kayak beyond Pier 26 and onto the wider river. He heads right, north, upstream, liking the feeling of his muscles beginning to work. The sun is hotter now. He wears his PAL cap. A good clean sweat breaks out along his shoulders and biceps. He passes the Chelsea Piers driving range, with its big saggy nets, where tiers of urban golfers hit balls toward the river. He passes the abandoned piers closer to midtown, scheduled to be demolished, for newer ones. He passes the docked museum aircraft carrier, *Intrepid,* and a while later Harlem, and then Riverdale, the last bastion of real wealth in the Bronx.

The shore becomes greener and the breeze cooler by the time, hours later, he passes beneath the low span of the Tappan Zee Bridge, far into Westchester, which missed becoming, by seven votes, the sixth county in the city of New York in 1898.

Voort continues north for two days, past Bear Mountain, past West Point. Nights he finds a bit of park, closed to the public, but by the time he goes ashore, everyone has left anyway. He does not have his badge, or gun, or cell phone. He does not check messages at home. He does not call Mickie, or Camilla. He sinks into the

rhythm of exercise, of aching shoulders and biceps, of
hot sun on the back of his neck.

*God, thank you for this river, for vision, for the ability
to feel heat and cold and emotion. Thank you for sound.
Thank you for complexity. Thank you for color and
movement, and for life.*

But if he thinks of anything else, while he works, it
is the stories his river rat uncles told him when he was
a boy, as they took him sailing up this same passage,
or chugged here on their tugboats, towing barges, past
the frontier towns turned mill towns turned yuppie commuter towns or private parkland for Rockefellers. Towns
with names of extinct Indians. Ossining. Poughkeepsie.

"This is where Washington retreated from the advanc-
ing British, up the Hudson Valley, at the beginning of the
Revolution," his uncles would say. They were fair-haired,
fair-skinned men, tugboat operators and policemen who
liked to smoke cigarettes and eat smoked cheese, smoked
sausages, hunks of bread downed with long-necked bottles of Knickerbocker beer. Men who would point out
the marinas and town halls and the squarish, blocky
walls and watchtowers of Sing Sing prison.

"And here is where Washington returned, years later,
and beat them. Did you know that his chief scout, in the
Yorktown campaign, was a Voort?"

At length, at dusk on the fourth day, he swings the
kayak east, toward the shore, at a forested stretch with a
small, solid-looking dock jutting into the silty water. The
sun lies between a gap in the trees on the far shore, huge
and orange.

Three children on the dock, holding fishing poles,
watch the kayak come out of the glare. Two boys and a
girl. All of them wear life jackets.

The littlest boy starts jumping up and down.

"Uncle Conrad!" he cries.

Voort paddles the boat in. When he climbs on the dock, the kids are all over him, laughing, holding his legs, perched on his shoulders.

"Will you stay a few days?" the smallest boy asks.

Voort's muscles are aching.

And Voort is thinking, I love these kids.

Don't miss the exciting new novel
by Ethan Black

ALL THE DEAD WERE WERE STRANGERS

Coming in a hardcover in September 2001.
Published by the Ballantine Publishing Group

For a sneak peak,
Please turn the page . . .

Meechum gives the driver thirty dollars, tells him to keep the change, and walks up a half-dozen cracked concrete steps into the modest but spankingly clean lobby. The linoleum smells of lemon polish. The potted palms are freshly watered. Reproduction lithographs of jockeys at Belmont Park racetrack; Angel Cordero, Julie Crone—the riders responsible for the hotel owner's gambling disappointments—hang by the freshly painted black, cage-style elevator that carries Meechum, all alone, to the third floor.

At Room 305, where a DO NOT DISTURB sign hangs on the knob, he runs his hand along the doorjamb; he relaxes when he locates, in the exact spot where he inserted them, three strands of his black hair, between door and jamb.

He inserts the electronic keycard, a modern surprise in these older surroundings, and pushes open the door. He'd left the light on. On the carrot-colored shag carpet he checks the undisturbed expanse of white talcum powder which, backing from the room earlier, he had sprinkled on the floor.

Meechum shoves the door forward, so it swings violently forward and strikes the wall. No one there.

When he enters, he stops and sniffs for any hint of

scent, aftershave, perfume, leather, that was not there before. Detecting nothing, he locks the door behind him.

One more night hidden, but at least safe.

It isn't until he enters the bathroom, and reaches for the lightswitch, that someone blindsides him from the left. An expert blow catches the side of his throat, and even as his hands come up protectively, and he's thinking *I can't breathe*, he knows he's leaving his belly open and the second blow comes fast, doubling him.

The ceiling is whirling. The floor rushes at his face.

He wants to fight but whoever is behind him wields enormous strength. He is helpless as a baby. His larynx seems crushed, and now the man is on top of him, and he feels another pain, sharp and sudden and *it's a needle* going in, by his collarbone, at the base of his neck.

When he wakes he's in the same room, and, senses sharpening, he sees that he's in bed. He reaches to pull the covers off.

I can't move my arms. They tied me.

The TV is on, loud. Very bad sign.

I can't breathe out of my mouth. There's something over my mouth!

"Meechum," a deep, older voice says, through the darkness in his head, and the pain.

There is a pounding between his eyes, and red bursts, dots, ebb and flow behind them. His throat is on fire, and when he tries to turn over, he can't move his legs either.

The voice says, "We lost you. But we found you. Like 'Amazing Grace.' Ever hear it with bagpipes? It makes you weep."

He opens his eyes. The light fuels his pain, spikes it higher as the voice, and vague mass of dirty brown lines above coalesce into a cotton sweater, as the voice says, plainly, matter-of-factly, "I'm going to loosen the tape on your mouth. Keep quiet or I'll kill you."

Close-up, the speaker is a study in contradiction. He is large, about fifty, with wide shoulders, giving a sense of physical power offset by the bulging stomach, as if he was once in superb shape but allowed himself to go to seed a bit. The left arm hangs at a slightly odd angle. The clothing is pressed, neat but not flamboyant. The wool trousers are the color of milk chocolate, selected well, off the rack. The V-necked cotton sweater is light beige, the crew-necked pull-over beneath that is white. He might be a corporate lawyer, lounging at home, on Sunday. But the whole subdued surface and soft voice are offset by the driving intensity in eyes of the palest blue, magnified by dark silver-rimmed glasses. The hair is steel-colored, cut short and receding from the large forehead. The face is round and Slavic, starting to go fleshy. The mass of creases at the corners of the mouth has a weather-beaten quality, as does the leathery skin, as if this man once spent an unhealthy amount of time in the sun. The entire effect is of a man put together over half a century in layers, each intense, reinforcing the other, until the final complex product was achieved.

Meechum realizes, *My clothes are hanging on a chair. I'm naked.*

And now he sees a second man, the one he spotted leaving the White Horse earlier, and the man is standing on a chair, holding the room's smoke alarm, which he has unscrewed from the ceiling. He appears to be replacing the battery. In his jeans and flannel shirt, he might be a building custodian who strolled into a kidnapping scene and began going about his business. He replaces the alarm.

The speaker says, "Hairs in the door? Really, Meechum. Charley broke in. I stayed outside and put the hairs back. You wrote something on a napkin, in the restaurant where you had lunch. You showed the napkin to the man in the White Horse. What did you write on the napkin?"

Charley wipes dust off his hands and approaches the bed, but stops as he breaks out coughing, a deep ugly sound coming from far inside.

Meechum says, "Napkin?"

The speaker sighs and reaches for a Windsor chair from the room's pine table, and swings it around so he can sit and drape his powerful forearms over the back. A talent at patience is indicated.

"Charley?" he says.

Leather Jacket moves fast, despite the coughing, whips down and replaces the tape over Meechum's mouth. He rears back and drives a finger, a mere index finger, into a spot on Meechum's neck. Meechum shoots up in bed, back arching. The pain blinds him.

"What did you write? Remember, no screaming."

Charley loosens the tape a little, allowing air in.

"Oh, God," Meechum gasps.

"God," the speaker remarks, "is a study in failed expectation." His expression remains bland, but the flatness of the voice shows suppressed passion.

Meechum thinks, *I must protect Voort.*

"Tonight's guests," blares the MC on the television, "are Jennifer Lopez! Steve Young! And that terrific actor, Tom Hanks!"

"Meechum, what did you write?"

The second man leans forward again, replaces the tape and shoves his finger into a new spot. Meechum screams through the fabric, feels saliva dripping down his throat. He can't breathe. Charley yanks him up in bed, enabling a trickle of air to reach his lungs through his nose.

"Meechum, in real life, unlike movies, people tell," the man with the twisted arm says as, eyes bulging, Meechum watches Charley undo the buttons on his flannel shirt, an act which, in its inexplicability, is more terrifying than anything that has so far happened in this room.

The MC says, "Please welcome the star of the new Disney hit, *The Mouse That Snored*."

"We're going to leave that tape where it is. I ask a question. You nod if you want to answer. Then Charley takes off the tape."

A few minutes later, Meechum forces out, through a world of agony, "Names. I . . . wrote . . . down names."

"What names?"

Meechum answers truthfully. "And the addresses," he gets out.

The speaker closes his eyes, calms himself, opens them. "Only those names?"

"Yes."

"No others?"

"No."

"You're sure."

"Yes."

"Charley, I'm not positive he's sure."

Meechum convinces them, at length, that he is sure.

"And who did you give this list *to*?"

"A . . . policeman."

The speaker sits absolutely still, his breathing remaining steady, his gaze never leaving Meechum's face. A small bright light flares and dies in his irises. His tone never rises, never changes. He is perfectly in control. He says, "A New York City policeman. Just a run-of-the-mill municipal policeman. That's what you're telling me?"

"A detective."

"And *why* did you tell this detective you were giving him the list, if that's *all* you told him?"

"I asked him to . . . I wanted him . . . to check . . . the names . . . to check the names."

The speaker runs a hand over his short gray hair.

"You're asking me to believe that you just gave him names and didn't explain it," he says, as much reasoning to himself as repeating information. "You're saying," he begins, but his frown is suddenly replaced by a look of understanding.

"You're saying you weren't sure you had anything to tell him yet, so you were protecting people until your suspicions were confirmed. You didn't want to divulge more unless you were sure it was real."

"Ye-es."

The speaker stands, and frowns. "Or am I fooling myself," he says, "because that's what I want to hear?

"Charley?" he says. "I'm not sure I believe him yet."

Several minutes later, when Charley has finished another round, the speaker says, "But how is the detective supposed to check the names out, if that's all he knows?"

"Make . . . calls. To friends in those cities."

"But why would the detective agree to this and even listen to you in the first place? He's got other things to do. Why pay attention to your request? A stranger walks off the street and tells a detective to 'check out some names,' isn't that what you said, and the detective, who I imagine has a million cases in backlog, legitimate cases, just snaps to attention and says, Yes sir, right away, sir, I have nothing to do and I'll just run off and do whatever nutty thing you want. . . . Is that what you're trying to tell me? *What aren't you telling me?*"

The tape goes back on Meechum's mouth. Through the foul taste of adhesive, he screams.

"I . . . used to know him," Meechum says when Charley loosens the tape again.

"As in, he's an old friend."

"Yes."

"And the name of this good old friend?"

Meechum shuts his eyes. He doesn't want to watch this time, doesn't want to see Charley, but he feels the hands at his mouth. He tries to bite, to whip his head away. He feels himself arching in agony, feels his spine cresting so far toward the ceiling that he sees it, in his mind, snapping in two.

Donotdonotdonotnotnot say Voort's name.

"Pretty strong," he hears Charley say with grudging admiration. "I didn't think he had anything left."

"Let's hear it for a great actor, who made sacrifices for his work. He put on thirty pounds for this part," the TV host says, and through Meechum's pain comes the tinny thunder of network audience approval.

After awhile Meechum passes out, and the phone starts ringing, which startles the man in the beige sweater. He does not like that someone is calling.

"Are you sure no one saw you come in?" he asks Charley, who now has his pants off, too.

"It's probably someone complaining about the loud TV."

"Probably," the speaker repeats, with some sarcasm. "Are you offering odds backing up this hypothesis?"

"You're the one who said to hurry." Charley breaks into coughs again. He has to wipe away phlegm from the corner of his mouth.

The speaker reconsiders, and subsides. It is the first time he has looked contrite tonight, and the change, in such a big man, a controlled and powerful-looking man, is profound. "You're right and I apologize. I took out my anger on you."

"Don't worry about it," Charley says.

"I mean it," the speaker says with real emotion. "After all you've done, and what you're about to do, I have no right to give you a hard time."

"I said forget it," Charley says.

"Thank you. Put on the pajamas and finish up. Take the pill. Give yourself ten minutes for it to take effect."

"My family?" Charley says.

"Already done," the man with the twisted arm says.

Charley pulls, from a plastic shopping bag, brand new, cellophane-wrapped green satin pajamas. He slides the trousers over his bare legs.

"Hey! Smooth," he says. "I always laughed at people who wore, y'know, pajamas."

He folds his shirt neatly on a chair. He lays his trousers over that. There is a ritualistic quality to his movements, as if he were a husband, married for years, about to climb under the sheets, onto his side of a double mattress, and pull out a *People* magazine, or channel clicker, or just, tired after a hard day, reach over and turn off the bedside lamp.

The man with the twisted elbow puts on a hooded coat of fawn-colored wool, button-up style. At the door, he turns and watches the lean man don his brand-new satin pajama top, then climb under the covers with Meechum.

"Charley, I'm sorry it came to this."

He turns his attention to the inert form in the bed.

"Meechum, I'm disappointed in you" is all he says.

Also by Ethan Black

THE BROKEN HEARTS CLUB

"[A] well-paced psycho-thriller debut."
—*Publishers Weekly* **(starred review)**

Breaking up may be hard to d.o.
But for these men, it's a killer.

hey meet every week in the dingy back room of a
ar in New York City. An informal group of men
ith one thing in common: They all suffer the sting
f a broken heart. But soon the anger turns to hate.
he rejection turns to rage. And the Broken Hearts
lub spins violently out of control—exploding into
urderous acts of vengeance.

etective Voort is assigned the case, determined to
atch an elusive killer who is always one death
head. . .who appears to switch identities with each
ew victim. . .and who knows how to cover his
acks with cold efficiency. Then Voort falls victim
 his own broken heart, as his ex-girlfriend
nknowingly becomes the target of a frightening
ew breed of serial terror. . . .

Published by Ballantine Books.
Available at bookstores everywhere.

The new Conrad Voort hardcover

ALL THE DEAD WERE STRANGERS

When an old friend suddenly vanishes, leavin
behind a cryptic list of names, Conrad Voort
drawn into a mystery involving the eerie deaths
unrelated strangers—and thrust into a race to sa
the next potential victim. But the search pits Voc
against an enemy even bigger than anything his s
crimes unit (or the NYPD) has ever encountere
And as two lethal adversaries prepare to face o
Voort is caught in the middle. . .forced to make a te
rible choice in order to stop an unspeakable crime

**"Greased-lightning adventures [that]
will keep you guessing and turning the pages
long into the night."**
—Kirkus Reviews

Published by Ballantine Books.
Available at bookstores everywhere.